QUARANTINE
THIRTEEN

Exploration Permit

Granted By:

N. Kelda

Date:

21ˢᵗ Trei 650

City of Amule

Also by Natalie Kelda:

☼ Inner Universe Series ☼

QUARANTINE THIRTEEN

Inner Universe Series: Book 3

Natalie Kelda

First edition November 2023

Cover design by Sophie Edwards
Edited by Jessica Netzke

ISBN: 978-1-7393016-1-3
ASIN: B0CK9PZF29

www.nataliekelda.co.uk

Chapter 1

The chair groaned when Tara pulled her leg up under herself. She used her bare knee to prop up her notebook, holding it with one hand while the other drew furious black lines across the smooth page. Her heart had yet to stop thundering from the nightmare that had woken her.

The aggressive scratch of the pencil on the paper helped. She paused, using the pencil to still an itch above her left ear. Then she continued drawing. Putting her nightmares into the notebook so she could shackle them there.

By the time her breath had evened, a maggot-riddled skull glared back at her from the page. She hated how well she could capture it. The dark hollows, the fracture where the brain had been scooped out. And there, under the grinning teeth, a hand poked out. Pieces of skin and meat left on it. A ring on the thumb winking. Gleaming with malice.

There had been other images in her dreams. Ones of blood and pain and intangible fear. But they were too blurred to allow for sketching. Too visceral for her to capture them. It was those hazier memories that haunted her the most.

She scoffed. Imagine being grateful to be mostly left with the vivid image of Edur's cannibalised corpse. It had been months. Over a year if she counted right. There had been some confusion about the days after they found what had been left of Edur and escaped the city of Ivory. Too much grief to bear and a sickness in her lungs she had thought would claim her.

Two loud knocks on the cabin door behind her, jolted Tara from the chair. "Stars burn me," she whispered and barely managed to snatch her notebook before dropping it. Closing it around the pencil, she put it on the desk.

Another double knock sounded; this time accompanied by a muffled voice. "Cap'n?"

"Sh! He's asleep." She hissed under her breath. Grabbing her trousers from the floor, she pulled them on before opening the door.

Fabian blinked hand raised as if about to knock again. "Ya's up? We've got—"

"Quiet," Tara said. She shoved the first mate into the hallway and shut the door carefully after herself. "Merlon's asleep still." She stuffed her shirt into her trousers.

"Runnin' him ragged, eh?" Fabian wiggled his eyebrows.

Tara groaned and rolled her eyes. "What is it? You didnae knock just to be insufferable?" Maybe he had, you never knew with Fabian. Humour was both his best and his worst quality.

"No." Fabian shook his head although he still looked suspiciously chipper. "Storm's incomin'. It's regular when

6

entering Fristate Galaxy but Cap'n likes being informed irregardless. And I thought ya'd wanna see since it's ya first time through here."

Deciding she couldn't be bothered finding and putting on her breast bandeau before her actual shift in a few hours, Tara gestured for Fabian to take the lead. She watched his back with a frown.

She couldn't get used to Fabian's short hair even though it had been eleven months since he chopped it off. He persisted that he wouldn't let it grow back out to the foot-long black ponytail he had once sported until he could be with his girlfriend, Mira, again.

But for that to happen, Mira would have to cut herself off from her family. He was a common sailor, but Mira was in the captain's tier and her family was unreasonably strict on tier mixing. *Assholes the lot of them.*

By the time they exited onto the deck at the other end, Tara had tied the scarf from her trouser pocket around her neck and sort of tied her hair back. But her hair never did what she wanted it to and would probably need adjustments soon.

On deck, Fabian spun and took the steps up the quarterdeck three at a time. Tara moved somewhat slower, letting her hands run over the smooth rail of the companionway. The breathing wood hummed with life under her fingertips, like the ship greeted her.

Lucia had taken a beating eleven months ago when they crashed on the harbourfront in Amule. Seven months of repairs rendered it impossible to tell where she had been put back together. The deck was stained darker than before. The red cherry-wood inlays along the railings had been extended

7

to door frames and detailing on the masts. She was beautiful and Tara had grown to love the soft song of her quivering breath.

Jara, the new helmswoman, was at the wheel. "I bloody 'ope he didn't wake you for that little storm brewing." She spat aside and used a mussed sleeve cuff to rub her nose. Her skin was almost the same sandy golden of the stones of Gulborg Castle in Amule.

Her large, dark eyes and pierced lips were always highlighted by several layers of immaculate make-up. Yet the crudeness of her behaviour remained at odds with her appearance. At least to Tara.

"Was already awake." Tara shrugged. The lack of proper sleep left her achy and grumpy. She turned to face the bow.

Then she closed her eyes and drew in a breath. She had to expel all those blood-soaked images still circulating in her head if she was to see anything. She had never had issues with it before. But with her sleep disjointed and mind full of last year's horrors, it had become a chore to focus enough to see the billowing, ever-moving energy surrounding the ship as they flew through space.

"Oi, tramp?" Fabian nudged her arm.

Tara blew out and opened her eyes. So much for getting a moment to concentrate. "What?"

"Ya's gotta open ya eyes to see the energy."

"Go get burned." She wriggled her fingers in the Squamate sign for 'burn'.

Fabian chortled and trotted off across the deck.

It didn't matter he had been joking like the two of them always did. His comment left Tara with an uncomfortable churn to her stomach. What if she couldn't concentrate enough anymore? Everyone aboard relied on her to see the energy currents they needed to follow for *Lucia* to fly fast and safely through outer space.

She adjusted her hairband. It only resulted in more of her brown hair falling into her face. Annoyed, she shoved the locks behind her ear and stalked off the quarterdeck and towards the bow.

When she reached the front of the ship, she placed her palms against the cool railing. She noted a dampness in the air. Merlon had mentioned that Fristate was a foggy, hazy galaxy so they had to be at the edge of it. They would stay on the less inhabited side, as far from the pirate-run Blacklock's Galaxy as possible while on their way to Jeweller City in the next galaxy over.

She had been to Jeweller City once before, last year, but they had bypassed Fristate by using a Tracker's loop-hole powder to travel straight to Amule. While they had crashed on the harbour, the events from that day that truly plagued her, was their prison escape through the disposer tunnels and the final fight against Lady Galantria. The last Star-Eater in Inner Universe.

A shiver coursed through her body. "Stop it," she mumbled to herself.

Once more, she controlled her breathing. *Stay calm. Tranquil. You're a navigator from a long line of navigators. Only you aboard this ship can see energy before it hits the sails.*

The thoughts did nothing but make her rage more when she opened her eyes and…nothing. All she saw was what everyone else did. No cold, turquoise streams of energy. She squinted, willing herself to see it.

There. Wisps of green and blue danced ahead. The strands were so faded. So feeble as she had rarely seen them. Either the energy here was obscured by the mist in the air, or she needed to try harder. She tilted her head, following the weakly shimmering threads of energy being pulled to the glowing sails and boosting the ship onwards.

Someone dropped a cleat, and it clattered across the deck. "Toss that up here, will ye?" Kieran called.

Tara glanced over her shoulder.

Gaunty, a slim sailor with short brown hair gathered in a neat, tiny ponytail just below the edge of the soft cap xe wore, picked the cleat up and lopped it at the boatswain dangling from the shrouds above. Kieran nodded a thanks and yanked his soft hat further down his forehead. His scraggly blonde hair poked out from under the hat but at this distance Tara couldn't see his chipped front tooth nor his crooked nose.

Turning her face forward once more, even the tiny flickers of energy had vanished from her sight again. Tara gritted her teeth. *Come on!*

Merlon didn't pay her to dawdle around but to see the energy so his ship and crew could remain safe even through storms like the one swirling in glittering grey clouds ahead.

Without trying to employ her navigator's vision it was clear the storm wasn't large, but if she could home in on the energy, she could tell Jara which side of the clouds had less turbulence.

"What's the verdict?" Jara shouted as if she had heard Tara's thoughts.

Tara's fingernails bored into the rail. *Concentrate.*

They would hit the storm in minutes. *Lucia* already groaned and rolled. The sails rippled with colours, flaring brighter when more energy hit the powder treated canvas. But everyone could see the colours on the sails where energy stretched the fabric taut.

Sailors shouted. Someone rolled a barrel across the main deck. The rumbling laughter of Boomer echoed up from the forecastle below.

Tara stuck her fingers in her ears and stared so hard her eyes began watering. There it was. Tiny flecks of turquoise amongst the pale grey haze. Was the energy more even to the left? There was almost some darkness there. She needed to weed out all the other things and see the energy clearly, like she used to. Tara blinked and the currents of energy had vanished from her sight.

She lowered her hands. Nothing worked. She had tried blocking everything out. Controlling her breath. Grounding herself by holding the rail and feeling the solidness of the deck under her feet. All the things they taught during the first year in navigator's school. Tools she hadn't needed to employ for nearly two decades.

"Go..." she paused, swallowed, and managed to raise her voice. "Go left, ten degrees downwards." That best be right, or Jara would no doubt think Tara had only got the job because her and Merlon were dating.

But that wasn't why. She had always been the best in school. The one with the clearest vision for energy. Apart from Lanier whose family was one of the purest lines of navigators known. He had transferred schools from Fristate's capital, Intrapolis, when his parents moved to Amule.

Tara still remembered the day he arrived. Since Amule's school only ever had around forty students, Lanier had been in her class despite being a couple of years older.

She had thought him cool. That dark curly hair contrasting skin that was decidedly paler than everyone else's.

At aged seven, she had only lived in Amule for a few months and was also a new kid. And she got teased for having a Trachnan accent so when someone teased Lanier for his Fristate lilt she had told the teachers. But Lanier didn't say thanks. Instead, he called her a tattletale and made everyone laugh at her instead of him.

Lucia tossed sideways, sending Tara staggering back into the present. Turquoise energy flitted in and out of her vision. She could only see it strongly for tiny one-second intervals. But she saw enough. Hopefully.

"Jara! Fifteen degrees to starboard and five up. Kieran, Derek! Get out of the shrouds." She caught a halyard and held fast.

The ship groaned, the breathing wood whining in the sudden gale force. Tiny shimmering particles speckled the cool air. The energy was too strong. Even though Tara could no longer focus on it, the brightness of the sails told her. They needed to divert some of it.

She let go of the line and ran to the windlass. "Fabian, the diversion anchor needs out."

"Gotcha." Fabian nodded and sprung to the second handle of the windlass' chain wheel.

Together they turned it. The anchor chains clicked out. With each link lowering the specially treated wooden anchor, more energy was diverted around the ship, away from the sails and slowing them. The pressure eased and so did *Lucia's* tossing.

"Fifteen percent diversion!" Jara yelled, her words all but swallowed by the howling in the rigging.

Tara's skin prickled. She looked up. The turquoise of the energy flared then receded and turned first dark teal, then black. "That's nae right."

"What?" Fabian looked up. The anchor clicked out to fifteen percent diversion.

"The energy it's…" Dread ate Tara's voice. She had seen that energy thousands of times. But never in the darkness of space. Hadn't seen it after the last portal on Amule's harbour was destroyed. Not since portals were outlawed to protect against outside invaders like Lady Galantria of Ivory.

"Tara, what's wrong?"

She met Fabian's gaze. "It's a portal storm."

Chapter 2

Tara should have focused better. Seen it sooner. She could have diverted them from the portal storm in time. But she had failed. Her navigator's eyes hadn't picked up the blackness amongst the turquoise. *Pull yourself together. You can't control everything.*

"Ha! Good one." Fabian snorted, a flicker on uncertainty in his dark eyes.

Tara shook her head. "I'm serious. The energy, it looks like a portal. Black. Empty. A void." But what if she was wrong? She saw no energy at all now however much she willed herself to.

Fabian glanced ahead then met her gaze again. "What do we do?"

"I donae know." Tara's throat constricted. Portal storms were supposed to be myths. But with everything that happened last year, she could hardly have expected differently. *You really thought life would get easier when you know it always gets back at you?*

If she screwed this up everyone might die. Or crash. The entire ship was breathing wood, the very material portal powder worked on. She wasn't sure a full ship could portal but with the sort of luck they had it could, and they would portal somewhere unplanned. Somewhere hostile.

"Tara, what do we do?" Fabian's knuckles were white for how hard his fists clenched.

The horrors they went through in Ivory and beyond had changed him. Yet being unable to be with Mira had had the most profound effect. With his shorter hair had come a melancholy. A realisation life was unfair. And she hated that his jokes never hit as hard as they once had. That his smiles and laughter held a hint of the same sadness that haunted her mind.

She turned to look past the bow. *See. Find a solution.*

Of course, her vision remained patchy. The blackness was only growing. The ship rolled and she staggered, catching herself on the railing. A line snapped and whipped in the air. Something disturbed the energy.

Tara whirled. "There's something else here."

But Fabian had sprung away to help Gaunty tame a halyard. "All hands! Turn her 'bout! Tack to starboard."

While Tara had wasted time trying to see what she no longer could, Fabian had rushed into action. He had become a star-cursed good first mate while she had turned into a star-mad fool who couldn't do the one thing that would help *Lucia*.

Sudden, high-pitched clicks and whines left soundwaves dappling against the sails. And something huge stole the

15

energy. She couldn't quite see it, but the sails told her. Dragons!

She realised too late what would happen. "Fabian, donae! Stop turning!" The wind took her voice. Nobody heard her. *Useless. Always so useless.*

Tara sprinted across the forecastle deck. Her arms flailed and she shouted, cursing that her voice was so feeble from fear.

Lucia cast about, throwing everyone stumbling across the decks. Those in the rigging bobbed. "Kieran, Karl get down from there!" Had she not already ordered everyone down?

Only the former turned his head towards her. 'Get down,' she gestured with Squamate signs. Kieran nodded and waved at Karl, but he didn't see, too busy adjusting a luffing topgallant sail.

The clicks echoed all around. So many. And they were close now. *Lucia* swung round to port. Her hull groaning and rigging wailing. It was too late to stop.

Tara narrowed her eyes, rushing back towards the quarterdeck. Jara would need her. If she could make it in time…

"Turn back!" Tara leapt up the companionway. But *Lucia* was uncontrollable. The sounds of the enormous creatures were so close around them. Coming straight towards the ship. Dozens at least. Not just Visca and Vincent, the only two dragons Tara had previously met.

The masthead of the main mast burst and snapped. The stay tore and the breaking wood churned. Wood splinters bounced off something invisible beside the ship. The heavy piece of mast caught in the shrouds. Tumbling down. The great beast flapped its huge wings, glimmering for a second.

"Karl," Tara croaked.

He scrambled to get out of the way from the falling masthead. Not fast enough. Ignoring Jara screaming at her to help turn the wheel back, Tara rushed towards the main deck again.

The broken mast top hit Karl's shoulder. He ducked and shirked, but cried out loud. He lost his grip on the ratlines. The flags from the mast fluttered past him. The brown and black of Merlon's family standard wrapped around Karl's leg while Amule's pale blue banner with the silver star billowed onto the deck.

He fell. So slowly. Everything lurched. Flickers of the air – energy pushing away from under him – sparked turquoise.

Tara ran towards Karl. He hit the deck with a heavy clonk. His head whipped. A second thud resounded through the boards when his skull met with them.

Lucia seemed to shiver at the impact. Tara's right knee gave out. She grabbed Karl by the shoulder, forced him to roll to his back. He thrashed. Eyes dazed and blood gushing from a cut on the side of his head and his nose.

"Derek, help me keep him still." Tara waved at the young sailor. "Karl, keep still. If—"

"Dragons! Dragons everywhere!" Gaunty shrieked.

Their great shapes glimmered like a heat haze in Amule's streets. Each the size of *Lucia*. They were headed straight into the portal storm. And even with the inconsistency of her navigator's vision, Tara saw the energy their wings stole. The energy that made *Lucia* lose speed and rendered her

17

impossible to steer. Then the dragons winked out. One by one.

The air turned grey. A softness enveloped them. Sounds ceased to exist. The black energy grew. Faint, but it was there. *Lucia* was hit again. This time a dragon screeched. Xir frilled head became visible for a flicker. Xe shook xirself. Brilliantly coloured tail feathers billowed. The dragon continued straight, but *Lucia* rolled too much.

"We's tipping!" Jara bellowed.

Fabian shouted in the same moment. "Hold on!"

Tara grabbed Karl's arm and wound her free one around the baluster of the railing. The ship keeled. Her shoulder threatened to pop from the weight of keeping herself and Karl from rolling across the deck and fall overboard.

Lucia's wood cried at the pressure. Then the damp greyness around them vanished. The last flicker of a brightly coloured dragon passed them by as if it had pulled them through the portal storm to a new place.

The light intensified.

Tara blinked. Something was wrong. The energy was downwards. The way it flowed across the sails, like they were pulled down. It corrected the listing. *Lucia* swinging back upright.

Merlon staggered onto the deck, half-dressed and still stuffing his shirt into his trousers. No boots to hide his powder-burn scarred feet. The door clappered behind him when the lock didn't snap shut. "What in the stars—"

Tara fought to free herself from the baluster. A sharp light, starlight, blinded her when the last cloudiness vanished.

Humid heat enveloped them. *Lucia*'s rigging whined, the sails luffing with the pull from below.

Tara had to do something, but Karl's head lolled. Eyes rolling and delirious.

"I's got him," Derek said, grabbing Karl by the shoulder and pinning him on the deck.

Tara jumped to her feet, catching Merlon's arm when he reached for her. "Portal storm *and* dragons." Her voice was hoarse.

Merlon blinked once, twice. A flicker of panic crossed his face, then vanished, severe control taking over. "There's a gravitational pull. We're on a planet." He let go of her and spun. "Jara, lift us! Kieran, Gaunty anchor out at five percent intervals till we reach a hundred."

"Masts are burning," Jara shouted.

Tara twisted her neck. Smoke drew black streaks across a pale blue sky. *Lucia* shuddered. The anchor clicked out, but they didn't slow. She drew in a breath and yelled, "Anchor out at ten percent intervals!"

Tara ran to the railing. Karl groaned beside her, Derek trying to shift him towards the main hatch on deck. The ground below them came closer too fast. And it was shimmering green and light blue. Her heart punched at her ribs. It wasn't ground at all.

"Water! It's all water below us." She caught Merlon's gaze from across the ship.

Fear flickered across his face but once more, determination swallowed it. "Prepare for water landing. Get that anchor to one hundred percent."

Does anyone even know what a water landing requires? It wasn't like any Edge Galaxies had habitable planets or large bodies of water. Dread rose in Tara's throat. She forced it back. She would *not* let fear control her.

Smoke billowed from the bowsprit. The sails luffed.

Tara sprung to the halyards, trimming the sheets to control the sails before they ripped. The wind stopped howling and the grey portal shimmer that had coated the breathing wood had vanished.

"Cap'n there's an island!" Fabian shouted.

Merlon stalked across to the starboard side. He moved steadily, like the ship wasn't tossing and rolling. "Flat?"

Tara climbed into the shrouds to secure one of the snapped lines from the fallen part of the main mast. Boomer aided Derek and Karl was moved below. *Merciful stars, let him not be badly injured.*

The island was too far away. They would never make it.

"Tara," Merlon called, "see any energy we can use as a boost to reach that island?"

Burn me! She paused, fingers trembling on her grip of the rungs. She had to get this right. Why was it so hard? It had never been hard before.

The water below was turquoise, but not the right shade for it to be energy. She closed one eye. Was there an air current going across the vast water and then skirting around the island? Little swirls of the nodding trees flickered in her vision. Wind.

"Around seventy degrees down." *Please be right this time.* "The island's full of trees and high ground in the middle.

Flatter near the water. Keep anchor on eighty percent diversion."

Jara acted on her words instantly, pressing the altitude pedal. *Lucia* nosedived. The sudden pressure of the wind hitting Tara pushed her feet off the shroud rungs. Her throat closed. If she lost her grip she would drown. Or die on impact.

It went fast then. There was a boost forward. The island came up below. Tall, palms and big-leaved trees swished against the keel. *Lucia* complained at each treetop her hull broke in passing.

The hill rose before them. "Turn to port!" Tara shrieked. She fought to catch a rung with her feet. Someone seized her boot and pushed it into the shroud. She dared a glance down. Gaunty was there, patting her leg in reassurance. "Thank—" *Lucia* banked hard to port. Tara's words got swallowed in a renewed hiccup of terror.

Gaunty bounced in the shrouds below, now xe dangled, fighting to catch the rungs with xir feet like Tara had been doing a moment before. Xe scrambled down, using the strength of xir spindly arms.

And then *Lucia* hit the edge of the island. Tara lost her grip. She fell. The deck rose to meet her. Her knees slammed the boards. She rolled, fighting to get back to her feet.

Sand and water sprayed up before the bowsprit. *Lucia* howled. Her breathing wood crying from the impact.

Tara reached out and caught Gaunty's elbow. The ship's sliding slowed. Everyone staggered around, tossed against the rail and masts and ratlines.

Finally, they were still. *Lucia* groaned softly, a broken yard tapped quietly against the foremast. The sails hung limp.

"Fabian, casualty check," Merlon shouted. "Kieran, fires first then other damages. I need five people with bows as lookout in case of hostiles. Quick now!" His heavy footsteps, that had the slightest drag to them, thudded across the deck. He stopped to help Deyon back to his feet. Muttered something to the second mate then headed straight for Tara.

Tara helped Gaunty to xir feet. "Get to the sick bay when you can." She gestured at Gaunty's head. The skin had split near xir hairline, probably from the impact when falling the last feet to the deck. While it bled profusely, it wasn't a deep or long cut.

Tara used a line to keep her knees from giving way.

"Are you alright?" Merlon grabbed her shoulder a bit too tightly.

Tara winced and he let go. "Hit my arm." She rubbed it. "I'm fine." She felt woozy but there wasn't time for fuss.

"Thank the stars. I need you to help Yorik in the sick bay if you can." He had on that mask of authority he had worn so often last year.

We were meant to stick to safe airspace and now we've hit a portal storm! Tara didn't like those odds. The stars had something against her, that much was certain. But she nodded at his words.

Merlon's brow creased for a second, then he sighed and moved to the next crew.

Tara looked across the deck. The brown and black standard had dragged halfway into the hatch where Karl had been lowered down. Blood smeared on the boards. If her navigator's sight had worked as it should, she would have seen the portal storm sooner. And then Karl wouldn't be seriously injured. They wouldn't be on some strange planet who knew where.

Above the calls and feet thudding from sailors running back and forth, there was a rhythmic, terrifying sound like that of water hitting something solid but thousandfold.

The starlight winked across the blue and green waters that stretched as far as she could see. The biggest lake she had ever seen, and its drops crusting her face were salty. Where had they crashed this time?

Chapter 3

Tara nodded, brows furrowing while she followed Yorik's instructions. Deyon winced but didn't comment when she wiped the cuts on his elbow with a cloth dipped in an antiseptic mixture. He was the last to come into the sick bay. That meant damage assessment and scouting for hostiles in the vicinity was all but done.

Karl moaned, and Tara glanced at him. The Passiflora sedative had already kicked in and he remained unconscious. Her chest tightened at the blood staining his pale shirt collar.

Undeterred, Yorik finished applying a glue-like powder to the cut on Karl's forehead. It would stop the trickling blood and aid healing. "The collarbone's broke. Poss'bly right ankle too with how swelling's going up." Yorik had an accent that betrayed he had spent equal amounts of time around Amuleans and Haven Galaxians. He was short for a sailor, no more than five foot eleven with coarse black hair and dark ruddy skin.

Tara cursed herself for not spending her traineeship wages on a couple of healing classes. At least Yorik was better educated than her in the subject – the very reason Merlon had hired him.

The sailing tiers had a lot more freedom than most tiers when it came to how they tailored their career. Karl had extensive carpentry and shipwright courses for example. Using his personal interest as a gain not only meant he earned more than a common sailor, but also that he would have no trouble finding another captain to sail under. That sort of advantage was important during these times where the sailing tiers in Twin Cities Galaxy were saturated.

Tara gritted her teeth. Carpentry skills wouldn't help Karl now. "He'll be alright, will he nae?"

"Depends on his head traum'." Yorik shrugged. Yorik wasn't one to rub honey on his lips. He would speak the truth no matter how much it might hurt.

Tara held her breath against the hard thumps of her heart. *No more deaths, I've had enough of that. Tomaline, if you listen, shine on Karl today.*

"He'll be fine, pet." Deyon patted her hand. The same worry rumbling in her gut, glinted in his dark eyes.

She chewed her cheek but managed a smile. "Thanks, Deyon. I donae think we'll bind your cut. The bandage would only bother you."

Deyon twisted his arm, glancing at the pink and red of his elbow scrape. Then he nodded and got up. He stared for another few moments at Karl, whose foot was now wrapped in a pale gauze. Then the second mate left as quietly as he had arrived.

Tara turned on the stool. Her knee panged painfully. Without getting to her feet, she picked up the various jars, bowls and strips of bandages and rags from the foot end of the cot Karl lay in.

"What of your's knee?" Yorik said.

She shook her head. "It's fine, sore, but fine."

Yorik opened his mouth, probably to protest, judging by how his eyebrows shot up, but a knock on the open door spared her.

Merlon filled the doorframe, lingering outside the sick bay like he often did, probably fearing there was still blood or gore to be seen. "How's he doing?"

"If head traum's not bad, he'll be a'right. Won't walk for quite a while." Yorik got up, joints popping. He took the leftover healing tools Tara had gathered in her arms before she could fight herself up from the low stool. He put the gauze in the cupboard drawer but left the sick bay with the dishes of mixed ointments.

Since they had spent valuable water rations mixing up the powders and herbs, any leftovers would be bottled up in labelled glass jars for later use.

Merlon stepped into the small cubby the second Yorik had vacated it. Worry creased his forehead. "What about you? Are you badly hurt? It was quite the tumble. Gaunty sprained xir ankle again. Seems that foot never really gets to heal before xe gets a new injury." He held out a hand.

With a sigh, Tara took it and let him pull her to standing. Her left knee pulsed, but she forced herself to put full weight on it.

Merlon's frown deepened and without listening to her feeble protest, he wrapped an arm around her waist. "Yorik's looked at you?"

"Bruised knees. Donae want to waste painkillers until we know where we are." Despite her determination to prove her health, she leaned into him. He smelled of warm starlight and wood lye. There was something soothing about the firmness of his support when they left the sick bay. She couldn't quite walk without limping, her knees wobbly and weak.

"No sign of people thus far. I have no idea where we are," Merlon muttered. "Since we're on a planet or moon and the star's warm, I fear we might've somehow ended up closer to the Far Galaxies than I'd like."

Tara glanced at Yorik, scraping tinctures into bottles on the shelf outside the sick bay. She kept her voice low on the way back towards the captain's cabin. "There were dragons. A lot of them. They seemed to fly straight *into* the portal storm. I think they might have set the course."

Merlon's grip tightened around her. His jaw worked but it wasn't until he had eased her into the desk chair and closed the hatch after them, he replied, "The gravitational pull is strong. I fear we'll struggle to take off."

Tara adjusted her hair, trying to capture most of it in her hairband. The fiddling did little to still the nerves trembling her body. Even if she couldn't see the energy properly, she could feel it. A heaviness in her very bones. It would be worse off the ship. The breathing wood and sails of *Lucia* strained to keep the gravity similar to what it was in Amule where she had been built.

"Is the gravity stronger than on Ola and your Ma's planet?"

Merlon dropped into his chair on the other side of the desk. "I think so. I should've brought my Tracker compass."

He ran a hand through his black hair, pushing it back over his head. He looked older when concern narrowed his golden-brown eyes and left his lips pressed into thin lines.

The anxiety flickering in his gaze, the one he quite evidently tried to suppress and hide from her, left a pressure in her stomach. If her knee hadn't hurt so much, she would have gone around the table and pulled him into a hug. He always tried to carry it all by himself. Even more so since Adrien had been murdered by Lady Galantria.

"We'll find a way home," she said. "We made it back from Outer Universe, remember. Wherever we are, it cannae be as difficult as that." She hoped she was right. But the odds of ending up somewhere it was even more difficult to get home from *did* seem staggeringly low.

Merlon sent her a tight smile. "Maybe I'll recognise some constellations when it gets dark. If it gets dark." He frowned.

Always the pessimist. "You will." She put all the conviction she could muster into her voice. "How many repairs do—" A quick rapping on the door cut her off.

"Yes?" Merlon grabbed the armrests of his chair, already halfway to standing.

Tara turned in hers, not even considering getting up.

Fabian burst through the door. "Cap'n, Derek saw a being. A human kid he reckons. Ran off to the bushes when he called out."

Forgetting her pain, Tara shot to her feet. She grimaced at the pulsing in her knee. But it was tolerable to stand. She simply needed to not put *all* her weight on the left leg.

28

"Has Boomer made blast arrows?" Merlon rushed to his bow by the bunk. He pulled a pair of black leather gloves from a drawer in the adjoining wall cupboards. "We need to follow that kid and find someone who can tell us where we are."

Fabian ran through the cabin to the chamber he technically shared with Tara, although she primarily slept in Merlon's bunk. A clatter of arrows tumbling onto the floor preceded Fabian cursing under his breath.

Before Tara could hobble to the chamber door to the right of the cabin, Fabian reappeared from it.

He stuffed plain arrows back into his quiver. "Blasts are ready. Boomer'll be finishin' up the orange one now. Never know if they's got diseases."

"Good. Three teams of eight," Merlon said. "The rest stay behind."

Fabian nodded and vanished back out of the main door. After his promotion to first mate, he had become so efficient Tara sometimes worried he forgot to breathe. But then he would muck around on calm days, and she knew him again, if for nothing else then through the constant cracking of bad jokes.

Her bow and arrows were also kept in the chamber, so she entered it while Merlon shrugged on his quiver. She gritted her teeth and knelt to pull her shooting gloves out from the box under her dis-used bunk.

"Tara," Merlon called. "You're not going. Stay on ship to—"

"What!" Tara sprung up, fighting not to make a face at the pang the motion sent up through her legs. Merlon stood in

29

the door and raised a brow at her, nonetheless. "I'm nae that bad off."

Merlon rubbed his face. "I know," there was the hint of a sigh in his voice, "but I need you to stay with Gaunty and Yorik. Someone's got to watch Karl and *Lucia*. Deyon's team will stay close too, but I need at couple of people onboard who can shoot."

"Gaunty and Yorik can shoot." Tara stalked back into the cabin to glare better at Merlon.

Stars burn her if she didn't know he feared she couldn't run if they met with hostiles. They had an agreement. No mollycoddling, but he fussed anytime they were alone. It was cute when he made her breakfast or tea to help ease a headache. Less so when he grounded her after crashing on an unknown planet.

"Gaunty, who got a nasty rope burn on xir hand last week?" Merlon raised a brow.

Tara blew out. "Burn it." She had forgotten that.

Gaunty wasn't a wuss, but the rope burns were still leaky. Tara had glimpsed them when Yorik re-did the bandage yesterday. *Gaunty's tough, unlike Karl, he's the biggest wuss*. Tara sighed. This time Karl had every reason to bemoan his injuries. She couldn't wait for his whinging. It would mean he was on the mend again.

"Please, stay." Merlon squeezed her arm. His eyes sought hers and held her captive when she gave in and met his gaze. "Make sure *Lucia* remains safe."

For someone who kept his emotions bottled up most of the time, intensity shone from the burnt ochre depths. Tara's chest fluttered. He wasn't truly referring to the ship's safety. "I will."

Merlon's hand slipped behind her neck. She leaned in, closing her eyes when he pressed his forehead against hers.

He let go, turning towards the exit. "We'll be careful."

"Merlon." She caught his hand, pulling him back towards herself. His arms wrapped around her as hers did around him. Her lips tingled when they met his. Warmth spread through her body, then he broke away, panting lightly. Longing winked in his eyes, but agitation blotted it out fast.

"Keep safe until I'm back." He squeezed her hand and left the cabin.

Tara couldn't keep up with his strides so she allowed herself all the grimaces she could while she limped through the corridor to the main deck.

She blinked at the golden, bright light outside. Fabian had already divided the crew into three groups. The sailors shuffled around, anxiously glancing across the sandy stretch to where the dark green bushes and trees swallowed the pale, yellow grains.

Tara hobbled across to the port side. The almost turquoise water looked a couple yards deep there. On the starboard it was simply wet sand. The land rose slowly up towards the trees that drew a blurred line fifty yards away.

Huge leaves and palm fronds made up the dense growth. Vines hung from some of the broader branches, others crept across the sand, stretching thin fingers towards *Lucia* and the salty water beyond her hull.

"Derek, your group is with me, where did you see the kid?" Merlon stood by the rope ladder that dangled over the railing on the starboard side.

While Tara stayed onboard, Gaunty and Yorik both at her side, Derek led the rest of the crew to the trees. Apart from a particularly tall tree, Tara couldn't see distinctive features at the spot they stopped.

Was it a date palm? She had seen something like it in Amule but there were so many tree species and since her da sneezed if he got near trees in flower, they had never done picnics at the orchards like many Amulean families did during holidays.

Her stomach hardened to a rock. Most of the people she cared about disappeared into the greenery. A series of freak accidents and possible disasters played through her mind, but she caught herself in the doom and fought it back. She would *not* let her fear rule her.

"They'll take care," Gaunty said.

Tara let her hand drop from fiddling with her hair. It would never stay in that bun anyway. "I know." She nudged Gaunty's arm. "Thanks though. I'll go sit by Karl. Call if there's the slightest hint of movement."

Karl remained fast asleep for so long Tara picked a hole in the frayed blanket Yorik had folded up and put aside. With the muggy heat of this planet, Karl had sweated through his shirt and trousers, drops pearling on his brown skin.

Tara didn't doubt he would be asking for his sarong the moment he woke. It was so sticky even she considered finding that one skirt she – probably – had packed.

The creak of the steps into the hold flung her from her seat. She caught herself on the sick bay cupboards, gasping at the sharp pain shooting up her leg.

Yorik entered, raised his eyebrows, and sighed. "You ought'a take some painkillers in the least."

"Tomorrow, if I'm still in pain." Tara straightened. "They're back?"

"Not the Cap'n's group. But it's getting dark."

Tara swallowed. *Don't panic. He's fine.*

Leaving Yorik to watch Karl, she crawled back up the wooden ladder. She took her time and willed Merlon's group to have showed up by the time she went to the starboard side. The sky had turned dark orange. Pink streaks, clouds Tara realised, crisscrossed it. The trees were shadowy, their shapes indistinct and the air close. How was it still so hot and humid?

Gaunty held the rope ladder while parts of Deyon's group returned over the rail. They all looked as sticky and sweaty as Tara felt. Hair and clothes clinging to their bodies and the waterskins on their belts empty or nearly so.

"Found anything?" Tara offered her hand to Jara.

"Not a thing. Mango trees and coconuts, none with fruit. Not a sign o' people."

Tara weighed the pros and cons, but eventually started lighting the lanterns that hadn't smashed in the storm and rough landing. One by one, she rubbed the white light powder between her fingertips, pushing the plates full of the powder back into the glass cage with a tube inside. As the

33

powder pulled upwards, the light intensified, casting a cold glow across the deck.

Once finished with her task, Tara returned to the starboard. She took to staring into the growing blackness. Hopefully not hostiles but rather Merlon and his group would find the lights useful waypoints.

Fabian's group assembled below *Lucia* on the damp sand. Fabian and Boomer hovered nearer the trees, heads sweeping from side to side. From their abrupt movements and nocked arrows, she knew they too were getting anxious.

"Deyon, should we go search—" Tara stopped.

Fabian whooped and lowered his bow. He trotted towards the dark figures appearing from between the trees.

Tara let out the breath she had held for ten minutes when Merlon's familiar shape was amongst the shadows plodding back towards the ship.

Chapter 4

T hree days later, a hollow thud and accompanying pain stabbing up her leg made Tara jolt awake. Black swirls of nightmarish images clouded her vision. Her heart thundered in her ears. Where was the danger? She had to *see*.

"Tara?"

Her head snapped around, fists rising, ready to defend herself. Always primed to fight back. School had taught her that was one of the few ways to keep the taunting at bay. Sometimes at least.

She blinked. The nightmares receded. They gave way to the warm light and quiet hum of *Lucia's* cabin. Nothing had attacked her, she had shifted and hit the back of the bunk in her sleep.

Merlon spoke again when she slowly lowered her arms. "You're safe. You were dreaming." He stood beside the bunk with a logbook in hand, watching her with a concerned crease between his brows. "Do you need me to stay?"

Tara nodded. She hid her trembling hands under the sheets but made an effort to shuffle out from the dark depths of the bunk.

All those maggot-riddled skulls grinning at her. Blood coming out of the walls of the well she had once been stuck in. She hadn't ever been this plagued by such nightmares. But now, Lady Galantria's cold voice followed her into the well Lanier had forced her to jump into. Edur's meatless skull laughing and laughing.

They're dead. Lanier is long buried, Lady Galantria was burned for her crimes. She chose not to think about Edur, murdered, slaughtered, and eaten by the cannibals in Ivory. He hadn't deserved death. Nobody who had died in Ivory had. She stopped herself before she thought of Adrien and Patrice.

"Did…" Tara cleared her throat and tried again, this time managing to get her voice above a croak. "Did you sleep much?" She touched the bed beside herself.

Merlon reached in and smoothed some of the sheets before settling. "More than usual."

She lifted an eyebrow.

"Hey, don't look at me like that. Five consecutive hours is a lot for me." He smiled. The expressions softened his features and warmed Tara. It made her bones feel soft.

She leaned her head against his shoulder. "By rights, you shouldnae be functioning on so little sleep. I'd be crazed if it was me."

"You're saying that like I'm not crazed," Merlon said.

Tara snorted. Her breath and heart settled. His arm pulling her closer stilled those last flickers of sleep horrors. In the past few months, the nightmares had become infrequent.

Slowly but surely leaving her, but instead she couldn't see energy.

She straightened and looked out the bubbled glass windows of the ship's stern. Not even a thread of turquoise no matter how much she tried focusing. *I'd like to see a therapist talk back my navigator's vision, I bet it's harder than it was talking away the nightmares.*

She turned her head back to Merlon when he kissed her ear. "How's Karl?"

"Better. Yorik reckons he'll be out of bed by tomorrow. Then it'll be a matter of making sure he doesn't do too much until his bones are mended. He strained something in his left arm and hand too. Even whittling should be avoided for now."

She nodded. Karl had been chatty last night and not had as many sudden dizzy spells he had the day before. Still, Yorik had bid him stay in the sick bay until they were certain Karl's brain hadn't taken serious damage.

The hot, close air quickly made snuggling into Merlon's embrace unbearable. Tara pushed away and stretched with a yawn. "How're you nae dying of heat with all those clothes on? Do you nae have a sarong like the rest of the crew?"

"Not really a sarong kind of person." Merlon's lips twitched in a strained smile. The one that, coupled with his eyes suddenly avoiding hers, meant not to push the matter.

Tara sighed. Nobody aboard, not least her, cared he wasn't all muscle and without an ounce of fat, but he remained insecure about his body. She too had been bullied about her weight, although for the opposite reason. Bone-rattler had been one of the nicknames Lanier had invented for her and she could still hear the echoing taunts in the school courtyard. Those things could be difficult to shake.

She flicked the sheets off her legs and made to stand, using Merlon's shoulder as leverage.

"Gracious stars!" Merlon seized her hand. "It's got worse, should you even be out of bed?"

She frowned at the bruises on her legs. They bloomed black and purple up from her knees and another spread across her left hip. The latter had yellow and almost green streaks in it. A sure sign it was slowly but surely healing. She shrugged. "I'm sore but it's bruises, nae more."

Merlon didn't look convinced and sprung to bring her clothes from where she had dropped them on the floor, so she didn't have to take the three steps to them. She didn't have it in her to tell him to stop fussing. He was rather adorable when he was in this sort of mood.

It was a good thing too she kept her mouth shut. While she dressed, Merlon vanished with a promise of making her oat hot cakes for breakfast. He knew she hated cooking and Gaunty had been released of that duty while they were stranded on the island so xe could give xir sprained ankle a rest.

An hour later, all hands, bar Karl, were on deck, ready for take-off. Nobody had a clue where they were but maybe leaving this island and planet would help with that.

All they knew was the sudden dusk arrived every day at the same time and lasted ten hours. The constellations becoming visible at night didn't match anything in Merlon's star maps, and he had a lot of those. It was one of the things he collected and treasured. According to himself, it had started with a map of Twin Cities Galaxy he had inherited from his grandma.

Tara ran her shirt sleeve over her forehead, only partially to dab away the sweat trickling down her face. She tried to control her expression as she did.

Merlon stood beside Jara at the wheel, his eyes on Tara, face expectant.

She had to see where the energy was stronger. They needed to know the exact currents for the sails to catch enough they could lift from this high-gravity planet.

Tara put her back on Merlon. *Forget he's watching. Forget everyone's watching.* Why had it become so hard to do what she was born to? How could she justify belonging to the navigator's tier if she couldn't even see a flicker of energy? Gritting her teeth, she squinted towards the forest. Nothing.

Stalking across the main deck, she looked across the vast, salty lake. Ocean was what she had decided it was called. Ola had told her about oceans at some point and she had found the page in her notebook that described it was usually vast and salty.

She narrowed her eyes. Was that an energy flow or the turquoise of the waters reflecting in the air above? Thin threads weaved around her. If she could make herself see them clearer, she could tell which way they were moving, and the crew could change the sails accordingly.

"What's takin' ya so long, ya tramp?" Fabian drove a fist into her arm. "Ya's usually jumpin' at any opportunity to order us common sailors 'round."

Tara grimaced but held her tongue. *Just see the energy!* But she could catch nothing except faint glimmers here and there. More across the water though. There was maybe a downwards force, that brown aura of gravity weakening further out on the water. Or maybe she imagined things.

Finally, she stalked back to Merlon's side. "Can *Lucia* float? We need to get out there, where the gravity is less severe."

"In theory. But if the gravitational force is too high, I'm not sure." He kept his voice low, glancing at Jara who was the closest crew. "Can we not take flight from right here?"

"We can try," Tara said. As if she knew. Without her usual abilities she couldn't possibly tell any more than he could.

Merlon nodded once. "On your orders then."

Tomaline burn me! She had fought so hard to get those command rights last year when she was still a trainee but back then she had been able to see energy clear as anything.

If she messed this up, Merlon might well rescind those rights, at least until she proved herself again. He had promised to treat her professionally on deck and he was the sort of person who took promises and correct procedures *very* seriously. Didn't help she herself had been adamant he made that promise.

"Tack to starboard," Tara shouted. "The currents are stronger out there, above the water. Anchor fully in."

"Reel in the anchor at ten percent intervals. Let's not break the rigging by allowing too much energy to hit the sails too fast." Merlon barely raised his voice, but it carried easily across the ship.

Colour flickered past the sails in short gusts. Tara focused on them. If she tracked the energy moving across the strong canvas, she could maybe ease herself into the flows moving all around. That's how those who struggled in school years learned to see.

Lucia groaned and she pulled forward. The water splashed against her portside and she listed. Instead of raising when Jara pressed the altitude pedal by the wheel, the keel scraped and dug itself deeper into the sand.

Tara ran to the railing, leaning over it to see what was happening underneath. "Raise us more! Quicker with the anchor!"

But *Lucia* moved only a few inches forward at a time grinding herself further down into the soft, damp sand. She shook, the hull and keel protesting. The tremors going up through Tara's knees made her wobble and sent pain pulsing through her leg despite the painkillers she had taken with her morning meal.

"Hold on, she's struggling to lift off!" Merlon called.

Crew staggered and *Lucia* tilted even further to starboard, driving herself down and sideways. The ship groaned and shook as she lumbered forward.

"Anchor fully in!" Boomer shouted.

Merlon cursed under his breath. The sails bulged but there would be no taking off. Not while they were on land.

Tara clambered along the stern railing. She stared across the blue water. Waves left swirls of turquoise energy, air pushed up and tumultuously round by the water underneath. "We have to get her out there."

Merlon met her gaze. Then he glanced at the straining sails.

"Cap'n, we'll crash the trees!" Fabian yelled.

Tara spun. They were lumbering forward, simultaneously digging into the sand, and spraying it up along the sides of the hull. The palms were coming up fast. And the large boulders hiding amongst the sand.

"Anchor back out!" Tara ordered.

The chains clonked. And the windlass screeched to an instant halt. "It's stuck! Branches and sand in the way." Boomer shouted.

"Drop canvas!" Merlon roared.

Fabian and Kieran whipped out knives, chopping left and right at the lines holding the canvas. The sails glowed. They loosened from one side of their fastenings, luffing to the deck where Deyon led Derek and Gaunty's attempts at collecting the sheets before they flew into, and swept away, the crew rushing around.

The anchor chains began grumbling again. *Lucia* moaned, her trembling plod faltering. It sent Tara stumbling. She caught herself against the rail. No falling overboard. Mira had miraculously survived that when they crashed the planet Merlon's ma and her partner Ola had lived on, but Tara held no illusions she would be as fortunate.

For a panicked second, she thought she would continue overboard. Then her grip around a baluster solidified. And in that short breath, bright turquoise tendrils wound themselves around her. Everywhere. And strongest were the teal of a little pounding heart by the edge of the trees. She blinked and it was gone. All the turquoise of energy had vanished. And she couldn't see anything resembling a living creature under the palms. Fear had made her see things that weren't there. Probably.

The breathing wood sighed with relief. The ship lay still once more. *Lucia* leaned heavily to starboard, the deck hard to walk across without slipping to the right.

"Pure disaster. Grav'ty's too much 'ere." Jara waved an arm, her golden bracelets jingling.

Merlon's face was grim, lips drawn into thin lines and brows furrowed as he stared off into the distance.

Tara mentally prepared herself for a scolding. She should have seen that the energy wouldn't be strong enough. *Lucia* wouldn't have been damaged much by this take-off attempt but if they hadn't managed to stop, she would have. And now they had even less space to get her turned towards the ocean.

"We have to get her into the water without flying," Merlon finally said.

Surprised he hadn't blamed her, Tara dared meet his severe gaze. Something in his eyes softened slightly, frown easing. She had to get her navigator's vision sorted. He trusted her to see the energy, not make qualified guesses on the best direction. He could do that himself.

She made a false start. She had to come clean about her lacking abilities. Another flicker of teal at the corner of her eye broke her line of thought, but when she turned to look at the palms, there was nothing there.

Still, a lump that had formed in her throat stayed when she tried to swallow it. She couldn't shake the feeling they were being watched.

Chapter 5

The entire crew shuffled beside *Lucia*, kicking at the sand, or stroking the salt-crusted hull. They had crawled down the ladders once the sails had been furled to follow Merlon and Kieran on their external damage assessment.

Tara pulled her soft cap a little further down, trying to shade her eyes better from the relentless starlight. If they weren't going to work more today, she would change into her skirt. It was far too muggy to wear trousers.

"No need for repairs." Merlon paused between Tara and Fabian. He used the faded red scarf from around his neck to wipe his forehead and stuck it in a pocket. "We need to get her dug out and into the water." He patted the hull. The breathing wood seemed to sigh at his gentle touch.

Tara had never thought of ships as living creatures, but *Lucia* had a strange presence to her. Like she recognised Merlon was her caretaker. It made sense he had insisted she got fixed back up – reusing her original structures where possible – after their crash in Amule's harbour.

It would have been cheaper to sell her for scraps and buy a new ship, but with the inheritance Merlon had from Adrien, it had been possible to salvage her. It helped that the Foreign Affair's Chancellor's claims of city recompense were cancelled when he ascended to High Chancellor after the election. Of course, the cost had been that the trial against him for illegally branding Tara and Patrice had also been dropped.

Tara blew out a breath to ease away the pang of grief the thought of Patrice brought. The new High Chancellor, Horatio Corncockle, had indirectly caused her violent death and got away with it by bribing stars knew how many judges. But that was how politics worked. At least in Amule. Supposedly they were less corrupt in Fristate's capital Intrapolis. But the majority of Fristate Galaxy was in turn overrun by pirates from the nearby Blacklock's Galaxy. Nowhere was perfect it seemed.

"Derek, Yorik, shovels if ya will," Fabian said, bringing Tara out from her musings. "Good thing ya said to buy more shovels, Cap'n. Not always so dense it seems." Fabian slapped Merlon's shoulder.

Merlon raised a brow, clearly too stressed to even smile at Fabian's attempt to lighten the mood. "Be glad she shifted further onto land. I'm not sure we could have dug her free if she was in the wetter sand."

Tara glanced at Merlon's scarred feet. Sand stuck to his dark skin well onto his shins. From her own trip around the ship, she knew the sand seemed to swallow feet if walking too close to the water's edge. Slightly unnerving that.

"How're we gettin' her into the water without sinkin' further?" Fabian scratched the back of his head.

Tara stared at the sand. *Lucia*'s keel was buried and a good yard or two of her stowage was too. But Tara had seen how repairs were done on land one day she had hung out with Karl back in Amule. "We could use logs. Cut some of the palms and wedge them under. Like they do to move ships out of the shipyard warehouse to where the masts get attached."

"That could work, but how will we turn her about?" Merlon frowned from the ship to the trees and then the ocean.

"I'm nae sure but if we put trees to her portside and let a sliver of energy through the sails while they're tacked to starboard..." Tara shrugged, she was making it up as she went.

Merlon nodded. "Let's try it."

"Good thing ya bought more saws and axes too, Cap'n. Have you finally grown un-dense?" Fabian grinned.

Tara groaned inwardly, but had a hard time not chuckling, nonetheless. She would always take his stupid jokes over that melancholic seriousness he fell into too often these days.

The afternoon dragged itself along. The heat never let up, although a faint breeze and the shade from the tall palms and fruit-less mango trees provided minimal relief. They sorely lacked Karl, but he was stuck in the sick bay on Yorik's orders.

Unlike last time they had to chop down a few trees for emergency repairs, Tara had learned not to saw or use the axes without wrapping her hands in fabric scraps. It kept blisters from growing too severe from the unusual work.

"Do you need water refills? A break?" Merlon asked.

Tara paused, leaving Fabian to chop at the palm. "I'm alright, Gaunty swapped our waterskins nae long ago."

"Oi, Trachnan, I'll die if I's got to chop this on me own."

Tara snorted. "You're unkillable like a roach, suck it up, turd."

"Careful with the humidity though," Merlon said. "I think we'll get enough trunks today, but we'll wait until tomorrow to try moving again."

"Thanks, pops." Fabian grimaced.

Merlon's expression was priceless. The mixture of offence and humour flickering in his warm, brown eyes sent laughter bubbling in Tara's chest. Merlon attempted to scowl at her, lips twitching.

"We'll be fine." She waved dismissively. "Might take a break after rolling this back though." She turned back to the tree when Merlon shook his head with a small smile and stalked to the next group further to the right.

Fabian leaned the axe handle against his hip, watching her for a couple of moments. She could *feel* his eagerness to say something, probably planning to wind her up, but she ignored him. The sooner they had this palm felled, the sooner they could push it across the sand, and she could go cool her feet in the water.

"So…" Fabian finally spoke, the very tone of his voice betrayed she had been right. Mentally she steeled herself,

47

knowing full well Fabian was far too good at finding her pressure points and annoy the starlight out of her. "Ya didn't talk to him yet, did ya?"

Disregarding him entirely, Tara paused, shook wood chips from the rag bandage around her hand and resumed chopping. Sappy wood splinters flew around her face. She squinted, cursing herself for not having crawled back onboard to ask Karl if she could borrow his tinted glasses. They would have provided her some security against the wooden projectiles.

"Ha, knew it," Fabian said. "What's holdin' ya up? Told ya he's wantin' the same chat, no?"

Tara pretended she hadn't heard. Her stomach hardened. It was probably too soon to talk about. They hadn't had their one-year anniversary yet.

"Hey tramp? I's talkin' to ya!" Fabian used the butt of the axe handle to nudge her shoulder.

With a hiss, she straightened. "I have nae idea what you're on about but you're a stinking rat's turd."

She swung the axe at his face but kept her arm close to her chest, never actually in reach of him.

"Ha!" Fabian jumped backwards, chortling. "'Course ya know what I'm on about." He wiggled his eyebrows.

Tara sighed. Why was he like this? She didn't have a brother, most people in Amule didn't have siblings, but she was fairly certain Fabian was the epitome of a younger brother.

Fabian's smirk turned into a frown. "Seriously though, the two of ya's old. Ya better get ya wants aligned or ya's outta time before ya know it."

"Old!" Tara huffed. She had turned but twenty-nine last month. Of course, Ma had only been about to turn forty when she got diagnosed with the cancer that eventually killed her. The healers hadn't known if it was a heritable type. All Tara knew was her grandparents had all died by the age of sixty-four. That gave Da another eight years to outlive any of them. She really hoped he would.

The palm groaned, leaning heavily to the left. Fabian threw his axe, pushing at the trunk to control where it would fall.

Tara channelled her frustration into her axe and sent the palm tumbling with another two strikes. Fronds and leaves rustled. Wood crunched and the ground shuddered when it landed. The sap smelled fresh, watery even.

Fabian ran his shirt cuff over his forehead. "Mira and I already talked 'bout a kid, ya know. Had to agree on whether we'd have one or not. What with her family and us being inter-tier. Unless we got approved to adopt an orphaned captain's tier, our kid will be a common sailor."

Tara stared at Fabian. "What did you decide?"

"Mira wants our own." Fabian shrugged. "I don't mind either way. Me brother's adopted ya know and my parents have had less trouble with him than me so I's thinkin' they sometimes wish they'd stuck with him."

There was a tinge of hurt in Fabian's face and it made Tara scramble for ways to make it go away. "He's nae a first mate though." Tara nudged Fabian's arm. "And I'd say if anything, they're proud you won the heart of a captain. Pretty big achievements for an entertainer tier impostering as a sailor." That was an old joke. That Fabian should have been born in the entertainer tier with how much of a joker he was.

Fabian laughed. "I wish they were." The smile didn't quite reach his eyes.

The very fact he had moved out the instant they returned to Amule told Tara what he hadn't ever let on. Inter-tier relationships weren't looked well upon even if there were no laws against it. Stars, even Da hadn't been particularly fond of the idea of Tara dating Merlon although he had said his peace and then gone back to his usual quiet acceptance. Da had never even grumbled at hosting Merlon for dinner.

Fabian on the other hand couldn't be in the same room as any of Mira's family without them threatening to raise a restraining order against him.

"Have your family met Mira yet?" Tara said.

Fabian kicked at the downed palm. "Wasn't possible with her dad locking her away like that." His face suddenly grew cheerful, energetic even. "But I have it on good authority she snuck away from his watch and turned her ship from Twin Cities."

Tara blinked. "Wait, what? How do you know that?"

Lucia had left Amule three months ago. Tara had spoken with Mira shortly before, at which point she had been stuck on a small clipper sailing to and from Amule's sister-city, Trachna, with various trade goods. Half her crew had been Cobalt Senior's – her dad's – people, keeping careful watch that she didn't go near Fabian when in Amule and adhered strictly to the routes Cobalt Senior had determined.

"Let's just say, there's a very special rodent aboard her ship." Fabian beamed.

Surprise washed through Tara and it took her a moment to consolidate this new information. The Tracker rat that had forced her friendship on Merlon and Tara had left Amule a month before *Lucia* had. "Bailey is with Mira? Merciful stars that's nae going to go well."

Fabian flicked a hand. "Nah, it'll be fine. Mira knows not to listen too much to her."

Tara shook her head. The fact Mira had rid herself of her da's crew and turned away from Twin Cities to stars knew where already suggested Mira had caved under Bailey's force of chaos.

Bailey had probably snuck away from *her* da as well. Last Tara heard she was meant to do another year of undercover training. Whatever that meant.

Trackers weren't very forthcoming. In fact, they were thought to be barely more than a mythical, secret people to everyone except the few "initiated".

Lucia had run into a Tracker ship while in Outer Universe last year and discovered they were real. And that they in fact were talking animals of all shapes and sizes. According to General Rum, Bailey's da, *Lucia's* crew were under constant surveillance when in port, ensuring anyone who tried to speak up about the Trackers' true identity were killed before the knowledge was spread.

"Come on then," Fabian said and chopped the fronds of the palm. "Or are ya as scared of hard work as ya are talkin' to Merlon about kids?"

"I'm nae scared of either." Tara ground out. She shoved at the trunk, but another stump was in the way, and it only rolled backwards again. *Typical.*

Fabian grabbed the top, hoisting it over the stump that lay in the way. "Course ya are or ya'd already spoke to him when ya first mentioned it to me, two months ago."

"I'm still thinking about it, alright? It's nae like I've decided if I want to register partnership with him." Tara used her foot to push the trunk out from the shrubbery and onto the sand.

She had thought she wanted that with Sona. But that hadn't ended well considering Sona had been sleeping with another woman for stars knew how long. And then she had the nerve to say she thought they were in an open relationship when Tara knew the first thing, she always mentioned was that she wasn't up for that.

Fabian puffed and raised his brows. "Why wouldn't ya? Ya might be too stubborn to admit ya love him, but nobody else is fooled."

"It's nae so straightforward." Tara glared.

She tried to stay professional on deck, was it so obvious she adored him? But then again, the ship wasn't exactly soundproof and Fabian living in the chamber opening into the cabin probably couldn't help but hear half the conversations she had with Merlon.

"Listen, if you—" A branch snapped behind them, and Tara spun.

There was a flicker of teal before the energy receded to faint threads and wouldn't grow stronger no matter how much she stared.

"Ya think there is some fowl or pigs around? I'd kill for some meat. Sick and tired of grains and old potatoes."

Tara ignored Fabian and took a step into the bushes. She shifted the large green leaves aside with a hand.

There on a bare patch of sand was the imprint of a small, human foot. She met Fabian's dark eyes. "I donae think it's pigs or fowl watching us."

Chapter 6

Tara shook her head at Fabian. 'Do not shout.' She used Squamate gestures.

"We've gotta get the others." Fabian spoke under his breath. He had flicked the axe back into his hand and looked ready to sound the alarm or rush after whoever had left that little footprint.

Tara nodded and scanned the ground. She plucked a sizeable chunk of bark and lopped it at the nearest person rolling a palm trunk towards *Lucia*.

Kieran jolted and whirled. "Ow!"

"Sh!" She waved for him to hurry over.

Still rubbing his neck, Kieran trotted towards them. Something in their stance, or the fact Fabian's gaze kept sweeping the brush around them, made Kieran pause to pick up another axe. "What's happe'd?" His Haven Galaxy accent never failed to make Tara smile. Except for today. Nerves leaving her too anxious.

"That has." Tara pointed at the kid-sized imprint in the sand. "We're being watched. Quick go get the others. Donae all come running and be quiet or we'll never find them."

Kieran did a double take. "I knew Derek saw a'body! He's got good eyes."

"Yeah, clearly. Let Cap'n know but Tara and I'll lead. The rest of ya hang back." Fabian squeezed Kieran's shoulder. He turned to Tara. "Ya ready?"

She nodded. "There cannae be many or Merlon would've seen signs of people when scouting the other day."

A frown had built on Kieran's forehead. The talc cream lathered on his far too pale skin had crusted around his brows but created white beads of sweat across his face. "We could be wrong 'bout that. Only been once to n'other side of the island."

"That's why ya need to be ready as backup. Now go, time's wastin'." Fabian spun Kieran and the boatswain stumbled. But he picked up his feet and sprinted so hard the sand flicked up behind him.

"Come on then." Tara butted Fabian's arm with the handle of her axe. Between the axes and their eating knives they weren't exactly vulnerable. And Tara had trained a bit with Karl's axe to get the hang of the weapon that was vastly different from her cutlass.

She searched the ground for more footprints. At first, she noticed nothing, then her focus shifted, and she realised there were little indents and disturbed leaves and sticks leading away from where they had been felling trees.

Fabian let her take the lead without a word, probably thinking she followed the remnants of disturbed energy she *should* be able to pick up on. She didn't even bother trying.

Someone had moved in a haste and the further they got into the thickets, the more clearly the trail stood out. Broken leaves, a solid footprint. She touched the tiny piece of torn fabric stuck on the side of a palm. "You think it's a kid all alone? We've seen nobody. Nae heard a thing." Her own whispered words made Tara's stomach clench.

How would a lone child have got here? And how would xe have survived? There were no fresh water sources on the island. No food the crew had managed to scavenge in the three days since the crash and it wasn't for the lack of searching for those things.

"A child alone? I hope there wasn't a disease killin' the parents," Fabian said.

They exchanged a glance. A contagious disease could doom everyone aboard the ship. Tara gritted her teeth. "If we find them, you stay back. If they're ill, best find out by only risking one of us."

"Not a chance! Cap'n would truss me up if I let ya into danger."

Tara forced a smirk. "Ah, just admit you'd hate for me to get hurt."

"Ha! Never." Fabian's voice went up a notch.

Tara opened her mouth for a rebuttal, but a glimmer of turquoise, no, *teal*, moved at the corner of her eye. Her head whipped around. There, the faint pulse of something alive. Only it moved upwards *fast*. Into the crown on a huge tree, she didn't know the name of.

"What's ya navigator eyes seein', ya tramp?" The humour fell flat. Fabian licked his lips when Tara glanced at him. He clenched the axe, holding it high, ready to swing.

"Something's in the trees. Stay put."

"But—"

Tara paused him with a chop of her hand. "Wait here." She tucked her axe into her belt and set off down the slope towards the tree she had seen energy in. Hopefully her eyes hadn't tricked her.

Fabian followed in her wake, crashing through the undergrowth with the noise of a whole flock of school kids on an excursion in Amule's orchards. So much for telling him to stay put.

She didn't pay his protests any heed but jumped up onto the first large branch. An enormous black and orange beetle clambered up the rough trunk. Biting the rising panic back, she flicked it off with her forefinger and grabbed the next limb on the tree. *It's not the well. The bugs won't crawl into your clothes or hair. Keep it together!*

"Tara if somebody's up there…" Fabian paused.

Shouts rose from behind them.

Tara faltered halfway up to the dense crown of the tree. Were the yells coming from the ship? What if this was a distraction and there had been an ambush? Her heart stabbed at her ribs.

"Dragons!" the faint scream carried on the wind. Was that Derek's voice?

"Get down, they need us," Fabian snapped.

Tara cursed under her breath. She looked up. The leaves hid everything above her head from her view. But whenever she blinked, there was a faint flicker. Heartbeats. Two of them. Or was it three?

"Come on!" Fabian all but squealed. He shifted from one foot to the next.

Tara began moving back down. "Burn it! Start without me."

Fabian hesitated a second, then he turned on his heels. He stumbled up the hill, glancing back every two seconds.

Tara's feet hit the ground. The crown of the tree rustled. One of the branches groaned. Tara stopped in her tracks. She should get back. Help protect the ship if the dragons weren't the ditsy Visca and Vincent they had received help from when stuck in Outer Universe last year. But *someone* was up there.

The shrill voice of Visca cut through the leaves and set Tara's teeth on edge. The ship was safe then. She put her palm on the tree. "We mean no harm."

"Are you here to take us away to become lab 'speriments?" A small voice said.

Tara's stomach flipped. A kid, a young one too.

"Shh!" Someone else hissed.

"Elin, quiet," a third whispered. Only, the whisper was typical of kids and much louder than clearly intended. And those accents. Who did they remind Tara of?

"But how'll we knows without asking?" The first voice, Elin, replied. She sounded quite consternated. And so young. Tara wasn't good with young kids. Elin could be three or nine and Tara wouldn't hardly know to guess either.

"Cause they're Q-rebels. Look'it them!"

Tara's throat tightened. Q-rebels. She had first heard that term when they met Ola and Merlon's ma, in Outer Universe.

"They'll shoot us if they're Q-rebels," a voice said. Xe sounded a little older than the other two.

Tara swallowed hard. If these kids thought *Lucia's* crew were Q-rebels, there was only one answer to where the portal storm had taken them. Right back to Outer Universe.

Tara forced down the fear trying to cloud her mind. They had barely found a way home last time. Nearly getting killed in the process by the Trackers. If Merlon hadn't been clever and Bailey decided she liked them and talked their case against General Rum, they would all have been long dead.

"We're…" She paused, clearing her throat. "We're nae Q-rebels. Promise."

"Are you here to make us lab 'speriments then?" Elin asked.

How old was she? Tara hadn't exactly dealt with young kids before. She had tutored many youths in the captain's and navigator tiers but only in their final school years, age fifteen and up. "Nae, we crashed on accident. Where's your parents?" She realised they could be dead. Stars knew it wasn't uncommon for cancer to claim people early. "Or your caretakers?"

"Dead," the older kid said.

"My mummy's nut d-dead!" Elin hiccupped.

"They dun't want us." The second kid spoke quietly. "Nobody does." There was such heartbreak in xir voice, tears brimmed in Tara's eyes.

Who could not want their own kids? Xe had to have got that wrong. Those who dreamed of kids saved up their entire lives. Cried with happiness when they got granted a permit for one. And cried even harder if they managed to carry to

59

term or got the letter about being next in the queue for adoptions.

A sob precluded Elin's quivering voice. "That's nut true. Mummy said she loves me."

"*Your* mummy maybe, nut ours," the oldest one said.

Tara leaned her head back. She couldn't see them up there except for the occasional pulse of energy. Their hearts were beating fast. They were scared or ill. *Or maybe both.* She gulped. "Why nae come down and we'll sort you out? I'm sure your parents are star-mad with fear of where you are…my name's Tara, by the way." She added, hoping that would soften them enough to come down and show themselves.

The tree's upper branches complained. Its crown shook a little.

"Elin dun't!"

But a small, tattered shape came scooting down the trunk like it was her second nature. Her bare feet were blackened with dirt. Her trousers and tunic had probably once been a lighter colour but now looked the same brown and streaked grey of the sandy soil covering the ground. Blonde curls were a matted mess. And then she hopped off the last branch. She was tiny, her huge blue eyes staring up at Tara. "You promise you dun't make us into 'speriments? Mummy said that's what they'd do if *they* take us away."

"I promise I willnae do that. Ever." Tara's tongue felt dry. Elin's shoulders poked out in sharp angles. Her legs and arms were sticks. The hollows of her cheeks and black around her innocent eyes told of starvation. A lot of it.

Elin blinked. "Will you give us food?"

Tara couldn't speak. She nodded. With a hard swallow, she found her voice again. "How old are you? Elin?"

Elin's face brightened with a smile. Her freckled cheeks, star burnt and pale under the tan and dirt, dimpled. "Five and one half." She turned and looked up at the tree. "Balfour! Cary! They'll give us food! And dun't wanna make us 'speriments at all!"

"Elin, get away from that lady." Despite the kid's words, xir feet came into view as xe climbed down.

"I'm nae lady." Tara almost harrumphed before catching her tone. The only lady she had heard off was Lady Galantria. She had been a Star-Eater descendant. And she had killed Uncle Adrien. Those last fatal moments. The sword driving into Adrien's back – the blood coughed out when he rolled over on *Lucia's* deck – played in Tara's head. And Patrice would be alive had Lady Galantria not double branded her and Tara. *I didn't even get to say goodbye.*

The second kid hesitated, halfway down and clinging to a branch and the tree's trunk. Blood crusted down xir arms to the elbows. Xir hair under the dirt was probably as fair as Elin's. The blue eyes stared down with a melancholy and seriousness that should never be in a child's eyes.

"Are you siblings?" Tara looked from the kid still in the tree to Elin. Only high tier members sometimes got granted permits for multiple kids. Mira was the only one Tara knew who had blood siblings. Adopted second and third kids were a bit more common, like with Fabian's brother.

The kid in the tree shook xir head. "Cousins. My mummy's her mummy's sister."

Wealthy parents then. Made even less sense they had been abandoned. Unless there had been a disease. Tara frowned. It was impossible to tell based on their starved, grimy appearances if they were ill. "Come down and we'll find you some food. Would that nae be nice?"

"I'm Balfour. I'm eight. Cary's eleven. He's the one still hiding," the blond kid said. He looked like a boy. He slowly climbed down and placed himself beside Elin, little hand on her skinny shoulder. The protectiveness in his demeanour was evident.

Pain panged under Tara's ribs. She now understood why his arms were streaked brown with dry blood. Cut upon cut along his lower arms were far too regular to be a coincidence. She had tutored someone who had scars like that. Marks from difficult years. Only self-harm could explain it. But Balfour had said he was only eight!

His eyes locked on Tara's face. He yanked at the frayed shirt sleeves, tugging to hide the cuts, and twisting his arms so they were less visible. Too self-aware for one so young.

Tara forced herself to smile. She wouldn't mention it. Wouldn't make him feel self-conscious or embarrassed. He needed the help of a talk therapist. And a hug. But he looked about to dart right this moment so instead she leaned back her head and cupped her mouth. "Cary? Are you coming down? We'll go find you all food if you do."

Balfour glanced up the tree. "Maybe Cary better stay here. He did feed his daddy to the Sarco crocs."

Tara stared at him. "I'm sorry, *what?*"

Chapter 7

She had to have heard wrong. It was probably the accent. But when Balfour met Tara's gaze there was honesty in his face.

"Cary fed his daddy to the crocs. That's why they decided to put him here, on the island."

Tara fought not to visibly wipe her clammy hands against her trousers. What could she reply to something like that? She cast about for words, but a yell from near *Lucia* saved her. One eye still on Balfour and Elin, she turned.

"Tara!" Merlon sounded like he had already assumed her dead and was about to lose it. At any other time, she would have laughed at how quickly he panicked but the last couple of days had brought too many unpleasant surprises, she couldn't blame him for worrying.

"I'm here. I'm fine," she shouted. Tightening her hairband, she smiled at the two kids beside her. "Come, let's go have something to eat and we'll find out what to do." She made sure to keep her voice even when she raised it slightly. "Cary, you hungry?"

For three heartbeats, there was no sound. Tara opened her mouth to call again, but then Cary moved into view. He was, impossibly, even skinnier than Balfour and Elin although some of that could be due to his general lankiness. He leapt to the ground and stared up at her, a stubborn set to his jaw.

His skin was a little darker than the other two's. Not so dark he was suited well to living in a bright galaxy like Twin Cities, but of a similar golden hue most Fristate Galaxians had. Below his floppy, black hair that looked to have been chopped roughly with something quite blunt, his dark eyes held equal measures of grief and defiance. "*I* didn't feed that man to the sarco crocs. He was drunk and fell into the river, and I didn't call for help."

"But—" Elin started.

"And he was NUT MY DAD!" Cary screamed. Tears glimmered in his eyes, face red from rage, or upset.

"Hey, let's take a breath and uh…" Tara yanked at her hair already falling out of the leather strap again. She had no idea how to deal with kids this young. Why had she ever thought she would be qualified to have a child of her own? "Let's go get something to eat. How's that sound?"

Elin's chin quivered but Balfour took her hand and met Tara's gaze. "We would like food. If you have any."

That seriousness in his blue eyes kept throwing Tara. She gestured for them to follow, making herself turn her back on Cary.

Distrust shone from his every pore but if she showed him nothing but distrust too, that would never change. And none of the kids had anything but the tattered clothes on them. It was limited what their skinny, shaky limbs could do for damage.

"Tara what's...oh, that's unexpected." Merlon faltered at the top of the hill.

'Stay back. Sick maybe?' She gestured.

Merlon's brows drew together but he nodded. 'Do not touch them. Where are the parents? What do they need?' He moved his hands slower than when he spoke to a Squamate.

Tara had complained often enough he knew she couldn't follow otherwise. She had taken classes while in Amule, but her knowledge of the sign language was still limited.

Tara shook her head. She didn't know how to answer his questions with signs. "They're hungry. Did I hear Visca?"

"Yup. And Vincent. They didn't seem to remember why they came and haven't answered any questions but they're paddling around in the water." Merlon waited until Tara caught up, then he fell in step, not with her but the kids, while staying several paces from them. "Hullo you three. I'm Captain Merlon. What do you all like best, potato soup or porridge with dried figs?"

Tara side-eyed him. How did he manage to sound so casual seconds after discovering three starved kids on a desolate island? She hadn't thought he could still surprise her this much.

"Taytoe soup!" Elin's face split in a grin. She was missing a front milk tooth. The new one barely poking through her gums.

Merlon chuckled pleasantly. "Great! That's my favourite too. Are you all alone out here?"

65

Cary refused to meet Merlon's eyes, but Elin and Balfour bobbed their heads.

"Did you get lost? No bother, you're not alone anymore as we got a little lost too." Merlon chatted all the way back across the sandy stretch. He didn't seem to mind that all he got off replies were nods or shakes of the heads.

Tara watched him from the corner of her eyes. He tended towards being formal and a bit stiff around strangers. The calm ease he treated the kids with was a side she rarely saw even when they were alone. She gave into the urge and shifted closer, fingers brushing against Merlon's.

He glanced at her and grabbed her hand, giving it a squeeze.

A warm tingling spread up through her arm. She sucked in a breath. *No more postponing.* "Merlon, can we talk later? I—"

"Monster!" Elin shrieked. Her and Balfour stopped short.

Ahead, Vincent's large frilled and horned head poked up from the ocean like some terrifying limbless beast. Water dripped as xe shook xirself, the green knobbly skin shimmering.

Cary rounded on them, accusatory finger pointing at Merlon. "You're going to kill us! Run!" He yanked at Elin's free hand, hauling her and thereby Balfour after himself.

"Wait!" Tara set after them. "They're nae dangerous!"

Balfour put his heels in the sand. Elin cried as she got pulled from either side, Cary still trying to get her back to the cover of trees. But Balfour flew at Cary's face, breaking the hold the older boy had on Elin.

Cary blinked, terror darkening his face, then he spun and sprinted away.

"We mean no harm!" Merlon shouted.

Cary didn't slow down.

Balfour on the other hand, turned slowly. His knuckles whitened, fingers clamping around Elin's shoulders. "Please dun't hurt her. She's so very hungry."

Tara stopped two yards away. Her stomach was a hard knot, she had no words.

Merlon stepped past her and sunk to a knee. Before Tara could stop him, he reached out and gingerly placed his hands on top of Balfour's still holding the shivering, crying Elin upright. "We would never hurt any of you. That's a promise. You're safe with us. You're not alone anymore. Do you understand that?"

Balfour stared at Merlon's face for so long Tara thought he was going to break free and run again. But then he nodded solemnly.

"Good." Merlon slowly stood. "Come, we'll get you some food and maybe we can talk to the dragons if you're as brave as you look." He put a hand on Balfour's shoulder, guiding them towards *Lucia* where the entire crew amassed in the shadows on the starboard side.

Tara picked up her feet. Merlon clearly knew how to be around kids much better than she did. "I'll explain to the crew."

She trotted ahead. She had never dealt with young kids. Not since before her family moved to Amule from Trachna, leaving behind the chosen aunts and uncles of her parents, several of which had had kids younger than Tara.

And she had striven to forget her childhood. Both the one in Trachna she had lamented losing in the move and the

67

subsequent years of bullying in Amule. She knew how to speak with a fifteen-year-old and get them to take their education and exams serious. But a five-year-old? She had no clue at all.

Fabian was the first to speak. "The heck's happened?"

"Kids appeared, clearly," Gaunty said. Xe had a crutch under one arm, saving the sprained ankle.

"They're alone far as they say," Tara replied. "Cary's scared we'll kill them but he's so starved…I hope he'll return and get some food at least. We donae know if they've got any diseases."

Deyon sighed. "And 'course Cat'n ignored safety. Nobody else be that stupid. Stay clear until we's sure they's not spreaders."

"Derek, run up and grab the soup and water. And maybe some oat cakes," Tara said.

Yorik stopped Derek as the young man jumped up the ladder. "Only a half mug for each. No oat cakes yet. If they've starved awhile, their tum's won't deal well with rich food."

Derek nodded and rushed up.

Merlon paused a good ten paces from the nearest crew, hand still on Balfour's shoulder. "Everyone, this is Balfour, and the little one is Elin. Did Derek run for some food?"

"He did," Tara said and let her fingers drop from her hair when Fabian raised an eyebrow and jerked his head for her to go over to Merlon and the kids. She grimaced at him but went to Merlon's side.

"We's sure is no distraction for ambush?" Deyon spoke under his breath.

Merlon shrugged. "They need food and beds no matter what."

Tara knew she had to do *something* to help the kids, so she rolled two shorter stumps of palm trunks over and settled them in the soft sand. "Here, nae as comfortable as a chair, but you can sit on these." *Do they even want to sit down?* She hated this. Feeling incompetent and out of place.

But Balfour eased Elin onto one stump, slipping down beside her. It seemed he took her safety very seriously.

Tara felt awkward standing towering over them and knew Merlon would be reluctant to get down on the remaining log. Both because he would struggle getting back up with his thigh muscle never quite having healed from an injury last year but also because he tended to get too self-conscious if seats sank into carpets or protested his weight. *Like my chair doesn't groan too every time I sit or shift.* She hoped he would eventually believe her when she assured him that she didn't care.

So Tara shifted the second stump to the side. The look in Balfour's eyes, stopped her from moving it far though. He saw right through the fear of disease everyone tried to hide.

She sat, thanking the stars her leg injuries from the fight with Lady Galantria had been tended to by Amule's specialists and had left her with no mobility restrictions. "Derek's bringing some soup for you." Her words were so flat she cringed inwardly. How did Merlon weave in that warmth?

The loud slurps of wet sand being walked on made Tara turn her head.

Vincent's enormous body lumbered around the back of *Lucia*. Xir clawed feet sunk deep and left craters in the sand as xe pulled them free to take another step. Xe walked on all fours as usual, xir enormous body the width of *Lucia's* deck, and xir long neck allowing xem to stand the height of the ship's main mast should xe decide to stretch it up.

Xir mouth was beaked and a faded mint green colour with brown splotches covered xir rough skin. Xe came to a pause a good score feet away and lowered xir frilled head.

Balfour jolted on the log and Tara, without pausing to think, patted his knee. "It's alright. That's Vincent." *So much for keeping to a safe distance.*

Balfour didn't look convinced, but he stayed put, clenching Elin's hand so hard she whimpered and yanked to free herself.

"Visca, flight mate, am I seeing visions or is this ship in the wrong place?" The wispy voice of the great being was like a rustle of dry palm fronds in a breeze.

Visca responded in her shrill tone. "I smell humans, get away from there!"

"Ah but I seem to reminisce we meant to look for humans." Vincent tilted xir giant head. The neck frill was so heavy it pulled xir head further sideways, the long black horns nearly hitting the shrouds on the quarterdeck. "Were there not a portal migration for the younglings which got disturbed by a human ship?"

"Younglings always blame others of disturbances," Visca's disembodied voice replied.

Most of the crew shrunk away against *Lucia's* hull. While they had met the dragons a few times before, the huge creatures were so forgetful — and occasionally decided to try stepping on people — it paid to be mindful around them.

Merlon, however, moved forward. "Vincent, we've met before. What do you mean by wrong place?"

Tara pushed against her knees, biting her cheek against the dull ache that resulted in, and stood. She touched Merlon's arm and leaned closer to whisper, "The kids thought us Q-rebels."

Merlon's head snapped round to meet her gaze. "Outer Universe?" He mouthed.

"I think so," she replied under her breath.

"Gracious Tomaline! She and the rest of the stars must hate us," Merlon muttered.

Vincent took another step forward, lowering xir head. The beaked snout all but nuzzled first Merlon's chest, then Tara's. "Ahh. The kind one and the alpha. And you have bonded more since we last met. Those are your offspring?" Vincent turned xir head to Balfour and Elin, huddling against one another on the log stump.

Fabian had crouched beside them, whispering reassurances. "They're like big, ditsy sheep. Nothin' dangerous."

When Tara faced Vincent again, she realised Merlon was staring at her. Heat crept up her neck. The questions in his eyes were too personal to answer here. She cleared her throat and addressed the dragon. "They're nae ours. They were alone on this island. Do you know where we are and where their people might be?"

Vincent's eyes narrowed and xir nostrils flared. "Why are your offspring Outer Universe humans? Those are quite terrifying. Well…the older ones. These look too young to play with fusion and laboratories."

"Those are born here, Vincent." Visca flickered into view when she dropped her camouflage. Her wings were folded over her back, shutting off the energy-catching properties of the leathery skin. Her body had the same brown splotches of Vincent but her base colour was a stone grey, the ten-foot-long feathers on the tip of her tail different shades of purple and blue where Vincent's were pink, green and gold.

Tara found herself staring from one dragon to the next. Last time, she had been able to see energy so strongly, even when she wasn't trying to, the tendrils drawing towards and around the dragons had been visible at all times. It was odd seeing them like other people saw them, big and lumbering and without signs of the strength of their wings.

"Here?" Vincent looked at the sky. "Ah. Quarantine Thirteen. The one they'll bomb soon, if I reminisce correctly?"

Tara exchanged a glance with Merlon, and they spoke as one. "Bomb?"

Chapter 8

Tara clenched her hand to hide the trembling. "Vincent, what do you mean by; they'll bomb soon?"

The dragon blinked. Green eyes confused. "Are you quipping at me, human one?"

"You said someone will bomb this place soon." Merlon spoke through gritted teeth. He too had made fists, but Tara couldn't tell if it was fear or frustration that simmered under his otherwise collected expression.

"I'm quite sure they already did," Visca said.

Fabian shifted to stand beside Merlon. "Doesn't look bombed to me."

"Bombed?" Visca shrieked, her long neck snapping up, nose to the air. "What's that?"

"Are you the kind one?" Vincent directed xir beak at Fabian.

"This is ridiculous." Tara hissed. "Vincent, pull your green arse together and tell us where the kids' parents are and how in the star-cursed universe we can get away from this planet."

Fabian side-eyed her. "I agree. Didn't them Trackers mention Quarantine Thirteen? Or was it Erica?"

"Both mentioned it. It's where Outer Universe people put their sick people." Merlon ground out.

Vincent had tilted xir head again, what could possibly be described as a frown was on xir face.

Visca's body had taken on a sickly yellow and grey colour. Tara thought it meant she was disgusted or scared but she would have to check her notes from their last meeting where Ola had explained the colour communication of the dragons.

"Vincent, the humans ones are staring at us." Visca backed up.

"I reminisce these humans. But I reminisce them from Inner Universe," Vincent said. "Ah, is your ship run aground? Let me move it for you."

"No! Wait don't!" Merlon ran after the dragon, but Vincent took no heed.

Tara caught his elbow. "Merlon, watch it!"

Vincent's tail flicked, the huge feathers hit them, sweeping them both to the ground with a thump.

Vincent didn't notice. Rather, xe trundled straight into *Lucia's* side, neck curling sideways and huge paws rising to push against the starboard hull. The ship groaned. Crew sprang out of the way of the lumps of sand spilling from between Vincent's claws. Derek narrowly managed to leap off the dangling rope ladders onto the beach before *Lucia* twisted her bowsprit towards the ocean.

"Visca, dear, give me a claw's push," Vincent said.

Visca eyed Merlon, seemingly not hearing his shouts to stop, and stepped around the screaming, panicking crew.

74

"They've gone mad!" Fabian hauled Merlon to his feet. Then offered Tara a hand while Merlon rushed to Elin and Balfour, cowering between the fallen palm trunks.

Tara cupped her mouth. "Stop! You'll strand us!"

Vincent jerked and twisted round. Xe let the front paws drop from *Lucia's* stern. Xe turned and trudged back onto the drier sand, leaving the ship partially capsized in the low waves. "Kind one! You healed my chipped claw. I owe you a debt for that."

"That's a long—" Fabian shut up when Tara elbowed him.

If the dragons had forgot they had already assisted them last year as thanks for her putting antiseptic on Vincent's infected toe, Tara saw no reason to remind them. They needed all the help they could get right now. "Yes, that was me healing your foot. Do you think you can help us get off this planet as a return favour?"

Visca stayed a few steps behind her flight mate. She snuck closer, one tentative step at a time.

"The gravity is much too much for your feeble sails to allow you flight," Vincent said.

Visca poked her head up behind his shoulder, nodding. "Nothing short of a lot of portal powder will take you off here. Unless you want to engage with the Outer Universe humans."

"Nobody wants to engage with them. Even Trackers avoid them," Vincent said. "You best return those offspring that are not yours and use a portal storm."

Coldness spread through Tara's limbs. The likelihood of them finding a portal storm not once but twice in their lifetime was miniscule. Unless they were a regular thing on

75

this planet, but Ola had never heard of a portal storm before sitting in during a fright night of ghost stories Deyon had held in Amule.

"Where do we find a portal storm?" Merlon asked. "And where do we find their parents?"

Tara glanced over her shoulder and blinked in surprise, Elin was on Merlon's arm, face buried against his chest. Balfour still held on to Elin's hand, but he mostly hid behind Merlon, blond head peering up at the enormous dragons.

"You'll have to wait for a storm." Visca shrugged her wings.

Vincent shook xir head. "Flight mate dearest, human ones do not have centuries to wait for a portal storm to arise. And they are exceedingly rare on planets."

"I want my mummy," Elin whimpered.

Her little voice hurt something deep in Tara's chest. She shifted backwards, putting a hand on Balfour's trembling shoulder and stroked a curl from Elin's face. "We'll find your mummy." Squaring her shoulders, Tara looked back up at Vincent. "Can you help us take off? Pull on the masts, push from under the ship?"

"The wood would scream and break." Vincent shook xir head.

Visca nudged xir neck with her beaked nose. "We should go. There are humans ones watching us."

Vincent's green winked brighter, signalling a 'yes' before xe spoke. "Flight mate, we are talking to them." Vincent's tail lifted and brushed against Visca's, the huge feathers almost tangling.

"I reminisce," Visca said. "These were the ones who disturbed the younglings' first portal migration. We should help them."

Vincent's green brightened and they both vanished, camouflaging perfectly with the surroundings.

"Wait!" Tara took a step forward. Energy threads flickered weakly around her. There was no sound of the dragons taking off, but their voices could be heard above the crash of waves. No words, but the clicking sounds they seemed to use between themselves. Then there was silence.

"Great. Now we'll drown getting aboard." Gaunty grimaced.

Fabian was already sloshing through the water towards *Lucia*. "It's not too deep. We'll only lose shorties like yaself." He grinned over his shoulder.

Gaunty huffed. At five foot ten, xe was bound to be the butt of all height jokes amongst sailors.

"Rub ya feet bastards. Let's secure the ship, eh?" Fabian shouted. He launched himself at the dangling ladder and headed up.

The crew rushed past, none getting closer than five paces to the kids.

"Leave the sails furled, ensure she doesn't move further into the water until we're all aboard." Merlon called.

Derek inched closer, one cup of soup in his hand. "I, uh, lost the other."

"I'm just glad you didn't get crushed or drowned." Merlon smiled. He gestured at one of the logs and Derek put the mug and two spoons down, then retreated. Merlon held Elin out from himself. "Are you ready for some potato soup? I need to go secure the ship, but Tara will stay with you, alright?"

Elin nodded, clinging to him when he lowered her to the ground.

Tara cursed inwardly. She had no clue how to speak with these kids. Merlon seemed a natural and she would hate for him to see her stuttering and struggling to engage them. "Come, let's get you fed." Tara waved for them to follow. She hated the light tremble of her fingers. Why did her body always betray her nerves?

Balfour led Elin to the stump from before and sat her down.

Tara jerked her hand away when Merlon reached for it. He would notice the tremor instantly.

"You'll be right?" Merlon whispered with a frown touching his brows. "The two of us can't go near the crew until we know for sure the kids are healthy."

Stars burn it. He was annoyingly observant today. She ignored the first question. "We can isolate them and us in the cabin. And we need to figure out what to do about Cary."

"He's watching from the trees. Hopefully he'll come out soon. Might help when everyone else is back on the ship."

Tara glanced back, finding the face amongst the dark green brush. She didn't know what the truth was about the man who had fallen into a river, but Cary was a starved, lonely kid and stars knew she wasn't going to be the one to leave him here to die.

"Cap'n? Got a minute?" Fabian's voice carried from the ship.

Merlon held Tara's gaze for another second, then he made to turn away.

"Merlon?" Her fingers brushed his ear where the helix was missing from a sword cut and had healed in an uneven line. He paused, frown deepening when she grabbed his hand. "I'll manage, but thanks for asking."

His lips curled for an instant, warmth glinting in his eyes. He squeezed her fingers and headed for the ship.

Tara turned her attention to the kids. Balfour knelt before Elin, mug in hand.

"Balfour you'll…" Tara faltered. For a second, she had thought he was shovelling down the soup, but she realised he was feeding Elin who sat patiently, opening her mouth when the full spoon closed in. Tara's throat constricted. "Donae forget to save some for yourself."

Balfour continued spooning the mug's thick soup into Elin. "It's okay. I dun't deserve it."

"Balfour donae say that. You deserve food as much as Elin. Here, stop." Tara bit the soreness of her knee back and crouched beside them. She had to wrench the mug and spoon from Balfour's skinny fingers to make him stop feeding it all to Elin. "You eat the rest now, and we'll get you both more soon. Promise."

Balfour stared at her like she had said something crazy. Reluctantly, he took the spoon again when she offered it back. There were only a couple mouthfuls left, but hunger won him over and he greedily licked the spoon and mug once he had a taste of it.

"Donae ever think you donae deserve something, Balfour. Everyone deserves food and safety."

He used a grimy finger to clean the mug entirely. Watching Tara all the while, blue eyes sceptical and a tiny furrow between his golden eyebrows. She hadn't noticed before, but he too had freckles across his nose. Nothing like Ola, whose hair was more orange than yellow, but more than Amuleans tended to have.

Balfour put the mug on the log Elin sat on. "My mummy says I dun't deserve anything because I'm evil." His eyes brimmed with unshed tears. "Because I'm a monster," he whispered. Before Tara could react, he plucked a shell from the sand, driving it into the cuts on his arm, drawing blood when he reopened one.

"Stop! Donae harm yourself. Balfour, love, you're nae monster." Tara caught his hands and held them as tightly as she dared.

His chest heaved in short gasps. Eyes glazing over, he looked about to pass out.

Tara knew those signs. She rarely had a panic attack, but those she had, stayed with her. "Balfour, look at me. It's alright. You're nae evil. I promise you, you isnae a monster." She kept speaking and holding onto him, easing her grip to be more gentle.

Slowly but surely his breathing calmed. His fingers pressed at the sores on his arms. Forcing more of the thick blood out. He was so traumatised. Tara had no idea what she was supposed to do. He needed a healer and a talk therapist. Not someone who was as likely to help during a panic attack as to have one herself.

"My mummy says it's nut our fault we're bad." Elin sniffled. She reached out and petted Balfour's scraggly blond head with a tiny hand. "Remember she says we're just born this way. We dun't hurt people on purpose."

Tara gulped. "What do you mean? Hurting people, how?"

Cary huffed. "We're mutants."

Tara sprung to her feet, hand reaching for the axe still on her belt. *What does mutant even mean?*

Cary continued. "We're healthy carriers of the new pox. At least that's what the adults say. I think they dun't like that we can see more colours than them."

"The new pox? Is that a disease?" Tara forced herself to let go of the axe.

Cary shrugged but Balfour nodded and replied, "They dun't like Cary because he didn't drown fast. My mummy says it's our fault the soldiers come. That's why they sent us away. To stop the soldiers coming and attacking the village."

"Ha!" Cary leered. "Like the soldiers care about you. Your parents wanted rid of you so they could go home to Earth Seven."

"But *I* want to go home." Elin's chin quivered.

Tara knelt before her. "Hey, we'll get you home. Come, let's see what other food we have on the ship for you three. Are you hungry, Cary?"

Cary stared blankly at her. "I've only ate fisheyes for four days, so the little whingers didn't die."

Tara gulped. "So, that's a yes?" A sigh of relief escaped her when Cary nodded. Hunger was something she could deal with. All that other stuff, she was less sure of.

Chapter 9

Tara left the chamber alongside Merlon. Asleep at last. All three kids were tucked in Tara's bunk that she rarely used anyway.

Cary was probably feigning sleep but at least he had settled after around two thousand questions about their intentions. Whatever he had been through before ending on the island, Tara wasn't sure therapy, and a loving home would ever fully restore his trust in people.

He had refused to explain what Balfour meant with the comment about him not drowning fast. Whether someone had purposely tried to drown the poor kid or not, Tara understood why he remained so defensive.

Merlon closed the door carefully after them and Tara took a deep breath. Kids were stressful. Maybe she had only been in love with the idea of having a child. Babies were certainly supposed to be even more work and she wasn't sure she was cut out for *that*. She liked older kids and had loved tutoring teenagers, but she hadn't ever been much around kids Elin and Balfour's age.

She glanced at Merlon, did he want a baby, or would he be open to adopt or foster an older kid? Right when Tara thought she had pushed aside her nerves enough to broach the subject, there was a knock on the cabin door.

"Maybe move your chair to this side," Merlon said. "We'll have to remain careful until we know if we get sick."

Tara did as he suggested and placed her chair, the one that had been Adrien's, close to Merlon's. She slipped onto it, letting him take her hand when he sat too. "Come on in," Merlon said.

"Cap'n." Fabian stepped through with a nod, followed by Deyon. "How's the kiddos?"

Merlon nodded at the remaining chair opposite the table. "Asleep, for now at least. We'll have to decide what to do about them though."

Deyon shook his head when Fabian offered to pull an extra chair out, the second mate staying by the door. He rocked back and forth on his heels. "We's best not deal with 'em, Cat'n. Tara said they's already admitted spreading diseases and you's seen what happens if something spreads aboard a ship."

Tara squeezed Merlon's hand when he twitched. Judging by the severe expression, it had been bad. Far as she knew, he hadn't lost any crew during the lung rot epidemic in Moonside, but he and Deyon had seen the devastation in Moon City first hand. Merlon never spoke of it, but Adrien had mentioned the tragedy once or twice.

"We can't leave them." Merlon spoke through gritted teeth, but the pain was clear in his voice. "They have nobody. We've got to return them to their parents."

Tara studied his face. He hid it well, but his eyes shone with old hurt. "Merlon, their parents left them here. On purpose. This isnae like your parents leaving for work and nae coming home."

"Yeah, but kids invent stories all the time," Fabian said. When everyone's eyes turned on him, he shrugged a smile twinkling in his eyes. "Don't look at me, I never said I've been such an honest fella all me life as I is now."

Tara snorted. As if Fabian was honest even now.

Merlon groaned with exasperation although he would probably admit later, he laughed inwardly. "The point is we don't know. We do know there are no signs of people on this island so their caretakers must be elsewhere."

"We have nae idea where and the dragons mentioned bombing," Tara said.

Merlon turned in his chair to meet her gaze. His expression was unreadable, but she had the distinct feeling he was disappointed she hadn't backed him up.

"Cat'n," Deyon said, twiddling his thumbs, "if you don't mind me saying, we's got plenty trouble getting back into Inner Universe, again."

"Ah, well…" Fabian scratched the back of his head.

Merlon finally broke from gazing at Tara to frown at Fabian. "What haven't you told me about?"

"Don't look at me like that!" Fabian spread his long fingers. "I'm not gonna show ya my private letters but I *may* be writin' with Mira who is, in fact hostin' Bailey at the moment."

Tara rolled her eyes at her own stupidity. Why hadn't she thought about getting help from the Tracker rat? Or the rat's da, since help from Bailey often resulted in outright disasters. "Where's the letter tube? We need to send for her or her da."

The Trackers had an invention Tara had only heard of last year, shortly after discovering the Trackers were talking animals. Hollow wooden tubes that could hold a rolled-up letter and when someone threw it, thinking of a person – or Tracker – who they wanted to receive the letter, it portalled straight to them.

The letter tubes were incredibly handy, but Bailey normally only allowed a single one to be sent between herself and Tara or Merlon. It did explain why Tara had heard nothing from the rat for nearly four months. Fabian and Mira had probably hogged it for themselves. She didn't blame them.

"I don't have it," Fabian said. "Sent it back to Mira ten minutes before that portal storm hit. But she tends to reply within a week. Might be a little longer this time. She mentioned preppin' to enter a galaxy although she didn't say which."

Merlon stared at him. "I have a lot of questions about all that but at least we should have a means to get home. And it leaves us time to find the parents of the kids."

Deyon shook his head all through Merlon's speech. "We's done going towards danger. You's said so youself, Cat'n."

"But he's right, we cannae leave them here," Tara surprised herself. Despite trying to not make promises she couldn't keep, she continued speaking. "If there's any energy signs of their village, I can lead us to it. That cold energy of Ola's old equipment is highly visible." *For navigators who can actually* see, *you fool.*

Merlon's grip around her hand tightened. His palm was clammy. While he kept his face neutral, this meant a lot to him. An urge to do whatever it would take to give him the triumph of returning the kids burned in her chest.

"We's going to get in trouble doing that," Deyon grumbled. But he was far less argumentative than Adrien would have been and stared at his feet rather than challenging Merlon's glower.

Fabian ran a hand over his short black hair, a smirk on his lips. "Bah! We'll be fine. Cap'n's thick skull will protect us, eh?"

"Or your sleazy jokes might make you the main target so the rest of us can run," Tara said.

Fabian snickered, not in the least offended judging by his expression.

Merlon blew out a breath. "If we find the settlement, we'll approach carefully and run at any sign of danger. We leave the island once Tara has determined the most likely direction. Dismissed." Merlon waved his free hand.

Deyon nodded once and left without another word, but Fabian lingered in the door. "Cap'n, jokes aside, we've gotta be mindful and not let ya personal history cause trouble, yah?"

"We won't go near a settlement until we've heard from Bailey. And I expect the two of you," Merlon looked from Fabian to Tara, "to knock sense into my dense skull if I forget I said this."

Fabian nodded and pulled the door shut after himself.

Merlon immediately turned to Tara. "Thank you for backing me on this. I…probably didn't think it through."

The sincerity in his eyes left Tara's stomach fluttering. She covered his hand in both hers. How could she admit to him she didn't even know how she was going to see the energy of the village like she had promised?

To avoid her own silence getting awkward, she stood, pulling at Merlon until he followed suit, knees popping.

"I know this must mean a lot to you. You're thinking if you could've found your parents sooner…"

Merlon wrapped his arms around her, burying his face in her hair. "We can't *not* try and reunite them," he mumbled.

"Be prepared it might nae end as you hope. If the kids isnae lying, their parents abandoned them on purpose." She breathed in his scent. Warm starlight and salt from the ocean. Sometimes when her heart thundered and she didn't want what would come next, she wished they could stay like this, holding each other forever and never have to face their fears and nightmares.

She pulled half a foot away when his arms slacked enough to allow it. His eyes were glistening, but no tears had streaked his cheeks. She hadn't seen him cry since the day of his ma's funeral. It had been a beautiful hole-drop, but Merlon had needed strict supervision to ensure he didn't fall back into S-V abuse. Deyon, Fabian and Tara had taken turns staying with him for five days straight. But he had made it through.

Of course, Yorik still had instructions to keep the sedative herb locked away but far as Tara knew, it had been months since Merlon had last paced in front of the sick bay, fighting the urge to numb his emotions.

"We'll take that hurdle if it arises." Merlon spoke softly.

Tara blinked, what had she said? She had lost all thought of their conversation looking into his brown eyes.

His expression changed from anxious grief to a hot intensity. "Tara, what do you want from us? I know it's only been eleven months but…well, I'm nearly thirty-one and only one of my grandparents lived beyond sixty."

Tara's mouth went dry. What if she didn't know what she wanted? Or if she thought she did and said yes to the wrong things only to realise when it was too late to back out? She lowered her eyes, unable to look at him. The longing in his eyes would play tricks and she had to make this choice for herself, not opting for something only to avoid disappointing him.

"You don't have to answer right away." Merlon's voice was so quiet she could barely hear him. "Stars knows there's no point rushing while we're stuck in the wrong universe."

She stared at the star emblem on his shirt's chest pocket. The silver and gold threads had worn dull. A thread stuck out, frayed and stumpy. Instead of buying new shirts, he would curse his blurry eyesight for hours on end, mending and patching the fabric. He had received a sizeable inheritance from Adrien but had chosen to use the coin on renovating *Lucia* and, far as Tara knew, put away the rest. *He's preparing for the fees to get family permits and meeting the housing requirements.*

Tara had done the same for years, living with her da to save and working double hours as a tutor. Yet now she wasn't sure if it would be a good idea to get a kid. She was bound to mess it all up. Their relationship, the kid's life. Things never went like she wanted them to.

"I think…I cannae make the decision right now." She kept her eyes on his chest, searching for the right words. "I thought I knew but I need more time…I'm sorry."

She felt more than saw Merlon shake his head. "There's nothing to be sorry about." His voice was tight, nonetheless.

She looked up, finding him watching her. "I do love you, Merlon, I just donae know if I willnae mess up."

The insecurity that had reigned in his eyes melted away. "I'm pretty sure I tend to be the one who messes up the worst." He smiled and heat rushed up Tara's spine.

"I donae know, depends which things we're talking. Some areas you perform pretty well." She returned his smile, leaning in. Her arms wrapped around his neck and their lips met.

His hands slipped down her back, drawing her closer. Her heart thudded in her ears, blocking out all other sounds until someone cleared their throat loudly. She came away gasping for breath and glared at Fabian standing in the doorway.

"Teenagers." Fabian rolled his eyes dramatically then continued as if he hadn't walked in on them smooching. "Cap'n, there's a good wind risin' with evenin', and I reckon we can get *Lucia* into the water proper, should we?"

Merlon drew Tara closer with one arm but turned to face Fabian. He pushed his black hair back over his head, glancing at Tara through the corner of his eyes. "Yes, we need to get into the water and set a course. Are *we* needed though?"

Tara suppressed a laugh. Merlon did nothing to hide his annoyance at the interruption. She fought the urge to bite his ear. The heat radiating through his arm around her waist left her feeling drunk but there was no reason to remind Fabian just how long it had been since he had seen Mira. Tara wasn't sure they were exclusive, but Fabian didn't exactly have a lot of options on board the ship. Jara was the only other woman, and like Fabian, she didn't sleep with men.

"Depends on the direction the settlement's meant to be in, I don't—" Fabian was cut off by the chamber door creaking open.

Cary stood in the door, his eyes red from lack of sleep and hair mussed. "I know the way home but there's a storm coming. I feel it in the air."

"Burn us," Tara muttered.

Merlon let go of her and walked over to Cary, gingerly placing a hand on his shoulder. The kid winced but at least he didn't jump away. Merlon smiled down at him. "Can you help us find the way? You'll be safe back down here when the storm hits."

Cary stared up at him with a shrug. "If you have more food and promise nut to make them take me back to that cell."

Tara's stomach flipped. Had they kept the kid locked up? She found her fingernails digging into her palms. She really didn't care for the people they were searching for. But she owed it to Merlon to try and reunite the kids if any of them had someone that loved them.

She counted to five before trusting her voice to stay even and addressed Cary. "I'll get you an oatcake. Do you like hot tea as well?"

Chapter 10

Five minutes later, Tara offered Cary the oatcake and tea. He ignored the mug but scarfed down the biscuit so fast Tara's automatic admonishment hadn't left her lips by the time he had demolished it. "You donae need to worry, we'll nae let you starve."

"Then don't make me stay in the village." Cary stared back at her, no emotion in his face except for a tick at the corner of his mouth. He took the tea when she held it out again, but he didn't drink it. "The village is that way." He pointed to the port side, towards the horizon the star appeared from in the mornings.

Merlon gave Cary's shoulder a squeeze. The kid jolted and pulled away like he thought Merlon would grab him and throw him overboard.

"Easy, kid. Only meant a thanks for your help."

"I'd rather have some of those books on your shelves to read," Cary said.

Tara blinked, that was an unexpected request.

Cary continued. "Are any of them stories? I like reading stories."

Tara looked at Merlon. None of her books were fiction, rather they were a mixture of navigation and herb lore. The latter ones had been Patrice's and had been given to Tara by Patrice's parents after the symbolic hole-drop ceremony they had held in Amule.

While Patrice's body had been put to rest at a hole-drop in Ivory, the city she had been killed in, her parents had needed the closure. Tara pushed that memory away. She didn't want to start bawling for seemingly no reason.

Merlon shook his head. "I'm afraid it's all about sailing and constellations. You're welcome to look through them all but don't scrunch the pages."

"I'm nut stupid." Cary rolled his eyes. "I dun't want this." He handed the mug back to Tara and turned, stalking to the passageway door, and vanished below.

"Stars, he needs therapy," Merlon muttered, then he went up the quarterdeck companionway. "Let the sheets go! Jara, you know what to do?"

Jara huffed. "If a'body knows what to do punting around on top of water I's a blue sheep."

Tara joined them at the helm. "I donae know either, but I read there's places where they travel on water. Out Far Galaxies way, where they have more habitable moons and planets."

"What does the energy say?" Merlon asked, his expression softened when he looked at her.

Here it goes. Tara took a deep breath. She had to get this right. But no matter how much she stared, the energy stayed hidden from her vision. How long was this going to keep on? She couldn't keep her failure at her main task hidden forever and if anything, hiding it could endanger everyone. She opened her mouth to ask Merlon for a private word when turquoise strands danced around her.

She leaned her head back, following the dim whirls of energy. The air was moving from the island to the ocean in the evening breeze. They could use that, and then tack the sails to get moving in the direction Cary had given. "Straight ahead until we're free of the sand. Then tack to starboard to run with the wind."

"You heard her, rub it bastards!" Merlon shouted.

The ship came alive. Gaunty and Karl remained below, but everyone else had been called upon for the attempt at getting into the water proper. While the gravitational pull was still strong, the waves below seemed to send small disturbances upwards which the sails caught in a flare of colours when they were unfurled.

Tara bit back the desire to busy herself somewhere it wouldn't soon be evident she saw little more energy than everyone around her. She watched the sails carefully, filling in the gaps where she knew the energy coursing over them came from. She might not be able to see much right now, but she had spent her entire life watching energy dancing around the air and knew exactly how it tended to behave.

Lucia groaned, her hull shifting below them. The sails pulled forward. "Try the altitude rudder, two degrees up." Tara kept her gaze directed at the sails, moving her head in an attempt at tracking the turquoise flickering past her sight at every blink.

93

"Is the energy harder to read here?" Merlon sounded worried.

Tara glanced at him. She hated admitting a weakness, but this could work for now. Eventually she would have to tell him if she didn't pull her shit together and started seeing energy again. He would have to let her go when she did. He couldn't afford to keep a navigator who was no more help than a common sailor.

Suppose she could return to tutoring. Her teeth ground together at the thought. She had dreamt of travelling space her whole life and had forsaken doing so for ten years to care for Ma, only to no longer be useful onboard a ship the moment she started living her dream.

"Tara?"

She nodded, not trusting herself to not sneer when Merlon had done nothing wrong. Too often her nerves made her snap when she shouldn't.

Merlon gestured at the sails. "At least it appears to be strong."

As if hearing his words, wind howled through the rigging, hitting the sails with a huff of sudden silence. The ship bounced forward. Sand and water splashed below. The keel scraped across the soft banks. They rocked from starboard to port and slid further into the ocean.

Then they were free of the sand and *Lucia* rolled, sighing as if relieved the pressure against her hull had eased. And Tara stumbled with the unfamiliar, quick tossing from port to starboard and back. Even Merlon staggered, catching himself on the wheel and reaching to steady Tara.

"This will take some getting used to," he muttered. It was something coming from him. He had grown up on a ship to a higher degree than everyone else, being pulled out of school by his strict foster da at twelve.

Tara slipped from Merlon's arm and moved to the railing. Darkness was falling with the waning star but the deep green of the water below them danced before her eyes. Was there brown gravitational energy even out here, or was she imagining that?

The wind picked up fast. It howled across the water, hitting the sails and forcing the ship forwards. But *Lucia* complained, her hull shrieking. They moved with such speed the water cleaved before the keel. It stood up around the bowsprit and sides. Foam and ocean spray soaked everyone remotely near the railing.

Tara backed up, spitting, and shaking saltwater from her face. She had lost Cary's mug.

"Jara, turn to port then raise us," Merlon shouted. "We need to get out of the water."

Tara shook her head, a warning whispering at the back of her head. "I donae—"

"Bloody 'eck! The wheel's ten times 'eavier than normal," Jara exclaimed.

Merlon jumped and hauled on the wheel. It moved slowly. So slowly.

Tara stared from them to the water. Energy winked at her. *Oh, burn us.* "It's the water giving resistance! Donae turn so much. Anchor—"

Lucia wailed, her rigging pulling and body tilting to port. They turned too fast for their speed with the water friction below.

"Land coming up! Anchor out!" Deyon screamed.

A bright flash zigzagged the sky. Lightning storm. An ear-splitting thunderclap sounded seconds later. *Lucia* kept keeling further to the port.

The heaviness of a landmass' energy grew before Tara's eyes. Her fingers snatched for a hold on the railing again. But the wood was slick with water and sand.

She shrieked, but her voice was swallowed in the second roll of thunder. Lightning hit the rods on *Lucia's* masts, positioned there to direct the energy straight to the sails. The ship jumped with a cough of effort. When she hit the water again, a giant wave swept across the decks.

Pressure stole Tara's footing. She tumbled, the wave pushing her upwards. Then it pulled back.

Lucia still leaned to port. The railing passed Tara by. Her fingers brushed a rope. Stomach flipping as did her body. Energy flared in bright turquoise. Tara vaulted down towards the water.

Sounds ceased to exist. All but the roar of the waves. They reached to embrace her. Tara gasped in a breath. But she already knew the ship kept going. She was left behind. They would never find her. Not in time. She sank, arms flailing and panic turning her vision black.

She kicked and paddled. The ocean spit her into the air in a whirling froth. She stole another breath. Light bobbed on the horizon. Not the star, that was behind her, nearly hidden at the edge of the horizon. She kicked again, but this time the salty depths hauled her down. Fear slowed her movements. There was no salvation. She would drown here. Alone.

Green shimmered in the deep. The teal of a living creature. Her eyes stung with the salt, the pain sharpening her navigator's vision for a brief heartbeat. The outline of the being burned itself into her mind. Twenty feet long at least. That shape. She knew it in an instant. Long slender faces with a bulbous snout. Four short almost paddle-like limbs. The monsters of the galaxy river.

Panic forced her to kick harder. She gasped in a breath of water. iIt pressed into her lungs. She broke free for a second, coughing out water, heaving to breathe. There was the light. Land. So close. But the human-eating beasts were stalking her from below.

Think Tara, Ola explained swimming once. Images of Ola flashed by. His short red hair under a broad brimmed hat. The freckles covering his face and hands alike. How had he moved his hands?

Tara closed her fingers. Those river monsters had to catch her to eat her. She had promised Da she wouldn't die from joining Merlon's crew. He might actually lose his calm if she did. And Merlon would blame himself if she knew him at all. No, she couldn't die here.

She kept Ola's swimming motions in her mind. Held them firm and clear, trying to copy them. The water resisted, but she moved. Upwards, another stroke and lots of kicking. She exploded through the surface. Land was closer yet. The water took her there. The energy's bluish, thin streams pushing her along.

Something solid hit her leg. It threw her around. Tumbling in the foaming waves. Her hand grazed against a hard, knobbly surface. But it moved, swooshing her along. She kicked to find the end to the underwater world. There, she gasped for another breath.

A four-foot snout broke the surface before her. Teeth white against the greyness of night. The jaws snapped. Bashing together, water churned as the beast swiped sideways. The head struck Tara in the face. She spluttered; pain erupted by her ear. A high whine dulled the crashing waves.

She grasped the back of the creature. Snatched at the stubby front legs. Anything to stay behind its head where the huge teeth couldn't reach her. It splashed, body twisting and propelling forward, halfway out the water. She clung on. And the shore drew nearer.

The beast threw its head side to side. Then it dived.

Panic settled heavy in her chest. She hadn't taken a big enough breath. How deep was the ocean here? The teal of another monster flickered below. It's heart slow, measured almost. And a third and fourth monster beside it.

The one Tara fought to keep hold of, rolled underwater. Short front legs paddling under her grip. Her fingers slipped. Scaled skin or claws cut into her palms. She pulled her legs under herself, feet against the creature's back and the moment she glimpsed the lighter grey of the surface, she set off using the animal as her ramp.

Her arms pushed. Legs kicked. She sucked in air, coughing at the water coming down with it. Land was so close. A wave shoved her towards the sand and grass. Another swimming stroke. So tired. She was so, so tired. Her muscles screamed. Her head throbbed from where the beast had hit. Her palms stung. She would never make it.

The ocean brought her along. Then there was sand under her hands. She bobbed on the surface, crawling onto the shore. Splashing.

Water crashed behind her. She knew without looking back it was the monsters. Fear lent her strength. Panic spurred her cramping muscles into action. She leapt up and out. *No looking back*. She ran. Stumbling, coughing.

Grass wrapped around her feet. She kept going. Further onto land. She didn't stop running until a flock of birds took off, screeching, before her and her boot sunk into a stinking mudhole.

Tara dared a glance back. The beasts were on the shore, walking towards her on Squamate-like angled legs. They dragged long, jagged tails after themselves. Huge black claws on their fat toes and white teeth gleaming in the dimness of night.

Tara turned to the left, where lights glowed amongst buildings. A fence rose between her and the first houses, but she wouldn't let that stop her. Not while monsters stalked her. She brushed sand and water off her face and set off, trotting on the boundary between the grass and mud.

Chapter 11

Tara's ankle twisted for the hundredth time. Her lungs burned. She stumbled but her flailing arms corrected her balance. Another quick glance to her left. There, at the water's edge, the huge beasts followed along.

They had slipped back into the water, easily keeping pace with her. She could *feel* their hunger. Their intent to capture and eat her. Hungry yellow eyes stalked her every move.

Darkness cloaked their brown and green scales in a grey light. Faraway stars cast but a feeble, cold gleam over the water. The knobbly noses poked out, black shadows in the dimness. They moved silently, their spiky tails undulating from side to side, sinuously moving them along with barely a ripple of the water.

Thunder and lightning rumbled from far away. Out over the ocean towards where the island was. Not that Tara could see the patch of land when she glanced in that direction.

Keep going. She clenched her hand around the blood dripping from her palm. Scale or claw, the creature she had been scratched by had left a deep gash in her right hand. And more blood had dried, sticky and thick at her temple. But she felt the throbbing pain as no more than a distant sensation. It would hurt more once her heart stopped trying to break her ribs.

Squares of shuttered windows glowed in a warm light. Huge birds on long thin legs shuffled around to her right, seemingly not sinking into the gloopy mud hiding between the tussocks.

Then a barrier rose before her. Tall and indifferent to Tara's predicament and exhaustion. Wooden boards and a linked fence blocked her way to the first house of the settlement. She squinted. Those wires at the middle and top of the fence looked barbed.

Her gaze slipped back down, following the fence first to the shore where it turned, blocking off the dark waters for as far as she could see. There were gaps, but all were at parts where the fence almost stood *in* the water. She couldn't go that way without the beasts snatching her up for a snack.

She tracked the fence in the other direction. It required her to wade into the stinking mud again, but the birds seemed wary of her. She didn't like birds that nearly stood to her shoulders.

Especially not when their yellow bills were a foot long and heavy with sharp, red tips. One stab from those beaks and she would lose an eye. She had fought off enough angry geese grazing in the schoolyard to know birds *that* size weren't to be messed with.

The horrifying growl of a great beast sounded and water splashed. Tara lunged forward, away. At the corner of her eye, the huge jaws opened. Two-inch long teeth glimmered. Water, sand, and grass sprayed against her back. She leapt up the fence, boots scraping against the planks.

The beast's mouth chomped with a deep thump. The fence shook and tore. The wooden boards splintered below Tara's feet. She hauled herself further up. The barbs reached for her face. She swung her arm over the midway wire, biting her cheek when it scratched across her throat.

Tearing at the fence, the beast rumbled. Its teeth clanked, biting again and again like it hadn't realised it wasn't chewing on Tara but the wood and chain of the fence.

Tara pulled herself past the midway barbs. To her right, the top wires were missing, drooping on the other side. She shimmied towards the spot. Blood ran down her arms. Long, superficial cuts ran from her wrists to her elbows. There hadn't been time to roll down her sleeves before passing the barbs.

Her fingers threatened to give. Knee joints jarring with pain. The jaws snapped again, so close pressure slipped past her boot heel. Fear boosted Tara over the fence. But the chain links flopped with her weight, groaning inwards. She lost her grip and fell.

The ground met her with a warm thunk of hardness. Air expelled from her lungs. Barbs scratched at her but let go without digging deep.

She gasped. Fighting to roll back on her hands and knees. Crawling. Her vision lurched. There was a building. And the beast kept attacking the fence behind her without luck getting to this side.

Tara's fingers found the corner of a house. Rough wood left splinters in her fingers. She fumbled her way back on her feet. Heart quavering, she dared a glance back. The water monster had retreated. *Finally safe.*

Tara let out a breath, staggering around the building. The stars had watched over her for once.

"Hold it roight there!" a woman said. The motion and click of a shotgun getting loaded stopped Tara in her tracks.

Shit. The last thing she needed was a "trigger-happy" Outer Universe human as Ola would put it. Tara had spent months asking him about Outer Universe. Their culture was strange and full of conflicts and wars.

The Edge Galaxies hadn't seen real war in more than two hundred years and Tara had to admit to herself she was fascinated by how foreign everything Ola had experienced was. Right now, she was less fascinated but thankful she had some little idea of the history of these people.

"I'm disease free. I mean nae harm. The…water animals have been chasing me for half an hour." It probably hadn't been that long. Her clothes had barely begun drying but she felt like it had been a lifetime. Her body shook violently from exhaustion.

The woman still held the long gun to her shoulder. She wore glasses, maybe like those Erica had had that could make their feeble eyes see nearly as well as an Inner Universe human's. "We dun't want no Q-rebels here. Those who align with your crazy ideologies have already left."

"I'm…" Tara had to clear her voice, harking up a lump of slime before she could continue. "I'm nae Q-rebel. We're from another galaxy. Our ship crashed in the water. I need to find it."

The woman snorted. "I'm nut stupid, I hear your young earther accent fine. Bunch of Q-rebels the lot of you. Get going out of here before I fill your chest with scattershot."

"Please, I'm only looking for the ship I arrived here on and the parents to some kids we found, alone." Tara realised too late she should have kept her mouth shut. But her mind swam. Between the head injury, bruised ribs, and fatigue she was beginning to see double. Or was there a second person beside the woman with the shotgun?

The woman backed up two steps. The weapon in her arms drooped for a moment, then she directed it at Tara again. "I dun't know nuthing about any kids."

She spoke with conviction, but the moment of hesitation beforehand told enough. Tara could use the anxious worry seeping out of the stranger. But she had to be careful, or Tara *would* end up with a chest full of metal shrapnel.

"They're desperate for their parents. The little ones are Balfour and Elin. The older, Cary, needs a talk therapist and a loving home. I believe his foster da or caretaker is dead." Tara took care not to move. A step or stumble and she felt certain the gun would fire. "Point in the direction of one of their homes and I'll get out of your way."

"Ho! Funny one that," a man said and stepped from around the corner of the house. "Sure, we'll just point you to the cemetery and admit we know about Q-rebels' whereabouts? Never. Jonna, shoot her up."

Tara gritted her teeth, ready for the pain, but the trigger wasn't pressed.

The woman, her hair tied back and hidden under a pale scarf, glanced at the man. "She's practically dead already, Delun."

"She's either a government spy or infected Q-rebel, I dun't care if she's half dead, she needs fully dead," Delun growled.

Tara blinked. His face was blurry, and everything around him too. He had brown hair, maybe. The light from the open door at the front of the house danced and flickered. Like that of a fireplace. A fire would be nice and warm, but Tara had nothing but an eating knife on her and she had seen what a shotgun could do.

Guards, staggering with their entrails spilling between their fingers, flashed behind her eyelids. She grabbed the wall, gagging at the memory. Ola had shot at Lady Galantria's guards until he fell with a sword-wound that nearly killed him.

He had lost a kidney. The guards had lost...parts of their bodies to the shotgun. She hadn't been sad to learn the Trackers had removed the inside mechanisms of Ola and Lena's guns to avoid the technology spreading to Inner Universe. Ola still had one hanging in his study room, but it was an ornament, nothing more.

Jonna had lowered the gun by the time Tara blinked tears from her eyes and focused again.

"Get out of here. Somebody's gonna shoot you if you dun't," Joanna said.

Delun shook his head with a scoff. "Something's gonna eat her out there. It's a long way till dawn. Go hide in the fourth house up there." He pointed up the dirt street. "Was the boy's place. The blond one I mean. Parents darn well gone with them Q-rebels like idiots. Thought they'd get home quicker that way."

"We all miss home." Jonna nodded. "But I wouldn't have abandoned a child to go back." The sudden tightness in her voice told of a grief so deep, Tara hoped she would never understand it. The way Jonna pushed a fist against her belly, and Delun caught the gun and her arm both when she staggered, said it all.

"That Cary kid is crazy," Delun said, "but the little ones never did harm nut a one 'cept those who hadn't yet been sick." He began ushering Jonna back around the corner towards their front door. "Go hide in the house and leave at first light. Tell your ship mates to stay clear. Village is marked by government after the central rebellion. With God's blessing, they dun't bomb us like they did the capital."

The door shut and darkness swallowed the street. Tara swayed, holding on to the boards of the wall until her eyes had readjusted. Then she forced her legs to move. One foot dragging after the other. It wasn't far, but she had lost blood and her teeth chattered despite the muggy heat.

She found the fourth house after a decade or so it felt. The door proved unlocked. In fact, it stood wide open.

Tara fell up the two steps and landed on the wooden floor with a clonk. She fought her hands under herself, pushing to sitting. No way she would get back on her feet tonight. She shuffled on her hands and knees. The throbbing of her new injuries and bruised knee joints sent floods of agony through her body.

A soft resistance against her bowed head turned out to be a couch. Tara dragged herself onto it. She could use some water. Her throat was parched and acrid from bile rising so many times but never making it all the way out.

A stiff blanket fell from the back of the couch, and she wrapped herself in it. Scarf between her teeth to stop the loud chattering.

Despite her exhaustion, she couldn't sleep immediately. Instead, she stared up at the ceiling. It was made of wood if her eyes didn't trick her. It reminded her a bit too much of Ivory and the trembling city not far from there. Shivers that had nothing to do with her chill coursed through her body.

She remembered waking up after the blood transfusion too well. Could almost see Adrien's face in the dark. The way he had looked at her, tears he would never let spill brimming in his eyes. She had known before she could even croak out Patrice's name.

Hugging the coarse blanket, Tara rolled to her side. Patrice wouldn't want her to keep crying for her lost life. But right now, Tara was terrified, alone and in a dark dank place and all she wanted was to hear Patrice's warm voice calmly talk her out of her panic.

And she wanted to snuggle close to Merlon, even knowing he would get up after a few hours when his insomnia got too bad to bear. Gracious Tomaline! She wanted to see her Da again before it was his time to go to the eternal stars.

The darkness grew. Seemed to push closer around her. She pressed her eyes shut and pulled the blanket over her face. *I will survive this.*

She would find *Lucia* wherever she was. Merlon was alive. He would come looking for her as Tara would for him. He was the sort of stubborn who would never give up until he knew where she had vanished to.

She grasped at the thoughts. Forced them to the forefront of her mind. The darkness seemed to recede. The air flowing into her lungs freely once more. And her breath grew steady while her mind went afloat in a tangled mystery of dreams and nightmares.

Chapter 12

A sharp sound woke Tara. She jolted upright. The blanket rustled under her clenched fingers. The fabric was slightly sticky, stiff, and weird. It didn't feel like linen nor cotton and it certainly wasn't wool.

A panel on the wall opposite glowed bluish white. For a few moments, the energy radiating from it overwhelmed her senses.

The cold, metallic blue of what Ola called *electricity*. Of course, the Trackers had taken all his devices before letting them return to Inner Universe, but Tara had seen their energy enough she wouldn't easily forget how it looked or behaved. It was like a distant, lightly pulsing curtain of energy.

The moment sleep properly left her muddled brain, her vision restricted again. Cutting off the energy she had been able to see clear as ever for a few precious seconds.

What was *wrong* with her? She had to pull herself together and stop being this anxious weakling who couldn't do what she was born to.

Can you get kicked from your tier for being unable to perform your job? She didn't know. Maybe it would count as a disability, but she would rather not mention it to Amulean officials and get put on the public disability funding programme. If they didn't know, she would be able to tutor and at least retain a liveable wage compared to the meagre disability aid. They might even hold it against her if she applied for a child permit, although adoption shouldn't be hindered by it.

The glowing panel on the wall suddenly spread upwards. A loud noise rang out into the room. The sound bored into her skull in its three-note bursts. Screaming, Tara covered her ears.

The light rising from the panel flickered and she realised objects had materialised inside the light. A scene appeared, like an overview of what she imagined the monster infested waters, the muddy grassland and village looked like from above. Weird ships swooped around in the air, rigid wings and noses pointed. Then they flew straight at her.

Tara threw herself on the floor. Her bruised ribs stole the air from her. She gasped, struggling to draw a full breath. Pain spread along her left side. Her hands dropped from her ears and she rolled off her ribs.

The life-like images on the glowing panel kept changing. Smooth sail-less ships circled and dived over what she realised was a city. The grey darkness of the scene made it difficult to see. Where were all the colours?

These ships looked like the one *Lucia* had passed on the way to the research station Ola had once lived on. The ship Ola had said could shoot a single blast and blow-up *Lucia* so there wouldn't even be wood chips left. That ship had passed without noticing them. But these on the screen were less kind.

People were running in the streets. Little ants between the houses. The ships flew over, dropping pill-shaped objects that exploded upon impact. The white flashes across the screen blurred what had to be nothing but awful deaths.

The moving light-painting flickered again. Tara gingerly sat up, back against the couch and hugging the rough blanket to her chest. Her heart thundered. She couldn't take her eyes off the scenes. Constantly shifting. Changing and showing new people getting blasted. Parents clutching their kids to their chests, elders struggling along with canes and random household objects in their hands.

"This," a deep male voice boomed, "this is what settlements who join the Quarantine Rebels will see. Are your neighbours sheltering or feeding the Rebels? Report them. Are your teenagers considering joining the war instigators? Report them."

Where was the voice coming from? Tara stared around the room, panic mounting in her chest, but there was nobody else. Clothes lay scattered through a doorway that led into the next room. A bag lay discarded at the partially open front door which Tara hadn't remembered to close in her haze. A pale light shone through a thin curtain and the gap of the door. Morning.

Then the screen's images cut out with a static screech. A woman appeared. Her face flushed although badly lit. The angle was strange, like Tara sat under her chin and the woman was a giant. But the blue eyes and blonde curls made Tara's

111

heart skip a beat. Everything down to the dimple on the left cheek looked so much like Elin it had to be her ma.

The woman's eyes flickered from one side to another. Fear shone from her every pore. "I intercepted a message from Earth Seven. They're heading this way. Evacuate everything. We have minutes. For Lord's sake *run*." A child hollered and she turned, the picture winked out. The light seemingly bottling itself back up in the panel on the wall.

Outside, doors banged open. People screamed and cried.

Tara sprung to the window, still clutching that stupid, gross blanket. She stared at the people rushing into the streets. They held metal cylinders with images of tomatoes and beans on the sides and weird shiny bags in their arms. Some had shotguns slung over their shoulders, others carried smaller weapons of similar metal-barrelled style.

An old man shuffled along in slippers. The grey-haired woman on his arm still had a pale blue night cap partially stuck on her head. They brought nothing at all, tears streaming down their cheeks as they followed the stream of people all heading in the same direction.

Tara took one last look, wrapped the blanket around her shoulders to hide her Amulean clothes, and stepped out the front door.

Delun flew at her face. "It's your fault! You brought 'em here!"

Tara staggered, holding up her hands to keep him at bay. Only then did she see the crusted blood streaking her skin. She had forgot the shallow cuts running along her arms. Other wounds stung on her neck and forehead. Somehow her eyes hadn't been gouged out.

"Leave her, there's nut enough time already," Jonna hissed. She hauled at Delun, eyeing Tara like she thought she might jump them both. They moved past her, a small bag over Delun's shoulder and Jonna with the gun in her hands.

"Wait," Tara turned and followed the stream of people. "Where are you going? Where're we safe? Please." Her voice trembled. *What was going on?* The woman, Elin's ma, surely she hadn't meant those ships blasting everything were heading here. But from the fear in everyone's faces…

"Just git' it!" Delun waved rough hands at Tara's face, so she staggered into a person rushing past.

"Sorry," Tara muttered. The women didn't even glance her way but kept running, pulling a club-footed child after her who clearly needed to be carried instead of dragged along the dirt street.

Steadying herself against a wall and waiting until the dizziness subsided. Tara looked around but Delun and Jonna had vanished. *Stars burn me.* She hadn't survived those terrifying water monsters to get bombed by Outer Universe humans.

She picked up her feet, ignoring the pain slipping around her left knee, blocking the joint and leaving her limping. The initial cries and screams had subsided. Quiet, fearful determination was in the faces slipping past her. Then something rumbled. Everyone turned, staring at the spectacle coming round a corner.

The people rushed towards the odd vessel. Black wheels and a square body, like a wagon except neither human, goat nor horse, pulled it along. Inside the enclosed case, several humans sat. Tara staggered with the surge past her.

113

"Let us on!"

"Take my baby with you!"

Desperation glowed in the eyes of the people hammering their fists at the vessel. They clambered onto the back. The open trough filled instantly. But it kept moving and making a loud honking sound. Children screamed when their parents dumped them onto the back tray. Kissing their heads and saying goodbye.

Tara turned away. Tears spilled down her cheeks without her agreement. But she had no energy to swipe them away. Her heart was too torn apart at the scene. Her mind too terrified she would get caught in this war she had no place in. If this was what war was, she was grateful for the Trackers guarding Inner Universe, keeping these Outer Universe bombers far, far away.

She clutched the blanket tighter around herself and trotted up the street. Turning a corner, she glimpsed a gate ahead. People were rushing out through it. Other square, wheeled vessels moved out onto the grasslands tooting at the people trying to climb onto the roofs and sides and clinging to every little nook on them.

A door burst open beside Tara. A blonde woman stumbled out, a toddler in her arms. It was the same blonde woman from the screen. She wasn't a giant like she had looked on the glowing panel, but she *was* Elin's spitting image, and not much less starved from the looks of it.

Her trousers and shirt hung loosely around her frame, the fabric worn but of a nicer quality than some of the others Tara had seen hurrying past.

People rushed Elin's ma. "Bethy!"

"When do they get here?"

"Will they bomb us?"

"Can't you make them see the rebels have left?"

Bethy shook her head, eyes red. She had clearly already cried as much as she needed to. No new tears streaked her cheeks. "I can't do more. I tried. But without Mayor Thompson…" Her eyes sought an escape. She pushed to one side then the next, but people kept stepping nearer, screaming their requests at her like she was all powerful. "Please, I need to get Ramson to safety." She hoisted the toddler a little higher onto her hip.

Despite her pleas, nobody listened. People pushed closer.

"Leave her alone! Get out of here!" Tara blinked in surprise at her own yell. She stepped into the crowd around Bethy. "You're wasting time. Get to safety!"

In her attempt at pulling people away, she dropped the blanket from her shoulders. Those nearest her jumped away. They pointed at her shirt. Gesturing at Amule's many-rayed star embroidered on the chest pocket. She pulled the blanket back around her, but it was too late.

"Rebel! There's a Q-Rebel here!"

Burn it all. "And I'll spread a deadly disease unless you get out of here!" Tara sneered.

Gasps and a weird cross-like gesture spread amongst the crowd. The people parted. Finally, they resumed their run towards the gates. Suddenly Bethy, with Ramson writhing in her arms, was the only person standing before Tara.

"Sorry. I donae think I have diseases. And I'm nae a Q-Rebel."

115

Bethy swallowed hard. "You're nut even from Quarantine Thirteen or Earth Seven, are you?"

Tara shook her head. She glanced at the gate and Bethy nodded, accepting the information without further need for explanation. They set off together, trotting along the dirt road.

Tara panted. Her ribs burned. She wouldn't be able to keep up. But Bethy fought to keep Ramson in her grip and slowed down, keeping the pace at a panicked, brisk walk.

"I found your daughter, if Elin is yours that is."

Bethy stopped abruptly. "What? She's alive? You have her? Where is she?"

Tara stared at Bethy's fingers cramped around her wrist. She held back a grimace of pain. The cuts from the barbed wire opened anew from the pressure. "On an island. Balfour and Cary were there too. We wanted to bring them home. They miss you. And they're severely starved."

Tears gushed down Bethy's cheeks. Sobs raked through her body although she didn't make a sound. "My baby girl. They took her. And Balfour too! I knew they weren't dead. But even Mayor Thompson said he saw them get grabbed by a croc. He signed the death certificates! I'd told them so many times never to play by the river mouth. I knew Balfour never would. He was always such a good boy. Just wants to please. To be loved," Bethy babbled, sobbing loudly by the end. "My little baby girl."

"We have to keep walking." Tara twisted her arm free and grabbed Bethy by the elbow. She steered the crying woman towards the gates.

"Where are they? Are they safely away from here?"

116

"They're safe." *I seriously hope so. Tomaline, watch over Merlon and the ship until I find them again.*

Bethy stopped again. She seized Tara's arm. "Her doll! I can't leave her doll. Take Ramson." Bethy tried showing the kid at Tara. But Ramson, brown curls in a tangled mess around his head, shrieked and fought.

"I cannae. My hands…" Tara held them out. Blood, mud, and grass caked along her lower arms. Fresh blood dripped from her fingertips. Her hands shook violently. She would never be able to hold on to the child.

"But I can't leave without her doll. She'll ask for it. Soon as she sees me."

Tara stared at Bethy. It was irrational and ridiculous. But the woman was falling apart in front of her. "Where is it?"

"On the mantelpiece above the fireplace. Right inside the door. Please, there's time. The fighters haven't pulled over the first time yet."

Tara gritted her teeth. "Keep running. I'll get it." She turned. *This is how I die.*

She threw the blanket and legged it back down the street. The last stragglers stared at her passing. They knew she was star-crazed. It was evident from their faces.

She burst through the door, surprised when it swung open readily. But then, why would Bethy have wasted time locking it when she knew the whole village was being bombed imminently?

A high-pitched whine preceded a boom that shook the ground. Tara caught a picture falling from the wall. Bethy, holding a baby and with a younger Elin beside her. Smiling but there was a grief in Bethy's eyes.

Tara yanked the life-like painting from the frame and stuffed it in her trouser pocket.

A glass and metal lamp smashed on the other side of the room. Tara's heart didn't beat. Or so it felt. She held her breath, waiting for the blasts to claim her life. But they didn't come.

There, fallen over on the mantelpiece sat a hideous ragdoll. Tara snatched it up and spun back out. She ran for the gates again. She was the last one inside the village. The grassy plain beyond the tall fence dotted with people and a handful of square vessels, spilling over with children on the backs and roofs.

Then the ships passed. A repeat of the whining noise from before and the boom as they seemingly sped up. She would never make the gates. Her vision narrowed. The energy of the ships was cold, hateful.

Tara halted, stumped by a huge grate across the gate's ground. Strong winks of energy flickering every time she blinked. Dangerous amounts of energy. There was an energy-free, narrow walkway across the middle of it. Bethy stood on the other side, waving frantically at Tara.

The ships flew over them. Passed the gates. Bethy turned, eyes following the ships. She started running from the village, hugging Ramson to her chest.

Then pill-shaped objects dropped from the ships' bellies. Not on the village buildings. On the rolling vessels, halfway across the plain towards the distant smoke of another settlement on fire.

The vessels exploded. Grass, dirt, and metal parts burst into the air. Huge gaping wounds remained on the ground.

More and more pill-shaped bombs fell. Raining on the people now turning, screaming to run back to the village. Relentlessly, the ships followed, and so did the explosions.

Tara stood frozen beside the fence. Terror ruled her mind. It kept her stuck there, in the shade of the wood and wire palisade.

Fifty yards out, Bethy was at the front of the people running back. She held Ramson in her arms like she thought that alone would keep him safe. The horror on her face was plain even from the distance. And Tara couldn't move.

She watched, dread creeping through her insides when the pill-bombs caught up with the fleeing people. The mothers and fathers. The grannies and uncles. Their limbs tearing apart. Mud and grass blowing into the air with them.

The last bomb fell right behind Bethy and Ramson. Surprise in her blue eyes as she was thrown at the metal grate between the gates. Even in the chaos, midair, Bethy twisted. Her shoulder slamming into the bars instead of Ramson hitting them first. But it didn't matter.

She didn't hit the safety of the walkway. The energy inside the metal jolted through them both. Their hair withered and set on fire. Bethy's blue eyes stared up at the cloudy sky, a single tear escaping. Her body convulsing.

The energy winked out. Bethy lay still. Her eyes unseeing. Ramson in her arms, still like a toddler never should be.

Tara turned. Her stomach cramped and bile forced up her throat. She retched on the dry dirt. Gasping for breath, tears blurred the world around her.

Chapter 13

The spaceships flew over a third time. Tara wiped at her mouth and blinked to track the grey shapes moving across the sky. They moved so slowly compared to a wooden ship. Her fingers still clenched Ma's spiral-shaped silver pendant under her shirt. Today, it lent her no strength or comfort.

This time, the ships released tiny green cylinders when they were over the village. They fell, spewing a gas that reflected the atmosphere's light in a prism of colours. Hitting roofs and porches and the dirt streets, they bounced and rolled. The gas kept exploding from them.

Beasts sprung from under the wooden steps, from inside houses. Cat-animals similar to those Tara had seen amongst the Trackers and other, larger unknown long-nosed and floppy-eared ones, shrieked. They writhed in the dirt. Clawed at their necks and faces. The howls of their terror and pain cut through Tara's mind like shards of glass. She covered her ears, sinking to her knees beside the gate fence.

A woman crawled out from under a porch. She clutched at her throat, coughing. Her eyes met Tara's and she began dragging herself across the ground towards the fence where no gas cylinders had fallen.

But even as she did, and while Tara fought to her feet to run and haul the woman away, her eyes bulged, and she dropped. Her body shuddered. Foam spurted from her mouth, and she curled into a ball.

Tara jolted backwards. Her shoulders hit the wooden fence and she pressed between the rushes. This was a nightmare. There was no other explanation. She had hit her head when the storm began, and she would wake soon.

Except, the bile burning in her throat was too real. The pang at her ribs. The crust of blood under her fingernails. Her dreams were never so full of real sensations.

She pushed her palms against her ears and closed her eyes. The animals kept screaming. Thrashing and dying. She knew this had to be war. Nothing else could explain the terrors.

She understood now why everyone chose to accept Amule's corruption issues rather than risking a coup and fights. People might be stuck in whatever tier they got born into and only those with enough coin to bribe higher ups could progress easily in life, but they *had* life. Dying from starvation or murders like these villagers did was the least likely death in Amule.

Thirst was what drove Tara to dare a glimpse of the world eventually. Whether minutes or hours had passed, she couldn't tell. No movements. The animals lay dead. Others had joined the woman on the ground. People who had evidently tried to hide in their homes instead of fleeing the village.

Tara coughed. Blood speckled her sleeve cuff when she lowered her arm. Her lungs strained, like she had breathed in heat directly from a furnace. It was possible to burn lung tissue. Tara had been to a burn lecture before they left Amule, and the teacher had mentioned that. *"Commonly seen in tiers working with furnaces, ovens and stoves such as smiths, jewellers and occasionally cooks."*

There had been little heat from the bombs and gas alike, but from how everything had died around her, Tara could guess it was the gas that had burned her lungs, nonetheless. She pulled the scarf from around her neck over her nose and mouth.

Tara unfolded herself. Slowly. Carefully. Her knees throbbed. And her side, arms, and neck hurt. Everything did, really. She used the fence to pull herself to standing. Then she made the mistake to look back at the gates. Glancing at Bethy and Ramson who lay so still. Their blond and brown curls charred. Their lips cracked and eyes and noses bleeding.

Her stomach clenched. But she had nothing left to throw up. Even the bile had run out. Tara put her back on them. There were too many dead to bury. At least they hadn't burned. Their spirits would still find the eternal starlight if the long-legged birds ate them. The birds that were already pecking at scattered remains across the plains.

Tara turned towards Bethy and Ramson but closed her eyes. She put her thumb and forefinger together, then spread all her fingers in the sign of a star. "May your spirits travel safely to the eternal starlight," she whispered, her voice was hollow. So was her chest.

The village still oozed with the gas although most of the little cylinders had stopped spitting the lethal substance. What was she supposed to do? How would she find out if Merlon

122

was alive? Tara refused to think of what would have happened had the Outer Universe attackers seen *Lucia* and dropped a bomb on her deck too.

She stared at the hideous ragdoll in her hand. A single black bead stared back at her. Threads where the other eye had fallen out betrayed it hadn't always been one-eyed. The hair was knotted cloth that had possibly once been blue and orange, but dirt made it hard to tell the shade. The arms didn't sit at the same height. The stitching was terrible. Like somebody who hadn't ever learned how to sew had created it. Had Elin herself made it?

Tara tugged it into her belt and picked her way through the village, avoiding the streets where people lay dead. She skirted the places gas still slipped from the containers, seeping lazily onto the ground.

She needed food and water. Maybe a bag and blanket and a better weapon than her eating knife. She would decide what to do next, once she had found those basics.

The wind did its best to blow the rainbow gas away, but it seemed to cling to everything. A sheen coated the houses and when Tara touched it gingerly, her fingertip stung like she had touched a hot piece of metal. Her skin bubbled up in a blister. Would all food and water be contaminated too?

A whirring rumble reached her through the whine of her ears. Tara turned around herself. She had reached a square that partially opened to the water. Tall fences barricaded and kept the green, toothed beasts out, but there was a large rectangle that remained open to the water.

She narrowed her eyes. If she concentrated, she could almost see the tendrils of cold blue energy inside the tall lamp posts by the open rectangle of water. Two tiny wooden jetties reached out in the middle of the unfenced area. Two or three sail-less, low boats bobbed on the sides of one jetty.

The rumble wasn't coming from there. She turned towards the muddy grassland she had waded through while stalked by the beasts. Not there either. Maybe it was her ears playing her a trick. As she finished her full circle, a wink of metal shot up from the grassy plains outside the gates.

Tara's heart pounded. There, coming from the distant city of tall buildings that sent black plumes of smoke in the air, something moved. And it moved fast towards the village she stood in the centre of.

Despite her attempts at willing herself to take deep breaths, they became faster and shallower even though she failed to see the energy from the approaching vessels. Somebody was coming and she had seen enough to not want any more to do with Outer Universe humans.

The first four houses she tried had that skin-blistering sheen on their doors. Kicking them in and using her handkerchief to avoid more sores forming, she found the insides coated as well. A bloated man lay inside the open door of the fifth house she got to. His eyes were bloodshot, a trickle of red ran from his nose. He stared unseeing at the ceiling of his home.

Tara dry-heaved and she backed out.

She couldn't hide in the buildings. Her hands shook violently, and her ribs seemed to shrink around her lungs the more she thought about the horrors around her. A glance towards the plain proved time was running out. Fear squeezed at her throat. She ran to the last house before the water and jetties. The one Jonna and Delun had lived in.

A sob pushed up through her and escaped with a whimper. They had been scared but hadn't killed her. Now *they* were dead. Limbs and bodies torn apart when they had only tried to run for safety. Their hostility last night suddenly made sense. If this was the sort of society they lived in, Tara too would have been ready to shoot anybody who threatened to bring all this destruction on the community.

She staggered past the house and let herself succumb to the sobs pressing inside her chest. Too dehydrated for tears, her shoulders shook, and her sternum hurt so very much. How could humans be so awful? Did they not know they had blown up children and scared folk who didn't pull the trigger on strangers even when they feared it would bring their own doom?

The clatter of the grates by the village entrance came as Tara fought to regain control. Terror yanked the last sob from her breath, and she straightened where she sat. A second clatter then a third told of more vessels crossing into the settlement. Had they rolled straight over Bethy and Ramson? She didn't want to know.

A scratchy voice boomed so the window above her head vibrated. "Survivors to the main square. The Rebels have been eliminated. Rebels will bomb no more. You're safe now." The voice was odd. Metallic or echoey in a way Tara had never heard before. Inhuman almost. As if each syllable had been strung together by someone who didn't know to change the inflection depending on the word and context.

"Dun't!" Someone hissed.

Tara's hands clenched. She stared when a young man slipped from an older woman's grasp and stood. "They're Earth patrol." He squared his shoulders.

"And they're the ones bombing us! It's lies!" The woman snatched after him.

The man shook his head. Jumping onto the jetty from the sail-less boat, he walked towards the square.

Fear rushed through Tara's body, but he never glanced her way. When he passed out of her view, she stuffed her shirt collar between her teeth to keep from squeaking in panic.

"Hold it roight there!" A woman yelled. Same accent as Ola, but tone ruthless like his never was. Maybe this was why he hadn't wanted to go home. Why he, despite his grief over Lena's death, smiled and laughed so often. He had exchanged this terror and death with a calm scholar's life in Amule's castle with an occasional trip on Mira's schooner.

Tara felt certain she would trade to any tier, even the disposer tier who worked in the horrifying dark, damp tunnels under the city, if it meant she never had to see another war like this again.

The young man who had gone to meet the newcomers spoke up. "I'm disease free. Nut a rebel either."

"Put him in a pod," the woman growled.

Her voice sounded strange. Tara frowned. Where and when had she heard that strange muffling? She dared a peek around the corner.

The man got shoved into a tiny glass-like compartment on the side of one of the wheeled vessels. Dozens of grey and white-glad people filled the square. The large vessels had bars around the exterior and glimmered with such pristine cleanliness Tara got the impression they had been scrubbed shortly before wheeling here.

The strangers had clear apparatuses, *oxygen-masks* Tara realised, on their faces. They wore weirdly shiny fabrics and even their hair was covered in a strange helmet. With their grey jackets and white trousers, black gloves, and helmets they looked like strange puppets rather than humans. If not

126

for their faces behind the sheer breathing masks, Tara would easily have thought them another sapient species altogether.

"Squad One, secure the periphery. Two and Three, first two blocks." The woman who appeared to be in charge gestured left and right while giving orders. "Remember the last mutant kids should be dead but these villages tend to lie and hide them. Assume any survivors carry the pox."

Both the leader and all the other strangers carried large grey weapons with a blue light on the side of them. What had Ola called those? Something-guns. They shot blue lightning bolts that could melt skin off bones. Tara remembered *that*. Luckily, she had only seen a bolt melt a metal and glass frame of a building.

Last time, another Outer Universe scholar, Erica, had been near death when she threatened to shoot them with one of those guns. Tara had still had her perfect navigator's vision too. The guns held so much pent-up energy even glancing at it had left her with a terrible headache. *Suppose there's one good thing about not seeing energy well anymore.* She could look all she wanted and not get even a tinge of aching behind her eyes.

"Squad Five, check there's nobody else in the boats but dun't get eaten," the leader said.

Burn me! Tara realised a bit too late that the last group of four people stomped towards the water. If one of them glanced her way, they would see her instantly. She scrambled backwards, scanning her surroundings. She couldn't get to the water, and they were clearly going to search the boats there anyway. But there was a grassy bramble hedge to her left that almost stretched to the house wall she knelt by.

Before the squad had marched so far they could easily see her, she dove into the tall, yellow grass. Prickly, thorny branches embraced her. Scratching at her already shredded arms. She chomped harder on her shirt collar and ducked, crawling on her elbows to get further into the thicket.

"Check that sound over there." A man ordered.

Shit! Tara froze. And there not two yards from her face, a furious tri-coloured cat-animal stared at her, ears flat and tail fluffed. She had met only one cat-animal before. Major Miit had been steel grey and extremely arrogant. Not that all the other Trackers hadn't been arrogant too. Tara held up her finger to her lips. Instead of remaining quiet, the cat-animal beat its tail, and yowled at her.

Somebody sighed, heels turning. "Just a cat that escaped the gassing."

"That'll have to learn to fend for itself now." The man who seemed to lead the squad spoke. "Get back here and let's get to it."

Tara let out a breath of relief when the person withdrew from near the thickets. Her heart thumped so hard against the ground she almost feared it would burst through her chest and dig her a grave. But for now, she remained undiscovered.

Chapter 14

Tara winced at every metal crate and drum the squad kicked into the water. They spoke harshly, their large grey guns sweeping from side to side. They slowly made their way through all the clutter.

They seemed aggressive, dangerous. But hadn't the young man, now stuck inside that glass cage, said they were Earth Patrol? Those were the people Tara had thought were meant to be the good ones. She wasn't so sure anymore.

The cat seemed to forget about Tara and stared through the grasses, tail flicking. Xir brown, grey, and orange fur was matted. Xe had snot running out of the nose, but the yellow eyes watched the noisy people intensely.

"How do we get out of here?" Tara whispered. The cat didn't respond. "Hey, can you hear me? Do you have a letter tube?" She shifted, not quite daring to poke the animal. She had been clawed enough by Major Miit to never want more of that.

The cat jerked. Xir ears flattened and xe hissed. It was an ominous sound. The hairs on the back of Tara's neck prickled and she wrapped her arm around her head in case xe decided to attack.

"Are you...dumb or something?" Tara winced at her words but she needed a response.

Xe didn't respond. Trackers were too arrogant to stay silent when called stupid. Did non-Tracker cat-animals exist? Stars knew, because Tara had only ever encountered Major Miit before seeing the dozens dying in the gassed village.

Another drum splashing into the water snapped Tara's attention back to the squad. She used a fingertip to push some grass out of her field of vision. When she blinked fast, she thought there was a fifth heartbeat. That teal energy flickering with agitation.

It took her embarrassingly long to figure out where the woman from earlier hid. Inside one of the boats, under a piece of tarp. If not for Tara's, rather terrible, navigator's vision she wouldn't have known.

The four people searching around the docks didn't appear to notice either. Once they had kicked and tossed everything in the water, they stalked back and forth staring into the boats. One jumped in, the blue bolt gun humming when xe flicked a tap on the side of the weapon with a thumb. The safety?

Ola had shown Tara how to shoot his shotguns before the Trackers took one and rendered the other useless. A reminder of the life he had left behind.

A rat leapt over the boat's side when the person kicked at the ropes and nets. The gun went off. Tara's breath caught. Was that rat a Tracker?

The blue bolt exploded into the water, sending the liquid into the air with such force the boat rocked and the person inside staggered. Xir back hit the jetty and another squad member caught xir shoulder, hauling xem up even as the water splashed over the boat's sides. Steam rose, the water bubbling.

If that rat had been a Tracker, it was dead now. A shiver coursed through Tara. She eased her fingers open, letting go of the handful of grass and dirt she had gripped in her fight to remain quiet. She suddenly understood better why the Trackers were so paranoid about humans discovering them. Once more, she thanked the stars they also ensured Outer Universe humans never learned of Inner Universe.

The helmet-person who had been in the boat straightened on the jetty.

"Waste of shots that. It's nut like anybody's going to survive swimming through the acid bath." The woman who had grabbed the boat investigator spoke.

The investigator tugged at xir shirt and rolled a shoulder. "Gave me a fright that nasty thing. It's acid inside the barrier?" Xe nodded at the rectangle of beast-free water.

A line of small floating cylinders ran out towards the middle of the river, parallel with the jetties, turned towards one another in right angles and met in the middle. Now Tara looked closer, she noticed the water inside the rectangle of floating devices seemed to have a faintly blue-green shine to it.

"Acid or alkaloid, who cares. Long as it keeps those sarco crocs away," the woman replied.

Investigator nodded. "Foul creatures. I've never understood why anybody would release that sort on a planet we know'll be inhabited."

"They were meant to go extinct again by themselves after building the ecosystem." The man who appeared to lead the squad scratched his neck through the shiny fabric. "Dun't get all cowardly another time, sunlight here's not strong enough to recharge anything properly."

"This place gives me the heebies." Investigator sniffed.

The leader waved a hand. "We're dun' here."

Tara let out a breath of relief for the woman hiding in the boat. She had no idea what those glass cages on the square were, but the Earth Patrollers were rounding up the half dozen survivors inside. No matter what, Tara didn't want to be part of it and maybe this woman in the boat could help her escape the village and search for Merlon.

The squad made it most of the way to the square before the woman threw the tarp aside.

Don't move yet! Tara tried willing her thoughts to reach the woman. They didn't, of course. Rather, the woman hammered at a metal box at the stern of the boat. A roar of smoke and vibrating noise rose in the close air. Energy danced around the growling boat box. She cast off the mooring lines and grabbed a stick poking out of the box. The boat started moving away from the jetty.

Tara stared in disbelief. The woman had gone undetected during the search and *now* she revealed her whereabouts? She had to be in a serious panic to make that big of a mistake.

The squad turned as one. The escaping woman glanced back. Even from the distance, obscured by grass, Tara saw the fear in her eyes. The boat sped up. It slipped over the long edge of the rectangle keeping the acid water around the jetties. The metal box on the boat's stern tilted shortly and the greener water spilled into the muddy beast-water beyond.

A blue bolt flickered through the air. It seemed to grow and compress at the same time. Tumbling around itself, it flew at a dizzying speed. The woman didn't even have time to scream. The boat exploded in fire so hot, blue flames licked across the water. The water monsters – sarco crocs? – beat their tails on the surface and dove into the murky depths with angry hisses.

"Damn it, Hick! That was a civilian," a woman snarled.

Hick, the shooter, shrugged. "Or a rebel, they were running away after all."

"Search everywhere again," the chief woman shouted. "Hurry up, y'all. We've got some civilians needing urgent med care."

Tara stuffed her hand in her mouth and remained still while the squads swept through every house and shed once more. The young man was beating bloody fits against the glass cage, but no sound escaped the small space. Tara turned her face from the grief in action. Had that been his ma?

She felt sick but kept her fingers pressed over her mouth. Any sound and she might end up blue-bolted too. Her eyes hurt like tears tried but couldn't escape. Why were these people so cruel?

The cat remained by Tara's side, silent, angry, and panting like xe was getting sick. She decided xe wasn't a Tracker or xe

133

would surely have spoken up or tried to communicate with her by now.

At least an hour went by. The Earth Patrollers or whatever they were, meticulously checking everything. Once or twice steps came close, but nobody went through the grass and thorny shrub Tara lay in. Eventually the whirring of the metal and glass wagons started back up and they began rolling out, one by one, the squads hopping on the backs and sides, others filing into the boxed off fronts.

When the strangers were finally gone, Tara couldn't move. Her joints were too stiff. Her dehydration and hunger drove her to crawl a few feet, then collapse. She realised she would die here. The birds scavenging on the scattered limbs that hadn't been collected by the squads would eventually find and eat her too.

Time stretched. It would be a long, boring death. Tara fought until she managed to roll to her side, taking pressure off her sore ribs but instantly losing all sense in her right arm and leg.

Her fingers searched her pockets for the hundredth time. Nothing to eat and her water bottle wasn't on her belt. It was in Merlon's cabin, on the hook by the bunk. Would he still be searching for her? Or had he already been obliterated with blue bolts or eaten by sarco crocs?

With nothing better to do, Tara watched the cat roll up. Xe panted worse now. Xir bulging stomach convulsing and eyes half-closed as if in pain.

It wasn't until Tara jolted awake, much later with the star waning beyond the fence, she realised what was wrong with the cat. By then, five tiny cats lay against xir stomach. Their ears were flat, and eyes closed, but little pink, grey, and black noses seemed to know what to do, nonetheless.

No attempts to move closer had success, so instead Tara just lay there, watching the tiny little cats nursing. It took her a few moments to realise one wasn't moving. When the mother cat shifted, four crawled with her, giving out tiny squeaks until they once more nussled against her belly. A little grey striped one remained still. Tara reached out. Its body was cold and stiff.

The cat stared at her, eyes sorrowful. Tracker or not, she knew one of her babies hadn't made it. A sob broke through Tara's chest. She pulled the cold little cat into her arm, cradling it against herself. But it was too late.

She cried. Eyes dry like her throat and tongue. Hollering into the dirt and grass. She struggled with each painful, gasped breath but couldn't stop the sobs now they had taken a hold of her.

Why had so many people had to die? It didn't matter she hadn't known them. She had been there. Watched their limbs getting torn apart. Bethy and Ramson, fried on the grate by that energy Ola had talked about. The one Tara had forgot the name of again which Outer Universe people used for heating and lights instead of using powders.

After a while, she rubbed at her face although barely a tear had left her eyes. She placed the dead baby cat on the ground. Using her left hand, she scratched at the hard dirt. It would become grass and its spirit would travel to the eternal stars. If animal spirits did that. She dug furiously. Ignoring the pain of sharp rocks burying under her fingernails. It needed a hole-drop.

A tiny part of her knew it didn't matter. That the baby cat wasn't a stand in for the burials she didn't know if Bethy and Ramson would get from those Earth Patrol squads. But she kept clawing at the hard soil until the dent was large enough to fit the tiny creature.

"May the stars lead you to their eternal light," she whispered and placed it in the ground. The dusty earth crumbled and filled in around it.

The mother cat watched, quietly licking each of the remaining four in turn. *I never want to know that pain. The agony of losing my kid.* Tara's body trembled when another round of dry sobs raked through her.

With night came rain. Tara woke from those first cool drops hitting her temple. Her brain slow, she jolted. Rolling to her back, she stared at the grass bobbing heavy heads around her. The rain slipped past her cracked lips, wetting her tongue, and sparked memories of where she was.

A glow lit up the grey clouds from somewhere beyond the village. There was a faint smell of smoke on the wind. If a fire came through these dry grasses, Tara would burn. She had no power to move. No will to save herself. Nowhere to go even if she had the resolve and energy.

The rain grew heavier, and she let her jaw fall open, choking on the droplets hitting the back of her throat. But she kept her mouth open, greedily drinking every molecule. Within an hour she had become drenched. Her body shivered with the cold that came with being soaked, splayed on the ground.

It rained most of the night and Tara slept little. By the time morning goaded away the clouds, a heavy mist coated the air above her. Her thirst somewhat satiated, hunger gnawed at her bones. How long since she had last eaten? A day or was it closer to two? She had lost track of time.

Arms shaking, she rolled onto her elbows. Pain throbbed everywhere. She would never walk anywhere. Crawl maybe, but nothing more ambitious.

The cat jolted, cowering beside her. The four kittens – two grey, a black and a mostly white with orange spots on the head and back – cried from under her belly.

"I willnae hurt you or your babies," Tara said. Her voice was but a croak. It sounded foreign, like she had forgotten how it used to sound for how long she had remained silent. Maybe it was due to the pain and hunger.

The air near Tara's clenched hands vibrated. She blinked at the spot, a grey shimmer and the black of a portal winking in and out of focus. Then a tiny umber rat appeared. It shook itself, the fur going from fluffy to smooth and it sat up, running the whiskers through its tiny hands.

"Bailey?" Tara stared. She had lost it, surely.

The rat turned her head, nose quivering. "There you are. We've been worried about you and…uh-oh." Bailey nosedived between Tara's arms. The cat followed.

Claws dug into her skin and Tara jolted to sitting. Bailey scampered into her shirt between two buttons and the cat pounced. Without a thought, Tara jerked her arm and flung the cat off herself.

The cat rolled across the ground, curling up and hissing but not attacking again.

"Begone dumb-born cat!" Bailey shouted from inside the shirt.

Tara seized the rat through the fabric and held her firm to stop the tickly squirming. "She's nae going to leave. She gave birth last night." While keeping hold of Bailey with one hand, Tara stuck the other into her shirt and fished the rodent out. "Hide under my hair and be kind and say Merlon's on his way."

"Tuh! He doesn't know where to find you so of course he isn't. I'll go let him know to steer *Lucia* for the fire. Go to one of the boats and wait." Bailey wriggled free and leapt away.

Tara snatched for the rat. "Bailey, wait!" But she had already portalled away again.

The cat crept back to her babies, ears droopy and spine showing through her scruffy fur.

Chapter 15

Despair and hope mingled in Tara's chest. She had no energy to move. But they were on their way. Merlon was alive, *Lucia* couldn't be completely destroyed if she could be steered. Tara let out a breath as slowly as she could manage. Forcing herself to calm down.

Her legs wouldn't bend or allow weight. Her hands shook violently. Too little sustenance did that. Even skipping a single meal sometimes left her trembling and dazed but she had never been this hungry before. Not even after eighteen hours stuck in a well had she been this weak.

Somehow, she got a knee under herself and locked the joint. Her palms stung when she pressed off against the ground.

Partway up she realised she had no balance. She keeled, face hitting the grass.

The cat shot past her with a hiss. A small white bundle in her mouth. Tara rolled over, watching the cat vanish through the grass towards the two wooden jetties. Maybe she *was* a Tracker?

Tara lost sight of her behind a broken fence and returned her attention to getting herself to one of the boats. The village was so quiet. She dragged herself along by her elbows, not even attempting to get onto her hands and knees. *So tired.*

The cat scooted past again, then left with the black baby carefully gripped between the teeth. Tara had no idea how it didn't break the skin. Cats had sharp teeth and Tara still had scars from Major Miit's.

The wounds along her arms, shallow as they were, stung with the mud and grit she pulled herself through. *Focus on the task.* She had to get to a boat and then she could rest until *Lucia* came to collect her. She hoped they were close and that the Earth Patrollers weren't.

Fifty yards proved far away indeed when her entire body hurt, and she hadn't eaten in days. Halfway there, Tara slumped on the ground. She had left the grass behind. The cat ran back past her, collecting the third kitten and trotting back towards the jetty with the tiny bundle in her mouth.

Tara followed the animal, curious where it was moving to. The moment the cat stepped onto the jetty, *something* flapped and screeched behind Tara.

She jolted, twisting her neck, and preparing for a swift death. But it wasn't her the blue bird swooped on. The red-tipped beak was a foot long and sharp like an awl. The stilt-like legs kicked at something in the grass, the beak chopping down. Tara put two and two together too late.

"Nae! Donae!" She lunged at the bird.

But the huge wings were already beating for take-off. It swung its long, purple neck into the air, a tiny, mewling baby cat stuck in the beak. Tara leapt and crawled towards it. The bird got in the air, the legs trailing after. She reached and snatched for the legs, but it was too far from her.

The mother cat yowled. She shot past Tara, so fast dirt flew from her paws. Her claws slashed for the scaled feet. But she too, missed. The bird flapped faster, turning when others of its species swept towards it from above.

When they began a tug of war, Tara turned away, pressing her eyes shut against the tears welling up. Not even a day old and two had already perished. Tara rubbed her eyes and looked at the cat.

She sat in the grass, yellow eyes tracking the birds cawing and flying around above. Her tail flicked back and forth, and her ears were flat against her head. Then she turned, meeting Tara's gaze.

There was a grief, however distanced and strange, in the cat's eyes. Tara gave up against the tears and they poured forth. "I'm so sorry."

The cat only stared. Then she got up and galloped back out of the grass.

By the time Tara had regained strength and made it back to where she had been, the mother cat and her last three babies were nowhere to be seen.

So, Tara crept across the ground towards the jetties. She hated this place. Where everyone died gruesome deaths, they didn't deserve. Amule was shitty and corrupt, but at least nobody got bombed or gassed or picked off by terrifying

141

beasts. Despite Horatio Corncockle being the High Chancellor, it was to be preferred to Quarantine Thirteen.

The jetty was full of splinters, the wood dry and dead. But even if Outer Universe had had breathing wood, Tara wouldn't have expected anything but their boats to be made of it. Ignoring the small stabs of wood slivers driving into her skin she shuffled and dragged herself to where the nearest boat lay moored.

She rolled over the edge, quite unlike her plan to gently scoot into the boat. The four-foot drop was broken by a solid metal bar of a thwart.

Pain exploded against her arm that hit the gunwale. Air expelled from her lungs and the already bruised ribs left her gasping. The world blacked out for several moments, her head spinning from the agony.

Tara wrapped her fingers around the thwart, using it to correct herself to a sitting position. She didn't dare move onto the stern seat for fear she would dangle and tip overboard. Instead, she leaned against the hull, slowly stretching her legs along the bottom of the boat. The bow end was partially covered with some odd black tarp.

Sitting inside it, she realised the boat wasn't made of a material she recognised although the hull had looked like wood on the outside. Something between metal and that material Ola had shown her in his and Lena's home. Plastics, was it? Except this was in tiny bits and pieces seemingly melted together.

Tara gave up trying to guess what it was. Long as it kept that weirdly smelling, greenish water away from her. A rope that dangled off the jetty where the woman had cast off hung above the water. The parts that *had* been in the water were gone. The way it had dissolved confirmed some sort of acid was at play, and Tara understood why there was no need for a fence around the rectangular harbour stretch. She didn't entirely understand how the acid stayed in this area, but the outline of the barrier floats bobbed on the surface of the outer edges of the acid waters.

Every breath hurt and she didn't dare move should another flare of agony shoot through her pained ribs. Despite her determination to keep awake and watch for more squads, Tara nodded off almost instantly.

Faintly, she registered something splashing. But it wasn't close. Her eyes were so heavy, she couldn't be bothered to open them. Voices shouted at her. Begging her to do something. She jolted awake.

There, not a hundred yards from her lay *Lucia*. She rocked gently in the murky water's waves. For a full five seconds Tara thought she had fallen fully asleep. That she was only dreaming about *Lucia* come to rescue her. Then she picked out Merlon amongst all the people waving at her from the deck. Hope surged in her chest.

Fabian hung in the shrouds above, arms flailing for her attention. Her heart skipped a beat when she saw Karl, next to Gaunty and Kieran. He was back on his feet!

She pushed off against the gunwale. The cut on her palm from the croc beast split open. She sucked in air to keep herself from screaming.

"Tara!" Merlon's voice was the first she heard. Why hadn't Bailey come to her again instead of this shouting? Merlon turned, tapping Derek on the shoulder and the young sailor sprinted from the rest of them, vanishing into the passage under the quarterdeck that led to the cabin.

Why hadn't Jara steered the ship closer? Unless the acid water was so strong it could damage *Lucia's* breathing wood. That was possible considering how the wooden crates the squad had kicked in had vanished from sight. Tara hadn't noticed earlier but now she realised only the top of the jetty was wood, the stakes going into the acid-water were made of some shinier, grey material. Metal?

Tara crawled to the front of the boat and back. No sails or oars. She had seen drawings of oars, not unlike those used by bakers to place bread in an oven, but she wasn't entirely sure how she was meant to use an oar anyway.

Her eyes fell on the metal box at the stern. The woman had punched the box, but Tara couldn't see anything to punch. There were buttons on the side that faced her. They didn't glow like those on Ola's computers and other weird equipment. Had there been buttons that didn't glow? She couldn't remember. Eleven months was a long time and the fight against Lady Galantria had blurred the memories from the last trip to Outer Universe.

She pressed a few of the buttons, nothing happened. At the corner of her eye, a black spot vibrated in the air. Her head whipped around. It took her half a second too long to recognise the type of portal energy she had caught a glimpse off. The letter tube appeared, shooting straight at her face.

Instinctively she ducked. But her movements were slow and instead of avoiding it, she banged the wooden cylinder with her forehead. "Stars burn me!" Pain sprung out where the tube had hit. She would get a bruise there, but maybe she already had several in the same spot.

The tube clanged against the inside of the boat, rolling back and forth on the nearly flat bottom. She rubbed the sore spot and picked the tube up. At least it hadn't flown overboard.

Her hands trembled so much she thought she wouldn't manage to pop the lid off. Then she realised she was trying the wrong end. Why didn't the Trackers make a more visible mark than that tiny line etched into the end that was the lid?

A letter fell out. Merlon's hasty – and nearly unintelligible – handwriting covered the small paper slip. Luckily Tara had practice from the past few months when she helped fill in the travel log books he was required to complete as part of his inter-galaxian trading permits.

Sorry, Bailey has no more portal powder for herself. We can't draw nearer, Bailey says the greener water is acid? She says there's a switch (not the type of whip but a button?) on the side of the metal box. Flick that opposite of what it is now and press the front button that's green. Use the stick to steer, I suppose that's like a tiller on a smaller ship. Bailey said to press the handle at the side carefully, that's the speed somehow.

Miss you ✳

Tara folded the slip up and stuck it into her bandeau. There was no reason to be choking up seeing that little crooked star at the end of the note. But she missed him too, dearly so. She heaved in an unsteady breath and turned to the metal box again. A small tap was on the side, Tara pushed at it. It didn't want to move.

"Oh, burn me already," she grumbled. Her fingers were going numb, and she could feel her bowel roiling. While she had nothing to throw up, she would be star-cursed unlucky if she passed out now. The "switch" slipped between her fingers, changing the angle it sat at.

The buttons on the front winked to life. One glowed green. She pressed it and the metal box whirred with a cough. *Thank you Tomaline for shining on me.*

With no energy to climb back up and cast off the mooring lines from the bollards, Tara pulled at the lines until they slacked enough to touch the water. The ropes' fibres hissed and spluttered. They didn't dissolve instantly, but when her grip failed and the boat rocked back, the tug was enough to break them.

She shifted back to the metal box and pressed the handle on the side. The boat shot forward. Terrified, she let go. The boat instantly slowed down. Tara's heart stayed in her throat, but she had already sped halfway across acid waters. She pushed the handle gingerly and the boat moved at a bit more reasonable pace.

Right as *Lucia* loomed, a tiny mewl sounded from under the tarp at the bow. She squinted and there in the dark, the eyes of the mother cat stared back out at her.

"Burn me." Tara glanced back. The jetty was ninety yards away. And her head felt like it floated separately from her body, she was that close to fainting with exhaustion. She would never make it back there, let alone somehow get the cat to leave the boat.

146

Then the boat slipped over the strangely buoyant separation between the acid and salt water. The sarco crocs circling *Lucia* splashed their tails and dove into the depths.

Panic thundered in Tara's head. The cuts on her palms seemed to throb more. Those beasts were longer than the tiny boat. She didn't doubt they could flip it if they wanted to.

The bow bumped into *Lucia*.

"Tara, grab a rung." Merlon was already halfway down the ladder that had been slung over the side.

She fell forward, hitting that stupid thwart again but her hand tangled with the end of the ladder. The boat yanked backwards, away from *Lucia*. The rungs shook against her grip for every step Merlon moved down. Tears forced their way into her eyes from the pain of her split skin wrenching more apart. "I cannae hold it."

But then Merlon's boots thumped against the bottom of the boat, staggering for the briefest of moments. Even with a stiff thigh muscle he had better balance than anyone she knew.

With a quick move, he forced a ladder rung around a cleat on the boat, holding it in place by *Lucia*. He knelt, hands gingerly grasping her shoulders. "Stars, what's happened to you?"

"Water's full of beasts and the village got blown up and gassed." She tried to shrug but instead keeled forward.

Merlon broke her fall. His chest solid and arms soft as he wrapped them around her. "Please don't die," his whispered voice broke on the last word.

"I willnae," Tara muttered. He smelled the same. Of starlight and wood lye. She allowed her eyes to close. "Donae leave the poor mother cat. The sarco crocs will eat her, and she already lost two of her babies."

Merlon mumbled something she didn't catch, his arms sweeping her up. The boat rocked and the ladder groaned. Tara rested her head against Merlon's shoulder, the haze on her brain taking over now she was safe again.

Chapter 16

Muffled voices woke Tara. She couldn't seem to open her eyes. Her lips tingled lightly. Had she been hurt? The bitter taste of Passiflora lingered on her tongue. But the surroundings didn't smell like a healer's clinic.

Soft sighs and the deep groan of pressure against a hull triggered her memories. She was on *Lucia*. The mattress under her unfamiliar and hard. With that sensation came another. Pain. Dulled and faint but throbbing through her limbs.

Passiflora wasn't a great painkiller. It mostly helped put a subject into a heavy sleep. The fact her injuries didn't overwhelm her, told of other herbs having been used.

No numbness or nausea so probably not S-V. Yorik knew to only use it in emergencies anyway. Best keep it under that floorboard that lifted at the end of this very cot. Depending on how stressed Merlon was, he was likely to at least *think* about taking it. There was no need to tempt him.

"…should be awaking any moment but ever'body's a little dif'rent," Yorik said.

Merlon cleared his throat. "Sorry, I'll stop pestering you. I know you've done what you could."

Tara managed to open an eye a crack. Merlon stood outside the sick bay door, but she couldn't see Yorik for the door panel and bulkhead. Merlon crossed his arms, glancing her way. His face remained blurry, was his brows furrowed with worry?

She trying to move but failed. Her right hand began twitching though. The Passiflora wasn't quite out of her system yet.

"Tara!" Merlon rushed to the cot. He dropped to his knees, clasping her trembling hand. He gave it a gentle squeeze. "You've had me worried," he muttered and kissed her bandaged wrist.

She attempted to squeeze his fingers to let him know she heard him. But she couldn't get her eyes to open. Rather, her eyelids had slid closed once more and sleep seemed to tug at her to return to the quiet stillness the Passiflora offered. Fighting against it was pointless. Until she was less sedated, she couldn't eat anyway no matter how hollow her stomach felt.

"Thanks to ya, Yorik." Fabian's voice sounded from the hold, pulling Tara back out of the slumber. "Have ya seen Jara?"

Merlon shifted, his hands still encasing Tara's. Had seconds or minutes passed?

The creak of the deck under him swallowed Yorik's answer to Fabian.

"If you bet on whether she'd live…" Merlon said.

"Ha!" Fabian laughed. "I'm not cruel, Cap'n. Nay, it's them new crew as are easy pickin's. Thinks ya's not a big, messy sobber when it comes to ya favourite crew."

Merlon sighed. "You really ought to be more respectful and I *haven't* been crying." Then he muttered under his breath, "I prefer to wait until I know how much to cry."

Her snort and chuckle surprised Tara herself as much as it seemed to do Merlon. He jolted, squeezing her hand a tad too tightly. Her eyes finally agreed to open but she couldn't control her voice. She twisted and wriggled her fingers.

"Sorry." Merlon let go. Relief warmed the smile he sent her, although those creases of worry remained on his forehead. "How are you feeling? Do you need anything?"

Bailey's pointed face popped over the edge of the cot. "She's dehydrated and starved." The rat hopped onto the blanket that covered Tara, sniffing around and then settled to groom herself.

Tongue numb and dry, Tara could only nod. She had a faint memory of having water teased down before she was given the Passiflora tea but that had to be a long while ago and she was parched again.

"Run and get it then." Merlon waved at Fabian.

"And ya's the one talkin' bout respect. Ya have no manners…Cap'n." Despite his moaning, Fabian vanished from the doorway, wearing a wide grin.

Yorik entered in his place. "You fully aware?" He continued when Tara bobbed a weak nod. "You'll want this against pain. Bout'o come back as Passiflora leaves the system." He tapped an amber glass bottle that stood in one

151

of the wood insets of the herb cabinet's tabletop. "Pink ones are for the 'flammation, green is regular pain killer. One of each. Need me for an'thing else?"

Tara shook her head.

Merlon picked up her hand again. The way he tracked Yorik's every move, Tara knew he wanted to speak to her, alone. Or as alone as they could get. Bailey tended to be stickier than cherry sap gum.

Yorik nodded and left the sick bay.

Tara got an elbow under herself, and Merlon helped her to sit, readjusting the pillow for her. When Merlon didn't speak, she raised a brow.

Merlon licked his lips, gaze meeting hers. "I thought—"

Fabian's steps returned and he skipped into the sick bay. "Here ya go. Soup's cold but don't matter. Jug, mug." Fabian placed each item on the flat portion of the cabinet.

Merlon turned his head, doing a rather bad job at glowering. Not that Fabian paid him any attention anyway.

"How's ya doing? We feared we'd lost *Lucia's* Trachnan tramp, would've been a right sobfest, eh Cap'n? 'Course we did lose ya for a bit and ya look more than half dead, but that's little different than usual." Fabian beamed, not even trying to temper his obvious relief.

Tara took the mug of water he offered. The tremor of her hands resulted in a minor spillage, but she didn't care. She downed the water, coughing and handed the empty vessel back for a refill. "Still look better than you on a good day, turd."

Fabian laughed.

"I had Elin's rag doll on my belt, could you give it to her?" Tara pointed at the mass of her clothes on the stool at the end of her cot. She had been changed into a fresh nightie while she was out.

Fabian returned the mug, once more full of liquid. "Ya ought to hand her that when ya can. I don't know the story."

Tara tried to ignore the images rearing in her mind again. She couldn't talk about that yet, not without breaking down and she didn't want to wipe the smiles of their faces. "Did you save the cat and her babies?" She sipped the water more carefully this time.

Merlon nodded. "We did. They're in the lower hold. Thought it might as well take care of the mouse problem."

"Ha! *We...*" Fabian scoffed. "Ordered me to go get the beast is what ya did, Cap'n." He yanked at a sleeve and revealed swollen claw marks across his knuckles and up his arm.

Bailey wrinkled her nose. "It's extremely rude to bring a cat aboard without my agreement. And a dumb-born even! Tuh!"

"It's extremely rude to call her dumb-born," Tara snapped. "The poor creature lost two babies within a day of giving birth so have a bit of mercy."

"Kittens." Bailey quipped.

Fabian frowned. "What?"

"Baby cats are called kittens," Bailey replied. "And do not call rat babies kittens. We have pups, like dogs but ours are much cleaner and nicer than dog pups."

Tara met Merlon's eyes and mouthed, "what are dogs?"

He shrugged. Not something Tara had missed then. It was one of those things Bailey would mention that they had never seen or heard of. Bailey could make Ola seem ordinary for the weird things she would randomly bring up. And then she would turn around and feign ignorance if she remembered it was classified Tracker knowledge.

Tara's eyes fell on Bailey once more. She stomped around on the blanket, round, and round. Getting ready to settle which meant there would be no alone time with Merlon. But Tara longed to speak to him. Images of what she had seen were pressing on her mind and she hated crying in front of people, or sapient animals.

She caught the first mate's eyes. "Fabian, I worry the cat smells Bailey when she's so close to the lower hold hatch. Maybe it's best she's on deck instead?"

"Gotcha." Fabian winked. He tended to pretend he was rather slow, but it was rare Tara couldn't get him to catch on to her exact line of thought with a few select words. He elbowed Merlon, wiggling his eyebrows as he snatched the rat from the cot.

"Unhand me!" Bailey wriggled. "I find your jokes most tiresome and have missed Tara soft-hair."

Fabian stuffed her in a pocket, shoving his neckerchief down on top of her. "Jokes? Ya want jokes? Very well. A rat snuck into a bar…" He left the sick bay, closing the door after himself.

Merlon turned to Tara. "Are you alright?"

She took a deep, unsteady breath. She opened her mouth to say yes, but a strangled sob escaped her instead. Ramson's little dimpled cheeks kept flashing through her mind. His

154

mud-brown curls smoking from the frizzed tips. Blood seeping from his nose and eyes. Bethy holding him tight, even in death.

Merlon wrapped his arms around her, so gingerly she would normally have told him to stop treating her like something fragile. Instead, she howled into his shoulder, clinging to his shirt, and gasping for breath.

"Whatever happened. Whatever you've been through. I'm here," Merlon muttered. He pet her head and all but rocked her gently, never embracing her too tightly but still giving a squeeze every so often.

In the end, it was the pain of her ribs that paused her sobs. Tara pulled away, using her bandaged hand to mop up the tears. "The village. They all got blasted. Then those who had stayed hidden in their homes got gassed. This horrible, sticky gas that made them cough blood and blistered your skin like a hot flame."

Merlon stared at her. His expression frozen. But she recognised the terror flickering in his eyes. He took her head in his hands and kissed her hairline by the ear. Where a bruise throbbed. Had the skin broke when one of the crocs had hit her?

Tara pressed on. Suddenly certain she would implode if she didn't tell him what she had seen. "Elin's ma was there. With Elin's wee brother. But they...they didn't..." Tara shook her head. There were no words for what she had seen. "The kids, they're aboard still, right?"

Merlon's jaw worked. "Yes. Elin's been talking about her mum nonstop. The dad's dead. Sounds like it was just her mum, brother, and Balfour in the house. Did you find his parents? He keeps saying they wanted him gone. That he's evil and makes people sick and some earth patrol people shot villagers. Honestly, if Bailey hadn't assured me the kids carry no diseases we could get seriously ill from, I'd have started to believe him. He certainly believes those things himself." Merlon wasn't a chatty person. He rarely rambled but when he did, it was usually due to a flood of emotions.

Tara seized his hand. He trembled faintly, evidently trying to bottle up everything that threatened to surface.

"I don't know what to do with them if we can't find their next of kin." Merlon's words were but a whisper.

Tara swallowed hard. They were all dead or gone. "They're nae here. Nobody's here anymore. Someone came, rounded up the last ones. Stuck them in glass cages and left." *Except for the woman they shot.* "There's another town, bigger one. But smoke came from it. I think it's burning too."

Merlon rose and got the mug of cold soup for her. He settled on the edge of the cot. The wooden frame protested, and he winced.

Before grabbing the soup, Tara made a point of shuffling herself until the cot groaned again. Stars burn her if she would let him think his weight was something to be embarrassed by. "Thanks." She took the mug. "Bailey might be useful. She'd know some Tracker or 'nother to contact about the kids."

The soup was salty, soft potatoes and Manihot chunks thickening it. Tara felt like a kid on the first day at the festival of the Passing. She finished the mug too fast, stomach only then beginning to growl. "Let me guess, Yorik said to nae eat too much today?"

"Just for a few hours." Merlon took the empty mug, but he didn't move. He had two false starts, but Tara waited quietly. "I thought you'd drowned. That I'd lost you too."

His shoulders moved in an unsteady breath. "I can't take any more deaths. These last three years...I know we're at a crossroads, but that's different. If you decide you don't want to be with me anymore, it'll hurt, but you'd still be alive. Still be able to do what you want in life."

Tara swallowed. She would *not* cry again. She thought of the cat giving birth beside her. Saw Bethy's arms around Ramson. When she blinked the blur of tears away, there was Merlon. His face serious, harsh even in his attempt at hiding the chaos of emotion his eyes betrayed. And she couldn't imagine not having him here, beside her when she needed it most. "We're still exclusive, right? Until I decide?"

Merlon nodded. "I'd prefer that." He rubbed at his palm, avoiding her gaze.

"I donae know about a kid. If I mess up. If xe got hurt. Died..." She shook her head to drive away the image of Ramson's face but forced herself to continue before Merlon could interject. "I love you, Merlon, I willnae stand between you and a child but I cannae say if I'm fit to be that child's ma."

Merlon looked up. He stroked a lock of hair from her face. His fingers were warm against her skin and his hand settled behind her neck. The touch was so light she knew he worried he might brush one of her wounds by accident. "I love you too."

He opened his mouth to continue, but a sudden desperation came over her. Tara leaned forward, pulling at his

157

shirt until his lips met hers. His grip around her neck tightened. She pressed against him, but her side panged, and she had to draw back with a huff. "Stupid ribs." She reached under her loose nightshirt and yanked to remove the length of fabric that served as her bandeau. It pressed where it hurt most.

"If you decide to have a kid with me, or someone else, you'll be the best mum." Merlon smiled, watching her undress with a glint of desire in his eyes.

She pulled the bandeau out and tossed it on the floor. "I slept in the grass and mud." Looking at him through the corner of her eyes, she folded down her collar, well aware the top buttons had opened when she removed the bandeau.

"So, an improvement on four months on a ship with scarce water, I take it." There was a chuckle to his voice, but he hadn't moved to either leave or touch her yet.

She grimaced when her thigh jolted in a short-lived cramp. "Hand me the painkillers, will you?"

While he got up, turning his back on her to refill the water mug and pick out two pills from the bottle, she shifted and pushed the sheets aside. Her legs were bruised but there didn't seem to be any bad cuts.

He returned to the cot's edge, fingers slipping along the outside of her thigh, tracing one of her tattoos. "You should recover more."

She scoffed and swallowed down the pills with a mouthful of water. "I need a reminder of what's good in life."

He didn't respond but let his hand wander over and up the inside of her thigh.

Chapter 17

The sick bay's door creaked open a crack, waking Tara. Her body even more sore than when Merlon left, she glanced once then closed her eyes, deciding whoever was at the door would have to wait until she had finished sleeping. From how groggy she felt, she hadn't been asleep for long anyway.

The door creaked again. "Sh! Elin dun't go annoy her." Balfour's voice carried from the hold.

Feet patted inside and Tara held her breath. She wasn't ready to look Elin in her blue eyes and tell her how her ma and brother were dead and gone forever.

The girl's breathing became loud, close to Tara's ear. "Is she dead?"

"They said she's fine. Come out." Balfour pleaded.

Tara dared sneak a glance through her eyelashes. Elin's brows were drawn together, and she had lifted a hand, finger looking about to poke Tara in the face.

"She's nut breathing."

"Elin get away from her! If they think we killed her…"
Balfour's voice broke.

Of course, Outer Universe kids would think nobody could
hold their breath for ten to fifteen minutes. Tara let out her
breath and willed herself to try and breathe calmly like she
was asleep.

Elin and Balfour both squeaked and jumped back. The
former hit the stool Merlon had sat on earlier, the clatter
making Tara jolt upright despite her endeavour to feign sleep.

Elin met Tara's gaze steadily, her face splitting in a big
smile showing her missing front tooth. "You're nut dead."

Tara blinked, straightening herself in the cot and double
checked her nightie was somewhat closed after earlier. "Um,
yeah I was only sleeping."

"Are you better now? Where did you go?" Elin brushed
off Balfour trying to pull her back to the door.

Tara gulped. She couldn't break the news. Not while pain
made her dizzy and she was sitting, half-clad in the sick bay
cot. "I'm better but I still need lots of rest." Was it cruel of
her to not immediately tell Elin what had happened? Tara
pushed a lock of her hair behind her ear, fighting the urge to
fiddle with it.

"My hair got washed." Elin declared after watching Tara
failing to stop herself rubbing a few strands of her own hair
between her fingers to calm her nerves before she began
crying. Elin looked so much like her ma. Like her baby
brother.

"Can you braid it? My ma always braids it." Elin held out
a lock, slinking closer.

Balfour grabbed Elin's elbow. "Stop it, she said she needs rest, nut you annoying her."

Tara swallowed a lump. She couldn't even braid hair if she wanted to, she had never bothered to learn how. It was such a simple thing, and she couldn't give Elin even that after watching her ma die. "I'm sorry, I need to sleep."

Elin's chin quivered for a moment, but then Balfour steered her out of the sick bay. "You can ask when she's better." Then they had left, the door still ajar. Tara rolled over, pulling the sheets over her face, and allowed herself to quietly cry. Was there anything she was good at? Nothing she could think of, that was for sure.

Tara cursed inwardly and fought to catch the lock of damp hair trying to escape her fingers. She had slept another ten hours and felt better for it. Her body still ached absolutely everywhere and some of the cuts by her throat were hot and swollen, but she could think and move – slowly – again.

Gaunty had brought her a small portion of porridge not long ago and with a full stomach, she had enough energy to get properly washed and change into the clean clothes Merlon had left for her.

The salty water left her skin feeling oddly tight and her hair more textured than usual. That didn't help her attempts at a braid. Maybe she had it this time though.

The sick bay door creaked open a few inches. Bailey bounded in. The small tug of Tara's trouser leg warned the rat was on the way up to her shoulder where she often liked to ride whether Tara wanted it or not.

"Whatever have you done to your hair?" Bailey said. Her tiny rat hands poked at Tara's neck. Her whiskers tickled.

Tara fumbled to grab her leather hair tie. "I'm braiding it."

"Tuh-ra!" Bailey snickered. "That's no braid but a glorified twisty rope. You look silly. Redo it. I much prefer to sit under a messy bun."

"Stop, donae!" But it was too late.

Bailey had already pulled at a thick strand of hair, yanking it out of the braid that had taken Tara as long as washing and changing clothes.

"You're the worst," Tara said and let her hands drop. Her hair immediately unwound itself to fall an inch or two past her shoulders.

Bailey prodded her temple, so lightly the throbbing of the wound by her ear didn't become worse. "There, now put it in a bun and I would like riding on your shoulder much better."

"Ah yes, because your likes and dislikes are more important than anyone else's." Tara sighed and stared at her warped reflection in the medicine cabinet's glass inserts.

Bailey nodded sagely. "Of course, I'm the only Tracker aboard after all. Why did you get such a foolish idea to braid your hair anyway?"

Tara quickly tied her hair back in a bun. A few locks instantly found an escape, but she pushed them behind her ear and picked up the wash basin. "Elin asked for a braid like her ma used to do. You know we hasnae decided how to break the news to them yet."

At least Merlon had agreed they should wait telling Elin until they knew where the kids were going after their stay on *Lucia*.

Tara used a foot to lever the door open. She dumped the water through the hatch in the forecastle that led outside to the head. It was a scary place for a toilet, but Tara tended to use those slippery rafters under the bowsprit to avoid the dark, crammed dampness of the cabin's head.

Bailey spent the time washing herself, seemingly indifferent to Tara's explanation. Not that it was surprising. Bailey thought herself the most important being at any given time. Strangely at odds with how helpful she at least tried to be on occasion.

"I got word from my dad," Bailey said. She leapt from Tara's shoulder to a step on the ladder that led to the main deck. Turning, she stared at Tara with her black, beady eyes.

Tara's stomach formed a knot, but she started up the ladder. The ocean left *Lucia* rolling in a strange way that left Tara slightly nauseous and she suspected she needed fresh air to get rid of it. "What did he suggest we do with the kids? Is a Tracker going to help find their kin or someone who can care for them?"

"No." Bailey quipped. "He ordered them killed. The ocean is full of sarco crocodiles, and he thinks tossing them overboard would make for the quickest, most humane death."

Tara's fingers slipped on the ladder. She flailed, her stomach flipping as her balance wobbled. Then she caught hold of the ladder again, wrapping an arm around the side rail.

163

She bit back the cry of pain when the cuts on her arm sprung open once more. "We cannae! Kill them? Has he lost it? He knows they're little kids, right?"

Bailey started preening herself. "They've seen too much of you. The biggest one has looked at countless maps of Inner Universe."

"They're kids." Tara hissed through gritted teeth. "Even if they told someone about us, nobody would believe them. There are people who could take them somewhere safe. Has to be."

Bailey cleaned her whiskers vigorously, eyes closed and not showing any signs of listening. Tara poked her in the soft, brown-furred belly.

Bailey turned her nose at her in what was usually a display of annoyance. "Have you not seen plenty of Outer Universe humans the last two days? There's all-out war about to begin between the Q-Rebels and Earthers. Those kids are mutants. Halfway between Inner and Outer Universe humans in DNA. If we give them to the Earth Patrol they'll end up in labs. It might be safe but getting poked and prodded with needles on a daily basis is hardly a nice childhood."

"So, you're suggesting killing them is better? They need to be with their people." It wasn't like their childhood had been great up until now.

"I'm relaying my dad's orders. You're mistaking that for agreement with said orders." Bailey wrinkled her nose. She jumped onto Tara's shoulder.

Tara's teeth ground together but she resumed her climb to the main deck.

"You's up at last!" Karl's face brightened and he clip clopped on his crutches to the main deck hatch. "What's this about taking up the sick bay before I's hardly left, hm?" He grinned, offering a crutch to help Tara pull herself up.

She waved him away and bit back the grimaces. Her muscles screamed for a respite after the tiny exertion. It would be a while before she was back to normal.

Straightening, Tara glanced about. *Lucia* lay still in the middle of the ocean, far from the flat land Tara had cowered on. She wasn't sure how they had managed to steer and move through the force of the water but she suspected Bailey had helped figure it out.

"You'd warmed the bed so nicely I thought I'd give it a go too." Tara smiled, boring her fist into Karl's arm. "Good to see you back on deck again. I take it you're nae working?"

"Nah, Cap'n won't let me. Not that we's got much to do anyway moored up in the middle of all this water," Karl said. He wore a burnt orange sarong and thin white shirt. The former seemed a good choice with his right leg wrapped in thick bandages and a splint. Getting trousers on would be difficult.

With the humid heat, Tara was a little annoyed she hadn't thought to ask Merlon for that skirt of hers. Not that she had a clue where it could be. At least the breeze had stilled her nausea.

"We'll catch up later, Karl. Maybe do a game of dice if you willnae cheat too much."

"No promises," Karl said with a grin. He slapped her arm and headed for Gaunty leaning on the portside rail and seemingly staring out over the ocean's vast blue eternity.

"Tara?" Merlon called, standing by the bowsprit. He gestured for her to come over.

The urgency in his face had Tara glance at Bailey on her shoulder. The rat poked her neck as if to confirm. Tara's stomach threatened to clench so hard she would throw up regardless of the nausea subsiding.

Tara let her gaze wander across the ship while walking to the forecastle deck. Kieran and Fabian were entertaining Balfour and Elin, letting them have piggyback rides by the helm. Why were everyone else good at kids? She swallowed the lump in her throat and whispered to Bailey, "you told Merlon about your da's orders?"

"I did, yes."

Merlon met her halfway across the raised forecastle deck, grasping her arm gingerly. Nothing short of panic darkened his normally warm, brown eyes. "You heard?"

Tara could only nod, her throat and tongue suddenly refusing to cooperate. She looked back at the kids again. Cary wasn't on deck, but last she heard he was reading every book aboard. She could understand that, although there wouldn't be much in the way of adventurous stories, space-navigation books could still provide some little respite from his reality.

"Cary is buried in Deyon's stash of ghost stories," Merlon said as if he had read her mind. "He's a bit recluse but seems a good kid. They all do." There was a tightness to his voice.

Tara forced herself to take a deep breath. Her throat eased enough she could reply, "We cannae kill them or let anyone else do that. They've already seen so much. They're only kids."

"It'd be over my dead body," Merlon growled.

166

It was a long time since she had seen that flare of anger in his face. Not since the former Foreign Affairs Chancellor managed to stop the branding trial and had easily won the High Chancellor vote. Granted, she had been throwing things that day too. Patrice would never have justice for what Horatio Corncockle had caused and then got out of. He was more slippery than an oiled rat.

Bailey yawned loudly. Tara twisted her neck, wincing at the pang of pain the movement resulted in. The rat began lazily washing herself again. It was clear Bailey had something on her mind, but she wanted one of them to ask her. *She's always so dramatic.* Tara caved instantly, nonetheless. "What is it?"

"The solution is simple. We make the kids take a blood vow to never speak of their lives here on Quarantine Thirteen and bring them back to Inner Universe. Amule has plenty of people waiting to adopt, any of whom you can pawn them off on."

Merlon made a sound that could only be described as a strangled huff. "Blood vow! They're kids."

Dizziness washed over Tara. She caught Merlon's elbow and held onto it to keep from staggering.

That first year after immigrating to Amule suddenly pushed up from the depths of her memories. She had been told to stop comparing the buckwheat porridge with Trachna's more common quinoa dish. And to change her accent "to fit in better". The latter had only resulted in the bullying getting worse when she struggled to pronounce the vowels like an Amulean.

In the end she had clung on to her Trachnan accent and even after twenty-two years, she retained it. "I willnae let anyone tell them nae to talk of their birth culture. Never."

"You're being awfully emotional about some kids you're trying to get rid of." Bailey jumped to Merlon's shoulder.

"We're not wanting to pawn them off or get rid of them. They need a loving home, not whoever bribed the orphanage the most to get ahead of the queue." Merlon looked ready to explode, his glower at Bailey had the rat turn her head away.

Tara frowned. "Not everyone on the wait list use bribery. Kieran and Hakim certainly hasnae."

"Which is why it'll probably be ten years before it's their turn," Merlon said. "Rochester fostered me, which was the only way I could remain in my tier. If I'd been under ten, they'd have adopted me out to whoever was on the top of the list. Not to mention, they'll separate them. More kids placed in different families means more coin for the orphanage."

Tara stared across the ship to where Balfour now stood with Elin by the railing. Her little hand was in Balfour's. He pointed and chatted about something or other across the water.

Balfour who already had plenty of scars and cuts along his arms. Despite his young age, she didn't doubt he would harm himself even more should Elin be removed from his side. Merlon was right, they would most likely be separated and she couldn't bear the thought of it.

Tara faced Merlon. "Alright, we cannae leave them here. The Trackers will kill them and Amule's orphanage will sell them to the highest bidder. How's Fristate for adoptions? We've got to help them somehow."

"You could always keep them," Bailey piped. "As their rescuers, if you pretend their parents were killed by pirates rather than Earth Patrol you could apply for fostering permits for all three if you were registered partners."

Tara's hand shot out to swat the rat, but Bailey dove off Merlon's shoulder with a cackle a rat shouldn't be able to make.

"Lennie might be of help. He spends more time in Fristate," Merlon said. There was the hint of hurt in his eyes and he avoided meeting Tara's gaze. Clearing his throat, he continued. "Only problem is, we still don't know how to get away from this planet."

Tara clenched her fists until the cuts on her palms threatened to burst back open. None of it mattered if they never got out of here. If they were stuck forever on Quarantine Thirteen, caught in the crossfires of the war between Q-Rebels and Earth Patrollers.

Chapter 18

After a long silence, Tara turned to Bailey, sitting on a low rung of the forecastle shrouds. "How do we get away?"

"Why are you asking me? I had a very small supply of refined portal powder and used it up finding *Lucia* and then leading Merlon to you. If I ask my dad for more, he'll send someone with it. Commander Rye or some other Tracker who'll see to it the kids definitely don't survive the day."

"Burn it," Merlon grumbled. "We've got to have other options. You were with Mira before coming here, right? Is there any way sending a letter to her could help?"

Tara shook her head. "How's she supposed to do anything? She has nae access to portal powder. And we'd need a *lot*."

Merlon flexed a hand, but it instantly turned into a fist again. He took up pacing the forecastle. "Lennie could maybe gain access to some." He stopped in front of Bailey. "Would you know how much to ask for?"

"Perhaps, I don't know the strength of human and Squamate portal powder, I only know it's terribly badly refined. We'd need sacks full of it I suspect."

"And that leaves the question of how we'd get it from Fristate to here," Tara muttered.

Merlon rubbed his face. "If we—" Feet thumped up the forecastle steps, pausing Merlon.

Elin ran across the deck. Her curls bounced like ripe grain nodding in the field. She wore a colourful, long tunic, and trousers both of which looked to have been made from one of Karl's countless sarongs. A rope belt tightened the tunic around her far too skinny waist, but her face glowed with excitement.

Three days of constant access to small amounts of food had already restored her energy to what Tara took to be more normal levels for a five-year-old.

Balfour followed much slower, his feet hitting and scuffing the steps up to the forecastle deck. While he too had more life in his eyes, that dark grief remained. He and Cary had starved and clearly been treated worse than Elin. Tara didn't doubt their recovery, physically and mentally, would be longer.

"Fab'an says you have a gift for me!" Elin could hardly stand still. Her fingers wriggled eagerly. "Is it mummy? Or Ramson? Did you find them?"

Balfour caught up. His hair, like Elin's, had been cut shorter and more evenly. Judging by the style of the haircut, it had been Boomer's doing. He was rather good at cutting hair and trimming beards and earned himself a few coppers

171

from crew who wanted to remain preened despite the long months of travelling through space.

"Dun't you remember seeing the smoke I showed you? The village is burning." Balfour spoke quietly. He stared at his feet. "It's my fault. Mummy said I'd bring the people with guns if I stay in the village."

Tara's stomach twisted. Her hand froze, halfway to the ragdoll she had tucked into the back of her belt. What was she supposed to say? It couldn't have been Balfour's fault that the village was gassed and bombed.

She stared at the horizon, where land showed as a faint brown slip between the blue of the sea and the peach and green of the sky. The smoke from something burning tainted the air a murky beige. She assumed it was the larger city, it made no sense to burn the village now when everyone was already dead or wheeled away.

Merlon knelt before Balfour, grasping his arms, and seeking the blue, sad eyes of the kid. "It's not because of you. Bad people will do bad things no matter what. I promise you, Balfour, you have nothing to do with the fires."

Balfour sniffed. His shaky fist wiped a tear from his freckled cheek.

"Hey," Merlon smiled at Balfour. His face grew so mild and warm Tara felt like he was a different person, and it left her heart thudding harder. "How about you help me set a new course? You were really good at helping Jara at the wheel the other day. I think I could use some of your expertise."

Balfour blinked. "I can-I can help you?" he hiccupped.

"Like you helps me climb trees!" Elin beamed. She patted his hand. "You is very good at helping."

172

"It's you are. You *are* very good," Balfour mumbled.

He rubbed snot off on the sleeve of the tunic that matched Elin's with the blue and yellow fabric hastily stitched into a shape and size that fit him. His shirt was a little shorter, revealing a braided leather cord used for a belt to keep the stumpy trousers up. They needed proper clothes, but at least they weren't in the threadbare rags they had been in on the island.

With all the dirt and grime washed off, they had fairer skin than Tara had realised, and she found herself worrying they needed hats and talc cream to protect from the rays although the faint mist in the air on this planet would probably ensure they wouldn't burn too fast.

Merlon pushed off on his bent knee and strained back to his feet. He shook out his right leg, the old thigh injury probably paining him. He held out a hand. "So, are you ready to help set sail?"

'Where go?' Tara gestured.

Merlon answered in single-handed sign language. 'Further away from settlement, we have to try something.'

Balfour gingerly took Merlon's hand, and they walked back towards the helm.

Tara nodded to herself. Doing something was better than nothing even if they had no idea how to get off this planet. A tug on her shirt pulled Tara's attention from them.

"What gift do you have for me?" Elin stared up at her, large eyes questioning. "Did you find my mummy?"

Tara swallowed hard. She caught Merlon's gaze from across the ship and signed, 'tell family dead not now. Night?' Her Squamate wasn't great, but Merlon nodded.

173

'We will tell them later, together,' he responded.

Tara sent Elin a strained smile. She didn't look forward to that conversation. Hopefully she could distract Elin for now. She had forgot the picture in her pocket and wasn't sure where Merlon had taken her dirty clothes, but she would find that for Elin later. She yanked the puppet from her belt and held it down to Elin. "I found your doll!" She tried to sound energetic, but it came across rather stiffly.

"Bitty!" Elin exclaimed and snatched it from Tara's hand. "Dun't worry, Bitty, I have you now. You is safe. You *are* safe." She hugged the ragdoll, rocking slightly as if to soothe it.

Tara couldn't speak. Emotion welled into her throat. This poor kid had become orphaned, was half starved to death and was about to be abducted from her birthplace. There had to be another way.

Didn't Outer Universe people have aunts and uncles and extra grandparents through their family friends? In Twin Cities Galaxy few had blood relatives beyond their parents and grandparents – who would often die before their grandchildren had a kid – so the nearest friends served as surrogates. It was a good system, everyone could choose people they fully trusted to help out when needed.

Adrien hadn't really been Tara's uncle, but she had always called him that. There had even been a small amount set aside for her in his will, the rest going to Merlon who in all but adoption certificate, had been his son.

"Look at all the rainbows!" Elin's thrilled voice snapped Tara from her thoughts. She followed the child's finger, pointing at the sails while the anchor was pulled in one percent and let through the smallest amount of energy.

Tara frowned. Ola had been quite adamant he couldn't see the colours on the sails. In fact, he had thought them plain grey. But Erica, the scientist they had rescued from a burned research station, had glasses that allowed both her and Ola to see the energy rippling across the sails' canvas.

They had agreed Outer Universe people had some difference in vision so by all rights, Elin shouldn't be able to see anything but grey. "They're pretty, which colours do you see?"

"I see green and red and purple and—"

Balfour burst between them, clasping a hand over Elin's mouth. "Dun't tell them!" Fear made his eyes round and large. "Dun't you remember that's why they put us on the island? You dun't wanna go back to the island, do you?"

Elin shook her head. Tears welled and spilled instantly.

"We willnae ever put you back on the island," Tara said. Her chest hurt. Why would anyone put them on an island for seeing some extra colours? Everyone in Inner Universe would have been exiled if that was such an issue.

Elin began sobbing. Balfour wrapped his arms around her, staring up at Tara like he didn't believe her for a second. "They said that too. Then while Auntie Bethy was working, they took us. Mummy said it was my fault, so daddy took us to the island."

Tara was lost for words. What could she possibly say when these kids had seen nothing but lies and deceit, and from Balfour's own parents!

She caught one each of their shoulders. Willed herself to look calm. Ignored the fear screaming in her head. She would mess this up. She always did. She wasn't any good with being soft and tender and kind. Couldn't switch over like Merlon seemed to when he spoke with the kids. "By the stars and Tomaline's grace, I promise you, we willnae leave you alone anywhere."

"B-but…Mummy said so too. I want my mummy! She promised to come for me if people took me away. She promised," Elin howled.

Tara realised she couldn't lie. Elin wouldn't stop asking for her ma until she knew and understood she wasn't going to come for her. And Balfour already watched Tara's face like he knew without her having said anything. "Come, let's go to the cabin and have something to drink. You like coconut milk, right?"

Elin sniffed hard and nodded.

Tara didn't manage to gesture for Merlon, but he appeared a second after she had scooted the kids into the cabin. Sometimes he could be surprisingly attentive when she least expected it. She held his gaze as she spoke quietly. "I promised coconut milk while I tell them where I was. Cary might like some too."

Merlon nodded once and squeezed himself through the tiny hatch that led directly into the hold and the nearby galley.

"Cary?" Tara called softly.

Feet patted from inside the chamber, the open door soon revealed the eleven-year-old. He had a book in one hand. The black bags under his eyes betrayed that he hadn't slept much in the past three days. Tara noted to herself to suggest Merlon

176

chatted with the kid – he knew best what it was like to struggle with sleep.

Cary scowled at her. "What'd you want?"

"Merlon is getting some coconut milk. Now I'm up, I'm going to tell you what happened in the village."

"Are you letting them put me back in the cell?" Despite his face staying almost nonchalantly indifferent, there was a touch of panic in his hazel eyes. The book trembled ever so lightly in his grip.

Tara scrambled for words that could convince Cary they wouldn't dream of doing that. But she realised none would gain his trust like showing him every day he was onboard that they never would. "We willnae let them. Will you sit while I explain?" She slowly pulled out her chair and helped Elin onto it. Balfour squeezed in beside her.

Cary crossed his arms, hugging the book. If Tara wasn't mistaken, that was one of her books on Twin Cities' most famous constellations, complete with the myths and stories involving them. Seemed he had managed to find one of the more entertaining ones after all.

Merlon returned with a clay bottle and three cups. He glanced at Cary, who remained in the chamber doorway, but didn't comment. The bottle clucked out the coconut milk, filling each mug in turn.

Balfour downed his mug instantly, Elin sipped slowly but constantly, and Cary only glowered into the cup after taking it from Merlon. Merlon returned to the desk and slumped in his own chair on the opposite side from Elin and Balfour.

Tara found herself pacing, working through her wording. There was no nice way to say this. The second time Merlon

177

beckoned her to sit, she obliged. She winced when her fingers found a cut on her scalp, and she gave up trying to push more locks into her bun.

Merlon raised a brow but didn't urge her to start, he knew she was gathering her thoughts.

She shuffled the chair to face the kids a bit more. Should she smile? Would that make her seem like a maniac? She probably shouldn't look happy while telling them their parents were dead and their home destroyed. She closed her eyes against the images resurfacing. The pain rising in her chest.

Letting out a deep breath, she began. "You know I looked for your parents? For your mummy, Elin?" She was quite certain she butchered Elin's pronunciation of 'mummy'. "She gave me your doll. She asked me to bring it to you. And she said she missed you terribly. She didnae know where you were. If she had, I'm sure she would have come for you. For all of you."

Tara had to pause. She wanted this over with, but Elin had shimmied forward, looking at her expectantly, not a hint of worry on her face. *I'm about to crush her whole world.* "Elin, your ma, your mummy she's—"

The cabin door burst open, Kieran rushing in. "Dragons are here. And they's saying we need prepping for portalling!"

Chapter 19

Tara blinked once. Twice. "Portalling?"

"Aye!" Kieran's arms flew up, panic evident in his face.

"Burn us." Merlon huffed. "Stay with the kids." He pushed past Kieran and ran out the passageway.

Tara sprung up, snapping when Kieran moved to follow Merlon as well. "Stay!" She rushed out of the cabin. The door boomed shut behind her and Bailey's voice reached her on her way out onto the main deck. Tara faltered, squinting against the midday light.

"...So you're saying, you flew to Portal Galaxy and just *took* all that powder? Sewers and bins, you might've ignited the last flames needed for war between the city tarillas! You must know the guilds have been fighting to push one another out ever since the last big portal powder mine ran dry." The little rat sat on her hindlegs on Fabian's palm. Her stumpy tail hung over the side of his hand, dangling with every shuddery movement of Bailey gesticulating at the two dragons.

Visca and Vincent hovered beside the ship. Visca's neck was twisted away, her body yellow and grey from disgust. Despite her beaked mouth not allowed for much in the way of expressions, her face left no doubt even if Tara hadn't known what the colours meant. Visca hated furred animals, especially Trackers.

Vincent on the other hand had xir usual mint green colour with brown splotches. Xir head was cocked to the side, inches from hitting the shrouds of the main mast. Those sharp, black horns on xir neck frill had snapped ropes before, injuring Merlon's ma in the process.

Boomer and Deyon seemed to have herded most of the crew to the port side, as far as possible from the potential danger of breaking rigging. Karl looked terrified, but then he had never quite got around to the idea the dragons weren't human-eating, fire spewing monsters like the stories said.

Tara stared at the huge canvas sacks in the dragons' clawed hands. One of Visca's black claws had torn a hole, a blackish-grey powder trickling out. Even above the slight murmur of calm water hitting the ship's hull, there was a hissing, bubbling sound. Tara leaned over the starboard railing and noted the powder set the water boiling. A white, thick steam rose from where the powder hit the surface.

"Do you not want to depart this planet?" Vincent spoke with xir dry, hollow voice. "We un-reminisced many times on the way to Portal Galaxy and back but contributed help in the end. These Outer Universe quarantine planets are terribly sad and barren of much good grass."

The dragons always spoke like this. With perfect enunciation but using words in ways that made little sense. It was evident this wasn't their usual language for communication.

Merlon stepped beside Fabian. "We do want to leave, but only using safe means. Would we be able to go to Fristate with this amount of portal powder?"

"We've a bad track record for portallin', Cap'n." Fabian said, then slapped Merlon's shoulder. "Ya's gonna give it a go first, eh? Maybe if ya hold on to a spare board from the hold ya'd get somewhere." The grin didn't quite reach his eyes and he licked his lips. He hid the fear well behind his attempt at joking, but it was there.

Tara joined them on the middle of the deck. Her heart thundered and she was willing to bet Fabian's did too. "If we *can* go to Fristate, there better nae be any portal powder left when we get there."

Since High Chancellor Horatio had banned the usage of portals in Twin Cities, it was no longer legal in any Edge Galaxies. Maybe with the exception of the pirate-run Blacklock's Galaxy. The punishment was life imprisonment, and she might not have ever been to Fristate Galaxy, but she had heard they were much less prone to bribery to let people off with smaller charges.

Bailey leapt onto her shoulder. "It might be safe. Or it might not. I can't say without taking it home and analysing it." She stroked one of Tara's locks that had escaped the bun, then turned her nose to the dragons. "Is it even refined?"

"We are dragons," Vincent said. "We do not consider ourselves with how you Trackers and people plot and mix these smelly dustings." Vincent lowered xir head, xir beak hitting a halyard. Xe pulled back before the rope snapped,

181

moving xir face carefully sideways until xe got to the larger gap where neither ratlines nor mast stays were blocking xir view of them.

Had Tara not known by now the dragons didn't eat humans, or indeed meat at all, she would have thought xe prepared to snatch and devour one of them.

"It must be little different from a storm and those are firmly reliable to find if you know how to see." Vincent added, xir eyes suddenly on Tara.

She cleared her throat, but a lump still blocked her from breathing. Did xe know she could no longer see energy like she once had? That all she caught were flickering and faint colours threading around xir wings that xe held still, partially folded.

Tara looked to the side. She didn't like the scrutiny in Vincent's emerald gaze. Xe definitely knew. She pushed at a few strands of hair, but they refused to go into the bun and stay.

"Vincent, dear, why am I bearing these bags?" Visca blinked.

Vincent broke from staring at Tara. Instead, xe tilted xir head at the sacks in xir own arms. Solid yellow coursed over xir knobbly skin. "I seem to have quite misplaced the memory thereof."

"It's portal powder, you brought it here to help us," Tara said.

Vincent's head whipped around. Xir wings spread out and xe soared backwards, up into the sky. Black, blue, and yellow – the colours of fear and anger – coursed over xem. For a long second, Tara was sure xe would camouflage and leave them helplessly stranded once more.

"Ah," Visca nodded. "I reminisce this ship. That's the smelly humans. The ones who caused and helped your chipped claw the other day. They do smell improved."

Tara exchanged a glance with Merlon. It seemed they still thought that incident was recent and not a year in the past. Their memories certainly weren't getting better.

Ola had hypothesised they were unfathomably old. One time he spoke to them they had apparently mentioned a stellar event three thousand years in the past. Tara wasn't certain she believed there were human records that old, but she wouldn't be surprised if the dragons were a hundred years old with how spotty their memories were. She had heard some Squamates grew that old.

Vincent lowered xirself again, tail curling sideways so the long feathers on either side didn't hit the water. "Your ship sings and cries. The salt water isn't wellbeing for living wood and too long a time in this sea will kill it. Portalling is the safest way if you want to take the ship with you."

Bailey scratched her side with a hind foot. "Tuh! You forget that portal powder reacts with water to create a gas that's terribly noxious, even for Inner Universe humans and certainly for my lungs that have no further evolutionary enhancements."

"It'll kill us?" Tara eyed the glittering stream of powder falling from the hole in one of Visca's bags to the ocean below.

Merlon frowned. "Wouldn't we be portalling away before that's a problem?"

Fabian shifted from foot to foot. He scratched the back of his head, the motion slightly odd because he didn't have the ponytail he had used to push up when he itched the spot. "Not sure I'd wanna chance it, Cap'n."

"We'll have to take a vote," Merlon said. "Bailey, any last advice?"

The rat stopped her incessant grooming and turned her narrow snout towards Merlon. She made a little movement that looked like a shrug. "I'm not going to advice one way or another. *I* only need to contact my dad again to get away from here. Suppose if the portal powder works, we might not die a horrible gassing death. I hate to admit it, but I don't have any better idea for getting the ship off this planet."

"Who said that?" Visca shrilled.

Bailey slid down Tara's arm, prompting her to raise it out so the rat could settle on her palm. "I did, you big nincompoop!"

Visca beat her wings, rising fast in the air. "Flight mate, they have a Tracker! We should begone before it runs all through our feathers."

Vincent turned xir head upwards to where Visca flapped frantically. When xe looked back down at the ship, xe blinked. "There are human ones staring at us, dear."

"Of course, there are!" Bailey spluttered. Her fur stood out to all sides. "Get your old, daffy heads in the now. You know them all the way back from when you helped them escape from the Star-Eaters of *Dödskalle*."

Black, blue, and yellow coursed over the dragons' bodies in rapid succession. Vincent hissed, "they know the dragon killers! We must flatten them!"

184

"Begone, dragon killers!" Visca shouted. Her paws flailed. The huge sacks of portal powder tore, and the glimmering powder trickled down.

"Uh-oh." Bailey pipped. "Hold your breaths!"

"Killers!" Vincent violently threw the last sacks at them, the motion shredding the fabric against xir claws. Wagon loads of powder tumbled towards the ship.

The water around *Lucia* erupted upwards. A sudden, urgent itch at the back of Tara's throat started a cough. The pain from her ribs stabbed at her side, bending her over and worsening the throbbing agony.

"Fristate! Think of—" Merlon didn't get further before the bright light of Quarantine Thirteen was swallowed in the cool grey haze of portalling.

Chapter 20

Tara wheezed, pressing her fist against her hip instead of her paining ribs. The screams from the crew, once again portalling unexpectedly, deadened. That strange silence where even Tara's own breath and heartbeat seemed to vanish. She hadn't been through a whole lot of door portals before they were outlawed, but it was a lack of sensations she would never forget.

Fristate Galaxy. She had to think of it, but she had never been there. It was supposed to be hazier than Twin Cities. The star shrouded in a mist that kept the galaxy dimmer and cooler and resulted in less cases of cancer too. The only reason it always remained the second-most populated galaxy was because of its immediate neighbour; Blacklock's.

That galaxy was run by pirates. They raided throughout Fristate, stealing ships and goods as often as kidnapping people and Squamates to be sold off to the slave trade in the Far Galaxies.

Merlon had explained all this while they looked over the maps in preparation for their entry into Fristate. The only reason they had planned to stop by one of the outposts nearer Blacklock's was to pick up Lennie, Merlon's Squamate friend, before turning towards Jeweller City in the much safer Dark Galaxy.

Sound returned. Tara drew in a breath, the scratchiness at the back of her throat eased again. She realised Merlon had a cramp-like grip on her shoulder. She leaned against him, still panting in shallow breaths from the pain. Her ribs weren't terribly bruised, she had had worse before, but they sure didn't like coughing and it left her dizzy.

The greyness receded, but only so much. A white mist remained around them. It rendered the darkness of space a dim leaden colour. *Lucia* groaned. Then her rigging and sails began luffing. Tara's feet lifted off the deck. Her stomach seemed to jump into her throat. Bailey's claws dug into her shoulder.

"Anchor in!" Merlon yelled. "Get the anchor reeled in!"

Of course. With the anchor wound out to ninety-seven percent energy diversion, the sails couldn't catch enough for the ship to remain flying through space nor indeed uphold the atmosphere the breathing wood attempted to create around the ship. Tara turned her head, snatching for the nearest halyard to avoid flying overboard when the ship plummeted.

Deyon was already at the cathead. But the old man struggled to wind up the anchor alone. Tara staggered towards the forecastle deck.

187

"Not you, with your injuries." Merlon snapped. "Fabian, grab her."

Merlon shoved Tara into Fabian's grasp and stumbled along the rail up to Deyon. With Merlon's help, the anchor chains clicked. The whine of the ship only grew louder. Tara wrapped her arm around a halyard. "Help them." She twisted free from Fabian's hand.

"Don't fly overboard." He leapt across the deck, feet barely touching the boards. At one jump, up the last steps to the forecastle deck, his feet didn't return down, and Tara's heart thumped hard against her sore ribs. But Fabian caught the ratlines, working himself back down and grasping the windlass' handle. He shooed Deyon aside. Between him and Merlon, the chains began winding in faster.

Lucia's cry eased. The sails glowed with colours coursing over them once more. Their descent waned. The slowly downwards movement continued even after they got past the seventy-percent mark. Jara was by the helm, already pushing the altitude pedals, altimeter in hand.

Tara peeled her fingers off the rope, wincing at the blood that had soaked through the bandage on her palm. She kept splitting open the cut on her right hand. It would take forever to heal.

Merlon let go of the windlass. "Everyone still aboard?"

Fabian straightened, his eyes swept across the deck, lips moving in a silent count.

"Capten!" Kieran rushed out through the passage door. "What's…oh we's not on no planet no more."

"Kids alright?" Fabian called.

188

A knot formed in Tara's stomach. Whether they had wanted to or not, they had taken the kids back to Inner Universe.

As if to answer Fabian's question, two blonde heads popped up behind Kieran. "Are we on a giant swing?" Elin asked, eyes large and excitable rather than terrified.

Kieran laughed and shook his head. "No, but sure felt like it, ay?"

"All accounted for, Cap'n," Fabian said.

A sigh of relief spread across the ship. Merlon clapped loudly. "All hands to stations. Get that main sail trimmed. Hurry up, you bastards!" He walked down from the forecastle deck, gesturing left and right while continuing to dish out orders.

"Are we in Fristate then?" Tara asked when Merlon took a break from shouting commands.

He stopped beside her, glancing up at the grey air. "It looks like it. Smells right. The fog I mean. But I can't tell where yet. I don't like how dim it is. If we're closer to Blacklock's than Intrapolis city…"

"It—" Bailey sneezed on Merlon's shoulder, shook her head, and continued. "It's Fristate. I've only been once, not long ago but I'd recognise the smell anywhere. Lots of light powder in the mist." Bailey leapt to Tara's shoulder and yanked at her hair.

"Do you know where?" Merlon said. The tightness in his voice made Tara anxious. He was a worrier, but in this case the danger of being close to a pirate run galaxy *was* significant.

Adrien had been a victim of a pirate kidnapping once. He had never told her anything about his time away, but Da had

189

let on what little he knew over the years. Adrien had been gone for over a decade. Returning a different man. All because the captain Adrien had sailed under hadn't taken a warning about pirate traps in Haven Galaxy serious.

"Escuse me." Elin tugged at the elbow of Tara's shirt, making Bailey peer down at her. "Has we gone to find my mummy?"

Balfour pulled at her. "Nut right now, Elin. You know about disturbing adults talking." He had a slight reprimand in his tone. Brows furrowed.

Tara noted there was fresh blood on his fingernails and one of the dozens of cuts along his lower arms had red smears along it. She had no idea how to address his self-harm. He badly needed a professional talk therapist. But that required they found out where they were.

"It's alright, Balfour, we're just—" Merlon broke off, spinning and staring up at the sails.

Bailey went rigid. "Something's wrong. That *smell*."

Tara blinked. She realised far too late the energy was acting odd. But she couldn't see it outside the colours on the sails or she would have known to warn them. The glowing waves on the canvas was pushing downwards, uniformly. She had read about this. "Pirate trap! Tack to…" She blinked and blinked, was there energy to the port? "To port! Tack to port!" If she was wrong about this…

The energy pushed them forward and down. *Lucia* moaned, her square rigging slow to be tacked to the side and her turning even slower. Then the sails went dark. They had moved too late.

The air became stagnant. There was no energy. None at all. Only grey, dark dimness. They dropped. The sails luffed and the rigging wailed at the air pressure of the trap. The energy of the wind passing them dissipated rather than being gathered in the sails.

Elin screamed. Everyone did. Balfour wrapped his arms around her, hunkering down on the deck. Tara threw herself at them. She caught them both and kept them on the ship when the drop began lifting everyone's feet off the boards once more. *Please, Tomaline, shine on us.*

These poor kids had been through enough. They hadn't deserved any of it. She didn't want to know what sort of slavery pirates sold kids into.

A flicker of colour went over the sails, buffering them upwards for ten seconds, but so weakly it only served to soften the impact. *Lucia* hit solid ground with a thundering boom. Dust and gravel sprayed in the air. The sails billowed then went limp. No light, not as much as a flicker passed over them.

Tara stayed on her knees, arms around Balfour and Elin. Their little bodies trembled against her chest. She closed her eyes again, tucking her nose down into her neckerchief to avoid coughing from the dust in the air. And she waited. Waited for the shouts. The roars of triumph and glee, when the pirates realised they had caught a wealthy merchant ship. An Intergalactic Traveller no less.

But there was no yelling. No jubilant cheer from pirates that had landed what had to be months' worth of profits in one go. Slowly, scared she had gone deaf and would see the leering faces of their captors once she looked around, Tara unfolded herself from around the kids.

She blinked against the particles swirling around them. A coating of dark dust settled. Balfour coughed.

Tara's knees trembled too much for her to get up so instead she thumped Balfour's shoulder blades lightly while waiting for her nerves to calm enough she could stand. He wheezed like it was more than a bit of dusty air. For a second, Tara thought he would pass out like Ola had when they had landed *Lucia* on a research planet with bad air. But Balfour's face didn't turn red, and his coughing eased slowly.

Merlon held out a hand. "You all alright?"

"I think so." Tara took his hand, letting him pull her up so she didn't need to rely on her jellied legs.

A glance around the ship confirmed everyone already stood at their posts, bows and blast arrows ready, as were the cutlasses of those who weren't archers. Merlon never wasted time preparing for hostiles and with how the past year had gone, she wasn't surprised the crew were ready in an instant.

Elin sniffled and Merlon knelt, picking her up like it was the most natural thing in the world to carry a kid around on his hip. "Hey, you're alright. We're alright." He stroked her curled head.

Balfour pressed against Tara, and she put her hand on his shoulder. She didn't know what to say but he hid his face against her side, fingers boring into her shirt like he thought she would grab him and toss him overboard.

Tara cleared her throat but looked out past *Lucia's* rigging instead of speaking up. She would only make it awkward or say something that would panic the kids more if she tried to soothe them.

Bailey transferred herself back to Merlon's shoulder. She was more fidgety than usual but with the tiny thimble around her neck empty off portal powder, she had no way to escape whatever fate might befall the rest of the crew like she usually would.

They seemed to have crashed on a small celestial body. A moon perhaps. The ground was a murky dark brown. Gravelly rock and fine dust covered it. Large, black boulders and craters alike rendered the ground treacherous.

To the far left, behind the ship there was something resembling wood and stone huts. But they were broken. Even from this distance Tara could see the roofs had caved in, missing doors left gaping holes in the irregular, leaning façades.

"It's abandoned?" She glanced at Merlon.

He frowned, narrowing his eyes. "Is it buildings or boulders over there?"

"Broken buildings," she replied.

His sight wasn't great. He didn't pick up details at the best of times, even when they were kids, but since his cabin portal had exploded in his face, he struggled with everything at low lighting levels. His vision was only a little better than Ola's in the dark which said a lot, Outer Universe humans had terrible vision.

Still, it wasn't uncommon she ended up writing Merlon's logbooks for him when his eyes were too tired and no amount of light allowed him to read. His insomnia of course didn't help, neither did the fact he refused to use hats or tinted glasses to spare his eyes when they travelled in bright starlight.

"I don't smell people, but the air's so moony I can't say for sure." Bailey wriggled her nose, whiskers quivering.

Elin turned her head and stared at Bailey. "Why can the mouse talk?"

"Mouse! Tuh! I'm a black rat I'll have you know." Bailey pointed her nose at Elin, her face impossibly offended. A rat shouldn't have such expressions and it looked creepy at best, but Tara sort of liked Bailey's sass. She had become a lot less hazardous in the past year. "And I'm a Tracker, all Trackers can talk. Except the dogs but that's why we left them to their own devices out in the Ice Galaxies."

Elin's face lit up. "Dogs? Puppies!"

Even Balfour tilted his head out from Tara's shirt, frowning up at them. "Like Mr Brown? He was a really sweet puppy. I was sad when daddy said the crocs ate him." Balfour wiped at his nose.

"Your dad *fed* the puppy to the crocs is what happened." Cary huffed.

Tara jolted a little. Where had he appeared from? Balfour's chin quivered and she knew she had to try and smooth things over; however awful Cary's claim was. "I'm, ah, I'm afraid we have nae puppies, but we have a cat and her…kittens." Tara had no idea what puppies were, and nobody seemed to want shedding further light on that but from the sounds of it, they were animals of some sort.

"KITTENS!" Elin squealed. "I wanna see kittens. Now!" Her arms flailed.

Tara found herself smiling. "They're down in the hold. But the ma cat isn't very friendly."

Merlon had to let Elin back onto the deck to avoid getting knocked out by a rogue fist. He fixed a stern gaze on Cary. "What you said wasn't very nice at all—"

"It's the truth," Cary interjected. "Saw it myself." He shrugged. He acted indifferent, but Tara noted the shiver coursing through him and the slight avoidance of Merlon's gaze. He hadn't been lying, but brutally honest. Not that it made it right telling Balfour. The poor kid didn't need to know his parents were even more vile than he already knew.

"In any case," Merlon continued, "to make up for it, you can take them both down to the lower hold and look at the kittens. Just remember the mum cat is a bit scratchy."

Cary made a face. "I dun't even know where that is."

"Karl does." Merlon nodded at the sailor clambering out from the forecastle. "He'll show you and stay with you." Turning to Tara, Merlon added in Squamate signs, 'they will be safer down there.'

She gritted her teeth and gave Balfour's shoulder a squeeze as he took Elin's hand and turned towards the hatch in the middle of the deck. If pirates had only been slow to attack, she doubted the kids were safe anywhere aboard.

Chapter 21

Tara adjusted her cutlass on her belt and stepped towards the ladder hanging over *Lucia's* portside. Fabian, Boomer, and Derek were already on the ground, a bucket of unlit blast arrows beside them and regular arrows nocked on their bows. Bailey had forsaken Merlon's shoulder to ride along with Fabian.

"You shouldn't disembark, with your injuries you won't…" Merlon faltered, worry creasing his forehead.

Tara glowered. She had decided against trying to use her bow while her arms and hands were covered with cuts, but she didn't want to hang back while people she cared for went into possible danger. She had given in on the island, but she wasn't going to make a habit of that. Besides, if she was too quiet and work avoidant, Merlon might suspect she couldn't see energy. "I'm a little injured, nae dying."

Merlon made a choked noise that sounded suspiciously like a held back groan of frustration. "Let me rephrase that, as the captain, I order you to stay aboard." Tara opened her mouth to protest, but Merlon continued in a rush. "You stay aboard until we've determined we're in the clear. You're always after me for working through injuries so try and listen to your own advice."

Tara ate the snap remark she almost threw at him. She was well aware half the crew were watching them and things would get awkward if she disobeyed a direct order.

However much she hated being left behind on *Lucia* again, she didn't want to force Merlon to give her a punishment to avoid the crew whispering of favouritism. She ground out a question instead. "What's the procedure if you bump into pirates or get captured?"

"Try and find energy to escape." Merlon slipped on his shooting gloves. "Boomer has a pink coloured blast. If you see that, you'll need to run. But the lack of energy is the whole point of these pirate traps so I'm not sure how we get out, even if nobody's home." He swung over the side of the ship.

Tara bowed her head in acceptance. She willed herself to keep from pushing the loose strands of hair back into her bun. Her fingernails dug into the railing while she watched them leave the safety of the ship. She hated being stuck here, having to watch them possibly wander right into the swords of pirates.

Opposite the broken buildings, a tall rock formation rose. Tara had never seen a mountain, but she thought the cliffs might be that. They reached twice as high up as *Lucia's* main mast and were the largest boulders she had ever seen. Even the rocky parts on the island the kids had been on hadn't quite been that tall and much less sheer.

She squinted. Was it energy over there, where she could see the edge of a black gap in the cliffs? Her gaze wandered back towards Merlon and the others. If there were pirates in small ships hiding in that hole inside the mountain…

"What do you see?" Gaunty nudged Tara with an elbow.

Tara glanced at xem, then focused back on the hole, the *cave*, she remembered the word from a book about Moonside which Merlon had lent her. There. High up, above the tip of *Lucia's* masts. A faint flicker of teal leaked out. The teal of heartbeats. Of bodies emitting heat.

"Merlon," she roared, "get back! Someone's there!" Her words didn't carry. Rather, they seemed to bounce back towards her. Merlon and the others didn't turn or react.

Tara swung over the railing.

"Don't—"

"I have to warn them." Tara pulled her arm out of Gaunty's reach, slipping down the ladders so fast she almost lost her footing, twice. Her feet hit the ground and she cupped her mouth. "Merlon! Fabian!" They crept along the scattered boulders, never glancing back.

It wasn't till she tried running she realised there was a certain weightlessness to everything. The gravity was off, barely even there and yet it held the ship firmly on the ground. It had to be the effects of the trap. However, it worked to cut off energy, it also disturbed the sound and gravity.

She kept shouting. They still didn't react. She had to slow down, trying to move faster only seemed to delay her movements. Then, between her gasping breaths, Fabian's incessant chatter reached her.

"…they sure are lazy pirates if they're expectin' us to hand ourselves over. Were's the fun in that? No fightin' and screamin'?"

Boomer responded with a huff. "I's heard pirates don't like wisecracks. Cuts their tongues out."

Tara snorted. Fabian deserved that one. Half a second later she stepped through an invisible barrier. The air instantly felt less stagnant, although still not very pure. The sounds from the ship subdued to a point she had to glance back to be sure crew were still there. Gaunty's shouts for her had suddenly muffled to non-existence.

The crunch of her next step sent Derek spinning, arrow pointing at her.

"Donae shoot me!" Tara held up her hands, muscles tight in the heartbeats it took until Derek lowered his bow without loosening at her.

Merlon turned, his brows drawing together, thunder growing on his expression. "Didn't I—"

"Sorry, but there's heartbeats. In that cave. Near the ceiling." Tara pointed. "I tried shouting but you didnae hear. Some sort of barrier blocks the sounds."

Having covered fifty yards across the ground, the protruding rocks no longer hid half the cave entrance from her sight. It was little more than a black mouth and jagged teeth although the very middle seemed flatter, like someone had chipped away and cleared the space just enough smaller ships might fit through. Ships like what pirates often used, fast clippers that were hard to outrun or catch up with.

Merlon turned his head and narrowed his eyes at the cave. Since Tara couldn't see the pirates or their ships, Merlon most certainly wouldn't see anything. He waved the others after himself, trotting back to Tara. "Can you tell how many? Are they moving towards us already? Surely, they'd have heard us crashing."

"I cannae say how many." Tara shook her head. "But listen, you cannae hear anything from inside the energy vacuum of the trap."

Fabian stared from the cave to the crushed buildings and then *Lucia*. "They sure are terrible at their job if they've got nobody on lookout when ya can't hear."

"Maybe that's why they're pirates. Too incompetent for anything else." Tara shrugged. She didn't like the nervous crease of his brow. He was the one who was supposed to crack jokes.

Fabian gave half a chuckle but didn't one-up her joke like he would when he was less worried. Rather, he gestured at Boomer, waving the impressively large, yet gentle, man after himself and headed straight for the cave.

"Fabian," Merlon hissed, paused to clear his throat, and continued in a steadier voice. "We don't want to alert them if they've not noticed we're here."

Fabian paused, rare annoyance coursing over his face. "We're not escapin' without a sound. There's no bloody energy so if there's pirates I wanna hit them with blasts before they get a chance at catchin' us in our attempts to take off." It wasn't like him to sneer, and certainly not to forget addressing Merlon with "Cap'n".

His anxiety made Tara's own roar to life. She was glad the bandages around her hands wicked away the worst of the cold sweat dampening her palms.

"I don't smell any humans except you lot." Bailey's nose poked past the collar of Fabian's shirt. "And cave bats. The big ones."

"Oh…" Tara squinted at the cave, but her heart was thumping even harder, sweat gathering between her shoulder blades too. She couldn't even see *hints* of energy now. Not that she could tell the difference between a human and a giant cave bat's heartbeat anyway.

Gravel crunched. Tara leapt round, fumbling to pull her cutlass.

"Don't cut me!" Kieran's feet skidded across the ground to a full stop, hands in the air. His scraggly blond hair mussed like he had evidently just removed his hat which now poked out of a pocket in his trousers.

"Stars burn you, Kieran. I nearly ran you through," Tara said. Her hands trembled when she returned the sword to its scabbard. She noted everyone else were also lowering their weapons again.

Kieran blinked. "But I shouted ye while jogging. *None* of ye heard me?"

"Tuh! It's a vacuum." Bailey tsk'ed.

The confusion on Kieran's face only grew more severe so Tara explained. "The lack of energy around the ship somehow muffles sounds from inside the trap."

"Ah, why'd ye not just say that." Kieran glared at Bailey. Unsurprisingly, he was also a bit curt while on high alert.

The rat paid no heed, but prodded Fabian's neck. "Come on then, let's explore and shoot us some pirates if they're hiding in the bat guano."

"Hang on." Merlon held up a hand. "Why did *you* ignore orders?"

Kieran ruffled his own hair. "Ah well Capten, I noticed energy does catch on the sails if you touch them or make noise near them. If we could shake them enough to move the ship or something…"

Merlon stared past Kieran to *Lucia*. "Good observation but I don't know how we'd do that. I doubt we can shout loud enough to move *Lucia*. We still ought to ensure this place is abandoned while we find a way to get enough energy to the sails. Boomer, light up a blast. Fabian, Derek, switch your arrows for blasts too. Kieran hang back with Tara."

Merlon swapped his own arrows as he spoke. The regular one went back into the quiver on his belt, and he plucked one of the heavier blast arrows from Boomer's metal bucket. A small fabric pouch had been tied around the arrowhead.

They were quite different to shoot than regular arrows. They had a tendency to seek downward due to the ballast at the tip. Tara had taken a course shooting dummy blast arrows once upon a time and had found herself thankful last year when they were being pursued by the cannibals of Ivory city. She hadn't been allowed to shoot much – still weak, and sick after the blood transplant that had barely saved her and Mira's lives – but she had been able to sub for Fabian who had a dislocated shoulder at the time.

Tara kept her hand on the hilt of her sword, stalking after the four with bows. Kieran stayed beside her, his cutlass a few inches out of the scabbard already. He had a nervous disposition, but he could suppress his fear rather well when under pressure.

Tara suspected he would eventually take over the second mate role once Deyon decided to retire. Merlon certainly gave Kieran enough extra responsibilities above his boatswain rank to suggest as much.

The cave rose in front of them. Tara fought to get her navigator's vision to home in on the energy, but the harder her heart pounded, the weaker were the flickers of energy she caught. And the four men ten yards ahead of her didn't help. Their quickened heart rates emitted an irregular energy, rising into the air and blurring that of whatever was near the jagged ceiling.

Merlon inched behind a large boulder, peering right into the cave. He hadn't lit his blast arrow. Boomer's lone, glowing, burning one was already plenty visible in the dim greyness of Fristate and they didn't exactly want to draw attention.

Boomer moved in line to Merlon's right, Fabian and Derek sticking near, heads sweeping back and forth.

Bailey leapt from Fabian to Boomer. Even though Tara saw the rat, she jolted. Boomer did a lot more than jump. With a choked grunt, the metal bowstring slipped from his fingertips. The burning arrow flew irregularly, diving fast. It hit one of the upwards pointing rock pillars at the bottom of the cave not twenty yards away.

The explosion flashed, blinding Tara. The boom shook the ground. She threw herself down. Pain erupted along her arms. Pebbles splattered over her body. She kept her eyes closed another few seconds then made herself open them again. Her breath hitched, she pushed against the hard ground. She shook gravel from her face and hair, blinking. Dust swirled and the white dots receded from her vision.

"Get down!" Tara yanked at Kieran, lunging for the hide behind the boulder Merlon and the others pressed against.

Merlon's eyes were shut, his hands trembling, but still holding the unlit blast arrow nocked to the bowstring. The flash of the blast would have rendered him temporarily blind. Even a flare of a powder lamp could do that. "Donae shoot us," Tara whispered in case he would have a scare from the sound of their scuttling.

She pressed against his side, allowing herself a moment of relief the steady firmness his proximity lent her.

"Are they coming?" He spoke under his breath, eyes still clenched tightly.

Tara opened her mouth, but the whoosh of something, a lot of it, made her twist her neck. Her muscles twinged. Huge black and brown shapes flapped into view. They screeched. Their wings sent swirls of uneven energy into the air.

Bats. Hundreds of them.

Chapter 22

The shrill cries of the bats drowned all other sounds. They kept coming. Out and up from the cave. The main group swerved right, avoiding the energy void-space where *Lucia* lay.

Tara rose, tracking the bats hitting the barrier she hadn't been able to see before. It gave off a cold energy. Not quite like Ola's Outer Universe instruments but almost. Magnetism. That was why it had a grey tint amongst the turquoise. The bats' echo-y shrieks hit and reflected against the field, their wings flapping to turn away. Then one hit the trap.

Ripples spread through the magnetic field that kept energy out. Confusion exploded the group of animals, dozens broke off, a few turning to head straight over *Lucia*. Her sails flared, energy pulsing from the slip stream the bats' wings and calls sent past the canvas.

Merlon's arm wound around Tara's shoulder, pulling her back down.

She lost sight of *Lucia* from the rocks between them and the ship. "Merlon wait, there's something—"

"Boomer, leave the bucket." Merlon spoke loudly. "On my command, you five run. Get the ship in the air. Get out. I'll hold them."

Tara huffed. "Donae be ridiculous."

"No way we're leavin' ya," Fabian growled in the same moment.

Tara raised a brow at him, almost smiling despite the panic rushing through her. That was something they could always agree on. If she ever failed at protecting Merlon, Fabian would be there, ready to step in.

Boomer clung to the bucket of blast arrows. "Can't get the bloody ship in the air anyway."

"We might." Tara massaged the frown between her brows. If three bats could generate enough energy to make the sails flare that much…

Her breath caught. She had seen energy! It had been clear as anything. The pale greyish blue of the magnetic vacuum, the clear turquoise spirals of the wind turbulence the wings had created. She sprung to her feet, heart threatening to break her ribs. When she directed her gaze at where she *knew* the field was, she saw nothing. Foggy air and a dust swirl outside the vacuum. But no energy.

Merlon yanked her down once more. His fingers trembling against her arm. He caught her eyes when she turned her head. "What did you see? Have the pirates snuck onboard?" His expression was unyielding, but dread flickered in the golden-brown of his eyes.

Tara twisted round but the boulder blocked the cave. Pirates. Why hadn't they welled out along with the bats? They couldn't have missed the blast even if they hadn't seen *Lucia* crash. Could they truly have the luck of having fallen into an abandoned trap? She shook her head. "I donae—"

"No sign of pirates." Bailey landed on Merlon's shoulder.

Tara pressed a fist into the sore spot on her ribs to avoid screaming in a fright. "Seriously, be done with all the jumping."

Instead of replying, Bailey scratched her ear, licked her toes, and scratched again. Merlon gagged. Tara wasn't far off from the same sentiment.

"They'd attacked by now, wouldn't they?" Kieran craned his neck.

Fabian shrugged. "One way to find out." He stood, stepping around the boulder before Merlon had scrambled to his feet.

Tara held onto Merlon's arm, using him to pull herself up. Her joints were beginning to ache again, the rush of fear subsiding.

"Fabian, slow down," Merlon said, then he muttered so low only Tara could have heard, "Stars, if I need to replace my first mate so soon again…"

Her stomach clenched and she bit back the twinge in her knee, skipping to stay beside Merlon. No matter how much she tried not to, a limp snuck into her walk.

Merlon glanced at her and shortened his strides without a word. His fingers holding the nocked arrow twitched and she knew he wanted to wrap an arm around her.

Fabian paused to set alight his blast arrow and they all caught up with him. Then he continued stalking straight into the cave, arrow nocked once more. The small flame cast flickering shadows on the rugged walls.

"That's something of a mast." Boomer nodded.

Tara followed the indication. There, near the right side of the cave the tip of a mast lay. The wood was grey and dead. It had been there a long time.

She looked up, searching for, and easily finding a broad rock protrusion on the ceiling that had several huge marks from being struck. While *Lucia* would never fit in here, cutters and other small, short distance ships had clearly been flown straight into the cave.

She blinked, eyes adjusting to the darker lighting beyond the first few yards. The walls and edges of the ceiling were marred with similar contact points. Old rigging, a piece of canvas that still flickered weakly with colours of stray energy and wood splinters enough to assemble a full ship littered the floor.

Pirates *had* been here. Many of them, but it looked like the narrow entrance of the cave had damaged their ships thoroughly. The soft gravel of the middle of the floor still had stumps, some smooth but many others with sharp edges. Rocks that had marks from being roughly chopped down in an attempt to even out the landing.

Tara glanced out, the magnetic field started nearly a hundred yards straight out from the cave, the only way anyone could get in here, would be by flying *through* the vacuum. Risky, it would leave the ship without steering abilities when it was most crucial. The whole setup spoke of desperation. Quite different to the stories of cunning traps and lures the newspapers tended to talk about.

"I think I know this place," Bailey said. She scuttled over Merlon's arm and leapt to Tara's.

Tara paused. She didn't like the growing darkness, and while there had been no signs of water anywhere the cave air had a dampness to it she really didn't appreciate, even if there was plenty of space around her. "You've been here before?"

Bailey snorted. "Tuh! Of course not. I've *read* about it. I specialise in the Edge Galaxies for my surveillance studies. Fristate and Blacklock's have interesting history and every locale is described in detail. This is Cave Fourteen. Also called Narrow Cave. Old pirate trap. One of the first. Long since abandoned for reasons you can probably guess." She nodded at a piece of canvas, dull grey and threadbare barely a flicker coursed over it.

Merlon groaned, he turned and came back to them. "You couldn't have said that before we wasted an hour panicking?" He raised his voice and called, "At ease, the rat has just remembered she knew this is an abandoned pirate cave."

"Tish tosh, fear keeps you alive."

Tara only half-heard Bailey's words. The rustling of something large, something with many legs was overpowering her.

"Dark, dank and bugs," she whispered. She wasn't in a well. There was all the space around her she could want. The ceiling was nearly two hundred feet above, having kept rising beyond the much lower entrance point. The walls on either side were another hundred feet apart. Forty yards inside the cave, everything seemed to expand outwards.

"Tara, are you alright?" Merlon's hand pressed her shoulder.

She stared at it. Why was Merlon trembling so much? His fingers were warm through her thin shirt. But that *scuttling*. Her eyes sought the darkness. There, air movements. Flickers of colour the quicker she blinked. Cockroaches. Or cave crickets. It didn't matter, they were huge, and she could already feel their spiky feet digging into her hair. Crawling under her clothes.

She whirled. Merlon's hand ripped from her as she sprinted away. There wasn't air. Nothing entered her lungs when she tried to pull in a breath, then another. Rocks grappled her feet. Stumps of old, cut-down pillars tried to trip her up. She had to get into the grey light outside. Had to escape the dark, dampness of the cave.

The ground billowed under her. Then a boulder rose towards her face. She caught herself. Palms panging. Pain shot up her arms. It was like a jolt of energy. Restarting her heart and lungs. She gasped for a breath. Drew it down, forced it to stay, then released it. Blinking, the world stopped spinning. She was a few feet from the exit. Panting heavily, her eyes fell on Merlon.

His hand was on her arm again. Worry creased his brows. Only then did she realise *he* hadn't been trembling. She shook so hard it made his entire arm quiver with her. His lips moved. It took another ten seconds before her mind had turned the words over enough to understand. "You're safe. You're not in the well."

Tara nodded, slowly. His fingers twitched against her arm. She could see his longing to throw his arms around her, but he didn't. Closing her eyes, she thanked the stars. For Merlon understanding and for not having a worse attack. When she opened her eyes again, her breath was nearly at a normal rate.

"Donae hold me too tightly," she muttered and put her head against his shoulder. Merlon embraced her, so tentatively she pressed herself closer. He knew not to encase her. She had only had two other panic attacks this past year, they weren't so frequent as her other nightmares now, but he had learnt quickly and without judgement.

"Our therapists are going to be so annoyed when we get home," Merlon whispered. Then he switched his accent to a bad replica of Tara's Haven Galaxian therapist's. "All that 'ard work and the twe of ye go get yeself into storms and pirate traps and gain new trauma all over."

Tara chuckled, wiping her eyes as she pulled a little away. "I think she'll agree with Da, we each get into enough trouble on our own and twice as much together."

"We also overcome it together." Merlon placed a hand on either side of her face. His eyes held her captive, emotion burning in the brown depths. Right when she thought he would say something more, he faltered and kissed her forehead instead. He stepped back. "Let's find a way off this planet…moon, whatever."

Tara clenched her hand around Ma's pendant under her shirt. She hated that Merlon was trying to give her space to decide. It wasn't him she was doubting, it was herself. Her ability – or lack thereof – not to mess up their relationship. Not to mess up a kid.

Weren't panic attacks proof she could never manage motherhood? How could she be there for a kid if she could lose control of herself because of a little damp darkness and the scurrying of bugs?

"You're making yourself anxious. I can smell it." Bailey's voice was the quietest mumble in her ear. So soft and kind Tara almost thought she had imagined it. But Bailey continued. "Whatever you're thinking you can't do, it's just a mind game. Don't listen to yourself." Then she yawned loudly and said, "those bats will return to their roosting grounds soon enough. I'd prefer not to get pooped on when that happens."

Tara swallowed hard and let her hand drop from the necklace. She wasn't sure Bailey was right. She didn't know Tara's penchant for messing things up. But she forced herself to stop thinking about it. *Stick to the current problem and solution.*

Tara cleared her throat. "About those bats, I have an idea that might get us out of here."

Chapter 23

A day later, Tara's plan had yet to come to fruition. Minor repairs had however been performed and they would be ready to attempt their escape imminently.

Sitting on the sick bay cot, Tara teased the bandage fibres from the cuts on her right palm. She grimaced. The wounds hadn't been deep when she got them, but every time she had climbed, lifted, or moved something it seemed like she had made it worse.

Karl, also sitting on the cot, leaned closer. A frown built on his dark brow. "Looks gnarly that. You's in need of help?"

"Can you reach the antiseptic? It's the bottle with the orange lid," Tara said. She dumped the dirty bandage on the floor and picked up the soft cloth from among the items she had laid out between herself and Karl on the cot.

Karl didn't need anything in the sick bay, Yorik had already adjusted the splints earlier, but he had come along to keep Tara company. She suspected he was bored to death. Merlon had barred him from even working on smaller carpentry-based adjustments across the ship and if there was something Karl hated, it was idleness.

"That's got a pink lid, you dunce." Tara handed back the bottle she had absently taken from Karl.

He harrumphed but replaced it with the right one. "Looks nearly the same. It's a grimy pink that. Someone ought'a repaint them."

"Maybe Merlon will let you do that. Not sure we have any paints or pigments though." Tara shook the bottle well before removing the lid and wetting the cloth with the watery tincture.

Gritting her teeth, she pressed the fabric against the main cut. Despite her mental preparation, the fizzling sting left her gasping. She quickly disinfected the other minor cuts and sighed with relief once the liquid dried back up with a few waves of her hand.

Tara dampened another corner and repeated the process on her left palm. Thankfully the cuts there were healing better, courtesy of her using that hand less, so the pain of the antiseptic wasn't nearly as sharp. By the time she finished, she was surprised to find Karl had returned the bottle to the holder on the cabinet and sat ready with the clean bandages she had put on the cot.

"No whinging," Karl said, raising a finger in reprimand. "You isn't a weakling for getting help."

Tara snorted, holding back the remark she had been about to blurt out about being perfectly capable of bandaging herself. Patrice had admonished her about that for years until Tara had got used to letting her deal with any injuries, but with her dead…

Tara swallowed hard and looked away from Karl's overly meticulous bandaging. The grief hit her like a boulder in the chest. Her eyes stung with tears, and she blinked ferociously. Crying was silly. It wasn't even the anniversary for Patrice's death yet. That was in another week or so.

The quicker Tara blinked to keep the pressing tears at bay, the more images flooded her mind. Patrice's still body. Her skin having lost that golden glow she had guarded jealously by wearing big hats, long sleeves, and talc cream whenever the starlight was bright. Her brown eyes never opening again. Lady Galantria, indirectly her murderer, hadn't even bothered showing up for the hole-drop although her less cruel partner had.

Someone dropped a barrel in the hold. The deep boom jolted Tara from the funeral in Ivory. Flashes of the past week took over. The villagers streaming out of the front gates. The pill-shaped bombs dropping. Limbs scattering with grass and dirt. And Bethy's still face. Arms hugging Ramson even in her death. Sobs broke through Tara's guards.

Karl's beefy arms wrapped around her. "There, there. Get it out, darling dear." He patted her back, rocking her back and forth.

She had longed for adventures not two years ago. Had jumped at the opportunity for an intergalactic journey that could take years.

She had even hoped she could guilt Merlon into giving her command rights despite only being a trainee. While that *had* worked, it seemed like casualties had shot up from one freak accident to everyone she cared about getting hurt or killed in an endless stream of suffering.

215

It took her embarrassingly long to recover some semblance of control. Tara writhed until Karl eased his too tight hug. His rough thumb wiped a tear from her cheek, and he sent her a small smile. "See? You's always hollering like a babe."

"And you're a bastard." Tara huffed but couldn't help laughing. She nudged his arm. "Thanks though. This past week, this whole *year*…" She shook her head, not wanting to tease another flood of heart-breaking memories to the surface. "I feel like I bring death everywhere I go."

Karl's face grew serious. "You saved three kids from certain death. If we'd brought them back to that village, where do you think they'd been now?"

Tara threw her arms around him again. She had lost Patrice and Adrien but gained so many new friends aboard *Lucia*. She realised, if she broke with Merlon she wouldn't see much of Fabian, Karl, Gaunty or anyone else anymore. The choice seemed to get harder the more she mulled it over. And it was all down to her being inept with children and well, romantic relationships.

"Thanks." She sat back, forcing herself to stop worrying about Merlon or kids or anything beyond the next task. "Do you think you can bandage my right hand too? Must be about time to try the plan so I need to lay topside soon."

Karl nodded and picked up the second bandage. "I's not understood what this plan is about but if it gets us back in the air and out of this pirate trap." He shrugged.

"It should. Did you nae listen when we went through it earlier?"

"There's a crooked baluster on the quarterdeck rail right where Cap'n stood, and I's not allowed to fix it."

216

Tara laughed. Typical Karl. His mind had probably been circling endlessly around that baluster being off instead of paying the least attention to Merlon's explanations. "Right, so we'll be five on the ground. Me to see the energy, mostly, while Fabian shoots a blitz arrow as far into the cave as possible—"

"I knows you's Trachnan, but please stop them big gestures while talking, I's tying a bandage on your hand," Karl said.

Tara rolled her eyes but took care to keep her right arm still, however odd that felt. "Anyway, the bats will flee the cave due to the flash and bang. That's when Derek, then Yorik will shoot more blitzes to direct them *into* this vacuum. Kieran will be on the magnetic field's border. He's shooting to get the bats right over *Lucia*. Their wings and cries create lots of turbulence. Hopefully enough to shift *Lucia* out of the vacuum. Bam, we're off."

Karl tucked in the end of the bandage and straightened. "Your plan?"

"Merlon's, Fabian's and mine." She had provided the concept, Merlon and Fabian had worked out the details since they knew the ship better.

His forehead creased. "But how's you getting back aboard?"

"Ladders. And Jara's turning back to pick us up should the plan go better than expected and *Lucia* can take off properly from the energy the bats send her way."

"Cap'n's not on the ground with you?" Karl raised a brow.

Tara used Karl's shoulder to stand, then held out a hand to help him up. She handed him the crutches Gaunty had

217

given up so he could get around. "We might need to run to catch up with *Lucia*. She doesn't turn well, as you know."

"Ah, yes Cap'n's not a fan of running after that leg injury." Karl nodded.

Tara led the way out of the sick bay, closing the door after Karl. "He worked too soon after getting injured. He willnae let the crew see but it pains him a fair bit. Gets cramps most days after long hours working…stop looking at me like that." Tara gave Karl the mildest shove.

"I just thinks it would make sense to have someone else on the ground than you." Karl headed for the hold hatch.

Tara shrugged and climbed up first, carrying his crutches while he slowly made his way to the main deck. A rush of activity broke out at the same time she handed the mobility aids back to Karl.

Merlon joined them by the spot where the railing had been pulled aside to allow for easier access to the ladder rolled out to dangle down to the ground. Extra rungs had been attached to provide a longer reach for when *Lucia* – hopefully – took off from the ground.

"Is Bailey still sulking?" Tara asked.

Merlon sighed. "Yes, she wants to steal the letter tube but the moment we're out of here I need to send it to Lennie. He'll know the safest course to Outpost 8. With those regime changes in Blacklock's…getting off this moon won't be our biggest problem."

Her stomach clenched and she muttered, "seems our troubles are never-ending."

"Are you sure I shouldn't send someone else down?" Merlon said.

Tara pulled her bow over her shoulders and pushed the quiver along her belt, so it was behind her for the descent. She only had four blitz arrows in there, but the long shafts and fletching could easily get in the way. "They willnae hear me if I remain inside the magnetic field."

She didn't tell him she wouldn't be of all that much use. Apart from the short-lived moments when the accidental blast had scared her, her navigator's vision had receded to mere flickers once more. Still, those glimmers of energy were more than anybody else saw.

"Is it dangers?" Elin peered past Merlon's leg. Her blue eyes were round, chin quivering.

He glanced down at her, patting the curls that had escaped the plait Fabian had done. "Tara's got very good eyes. Even if something's dangerous she'll see a way to be safe."

"I donae know about that." Tara frowned, realising too late her words freaked Elin out even more. She ought to keep her mouth shut.

Balfour rubbed his nose. "So you're nut coming back? Like the other adults?"

Maybe he saw the panic growing in Tara, but Karl stepped forward and nudged Balfour's shoulder lightly. "She'll return to us. But why don't you both come along, and we'll see to the kittens? It's going to be busy up here and you doesn't like all the shouting, does you, Balfour? Then we'll go back up when Tara's back."

Merlon nodded his thanks, transferring Elin's pincher-grip from his sleeve to Karl's large hand. Balfour lingered a moment longer, staring at Tara to such an extent she almost began squirming. It was like he tried reading her mind's innermost secrets and she was certain he would find her wanting.

"Come on you." Karl tapped Balfour's leg with a crutch.

Slowly, reluctantly, Balfour turned. "They always say they're coming back," he mumbled. Then he took Elin's hand, looking up at Karl who towered above the kids. "Do you want me to carry your crutches down the steps?"

Tara shook her head. That kid was always so thoughtful.

"Hey," Merlon said, squeezing her arm. "You're good?"

"Oi! Tramp, why's ya takin' a lifetime?" Fabian called at the same moment and waved from the ground.

Tara glanced over her shoulder. "Let me finish plotting how to leave you behind, turd!" She faced Merlon again and let out a breath. "I'll be fine. Try nae to leave us all behind if this works better than we expect."

Merlon smiled, his eyes remaining worried. "We'll turn back if that happens. Wouldn't dream of leaving you here."

Eventually, Tara made it to the ground, and they took up their positions. Striking the long spark-light on a rock, she placed the wooden stick in a crack of a rock. She angled it to allow her easy access to light the tiny pouch of blitz powder tied to the tip of the first arrow she drew. She should only have to shoot a single arrow and hoped that wouldn't mess up her healing hands too much.

"On ya call, tramp," Fabian shouted from near the cave entrance. He had the furthest to run to get aboard before Jara would have to turn *Lucia* back around while avoiding the vacuum and boulders alike. Luckily, he had long legs and was a good sprinter over short distances.

Tara turned her head. "Everyone hear me?" When Kieran, Derek and Yorik all nodded, she looked back to Fabian. "Alright, get the bats flying if you're not too poor of a shot, turd."

"Ey! I took extra archery classes, can't have the navigator outdo the first mate."

Tara opened her mouth to let him know she *did* outperform him in every way, but his burning arrow was already in flight. It landed deep in the cave, exploding in a flash of light and loud bang. Unlike blasts, blitz arrows did little damage despite sounding and looking flashier.

Surprisingly, it worked exactly as intended. The colony took to the air with loud screeches. Their huge wings in comparison made little noise when they poured out of the narrow cave entrance.

Fabian sent another arrow almost straight upwards. Yorik loosened his not a second later.

The projectiles exploded when they hit one another, and the flock turned sharply to avoid the flash. Yorik was about the best shooter Tara had ever seen, even better than Kieran.

Tara forced her breath to slow. She waited for the tail-end of the group, then sent her first arrow to hit Fabian's third shot and thanked the stars when she barely did hit. Her fingertips thrummed but she had borrowed Gaunty's arm braces, and the leather protected her scratched skin.

Yorik hit Derek's first arrow in yet another spark and boom.

The bats squabbled, flapping wildly into the energy vacuum. Then the group began turning.

"Again, Derek," Tara yelled. "Kieran, keep them moving forward over *Lucia*!" She picked up her spark-light, lighting a second arrow as she ran back towards the ship. The sails were flaring. The ship lifted, bumbling along the ground. "It's working. Keep the bats moving."

Derek loosened again. This time it was Kieran who sent an arrow to meet it. Another flash urged the bats close by *Lucia*.

Fabian caught up with Tara, slowing only to take her spark-light and let her send off a second arrow. Yorik didn't even need to stand still to shoot an arrow that hit hers mid-flight. She suspected Merlon would have hired him even if he hadn't had level two healer's courses under the belt too.

Her boot scuffed on a rock, halting her trot so abruptly she tumbled forward.

Fabian caught her arm before she slammed into the ground. "Come on, can't leave ya here, can we."

Lucia slid across the ground, her sails luffing. The last bats were nearly through the vacuum. Something flickered beyond *Lucia*. A flare of colours. The bats turned, doubling back before veering sharply away from *Lucia*. Tara blinked, behind *Lucia* a ship was coming straight at them.

She swung her bow over her shoulder. *Lucia's* muffled groans reached her the instant they passed into the vacuum. "There's another ship."

"Oh crap." Fabian panted.

The ladder slipped across the ground. Derek was at the top. Kieran caught the bottom rung, waving for Yorik to jump up after himself.

"Look at the flag." Fabian grabbed Tara's arm again, yanking her along. "It's pirates."

Chapter 24

"**B**urn us, burn us!" Tara stumbled across the rocky ground.

Yorik reached the ladders. The bats were swerving away again, but *Lucia* was about to hit the barrier that kept energy out. Once the ship had re-entered normal space, she would leap forward, her anchor fully reeled in, and all sails primed for flight.

Fabian kept pulling Tara along, steering left, far ahead of where *Lucia* was but if the ship picked up speed, they would still struggle to catch those ladders in time. The bowsprit broke through the invisible magnetic field with a flash of turquoise.

Tara faltered, blinded. The timing of her energy vision working was impeccably awful.

"Keep goin'!" Fabian hauled her by the sorest spot on her arm.

Tara staggered along, rocks grabbling for her feet. She blinked away the dots blurring her surroundings. The flying

223

jib was the first sail to reach the outside. A flare of colours danced across the fabric. *Lucia* bounded over the ground, leaping into the air. The ladder lifted. The last rung left the ground.

"Run, run, run!" Fabian shrieked.

Behind *Lucia*, the pirate ship became fully visible. A fast, gaff-rigged cutter. The wood was dyed black, purple, and grey, hiding the hull against the grey mist of Fristate, only the glare of the sails and the blue jagged edges at the top and bottom of the black flag betrayed its existence. And the ship was turning for a pursuit.

Fabian kept shouting. Tara could no longer hear his words. Her ears whooshed. Her chest felt about to explode. The pain in her body ceased to matter. Ceased to exist. She twisted from Fabian's grip, sprinting. They had to catch that ladder.

Lucia groaned. She turned to port, towards them, but only a few degrees. The main sail caught the energy. Someone worked the anchor, slowing *Lucia*. Merlon stood at the gap in the railing, screaming. They were so close. Boulders came up, *Lucia* screeched, and her hull twisted upwards. The ladders rose further.

Fabian lunged. He caught the second rung. "Tara! Grab the—"

She leapt at his outstretched arm. Her legs pedalled the air. She flailed. Her fingers closed around his lower arm. He flexed, heaving her upwards even as their grip had barely cemented. Tara's free hand caught the lower rung.

"Get up! Boulders!" Merlon's cry trembled down.

Fabian pulled at her. "Up, up!"

But her muscles were screaming. Her head roared from overexertion. "I cannae."

The ladders bounced. Fabian kept tugging at her, his foot found the last rung. Her little finger caught between the wood piece and his boot. She howled. Then the pressure eased.

Fabian crawled upwards.

Tara could do nothing but cling to the bottom two rungs. Lungs burning. Muscles like liquid iron and jelly. A boulder hit her dangling legs. The ladders bounced off. Her trousers, and the skin underneath, scraped across the rough surface. She barely felt it. Everything else hurt so much already.

She turned her head from the next rock cropping up ahead. There was no reason to watch what would either kill her on impact or force her grip off the ladders. In either case she would be dead soon. And she was too tired to care.

The pirate ship hit the vacuum when she looked towards it. Had so little time passed? Mere seconds. The sails on the cutter went dark. Little people, like grains of brown rice flitted across the main deck. They kept working like they expected the ship to keep flying. She realised it *did* since they had come in from the side at full speed, they had enough momentum to keep going.

But the last-minute turn to follow *Lucia* had put them at a dangerous angle. Those big boulders right outside the cave that Jara's steering had narrowly kept *Lucia* from hitting, stretched their greedy fingers for the pirates' cutter.

They didn't brace in time for the ship hitting the rocks. Wood splintered. The hull broke open by the stern. People were tossed about, and the ship keeled to starboard.

It stopped abruptly, only the topsails stuck out from the magnetic field. They wouldn't manage to follow right away. *Lucia* could make it away yet. With a head start, they could be safe.

Blinking, Tara swung against *Lucia's* singing hull. How had she got this far up? She hadn't been turned to mash against the boulders like she had thought she would.

The sighs of the breathing wood slowed her accelerated heart. She kicked, boots scuffing across the boards, but she couldn't bend enough to catch the bottom rung with a foot. Her ribs screamed in protest at the attempt. She didn't dare unwind her arm from the ladder to crawl upwards or she would drop to her death, her fingers powerless and twitchy.

The grey rocks were getting small fast. Cave Fourteen and the moon it sat on vanishing when they pulled out towards space. Would her hair catch on fire if she remained on the side of the hull while leaving the weak atmosphere?

Hands grasped her. Hauled her body onto the main deck. Tara flopped, every muscle in her body crying for a break and refusing to shift her limbs. Strong arms drew her close. She closed her eyes and breathed in Merlon's familiar scent. Starlight and wood lye. Safe. Long as he held her, she remained safe.

"Stars burn you. Don't you just give up like that," he muttered into her hair.

Deyon cleared his throat. "Cat'n? Pirates might have grounded themselves but we's best get back to full speed."

Merlon pushed a leg under them both, hoisting her as he stood himself with a grunt of effort. His right leg trembled against her. A sure sign he had overexerted the old injury of

226

his knee and thigh. "Fabian, get her below please. I need you back up until we're in the clear. Tara," Merlon waited until she raised her head and met his gaze. "I need the letter to Lennie sent sooner rather than later. It's in the locked drawer."

"Of course." Her voice was coarser than a raw block of sandstone. She grimaced at the flare of pain when Merlon transferred her to Fabian who unceremoniously grabbed her wrist and forced her arm over his shoulder.

Fabian didn't waste time letting her hobble along, but almost carried her through the passage to the cabin.

He plonked her in her chair. "Ya scared the starlight outta me, ya stupid tramp." He slapped her arm, relief in his face.

Then mischief washed it away. "Have fun with the grumpy rat." He winked, skipping out of the door when she swung a very weak fist at his side. "Ya owe me one!" Fabian slammed the door.

"I owe you so many I'll be broke." Tara rubbed her face. She stayed in the chair for a long minute, gathering enough slivers of strength to move around the desk. Eventually, she forced herself up, using the table to keep herself upright and shuffled along. She dropped into Merlon's chair on the other side.

Reaching for the top drawer, she froze. A letter opener and…a wire from the powder lamp's stopper stuck out of the keyhole. The drawer gaped a couple of inches.

Tara yanked it fully open. The inside looked mostly untouched. Merlon's logbooks and the little stand for the inkwell was stuck in the corner chamber where it should be, with the pen wedged under the top logbook's leather closure.

Two things were amiss. The loose papers Merlon kept for letters had all scattered from the neat pile they usually were in. That could be from the rough take off, but the topmost sheet had been a letter containing their approximate coordinates based on the current constellations around them. It wasn't there.

Neither was the wooden letter tube Trackers used to send correspondence. The one Merlon had planned to use to send the letter to Lennie in hopes the Squamate knew the safest route away from Cave Fourteen. With pirates on their tail, they needed that route more than ever.

"Bailey!" Tara hissed and stood so abruptly the chair fell over. The cabin swam. She had moved too quickly. To avoid falling over, she seized the desk's edge until the dizzy spell subsided. She needed a nap and some water. Merlon's waterskin hung on the hook on the side of the desk so she grabbed that and drained it.

"She's *very* thirsty." Elin's little voice jolted Tara.

She lowered the waterskin to find Elin and Balfour peering out from the chamber door. The latter opened the door another few inches. "The talking rat broke into the desk."

Tara glanced at the drawer. She had guessed that but maybe Balfour had seen more. "Did she take a wooden tube? About this big?" Tara held up her hands six inches apart.

"She muttered about letters and friends and…not friends. Then she pushed the tube off the table, and it vanished," Balfour said.

Tara sighed. "Typical."

Balfour ducked his head. "I'm sorry. I was scared of her. Mummy says rodents have even nastier diseases than me."

228

Tara walked over to the chamber door. Balfour hid behind the door, cowering like he expected her to be mad at him. Like she was going to strike him. "Balfour, it isnae your fault. You donae have nasty diseases. Bailey's...difficult. You donae need be afraid of her, but I'm glad you told me what she did."

Balfour blinked up at her, incomprehension on his face. He offered up an arm, turning his head aside. The very way he did so, twisted Tara's guts into a tight knot. He was *still* expecting her to hit him. Whoever his parents had been, they should never have been allowed to have a kid.

"Balfour, listen..." She sought the chamber beyond him for words. Her eyes fell on the life-like painting of Elin, Bethy and Ramson which Tara had stuck to the powder lamp in the bunk the kids shared. Bethy's sad smile was no help. Neither was Cary, who was on the floor beside the bed.

How could Tara phrase it so Balfour understood nobody would hurt him? He hadn't even done anything if not helped her by telling what had happened!

She sunk to her knees, her stomach clenching painfully. Gingerly, she placed a hand on each of his bony shoulders. "Nobody here will ever hurt you. I'll never hit you. I promise, on Tomaline's warm light, I'll never allow you to be hurt like that."

He met her gaze without flinching. Anything but belief tumbled around the depths of his blue eyes. He rubbed his runny nose on a sleeve cuff. "Okay."

"Good. Here, use a handkerchief, yeah?" She produced one from her pocket that she hadn't needed anyway.

He took it, frowning. "It's fabric."

229

"They're like the people in old stories," Cary said, straightening from the floor beside the bunk. "Wooden boats, no electricity. They'll probably hang or torture us if we steal."

"W-what?" Elin's eyes grew huge.

"Or chop off your hand. I read a book once where they did that to someone who stole bread."

Tara scrambled to gather her thoughts for a reply. *Stars, what is it with this kid trying to scare the other two constantly?* She shook her head, using the door frame to stand. "Those things were outlawed many, many years ago. I'll be very disappointed if you steal, but nobody will torture you, ever."

"We stole the cat." Cary shrugged.

"What?" It was Tara's turn to stare.

Elin giggled, fingers twitching. "The grey kitten is Spot and he's mine!" She jumped up and down.

Only then did Tara understand why Cary had been on his stomach, staring under the bunk. The flicker of small heartbeats sent swirls of energy out from underneath. A pair of yellow eyes watched her carefully.

"We can put it back." Balfour avoided Tara's gaze, once more looking like he mentally prepared himself for an assault. He seemed to curl in on himself, making his body smaller, less of a target for the slap of an unkind hand.

Stumped, Tara asked, "what did Bailey say to the cats being up here? She's nae friends with the mother cat."

"The rat? She left," Cary said. "The black kitten is mine and I'll scream if you take her from me." Cary, unlike Balfour, glared at Tara. "Balfour can have the white and red one and

230

you can keep the mummy cat when she doesn't like the kittens anymore."

"Um, alright. But I donae know if we can keep them at all." Could people eat cats? She wasn't sure they would be allowed to bring a new species to Amule unless it had usage.

Merlon had often mentioned how difficult it had been to get the horses of his former girlfriend imported. He had been forced to agree they could be butchered for meat, hides and glue once they were no longer useful to farmers working in the fields. Despite that, the old stallion remained alive, and Merlon went up to feed it expensive apples once a week when they were in Amule.

"Tuh! Cats will be allowed alright." Bailey sat up on the chair inside the chamber door.

Tara had no idea where she had come from, but Bailey tended to be like that.

Bailey continued unhindered. "Cats are rodent killers and will be considered very useful. As long as you make sure they never touch a chicken or duck..." She made a shrug-like gesture. "Nasty things, dumb-born cats."

Tara snatched at the rat, but Bailey leapt over her hand and up her arm. "You better have sent a letter to Lennie—"

"Lennie! Ha. Never. I sent one to someone much more helpful. If we don't get caught by pirates beforehand, we're to meet in Outpost 9."

Tara gritted her teeth. "We needed that letter to ask for the safest route to *avoid* pirates."

"Bah, you'll be fine." Bailey began washing herself.

Tara rubbed a sore spot on her arm. She really hoped they would.

231

Chapter 25

Two days after they escaped Cave Fourteen, the pirates still hadn't caught up with them, but Merlon had asked the crew to spar and refresh their sword skills daily.

The clang of sword blades striking one another sent a pang through Tara's head. The cut above her ear from the sarco croc's thrashing was healing. With the skin pulling together tight, it left her with a constant, low-level headache that made her grumpy.

She shifted her legs closer towards herself, using her knee as the support for her notebook, drawing furiously. Edur's clean-scraped skull had given way for new scenes in her nightmares.

She hadn't thought it possible to dream about anything more disturbing than Patrice and Edur being maggot-riddled corpses dumped deep in the ground under Ivory but last night had proved her wrong. She had trusted she had gone free after five nights without nightmares but the horrors she had witnessed on Quarantine Thirteen had caught up with her at last.

Ramson's charred curls looked lustreless when drawn in pencil. She would paint it in full colour at some point. It would help get the images to leave the darkest corners of her mind but her pigments and oils were back in Amule. Pencil drawings would have to do for now. She stared at the unseeing eyes she had put on the page. The dimple on Ramson's cheek. Nausea rose and she slammed the book shut.

Her eyes refused to focus on the main deck in front of her. She leaned back against the raised quarterdeck, stretching her legs in front of herself. The wood felt warm beneath her. *Lucia* hummed quietly like she too was relieved they had escaped Cave Fourteen without a pirate pursuit.

If Merlon's Fristate maps were precise, they would reach Outpost 9 in another day. Or rather a bit more since Fristate Galaxy operated on twenty-four-hour days instead of the more usual twenty-six.

No amount of questioning had budged Bailey to reveal who she had sent the letter to. Tara hoped it wasn't anyone who would cause them more trouble. With Bailey's track record, that was, however, by far the likeliest outcome.

"No sparring today?" Gaunty sat down beside Tara, jerking her from her thoughts.

She shook her head. "I want to, but my hands need time." She turned over her right hand to show Gaunty.

She hadn't rebandaged most of her cuts today, hoping fresh air would help the healing along faster. The cuts weren't deep, but the constant tearing anytime she used them left her with two frayed, crusty wounds that ran the length of her palm. "Even if my hands were fine, I think Merlon's seen too many of my bruises. He'd lose his cool if I tried sparring."

Gaunty snorted and crooked a smile on xer thick lips. "Do as he says, not as he does."

"Exactly." Tara couldn't help smiling. She turned her gaze to the match before them. Fabian had stepped in after Deyon's short attempt at keeping up with Merlon. He never bragged, but Merlon was about the best person Tara had ever seen wielding a sword.

With the pirate threat being very real, everyone but Karl and Tara had been training for at least half an hour a day. It probably helped work out some of the nerves that had built up aboard in the past week of unexpected events.

Gaunty nudged her arm and pointed. "Them kids are quite fascinated. Karl mentioned he might be able to craft a wooden sword or two for 'em."

Tara leaned forward enough she could see Elin and Balfour. They sat at the bottom of the portside quarterdeck steps.

Cary was at the top of the companionway but while the two younger kids were gaping at the sparring match, Cary had buried his head in a book. From the cover art, Tara took it to be *Gateway to Amule*, a famous cookbook everyone seemingly owned, except Tara. Judging by the notes sticking out from between pages, it was Merlon's much used and dearly beloved copy.

A sword clattered on the floorboards. Fabian held up his hands, the grin on his face not quite reflecting in his eyes. Tara frowned. He had remained nervous since they left the

234

cave. Everyone was a bit frayed but she had a feeling it was more than the pirate threat. Something about how his shoulders slumped when he thought nobody was watching.

"Where's your head? I was going as easy as I could." Merlon used the tip of his sword to flick Fabian's into his hand, then handed the cutlass over to the first mate.

Fabian grimaced and shook his head. "I'll do better tomorrow, Cap'n."

"No bother but do better if we run into pirates." Merlon had no annoyance in his voice, then he turned. "Gaunty, you're up. Need to teach you stationary defence if your ankle's still sore."

Tara lent Gaunty a hand and xe stood with a sigh. "It'll be my sword on the deck in two seconds, just you watch me."

"You'll be fine." Tara waved xem off.

Fabian flopped onto the spot Gaunty had vacated. He rubbed his face while grumbling under his breath. "Goin' as easy as he could, gah."

Tara leaned forward and stuck her notebook into her belt at the back of her trousers before drawing her knees halfway to her chest again.

She waited when Fabian glanced her way, avoided meeting her gaze and then *still* didn't spill whatever was clearly on his mind. Giving him another couple of moments to talk, she grew too impatient and poked his arm, right where she knew he had gained a recent bruise.

"Oi!" Fabian winced and flapped a hand at her face. "Ya's a menace."

"Donae be ridiculous, I've nae started menacing you yet." She grinned but to her surprise, Fabian looked away again.

235

She bumped him with her shoulder and waited until he reluctantly met her eyes. "What's up?"

He made a face and picked at the boards they sat on. The breathing wood was too smooth, and all his fingernail's scratching resulted in, was a bit of the lye coming off. Tara cleared her throat in a carefully questioning way.

Fabian sighed but spoke at last. "Me brother's in Fristate. I don't know where of course but this year he's here. I wasn't keen stoppin' extra to pick up Lennie and now we're on the wrong side for gettin' to Dark Galaxy so we'll have to make stops everywhere. It'll be a wonder if we don't bump into him."

"I thought you got along fine with your brother? I know your parents were a bit difficult until you got work on *Lucia,* but they seemed lovely anytime they brought food round." Tara paused, pursing her lips. She tried to recall if there had ever been a point his parents hadn't acted supportive when visiting the house Fabian shared with Karl, Deyon and Merlon.

She knew they had taken Fabian's relationship with Mira relatively well, despite the fact Mira was from the most influential captain's tier and her family did *not* agree with inter-tier relationships. If Cobalt Senior decided to make life hard for Fabian's entire family, he barely had to break out his bribing coin. A word or two from him, and all of the Atare family would be jobless.

"They're fine. They were never difficult but sort of…well they wanted me to stop makin' trouble I suppose and had pretty terrible ways to try and go about that." Fabian continued picking at the planks, keeping his dark eyes firmly away from Tara's gaze.

She didn't prod him again when he fell silent. Turning her head, she watched the sparring. Merlon was indeed disarming Gaunty, but only when xe messed up the no-step defence Merlon had shown xem a moment earlier.

"Me brother used to stand up for me anytime I needed it." Fabian spoke quietly. "Ya didn't meet him 'cause he didn't take to the news 'bout Mira like me parents did. He thinks I'm goin' back to rash and poor decisions. We had a big row right before he left for Fristate."

Tara squeezed Fabian's arm. "I'm sorry...wait, was that the night you came home a drunk, blubbering mess?"

"Ha!" Fabian chortled without mirth. "Yeah, Mira's dad shut the door on me face and then me brother did the same and I thought drinkin' would help. Instead, it reminded me of Edur and then *that* night was ruined."

Tara's throat closed and she had to swallow several times before she could speak. She put an arm around Fabian and gave him a sideways hug. "We all have nights like that. Maybe he'll feel different if you do bump into him here. Why's he working Fristate anyway? He donae have a daughter anymore?"

Horror washed through Tara, but she didn't manage to stop herself before uttering the last sentence. What if the kid had died? Way to make Fabian feel even worse about the fight he'd had with his brother. She pulled her arm free, maybe she should just leave. Everything she said these days resulted in more distress.

Fabian sent her a half-smile. "Still has a daughter yes. He's the third legal guardian. She's got additional needs, quite expensive herbs, and such. Fristate's got better wages 'cause of the pirate plague so they takes turns out here. Not sure how they'd have managed if only a couple but two dads and a mum works."

"Kids are expensive." Tara nodded.

Fabian shrugged. "Mostly for lower tiers. We might get allowed permits and fertility pills for less but all the rest costs the same. *You* don't get to pull the poverty card so get that out of your noggin'." Fabian tapped her head with a knuckle.

Tara stuck her tongue out. He was annoyingly good at guessing what went through her head sometimes.

"So what're you doin'?" Fabian said.

"With what?" Tara didn't like the grin that had returned to his face. It seemed it had helped voicing his concern to such a point he was no longer feeling down. She envied how fast Fabian moved on. He never lingered on his sorrows and hardships.

He nodded at the quarterdeck steps. "With them? Ya's not lettin' them be sold at an orphanage, surely? They'll find good homes that way sure, but they'll never be allowed to go to the same family. Would break Balfour's heart no doubt, gettin' separated from Elin."

Tara's stomach flipped before she had even glanced at the kids on the stairs. Elin's head rested on Balfour's knees. Her hands were cramped around the hideous rag doll while Balfour petted her head tenderly.

Elin and Cary had been a bit rough with the kittens, but Balfour had held his as gingerly as had he thought it a blast bomb about to explode at a wrong touch. He seemed so fragile. She wasn't sure he wouldn't do something more drastic than cutting himself if an orphanage placed him and Elin in separate homes.

"I donae know," Tara whispered. It was her turn to avoid Fabian's gaze.

He leaned back, stretching his legs out and folding his arms behind his head like he was about to go to sleep. "Well, Cap'n is only waitin' for ya agreement, and he'll keep 'em in a heartbeat. If I's got no doubt, I can be a good parent, ya really has nothin' to worry 'bout."

Tara shook her head, words failing her. A sick feeling spread in her gut. They needed so much, and she wasn't sure she could give it.

And she had watched Elin's ma die. Witnessed the entire village being blasted into nothing but mush and body parts. She still hadn't told Elin her ma was dead let alone confirmed what Balfour and Cary already knew, that they had been unwanted by their birth families. Not that they ever needed to know that part.

No, Tara wasn't sure she wouldn't mess up a kid with much less trauma, but she surely would do everything wrong when trying to help these kids. She already *had* messed up a million times over. If she couldn't even do her job and see energy properly, how was she supposed to take care of a whole little person?

Chapter 26

As if she felt Tara's gaze, Elin sat up on the step. Tara looked away, but it was too late.

Elin sprung up with such vigour Balfour jumped in a fright although he didn't stand from what Tara could see out of the corner of her eyes. Bare feet patted across the deck. Elin stopped before Tara, ragdoll pressed under her arm and bouncing on the front of her feet. "Will you braid my hair like my mummy dids?"

Tara swallowed hard. "I'm nae sure I can braid it like your ma does." She glanced at Fabian.

He raised a brow but addressed Elin. "Tara's hands are still healin'. Maybe in a few days, eh? Sit," Fabian patted the boards in front of him. "Ya's gotta make do with me silly braids for now."

Elin hopped over to him, nearly doing a split when she sat. "Are you going'a make two silly braids?"

"Maybe I'll do *three*," Fabian said.

Elin giggled, barely able to sit still while he carefully raked his long fingers through her loose blonde curls and divided her thin hair into three sections.

'Thank you,' Tara gestured when she caught his gaze.

Fabian shrugged and answered with a single hand, 'you do it next.'

Tara concentrated on the button on her shirt sleeve. It hung loose for all the picking she had done, but Merlon would probably sew it back on properly if she asked. She hated all those boring tasks. Cooking, dusting the shelves, mending clothes. She would much rather go practise her rubbish guitar playing a bit more, or draw.

At least she was so good at drawing these days that nobody judged her skills there. Not that Merlon ever came with snarky comments about her lack of effort when it came to the things she had no patience for. Both Sona and Filip had used to drop comments about the tasteless dishes she whipped up in a hurry and Filip had forever been bothered Tara didn't put her hair up "tidier".

Not that Filip had lasted long, but Sona had practically lived at Da's for two years before she went off with what's-her-name and despite all those little things Sona had made Tara hate about herself, she had been heartbroken by the betrayal. It had taken Ma's death before Tara had a good look at how much Sona had nagged at and tried to change her.

Patrice had promised to vet anybody Tara considered dating after that. She had always been much better at judging people's true character than Tara.

They had only had one conversation about Merlon before Patrice was murdered. And that had been Patrice prodding

Tara about her feelings to ensure she was alright with Patrice trying to get in bed with him. Of course, Merlon had said no, and the relief Tara had felt had scared her a fair bit considering how mad she had still been at him at the time.

Merlon had long since explained why he hadn't showed to Ma's hole-drop. She had forgiven him that perceived slight months before he had explained though. With how much he struggled to stay off S-V even now, Tara understood why he hadn't dared go, in case it triggered a relapse less than a year after his near-fatal overdose.

"I can't tell if I'm somehow in trouble." Merlon held out a hand towards her.

Tara blinked, realising she had been staring at him the whole time. Beside her, Fabian was putting the finishing touches on the third braid. It seemed the silly part was that he had added a red leather string to the braids which made it easy to tie at the tips where Elin's hair was frayed and thin.

Tara took Merlon's hand, letting him pull her to her feet. "You're nae. Lost in thought is all." She stretched up, fighting the urge to let herself hide against his warm chest.

He tended towards melancholic seriousness and refused to go dancing with her, but he let her be herself. He wasn't jealous like Sona or raised eyebrows at her clothing choices like Isha. She was pretty sure he hardly even noticed how she put her hair up, unlike Filip.

Merlon asked no questions when she kept hold of his hand, ignoring their usual arrangement to act professional around the rest of the crew. His gaze shifted at the same moment there was a tug at Tara's belt.

"Fab'an says—" Elin's words were broken off when the notebook slipped from the belt and hit the deck with a thud. The pencil hit Tara's boot.

"Oh crap." Fabian blurted, clambering to his feet.

Tara turned, horror washing over her when she saw the pages it had fallen open to. Ramson's blackened face. The eyes shrunken back and his hair charred wisps.

Dizziness washed over Tara as she crouched to snatch the book. Her movements seemed slow. So slow Elin also reached for the book, fingers stroking across the pages. Tara yanked it away, slamming it shut and straightening so abruptly the ship seemed to spin.

"Why is Ramson looking so weird? What is wrong with his eyes?" Elin stared up at her. Tears were already gathering under her lashes, making the blue eyes glimmer.

Balfour appeared beside her. "What did you do? Why are you making her cry?" His tiny voice was full of accusation.

Tara baulked. She bumped into Merlon who caught her shoulders. "Do you want me to explain it?" He muttered under his breath.

She wanted nothing more. If she could, she would run away and hide and never look these poor kids in the eyes while telling them she had watched their ma and aunt die. That she had been there and done nothing.

Fabian held her gaze, he shook his head ever so slightly. He knew she was contemplating various escape plans. Then he looked at Elin and gestured for Tara to speak. He could be ruthless sometimes.

She clutched the notebook to her chest, her knees slowly

giving way until she was level with Elin and Balfour. Her tongue went dry and numb. She cleared her throat, but it didn't shift the lump stuck there.

Merlon gave her shoulder a squeeze.

Tara drew in an unsteady breath and met Elin's shimmering eyes. "Y-you know how I went to the village to find your ma—your mummy?"

Elin hugged her ragdoll tighter. Balfour's fingers whitened. His grip around Elin's arm began shaking.

"I did…find her." Tara continued before she lost the ability to speak. "She was so happy to hear you were alive. But then there were blasts dropping from the sky. Everyone was running out the gates, but your mummy remembered your doll and I promised to get it. So, I ran back to your house…I'm sorry Elin, but your ma and brother, little Ramson, they died with the bombs. I wasnae fast enough. I couldnae…" Her throat closed. Tears streamed down her cheeks. "They've gone to live beyond the eternal starlight."

Elin blinked at her, uncomprehending.

"What about my mummy and daddy?" Balfour asked quietly. He didn't look shocked. Tara suspected he had long since guessed, or perhaps Cary had and told Balfour of his suspicions.

Tara swallowed hard. "I'm sorry, Balfour, they'd left. I think they're alive but…I donae know where they are."

"They wanted to go home to Earth Seven." He nodded not a hint of surprise or sorrow on his face. "They said it was my fault they couldn't. They sent me to the island so they could go home. It was all my fault." His voice broke on the last word. The single sob that raked through him sent a jolt through Elin.

"Balfour that's nae—" Tara didn't get further before Elin threw herself into Tara's chest. Stumbling, only Merlon's hand on her shoulder kept Tara from falling on her arse. Elin hollered into her shirt, clinging on as if her life depended on it.

Tara hesitated, her own tears had dried up, instead a deep pain inside her chest grew. Unsure what else to do, she gingerly put her arms around Elin's trembling body. Elin howled even louder, fingernails boring into Tara's arms. And Balfour stood there, blinking rapidly, and wiping his nose time and again, putting on a brave face that made Tara feel even more sick for their grief.

Merlon knelt, knees popping. He put a large hand on Balfour's trembling shoulder. "It's not your fault. None of it would ever be your fault but it's alright to be sad. It's alright to cry."

Balfour shook his head, sniffling and barely breathing.

"Everyone cries sometimes." Merlon spoke calmly, he produced a handkerchief and offered it to Balfour. The boy shook his head again.

Merlon continued. "When my mum died, I was very sad and cried a lot. I still do when I think of her and miss her sometimes."

Balfour took the handkerchief, clenching it in a trembling hand. "You cry too?"

Tara nodded when Merlon did. Somehow, she found her voice enough to reply. "We all get sad and then crying helps."

Elin's sobs grew in intensity, and Tara found herself rocking the child.

"I'm evil. I dun't want to go home." Balfour dug his fingers into the scabbing wounds on his lower arms.

Merlon jerked forward, seizing Balfour's hands. "Don't! You're not evil. Balfour, look at me, hey, there you are. You're *good*. You helped set the course earlier, right? And you're a good brother to Elin."

"Cousin." Balfour sobbed. "Auntie Bethy said I need take care of her when we're playing outside, and I tried but they took us. And Auntie didn't hear me screaming. It's my fault they put her on the island and-and…"

Elin writhed free from Tara, slamming her little body into Balfour's, and hugging him tightly. "Dun't cry. You dun't do anything bad. I-I-I said I saw colours when you said I shouldn't. Dun't cry."

Merlon nudged Tara. "Maybe a nap will help. They didn't sleep much more than me."

She nodded, wincing with stiffness as she stood. Only then did she discover Fabian had sat down on a couple of steps below Cary, chatting to the kid who was still staring at his book but barked a response every now and then. Nausea welled at the realisation she had forgotten about Cary for a bit. Elin and Balfour's reaction had overwhelmed her to a point she felt like she too needed a nap.

"Come on." Merlon reached out and patted Balfour's shoulder again. "Let's go look at the kittens and if you want to talk, we can talk but if you want to just sit in the bunk for a bit, that's fine too."

Elin turned and climbed into Merlon's arms without a question. Balfour hesitated, not moving when Merlon stood, lifting Elin off the deck.

Tara feared her voice might break but held out her hand. To her surprise, Balfour took it after only a second's pause.

"Will you leave us somewhere so you can go home too?" He asked while they walked through the dim passage towards the cabin.

Tara stared down at him. Her heart thundered in her chest. What could she possibly answer that wouldn't turn out a lie in his eyes? "We willnae abandon you on an island. We'll never do that."

Balfour twisted his hand from her grip. "It's okay. You can say if you dun't like us, but Elin needs a new mummy now Auntie Bethy is dead."

Tara had no words. How could she make any promises when she wasn't even sure she was cut out to be a mum? She managed to croak out a weak reply, "We do like you, Balfour." But he strode into the chamber without hearing her words.

Chapter 27

"Outpost 9," Merlon said, handing Tara his spyglass. "I normally avoid this side of Fristate. It's expensive and full of pirates bribing the archons and other officials to look the other way while they moor and replenish their stores."

Tara looked through the lens. The outpost had the typical flat bottom, slopes slowly slanting up from the sickle-shaped harbour. Only a dozen rows of houses dotted the front towards the harbour, the rest seemed to be mainly fields of crops. "They've got more fields than Amule." She handed back the spyglass.

Merlon nodded. "They produce most of the grains for Intrapolis. And this is where everyone stops for a spell before turning whichever way they're travelling. Intrapolis' mooring prices are extortionate."

"So basically everything in Fristate is expensive and full of pirates?" Tara raised a brow. In Twin Cities, everyone spoke of Fristate Galaxy like it was a much better alternative to start a family. Intrapolis was supposedly around fourteen thousand people strong now, not far behind each of the Twin cities of Amule and Trachna.

Merlon crooked a smile. "There's a reason I never moved here. It would've been easier with my trade in Jeweller City, but we'd have to fly more months of the year to make up for the housing and mooring costs."

"There's boats flying!" Elin exclaimed.

Tara looked across the deck. She was on Kieran's arm although he was supposed to be furling the topmast sheets in preparation for entering the outpost. Balfour was hovering around the blond sailor, watching him like he thought Kieran would toss Elin overboard.

While Elin had bounced back and only asked twice for her mummy when they woke up, Balfour had withdrawn into a shell Tara had no idea how to get him back out of.

Cary seemed unchanged. He currently sat near the bowsprit. The slight rolling of *Lucia* having left him looking rather nauseated. He hadn't kept his breakfast down and even from where she stood at the helm, Tara could tell he wasn't reading the book he thumbed through slowly.

The kid had read almost everything aboard already, preferring the books' company to that of any crew, although Tara had heard him whisper to the cat and kittens sometime in the night.

"Kieran," Merlon called, "put Elin down and get into the shrouds. We're mooring in fifteen minutes."

Elin slipped to the deck and sprinted towards them. Curls bobbing. "Does you see the flying boats?" Excitement glowed on her face.

"I do, yes. *Lucia* is a flying ship too you know." Merlon smiled. He patted her head, resting his hand on her shoulder as he leaned down while pointing out through the railing since Elin couldn't quite look over the top. "You see that flicker of grey? That's where we're going. You'll be able to see the town soon."

Balfour halted a few paces from Merlon, he ignored Tara when she tried to wave him closer. His coldness left a sickening pain in her gut. She had tried to avoid making promises she might not be able to keep, but Balfour seemed to have decided this meant he was better off keeping himself distanced. The fact an eight-year-old could even do it so successfully spoke to the gruesomeness of life he had before.

Merlon guided Elin to look through the spyglass, but she kept closing either none or both her eyes, so Tara doubted she saw anything at all. Even if she could see through it, Elin kept tilting herself sideways, so the railing's balusters got in her way.

After a moment, Elin turned, shoving the spyglass at Balfour. "Look, look!"

Balfour reluctantly took the lens. Probably he only grabbed it because Elin had been about to drop it and he kept it from falling onto the deck. He gave Merlon a sceptical glance when he received instructions but then finally put the gilded lens to his right eye.

Merlon pushed the end of the spyglass, adjusting the direction. "A bit down, about…there. You see the—"

"It's a flying village!" Balfour gasped. He lowered the tool, blinking from the horizon to Merlon and back. He rested the cylinder on top of the rail, standing on his toes to be able to peer through the end of the brass tool.

Once more Merlon shifted the lens a tiny bit for him. "Yes, it floats in space. It's Outpost 9. Where we're going. You can see it with your bare eyes in about thirty seconds I reckon."

Balfour nodded, mouth open as he peeked through.

Tara felt displaced. She had nothing to add or help with. Merlon was a natural with the kids while she constantly fought to figure out how she was supposed to interact with them. Not that she was sure she ought to. Most likely, they would be taken into foster care the moment *Lucia* returned to Amule, or lay to in Intrapolis if that became their plan. Wouldn't it leave them feeling abandoned once again to be dumped in the nearest orphanage, destined to be separated to satisfy more than one wealthy family?

Turning, she decided to busy herself, helping with the preparations for arriving in the over-proportioned harbour of the small outpost. She cursed herself for not having bandaged her hands earlier, any halyard work would leave her wounds open and raw once more. Ignoring that knowledge, she headed for the nearest line that needed shifting to accommodate the smaller sails slowly being folded away.

"Tara, you're still not to work," Merlon said.

She winced, so much for trying to make herself useful. Finishing the knot around a cleat, she abandoned the ropes again. "I've got to do *something*." She hated feeling useless.

Merlon nodded. "The kids need name bracelets. We don't have any official papers for them, so I asked Karl to have a go at stamping their names and *Lucia's* registration number onto some leather straps. They need to go down to see him

251

for sizing. Once we catch up with Lennie, I'm sure he has a contact that can help creating papers."

"What are the papers for? They're nae ours." Tara frowned, glancing at Elin and Balfour who were taking turns peering through the spyglass.

Merlon didn't meet her gaze but stared at them when he replied, "No…" He drew out the syllable and for a second Tara thought he was about to say they should be, then he blew out a breath.

"We're in a pirate filled galaxy and they neither look like us nor have our accents. The odds of someone thinking they've been kidnapped for slavery, especially with how skinny they are." He shrugged. "Until we know what's best for them, I'd rather they stay with us and not be removed by overzealous law enforcers."

She couldn't decide if she was impressed or worried about how much thought he had put into this. She had the distinct feeling he would never forgive her if she said they should give these kids up to someone better suited to care for them. Of course, it wasn't Merlon who wasn't qualified…

"Fabian said there will be a bookstore." Cary's voice made Tara jump as much as it did Merlon. How had he crossed half the ship without her noticing? He was eerily good at moving quietly around. "I want more books or I'm telling everyone we *are* kidnapped."

Tara's throat closed up. "Why'd you do that?"

"There's no need. You'll all three get to buy new clothes and you'll get a small allowance to spend on whatever you'd like." Merlon sounded calm, but Tara saw the twitch at the corner of his mouth. "We'll find a way to return you to Quarantine Thirteen if that's what you want."

Cary huffed, he looked annoyed for a moment but then the ship rolled, and he hid his mouth behind his hand. For a few seconds Tara thought he would throw up, but he fought it back.

"Cary was never allowed to read back home because he stole books from the community hall," Balfour said. He held out the spyglass to Merlon. "We can see the town without this."

Merlon blinked, head whipping around. "Burn it! Tara, get them to Karl, please. I've got to oversee this." He spun on his heels, shouting commands as he trotted up to the helm where Jara called extra orders from.

Tara tore her gaze from Merlon and looked to the kids standing before her. Elin smiled expectantly but Cary and Balfour looked like they considered how to coerce her or run away respectively. She cleared her throat and attempted to smile. "So, let's go below and find Karl. He's made name bracelets for you."

"Why? I know my name." Balfour's brows furrowed.

"It's uh...let's get below first," Tara said and gestured for them to climb through the loading hatch in the main deck while gathering her thoughts. "It's in case you get lost. So, people know you belong on *Lucia*."

Balfour froze, halfway down the ladder. Cary helped Elin off the bottom steps, but Balfour remained stationary, staring up at Tara with a desperate longing. "I belong here? Mummy said I belong nowhere." His voice broke but he kept on. "She said the rebels is my fault. If I didn't spread diseases, they could go home. Mummy and daddy I mean."

Tara could only shake her head while trying to find her voice. Searching for the words that would ease the pain in his gaze. Why was she struggling to speak with the kids? She had never had trouble talking. If anything, she had been teased in school that she spoke too much and that had only resulted in her screaming louder.

It wasn't till Balfour moved off the ladder and Tara climbed down into the dimness of the hold she had formulated something tolerable for a response. "Everyone belongs somewhere. You're helping Captain Merlon. That's a very important job and that makes you belong here, right now at least." She could have swallowed her tongue at the final words, but Balfour didn't seem to have heard.

His face shone with genuine pride like she hadn't thought the traumatised kid capable of feeling yet. The grin splitting his face gave her courage to continue. "You donae spread diseases either. You seen anybody get ill onboard here yet?"

"Me." Cary all but gagged.

Elin reached up, touching his forehead with her little hand. "You's boat sick. Fab'an says earlier. And you says long ago you's boat sick when going to the island too."

Cary peeled her sticky fingers off his face with a grimace. "It's you *are*, and this ship is making me much worse sick than sailing to the island ever did."

"Right, being down here willnae help you feel better. Quick now, get to the forecastle and Karl can sort your bracelets so you can get back up in the cooler air." Tara herded them towards the front of the ship, through the door into the ever-smelly forecastle.

Karl had the three leather straps ready. He had impressed their names along the quarter-inch broad piece of supple leather and had already inserted a metal rivet on one end. Cary had his adjusted first, Karl punching a hole so it wouldn't be too tight but also wouldn't fall off easily, then the leftover end was cut down to only be one inch long. The moment it was on, Cary fled up the ladder to the deck, looking more than a little ill.

Balfour was next.

"It looks like you've been making more—"

Tara shook her head, pausing Karl before he made Balfour cringe even further. The kid withdrew his arm, fingers closing over the dozens of barely healed cuts. She had no idea what he had found in the chamber to make three new, blood-crusted wounds across his wrist with. Between her and Merlon they had removed everything that had even the slightest hint of sharpness to it first thing that morning.

Tara scrambled to smooth things over. "We're matching. I'm healing up now and so are you, right Balfour?" She smiled, turning over her arm and pulling her sleeves up more so her cuts from the fence wires were visible. Unlike Balfour's new cuts, hers were beginning to look halfway healed which was a relief.

Balfour stared at her arm like he hadn't ever noticed the scabs covering it. But then he nodded and reluctantly offered up his wrist again.

Karl measured the size, once again leaving a bit over an inch of leather past where he punched a hole for the rivet.

While Elin had hers fitted, Balfour ran a fingertip over the engravings. "What does IT501 mean?"

"Intergalactic Traveller 501. That's *Lucia's* registration name. If you get lost, you can tell people and the harbour officers will be able to bring you back onboard. Everyone will know where you belong." Tara breathed a little freer. The hostility had left Balfour's demeanour and it made it easier to speak with him without her mind screaming to abort and run every second.

Elin stroked her bracelet, now fastened around her left wrist. "I wish mummy has one. Then she dun't get lost so I can't see her again."

"She's dea—"

Tara seized Balfour's shoulder before he could finish. She knelt before Elin. "I wish she had too."

Elin sniffled and threw her arms around Tara's neck.

Tara could do nothing but hold Elin tightly when the child began sobbing. The loss of her own ma suddenly felt like a very short time ago and Tara bowed her head, shutting her eyes against the dull agony in her chest. "You'll see her again one day, Elin. Her and Ramson are waiting beyond the eternal stars with mine and Merlon's ma's. I promise you'll see them when it's your turn to go there."

She couldn't tell whether Elin heard or not. Balfour blinked, eyes shimmering. Tara grabbed his hand and held it while Elin cried and somehow, it felt like she was finally doing the right thing.

Chapter 28

Lucia groaned and rocked in a familiar way. They were laying to, putting the huge hawser ropes around the bollards on a jetty.

Tara eased her grip around Elin, her knees screamed for her to get up. The scrapes she had gained hitting the boulder when they took off from Cave Fourteen were swollen and sore today.

Karl had busied himself putting the leather scraps, and tools away. He was alright with the kids when all they needed was light entertainment but worse than Tara if they were anything other than mostly preoccupied by the kittens. Of course, he had never wanted kids, so it was less at odds with his life goals.

Tara had two false starts before she managed to speak beyond a hoarse whisper. "Do you want to go see what the town's like? We'll buy you some clothes and shoes. Maybe we'll go to an inn for a nice meal afterwards." She hoped she wasn't overpromising herself. Some outposts they had stopped at between Fristate and Twin Cities had barely had a store to their name, but some sort of meal should be obtainable.

"I'm hungry," Balfour said. It wasn't half an hour since they had been chewing on dry oatcakes but Yorik still didn't permit them full meals so Tara could understand why they would already be peckish again.

Using a beam-supporting post to pull herself to her feet, Tara eased from Elin's arms. She offered the girl a hand, which she took. "Come on then."

Balfour shook his head. "I'm *hungry*."

"We'll go get food soon. They might have chicken if we're lucky." Tara winced inwardly at her own words. Meat would be prohibitively expensive on an outpost like this. Still, if pig wasn't too extortionate, pork rinds would be on the menu more so than the cheaper poultry. Yorik had mentioned the kids' needed fats and meat alongside the grains, potatoes and yams that was all *Lucia* had in her hold right now. Hopefully Kieran would bulk up the food and water stores during this stay.

Balfour began trembling, his eyes unfocused. "You're going to leave us. Starve us. Just like Daddy did."

Tara lost her breath. His words like a punch in her gut. His own *Da* had left them on that island? She had thought he misspoke last he mentioned it, but she was beginning to realise his parents truly had been as cruel as he, without resentment, told her. No wonder he was so messed up.

Elin whimpered and Tara realised she held her hand too tightly. She carefully loosened her grip although Elin wouldn't let go entirely.

258

Tara shook her head. "We willnae leave you to starve. We'll go buy food first thing."

Balfour burst out sobbing. "I dun't wanna die of hungriness."

"Shh, easy. You willnae. Balfour…" Tara freed herself from Elin and tried putting her hand on Balfour's shoulder, but he slumped on the floor with a thump, rocking and hollering. She scanned the forecastle, but Karl had gone into the main hold and there was nobody else who could help her. Panic rose in her chest. What could she do to make him understand? To calm him back down so he could breathe instead of the shallow gulps that would leave him dizzy.

"Do you want the rest of my cracker?" Elin offered up a single bite-sized crumb of oatcake which Tara had no idea where she had kept.

Balfour's breath hitched and he blinked. Then he took a deeper breath and shook his head. "You should eat it, Elin, you need it more than me."

Even though his gaze remained slightly unfocused, hands trembling, legs pulled to his chest, he still put her before himself. His sacrifice hurt something deep inside Tara. She patted herself down but had nothing to offer. Mentally, she made a note to carry snacks in future to avoid this.

Bailey hopped through the doorway at the same moment. She sat up on her haunches, whiskers quivering. "We're ready to disembark."

"Balfour needs something to eat first." Tara stepped over the rat and pushed the door to the hold up.

Bailey skittered through. "Tish-tosh he can eat in town." She bounded across the floor, heading for the ladders up to

259

the main deck. "Come on quick! I want to see which of you first discover the friends I sent for. I'm surprised Fabian didn't yet…" The last sentence was a mutter and then Bailey had vanished again.

Tara ignored the rat, stalking straight to the galley near the stern and captain's cabin. After a short rummage she found three oatcakes. Elin was petting Balfour's frizzy hair when Tara returned to the forecastle.

He snatched and devoured his oatcake so fast Tara barely managed to open her mouth to ask him to slow down before it had gone. Elin nibbled slower on hers while Tara kept the last one for Cary should he be less nauseous once they stepped onto solid land.

"Do you feel better?" Tara knelt despite her protesting joints. "We'll go find an inn soon as well."

Balfour licked his fingers clean, eyed the oatcake in Tara's hand then nodded slowly. "I dun't like when I can't breathe."

Tara raked her mind for a good response, remembering how Merlon had dealt with it when Balfour was trying not to cry. "Nobody does. I also sometimes get so scared I cannae breathe. Mostly if I'm somewhere dark and damp. But if you're ready, we'll lay topside. I'm sure there's going to be so many things you've never seen before you'll forget that you were scared at all."

Nodding, Balfour unfolded himself. He didn't take her hand when she offered to help him stand, but he did take Elin's and led her to the forecastle ladders.

Tara followed them up, scanning the harbour they had moored in once she stood on the main deck. The flat plot of land stretched beyond the wooden jetties that hung into space so the ships could pull close without damaging their keels.

Sailors shouted. Barrels and carts rolled. It was busy and had to be day. With the light a constant grey, it was impossible to tell the exact time with Merlon's timepiece in the cabin still set to Twin Cities's hours. She knew he would adjust it once they had double checked in town what the time was here.

The harbour was expansive. Much bigger than warranted by the meagre town although that matched what Merlon had explained. This was a place ships took extended breaks between bringing goods to and from cities like Intrapolis and Amule, both of which had high mooring prices for foreign ships.

Most of the larger ships lay to on the left side of the harbour while the smallest clippers were at the centre and nearest the open streets. Opposite where *Lucia* lay, schooners and other mid-sized merchant ships hung by the long jetties.

"Fabian's sorting the paperwork, then we can disembark." Merlon paused beside Tara and the kids. "What's with you two looking so sombre?" He smiled down at Elin and Balfour.

Tara nudged Merlon's arm and signed when he glanced her way. 'He scared. Hungry. Gave one.' She held up the last oatcake. She couldn't see Cary, but he might have hidden himself in the chamber again, so she stuffed the cake into a pocket.

"I see." Merlon nodded.

"Hey, kiddos," Kieran called and waved a hand. "Ye want to help me tie this up?"

261

Elin yanked Balfour along, a grin splitting her face. Tara caught herself staring wistfully at Kieran. *He* had it covered when it came to kids. It was too bad him and Hakim would probably have to wait years and years before it was their turn on the adoption lists. They would make amazing parents one day.

Tara frowned. Maybe *they* could adopt the kids. She wasn't sure they had enough savings though. Adopting one child cost a pretty penny, three was most likely far above anything common sailors would ever manage.

Tara suspected her and Merlon could at most afford two depending on how much Merlon had left from fixing up *Lucia* – and if she would make up her mind already. With their income nearly four times higher than sailors' it had to be near impossible for Kieran and Hakim's to be approved for multiple kids.

Bailey climbed onto the railing and faced them. Her ears were flat along her head. "You're all boring! Aren't you excited to see who I sent for?"

"Not really no," Merlon said. His lips twitched when Bailey's fur stood out to all sides. He was winding her up on purpose.

Tara narrowed her eyes. Over by the schooners she spotted a ship with yellow sides and black masts that stood out amongst the more grey, purple, and otherwise drab fashion of Fristate ship colours. "Why does that ship look like *The Bounty*?"

Bailey began chittering, a sound Tara had long since learnt was her hysterical laugh. That could mean but one thing.

Tara stared at the rat. "You made Mira come *here*?"

"Tomaline preserve her!" Merlon gestured a star in front of himself. "Fristate is about the most dangerous galaxy on the Edge, and you convinced her to fly here within her first year of owning a ship? Here I thought you had become vaguely responsible at last."

Tara rubbed her temple, grimacing when she brushed against the sore cut over her ear. "Ola's still with her? I'm guessing you didnae tell him about the pirate nuisance."

Bailey lifted her front leg, scratching her side vigorously with her hind leg while she spoke. "No need. Long as no pirates attack, they'll be fine. Come let's go see who else they have with them. Kieran will want to come too."

"Kieran?" Tara exchanged a glance with Merlon. What was that about? While Kieran got on well with Mira and Ola, he wasn't exactly close with either.

But the rat only sniggered and leapt onto Merlon's shoulder. "Off we go then." There was no point trying to press her. Bailey loved playing games and pulling surprises. Tara didn't know if that was a Tracker thing or a Bailey thing although she suspected it was the latter. The short encounters with other Trackers, mostly Bailey's da, had been serious to a point of being terrifying.

"They're probably not onboard, it's dinner time," Merlon said.

Bailey sniffed offendedly. "I told her to wait. They would have arrived not six hours ago if my calculations are correct."

Merlon sighed and Tara followed him towards where Kieran had Elin and Balfour help roll up a line, or rather, they held the end while he rolled it up. Pride shone from their faces and Tara found herself smiling at the sight.

It was a simple gesture, but she filed it away for later. They basically needed to *believe* they were helpful. It reminded Tara of the teenagers she had tutored over the years. A handful of them could have done with an earlier introduction to how a ship worked.

Mira for example hadn't been aboard a ship since aged four and hadn't known where to start rolling up a line correctly. Even if the kids weren't able to do much now, they would pick up things along the way by seeing it done and it would boost their confidence too.

Fabian returned at the same moment they paused by Kieran, a wad of documents in one hand. "Bloody Fristate officials want me wastin' me life signing documents. Ya keep track of 'em, Cap'n." He slammed the sheets against Merlon's chest.

"Later," Merlon said, not even moving to grab the papers. "Run leave them on my desk and return in a jiffy. There's someone we're going to meet. Bring Cary up too so we can shop clothes and shoes."

Fabian frowned but when Tara nodded, he legged it to the cabin.

While they waited, Merlon ordered the crew not to stray alone but allowed them a full day off. Deyon and Karl were tasked with staying aboard for security. The latter whinged but only until Deyon sent him a raised eyebrow. It wasn't like Karl could go dancing with his leg in a splint.

A minute later, Fabian returned. Cary dragged his legs behind the first mate. He didn't have a book with him and Tara suspected Fabian had made him leave whichever volume of Merlon's five book set of merchant ship laws Cary was currently on.

Finally, Merlon strode across the gangway, pausing halfway across to the jetty. "Kieran, you're coming too according to the rat." He jutted a thumb at the bulge of his shirt pocket where Bailey had vanished.

She would have to remain unseen in the town.

Tara hadn't quite understood why Trackers kept themselves hidden away, but General Rum, Bailey's da, had promised a swift death if *Lucia's* crew revealed the true identity of the Trackers to the general public.

Oddly, Rum hadn't thought twice about revealing himself to Da nor to Yorik and Jara on the day they left Amule. It seemed his high rank meant he was allowed to introduce himself to new people, but Bailey was exceedingly careful she didn't get seen.

"I gone and done some wrong?" Kieran frowned.

Fabian knelt, letting Elin climb unto his back. "Ya's always done somethin' wrong. Can't ever live up to the old boatswain, eh?" Fabian thumped his own chest with a fist.

"I'd worry he'll replace *you*, turd." Tara shoved Fabian lightly and he flicked a little finger at her.

Kieran hissed, "Don't do that when the kids are looking, ye dolt!"

"Why?" Balfour looked seriously at them.

"It's rude so donae do it at people." Tara shrugged, Haven Galaxians were always so sensitive. No Trachnan would shy from rude words nor gestures. She turned her focus to the kids. "Come on, we're going to meet some friends and then go for dinner if you can eat more?"

Balfour bobbed his head. "I'm still hungry."

"Always hungry," Cary muttered. Tara handed him the last oatcake. It was gone in half a second. Him and Balfour seemed to inhale their food.

"Run, run!" Elin kicked her legs at Fabian, and he squealed like a pig, trotting across the gangway and onto the jetty where Merlon waited.

Tara offered Balfour her hand at the same moment Kieran did. Kieran muttered an excuse, but Balfour stared long and hard before finally taking Tara's and letting her guide him onto land.

Even when they walked safely on the harbourfront's main road, he didn't let go, his fingers clamped around hers as if he thought she would turn and run away.

Chapter 29

S talls lined the street front between the open harbour and the dozen or so rows of houses rising behind it. Most merchants were in the process of packing up, and Tara decided it had to be the end of the day. Fabian headed to the nearest stands, nonetheless, still carrying Elin on his back.

Balfour's eyes were glued to every booth with food and Tara only needed to catch Merlon's eyes for a second before he nodded, and they veered to the left to follow Fabian's route closer to the market.

"You can each have one thing," Merlon said. They paused in front of a food stand that hadn't yet closed for the night. Soft quinoa-sprinkled buns lay at the front, sausages, most likely of a mixed meat and lentil sort judging by the green tint, hung to the right. Small bags of various grains filled the back while traditional chilli pockets – fried lentil and chilli filled pastries – paraded along the left of the slanted table.

"Only one thing?" Cary stared intensely at the stall.

Merlon nodded. "One to eat now, we'll get a couple other things if you want for later, but remember we're going to an inn for dinner soon."

"I want that one." Balfour pointed at the largest quinoa bun on the entire table.

The stall holder, a squat beefy-armed man smiled. His teeth were blackened and one of the front ones had gone missing, his skin a much lighter brown than most of the sailor's milling around. He clearly spent all his days in the dimmest areas of Fristate, never getting exposed to the stronger, deadlier, starlight of neighbouring galaxies.

Cary picked a sausage which was cut straight from the dangling garlands. The vendor took Merlon's copper coins, grinning even wider when Merlon asked for a dozen chilli pockets to be wrapped up in waxed cloth.

"What 'bout your, littlest one'eh?" The Fristate accent was thick when the man smiled at Elin, still perched on Fabian's back.

Elin shook her head. "I want that one." She pointed at the next shop which, oddly, was a healer's equipment's store. The person running the booth was occupied with a customer at the opposite side of the table and didn't appear to notice.

"That's bandages, not food." Fabian frowned over his shoulder.

She nodded solemnly. "Balfour needs more for his arms."

Beside Tara, Balfour winced. He sidestepped, hiding behind her and Merlon, although he barely paused devouring the bun.

The man who had already served them smiled overbearingly, clasping his hands in front of his chest. "Rescued from'eh pirates A take it?"

Tara's mouth went dry. Stolen from their village, from their planet, from their *universe* more like it. She couldn't get a word over her lips, but Merlon saved her.

"Yes, it was quite the ordeal. We're just glad they're safe now." Merlon squeezed Cary's shoulder. "Let's have another quinoa bun and Elin can eat that when she's hungry." Merlon flicked another copper at the stall holder and received a wrapped bun which he, like the lentil parcels, handed straight to Kieran.

Elin twisted her neck when Fabian turned back to face them. "But I want that for Balfour!"

"We have plenty of bandages onboard." Merlon shook his head. "Kieran will buy more as well when he's restocking our supplies tomorrow."

Elin jutted her bottom lip out and for a moment, Tara thought she would start screaming. When she didn't, Tara breathed a sigh of relief. While the food seller had believed the lie, she wasn't sure everyone would.

"Are we goin' for that meal now? I could eat a goat." Fabian slowed and Elin wriggled until he let her slip down to the ground.

The harbourfront was busy, but not to such a point Tara worried the kids would get lost instantly in the crowds. Still, she waved Cary and Balfour in front of them, the latter taking Elin's hand as he finished off the bun which he, by all common sense, shouldn't have been able to eat so fast.

"Stay close, please," Tara said.

Cary didn't react, but Balfour glanced back, holding onto Elin when she tried sprinting off between the buildings.

"Cap'n?" Fabian raised a brow. "Dinner now, yeah?"

Merlon smiled. "We have somewhere to be first."

"Somewhere to be?" Fabian looked at Tara, but she shrugged, fighting to keep the grin off her face. Fabian hadn't noticed Mira's ship moored in the harbour.

He would be jittery with excitement when he did and Tara couldn't wait to see his face when he realised. The opportunity was too good to pass up.

While Tara was looking forward to giving Mira – and Ola – a hug, she would wait if it resulted in a bigger surprise for Fabian. She nudged Merlon, grabbing his hand to draw him nearer as they strolled on. She leaned close and whispered, "What d'you say we make a proper surprise of it?"

Merlon glanced at her through the corners of his eyes. A twinkle of humour lit in his gaze. He gave her hand a gentle squeeze and turned his head back to Fabian, currently walking backwards and watching them through narrowed eyes.

"Ya's up to somethin', I can tell."

Tara snorted. "Oh really? How'd you know I didnae tell him what he's got in store next time we're alone?"

Fabian opened his mouth to reply, but since he was walking backwards, he didn't see a sailor carrying a sack of flour. He stumbled into the woman and received a shouting like no other.

Merlon let go of Tara to haul Fabian along, growling at the first mate. "Quit making trouble. This place is full of pirates. There's a reason we never moor here, and I'd rather not end up thrown over a jetty."

Fabian ducked his head. "Didn't mean no harm, Cap'n."

"Take the kids, you and Kieran go get seats at that inn over there, looks less crowded." Merlon pointed. He was good at pretending to be annoyed with Fabian.

Fabian followed the indication, frown deepening on his forehead. "But wasn't we gonna go somewhere? And I reckon it's quiet 'cause food's barely fit for fowl."

"*You're* too much trouble to go anywhere important, obviously." Tara flicked Fabian's ear.

His hand shot up and he carried on like she had boxed him. "Hey!"

"Kieran," Merlon called, and the blond sailor turned back, pausing Balfour and Elin with a tap on the former's shoulder. Merlon continued. "They can share a meal. Monitor none of them eat too much or too fast. Yorik reckons they need another week or two to adjust, especially if it's fatty and rich food."

Kieran nodded. "Sure thing, Capten."

Fabian held out a hand, but Merlon only stared at it. "You're paying, Fabian, for all of us. Maybe that'll stop you cultivating trouble."

"Hardly," Tara said, grinning.

"Cap'n!" Fabian moaned, but he moved his hand to Balfour. "Alright, kiddos, the retirees are grumpy so let's go find food."

Tara huffed, "Retirees! I only turned twenty-nine last month."

"Exactly, ya's ancient." Fabian winked over his shoulder, probably dying to skip along to annoy her even more, but couldn't since Elin had taken his hand.

271

Merlon sighed. "Keep an eye on him, Kieran. Something tells me he's only going to get more annoying when he finds out the surprise."

"There's a surprise, Capten?" Kieran blinked.

Tara took Merlon's hand again. "You'll see soon enough."

Kieran took the cue and trotted after Fabian and the kids. Bailey muttered from the breast pocket at the same moment, "I can't believe you're ruining the surprise. They're meant to be there, you know."

"We'll take Mira and Ola for dinner. All the better of a surprise," Merlon said.

Tara nodded. "I cannae wait to see Fabian's face. And I get to hug her first. That'll drive him mad."

"Why do we need Kieran too though?" Merlon glanced down at the pocket Bailey hid in.

"Let's see if you can guess it."

Tara fought to think who or what it could be.

Kieran had no siblings, adopted or otherwise. His parents were still in Haven Galaxy, but he didn't get on with them, they had wanted him to stay in their home galaxy, not move to Amule and especially not to work on a ship that travelled much further afield.

He did have a family friend turned aunt in Trachna. Tara hadn't met her but was pretty sure she would be in the same circles as Tara's step-grandpa. Not that Tara had much of any contact with him.

But why would that aunt be here? It seemed rather far-fetched even though Mira had been bringing goods between Amule and Trachna for the past eight months. Or less, Tara corrected herself mentally. It had to have taken a few months for Mira to reach Fristate.

"I donae know," Tara said eventually.

Merlon turned down the jetty *The Bounty* lay moored by. "Me neither. My best guess is that bonus aunt I can't ever remember the name off, but I'd be surprised if either you or Mira even know about her."

"Tish-tosh, no fake aunts," Bailey said.

Tara poked the rat through Merlon's shirt pocket. "You seriously need to stop degrading us. Chosen extra family is the best." Her heart squeezed tightly for a second. Adrien had been her most beloved uncle. He had meant more to her than the grandparents she only saw for two weeks every few years. She hadn't even been to the hole-drop of her last grandma since Ma had died the month before.

Merlon slipped an arm around her waist and held her close, slowing their pace. She bit back the pain of their loss. Merlon knew exactly where her mind had gone, and he missed Adrien even more than she did. She allowed herself to lean her head against his for a moment.

Bailey chittered wordlessly for ten seconds then finally spoke again. "Who did Kieran register partnership with before *Lucia* left Amule?"

Merlon stopped in his tracks. "Hakim? Stars, how did Hakim end up on *The Bounty*?"

"Not my doing. He was in Trachna but wasn't satisfied with the captain he sailed under. Ship got sold to a prickly geezer or something and the crew walked out. Mira bumped into him while she was assembling her own crew after firing the ones her dad had given her. Easy hire."

Merlon nodded and resumed walking. "That happens a lot. A ship changes hands but the crew don't get along with the new management style. Kieran's going to shine like a star when he sees Hakim."

Tara's stomach did a flip, and she tightened her grip on Merlon. Words escaped her before she could revise them. "If I didnae expect to see you for nearly a year I'd be shining too."

Merlon stopped, taking her face in his hands, and searching her gaze. "I love you too, Tara." He let go, intertwined his fingers with hers and kept walking towards Mira's merchant schooner.

Tara's entire body burned, starting from the places he had touched her and where his hand still rested in hers. She had no idea how she could give him up if she decided she wasn't fit to have a child.

A small voice at the back of her head was nearly drowned out by the worries shouting from all sides, but she heard it, nonetheless. *You've not messed up so badly the kids hate you yet, maybe that's a sign.*

Chapter 30

Tara paused when they reached the bowsprit of *The Bounty*. Her fingers still tangled with Merlon's, she caused him to falter too.

Nobody was on deck. Tara tried to focus her sight, hoping she could pick up the faint pulse of heartbeats and warm bodies inside the hold of the ship.

Nothing.

He glanced back at her. "You alright?" The hint of a frown built between his brows. "If there's anything—"

"I'm fine." Tara managed a smile. She had hoped her navigator's vision would have returned by now. Why did it keep being so elusive? "Come on, they must be below deck."

Merlon watched her face when she stepped around him, pulling at his hand to make him walk again and stop watching her like he was piecing together she had an issue. She knew she ought to tell him – he wouldn't laugh – yet the words never wanted to leave her tongue.

Whether he was guessing what was wrong or not, Merlon didn't comment. Rather, he stamped twice on the gangway, staying on the jetty.

Tara was sure Mira wouldn't find it rude to have her former mentor come aboard, but courtesy bade captains wait until they had been invited onto another's ship and Merlon could be a stickler for rules – unwritten or not.

Not willing to let go of him just yet, she stayed by his side while they waited for a response. Time stretched into days. It seemed to take a lifetime before the door under the quarterdeck swung open.

A cropped blue head was the first thing Tara saw. She stepped on her own feet, only Merlon's hand in hers kept her from rushing to Mira. The captain of *The Bounty* took the three steps up from the cabin, appearing from behind the door.

Mira's gaze scanned the ship with brows drawn together, then her eyes caught Tara's and her frown washed away with a grin. "Tara! Merlon!" She rushed across the deck.

Tara freed herself from Merlon's hand and leapt across the gangway, meeting Mira halfway. She threw her arms around the younger, but both taller and curvier woman. Mira's right arm wrapped around her in turn, squeezing her so tightly Tara blinked in surprise. "You've trained."

Mira drew back with a chuckle. "Have to, it's bloody hard working with one arm but stars know I won't let that stop me." The turquoise specks in her brown eyes sparkled. Those dots had appeared along with the blue hair after her life-saving blood transfusion in Ivory.

"And you cut your hair, I did say it suits you with a shaved head." Tara still held Mira by the shoulders, taking her in.

She looked happier than the last time they met. It had been nearly six months ago and Mira had still been getting used to her new life as an amputee. That hadn't been what made her look sad though. It had been her da forcing her and Fabian apart, arranging the Trachna-Amule trade deal despite Mira's continued wishes to travel further afield. But Cobalt senior was an influential man and not one to easily dismiss.

"You look like you've settled well, she's a pretty ship." Merlon smiled. He patted the black railing of *The Bounty* and stepped onto the deck.

Mira beamed at him. "Thank you. I hated her at first, I did tell Dad I only wanted a cutter, but you know what he's like."

Merlon nodded, his smile turning wistful. He had been butting heads with Mira's da – and her oldest brother – most of his life, mainly because Merlon preferred the company of his common sailor crew to that of others in the captain's tier. The snobbery of the Cobalts wasn't something Tara could fathom. Tara's family had always had friends amongst a variety of tiers. *If they're solid people, they're solid people*, as Da always said.

"You've got to tell us how you got here. What did your da say?" Tara let go of Mira's shoulders, fighting the urge to grab her hand instead. She had spent three years mentoring Mira, but it was their trip to Ivory, where Patrice and Adrien died while Mira's hair turned blue, that had made Tara truly appreciate her as more than a clever, cowed kid.

Mira stretched her neck. "Where's Fabian? I thought he was hiding to try and give me a fright or something. And what's happened to your head, and your hands!" She grabbed Tara's hand and turned it back and forth to take in the cuts and scabs.

"I took a tumble." Tara gritted her teeth. She would rather not think about it. "Fabian donae know you're—"

"Oh! And wait till you see who showed up wanting a job when I was about to leave Trachna. I'll just get Ola too." Mira spun and rushed off.

Tara sighed. Mira had terrible attention span when she got excited. That had been how Tara ended up tutoring her. She had quickly discovered Mira wasn't at all lazy or dumb as some of her teachers had said, but simply needed to learn in a non-linear fashion.

Staring back towards town, Tara tried to make out the inn Fabian and Kieran had taken the kids to. If only they had been a bit older, she would have known better how to handle them. But she had never dealt with anyone younger than sixteen and there was a very large difference between a five-year-old and someone about to become an adult.

"Why are you nervous?" Merlon reached up and caught Tara's hand.

She grimaced, letting him pull her fingers from the mess of her hair that refused to stay in a bun. "Was thinking." When Merlon raised a brow, she let out a breath and explained. "I'm a good tutor, but only to older kids. I donae know how to deal with those little ones." She gestured at the town at large.

"Nobody who don't have their own kid yet knows, not really." Merlon shrugged. "And they've been through a lot so even people who *have* a kid wouldn't deal with everything

278

perfectly. Nobody would ever expect you to never screw up a few things. You know that right?"

The deck creaked and Tara made to turn her head, relieved to escape Merlon's calm, resolute gaze.

Despite that, he continued speaking. "Karl mentioned Balfour's panic attack. You're better equipped to talk him through those than most other people would be. Except maybe for you, Ola." Merlon bobbed his head at the wiry old scholar following in Mira's exalted wake. It would have taken him quite a bit to admit that to Ola's face.

Ola reached out a hand, shaking Merlon's as was the way of greeting in Outer Universe.

Tara gestured a star before giving Ola a brief hug. "How're you doing?" She stepped back, seeking Merlon's hand to calm her nerves.

How would Ola react to the story of how they came by three orphaned and abandoned kids? They were from his universe, probably even the same area judging by the likeness in accent.

"Achy but that's age for you," Ola said. "I do enjoy this dim starlight though. I can even roll up my sleeves for a while without burning. Now what's it I overheard, who's having panic attacks?"

Tara found herself shifting closer to Merlon. She didn't feel like revisiting the nightmarish day in the village. But it was too late. The limbs flying into the air. Ramson's brown curls singeing. Images flashed behind her eyelids when she blinked, and she was grateful when Merlon put an arm around her shoulders.

He gave her a light squeeze. "Long story short, we hit a portal storm and ended on Quarantine Thirteen. Picked up three orphans and got dragon help to get back here."

"Gracious stars!" Mira gestured a star in front of herself.

Ola blinked once. Twice. Then burst out. "Quarantine Thirteen! Blimey that's why Bailey vanished so suddenly?"

"Tuh! I don't vanish for no good reason." Bailey poked her head out of Merlon's pocket. "Where's Hakim? We've got a dinner to attend. And you better smuggle me some goodies." Bailey pressed a tiny paw against Merlon's chest.

He groaned. "You're not eating while *in* my pocket, that's disgusting knowing how messy you are."

"You can sit on my lap," Tara said. She had barely uttered the final word before Bailey had shot out of the pocket and dived straight under Tara's hair, snuggling close to her neck.

Ola still stared at them with raised brows. "You'll have to tell me ever'thing. I dun't know nuthing 'bout Q13. Well apart from the initial research into turning it habitable of course. It's where you got hurt? Looks nasty that cut." Ola touched the side of his head matching the spot where Tara had a wound over her ear.

Tara gulped. "M-maybe later." *Think of something else.* Cobblestones and weeds, like Lena had done. Except, Merlon's ma had got herself killed. Tara shook herself, refusing to let the panic run with her. She forced a smile. "Let's go eat and you can tell us how you ended up here when you wasnae meant to leave Twin Cities."

"Sure," Mira said. "I'll run get Hakim. I'm afraid Lennie wandered off for some business or other. I'm sure he'll be back soon though, so I'll leave a message with Dinai, xe's my new first mate and stars am I happy I got rid of Rocca. I'm sure she reported back to Dad about every breath I took."

Merlon stared after Mira as she vanished down into the forecastle in a flurry of motion. It took him several seconds before he muttered, "Lennie's here? We were meant to pick him up in Outpost 8."

"We bumped into him there while we waited for Bailey's instructions. Funny fellow, still dun't know if I'd trust him." Ola's orange brows puckered and his lips pursed. "Seems the sort who's willing to sell anything for the right price."

Merlon's lips twitched. "Did he try to pawn off Dainty? He jokes about that a lot but in reality, his kid is probably the only thing he *wouldn't* sell no matter the price."

"Are you implying he'd sell his partner?" Tara snorted. She was relieved the conversation had taken a turn and the ghastly images in her mind receded once more.

Shaking his head, Merlon turned and led Tara back down to the jetty. "Squamates don't believe in slavery. If only humans were as smart."

"Edge Galaxians are at least." Tara shrugged.

She slipped from Merlon's arm to wait and watch Ola and then Mira and Hakim join them. She nodded with a smile at Hakim. He was a quiet person and gestured a star at her and Merlon in greeting but didn't speak. Considering how much Kieran always babbled, Tara had often wondered how Hakim ever got a single word in.

Bailey shifted under Tara's hair. "Some of the Sand Galaxies have recently outlawed slavery. Maybe the regime shift in Jungle Galaxy will also finally see an end to slavery there, but with how abrupt the coup was…" Bailey muttered indistinguishably.

"I donae know where any of those galaxies are." Tara shook her head.

Bailey didn't respond and they set off down the jetty, towards the harbourfront and the increasingly lively inns and pubs along the broad street. Sailors were finishing their meals and continuing their drinking.

It would get rowdy later and Tara decided they should hurry with dinner and get the kids back to *Lucia*. Everyone was still – mostly – decent but there was no reason for the kids to add bar fights and alleyway sex to the things they had seen at such a young age.

"Which place is it?" Mira was positively bouncing. She kept running her hand over her stubbly head, adjusting the scarf around her neck and then the string tying together the left hand sleeve just above where her elbow had once been. The shirt was tailored to her, the left sleeve shorter and with a decorative, frilly lace a few inches below the closure.

Tara skipped past Merlon and Ola and linked her arm with Mira's. "Stop fussing, you look cute. It's over there." She pointed.

"I wish I'd put makeup on," Mira whispered and rested her head against Tara's shoulder for a moment. "Not that he'd notice." She laughed.

Tara put her hand on top of Mira's that still rested on her arm. "He willnae care in the least but for the fact you're here. I cannae wait to see his face! And Kieran's." She glanced back at Hakim whose face lit up at the mention of his partner.

Tara let go of Mira when they reached the door. Peering in, hoping to find Fabian and Kieran seated so they wouldn't see them enter the dimly lit room, she couldn't immediately find them.

Frowning, she stepped through the door. Where had they gone if not here? There was enough space both inside and, on the benches, lined up outside.

Then she discovered Fabian, pinned up against a wall and pawing at the scaled hands of a huge Squamate that hoisted him up by the shirt collar.

Fabian's voice carried despite the rowdiness of the crowd. "Listen, those kids are fostered by our Cap'n. We've done no smugglin' of child slaves so set me down, ya big tosser."

"Burn us," Tara muttered. This could very quickly turn into a nasty bar fight, seemed it was late enough for those after all.

Chapter 31

Tara gestured the others through the door. "Hurry up!"

"Can't leave him alone for a minute without getting into more trouble." Merlon grumbled the second he stepped inside. He strode forward.

A singing sailor jumped to his feet, blocking Merlon's path without noticing and swung xir beer mug backwards for one of the high notes. Merlon ducked, but not enough. The mug hit his eyebrow with a resounding clonk. His knees wobbled and he stumbled a step back.

Tara leapt towards him. The singing sailor whirled, surprise on his face. His flailing elbow hit and slammed Merlon's face sideways, right into the curved hook a yellow-stained powder lantern hung from.

Tara reached him as his knees gave in completely. "Burn you!" she hissed. The cuts along her arms seared, splitting open again while she staggered to keep Merlon from collapsing on the sticky, ale-infused floor. She was far too battered and injured to be balancing his weight.

"S'ry, s'ry! Eternal moonlight! I din't see 'im!" The sailor threw xir mug at xir friends and caught Merlon under the arms. Drunk Singer eased Merlon onto the bench beside one of xir mates. "Dimmest moonlight I din't mean hitting 'im." Xe wrung xir hands, reaching out to hold Merlon up when he almost keeled sideways.

Tara glanced from Merlon, dangling where he sat and blinking dazedly, to where Fabian still fought to get the big Squamate to let go. The commotion of Merlon taking a tumble had brought a surge of people to this side of the room, leaving Mira and Hakim elbowing their way towards Fabian with little progress.

"S'ry, I truly am." Drunk Singer made a circular motion with xir palm outward which, together with xir foreign accent, placed xem as a Moonside Galaxian. Probably not one who lived on this side of the Edge Galaxies permanently or xe would have signed a star like most started doing after a few years away from home.

Tara pressed Merlon's hand between her fingers. "Merlon? Can you understand me?"

His skin had already darkened by his brow, but the real thing that sent a jab of worry through her was the bleeding cut by his hairline. He had knocked his head into that iron hook with full force and if it hadn't been smooth and rounded, he would have hung himself like a pig after slaughter.

Merlon's eyes kept closing, leaving Tara to pinch the inside of his arm in an attempt at keeping him awake. She turned and grabbed Drunk Singer who stood dumbstruck beside the bench. "Run and get a healer, *now*."

"I, uh, 'course!'" Xe spun and ran straight into Ola. "S'ry!" Xe slipped past the scholar and vanished out the door.

"Ola," Tara called and waved him closer. "Do you have a handkerchief in your pocket?"

Ola produced one, quickly folding it up and pressing it against the profusely bleeding cut on Merlon's temple. "You're bleeding too."

Tara twisted her arm and glanced at the split skin. "It's fine, just old cuts sprung up again. Seems they'll never heal."

Shouts rose amongst the generally loud din and Tara stretched her neck. Was that Mira punching a Squamate in the face? Merciful stars this was going terribly. She tried to look through the throngs around her but still couldn't see Kieran and the kids. Where were they?

"Uh-oh," Bailey whispered.

Tara turned her head but couldn't see the rat still hiding under her hair. "What?"

"I hear, and smell, trouble. Mira and Fabian are in a fight. The kids are terrified. I suggest we go help."

"Burn it." Tara looked from Merlon to where it sounded like the fight was getting heated.

Ola waved her aside. "Go, I'll keep him awake until the healer gets here. Better stop that scuffle. I heard Fristate has severe punishments for starting fights."

Tara growled under her breath, but relinquished Merlon's hand and stood. She shoved her way through the crowd. An uneven circle had formed around Mira and Fabian, standing back-to-back and facing each their Squamate. At least none of them had drawn weapons.

Apart from the fact bringing weapons into a bar-fight wasn't ever a good idea, Squamates saw weapon use as a sign of weakness. If they had started a fight, they would finish it and the humans in the equation would not have a good time of it. She glanced back at Merlon. *Unless he's the opponent.*

Merlon had once fought for coin and while he had scars to prove he hadn't always won, the respect Lennie and his other Squamate friends treated him with, told enough. But he wouldn't win any fights with that wound on his head, and it seemed it was on Tara to break it up.

She pushed aside the last person in front of her and stepped into the open space the spectators had created. She swallowed the knot of nerves threatening to overwhelm her. "What's the problem here?" She squared up her shoulders a little belatedly.

Both Squamates, one a huge varanoid with a pink tongue flicking and long tail curled up and ready to whip, turned their heads and stared coldly at her. The larger had a long, streamlined head and body. The faint resemblance with the sarco crocs from Quarantine Thirteen had Tara trembling inside.

The smaller Squamate had brown scales with golden accents, tapering into long spikes beyond the broad head. They both wore shorts held up by gem-studded belts. Bracelets clinked on their wrists, and yellow gems had been drilled into the spikes of the smaller one while the varanoid had a nose-to-ear-hole silver chain dangling. The latter adornment suggested Silver Chain presented as a female. A blue nose ring on Spiky determined xe preferred neutral pronouns.

287

'They have child slaves,' Silver Chain signed. She flashed a thick leather bracelet on her arm. It had a metal plaque on it, but the engraved explosion on it meant nothing to Tara.

Fabian bristled. "I told ya, we don't have no slaves. We're bloody well Amuleans not some nasty Far Galaxians!"

'We are Far Galaxians.' Silver Chain signed, punctuating with a hiss starting deep in her muscular chest.

Tara cleared her throat and gestured once Silver Chain turned towards her. 'They not slaves.' Then she continued aloud, "I'm navigator Tara Polendi and those kids have been rescued far away from here. I'd suggest you back off. You have nae authority to beat up an Amulean first mate and captain."

Silver Chain shifted to fully face her. It was only then Tara glimpsed Kieran, Hakim and the kids pressed into a corner, a third varanoid Squamate watching them with a scowl. Kieran had Elin in his arms while Balfour hid behind Hakim, his blond mess of hair all Tara could see. Cary stood with clenched fists deepest in the corner and looked like he would fight nails and teeth if anyone got too near him.

'We are hunters, we have every right,' Silver Chain signed.

Burn me, pirate hunters? Tara swallowed hard. She refused to step back when Silver Chain stalked closer and loomed over her with the seven-odd feet of height that was clearly supposed to intimidate.

"You donae have rights to beat up honest sailors from Twin Cities. These children are under our care and protection."

Silver Chain narrowed her golden eyes. Her tongue flicked so close to Tara's face she caught herself moving to punch it away. A scar marred Silver Chain's neck, and dark lines broke up the reddish-yellow colour of her snout and throat. 'Where are their papers?'

"They donae have any." Tara ground her teeth together. "We *just* found them."

'That sounds like a very bad lie,' Silver Chain gestured. 'A pirate lie.'

Concentrating enough to understand each sign the Squamate used was beginning to wear on Tara. She was already tired, and her arms were on fire where the cuts had reopened. Her stomach growled from hunger and worry nagged at her every time she remembered Merlon still hadn't come to help, which meant he remained dazed and possibly suffering a concussion.

People pressed from behind her, eager whispers and bustling to get a better view of the show down. The inn had turned into a chaos of stinking sailors crowding in from the doors and faces glaring through the windows.

Nobody had stepped in to stop the disagreement, but Outposts were like that. Tara wouldn't be surprised if several law enforcers were amongst the people staring at her, themselves too engrossed to act, maybe unless someone pulled a weapon.

Finally Tara collected her mind enough to retort a reply, "If you're in doubt, ask the kids and they'll confirm they're nae slaves."

Silver Chain stepped forward, her eyeball staring down at Tara. For a second, Tara was sure she was about to have her neck snapped by the huge being. Then, without a word, Silver Chain turned and made a single gesture Tara didn't quite see.

The varanoid keeping watch, one eye on Kieran and the others and one eye watching Tara and Silver Chain, reached behind Hakim. Hakim tried to push xem away, but a tight grip of his collarbone with the Squamate's free hand and Hakim all but buckled. Balfour screamed as he got pulled into the open space.

"Let go of him!" Rage built in Tara's chest so suddenly and violently she had no time to prepare herself for it. It consumed her entirely.

She lunged past Silver Chain and caught the nostril of the Squamate who had snatched Balfour. She yanked the varanoid's head sideways and down, punching xir neck right where one of the large veins showed. The moment Snatcher's head rose, and xe stepped backwards to get out of her reach, Tara let go.

She reached for Balfour. He threw himself at her and she knelt, hugging him close. "It's alright, I've got you," Tara muttered, unsure where the words even came from, but she meant them as intensely as her heart thundered in her ears.

"You were meant to de-escalate," Bailey whispered.

Tara ignored the smartass rat and kept her hand on Balfour when she slowly rose to face Silver Chain once more. Balfour pressed against her legs, clutching her arm, and trying to hide behind it. "Go ahead, ask them if they are slaves or if we saved them from starvation."

Silver Chain cocked her head. Her tongue flicked towards first Tara and Balfour, then Snatcher who was giving Tara the stink eye. Spiky had watched with a cool air of indifference but Squamates were hard to read. Xe might be internally raging and ready to attack.

Tara was suddenly very glad Merlon had taught her a few tricks for fighting a Squamate. She had never had plans to use it, most Squamates were much less aggressive than humans, but it seemed to have come in handier than she had anticipated.

'We are done here.' Silver Chain turned and waved for her companions to follow.

The excitement fizzled out of the crowd when she strode through. People and Squamates shifted away, giving the three pirate hunters a clear path out through the front doors.

"That was even more scarier than watching the bombings on the tv holo," Balfour whispered.

Tara's knees threatened to give way, so she obeyed them and knelt in front of him again. "We willnae let anything bad happen to you."

"Thank the stars, thought we's dead for sure," Hakim mumbled from the corner.

Tara glanced past Balfour, forcing herself to stand up straight. Fabian and Mira were hugging one another tightly, sobbing or laughing or both. Meanwhile, Kieran adjusted Elin on his arm, and helped Hakim back to standing. The smile growing on Kieran's face sent Tara spinning back to scan for Merlon's face.

He wasn't on the bench. Her stomach dropped.

Then he was right before her, hand still pressing Ola's, now bloody, handkerchief to his forehead. "I'm sorry, I shouldn't have head-bopped that lantern hook." His smile quickly got replaced by a grimace.

"You should get back to sitting." Ola pulled out a chair.

But Tara threw her arms around Merlon. "Bad timing for injuries is sort of your thing," she muttered into his neck.

She let her hand drop to Balfour's shoulder when he sidled closer. The boy grabbed her hand and held on so tightly her throat closed. If things had gone wrong, those hunters could have taken the kids away to a random orphanage in Intrapolis or beyond. She hadn't determined what she thought best to do but she wasn't going to let anyone else make that choice for her.

"Who needed a healer?" A woman called.

Tara found herself laughing through tears and stepped back from Merlon. "Over here. Please." She held up a hand, relief warming her through.

Chapter 32

Law enforcement did appear in the aftermath, but Balfour refused to let go of Tara and after waiting for the healer to put a glue powder on Merlon's cut, they separated. Merlon and Ola went with Mira and Fabian to the enforcement office to place an incident report and Tara took the kids back to *Lucia* along with Kieran and Hakim.

Elin woke Tara twice during the night because Balfour was in a panic about the lack of food in their chamber. In the end, Tara pulled one of the spare mattresses from another bunk over to the floor by the kids'. Sleeping beside them, she could hand Balfour half oat cakes and nuts anytime he startled awake.

She didn't hear Merlon return but Bailey, who had initially gone with him, did wake her when she came back. The rat grumpily informed Tara that Merlon was catching up with Lennie and had declined to carry Bailey back to *Lucia*. The cat appeared around then, and Bailey left in an angry huff to avoid getting eaten.

293

Despite having hit his head and then staying up late, Merlon was awake and sat by his desk when Tara tiptoed out of the chamber the next morning. He didn't notice her but stared at the open logbook in front of him. A floorboard creaked and he looked up, the frown between his brows giving way for a smile. "I was worried where you were until I checked the chamber. Did the kids struggle sleeping?"

"Balfour's getting panic attacks when he wakes feeling hungry." Tara shrugged. She remembered the months after she had been stuck in the well. Waking up in the dark, she would freak out, thinking the sheets were full of scurrying bugs.

"Donae scratch the cut." Tara flicked Merlon's shoulder and sat on the armrest of his chair. Her night tunic rode up her thighs.

Merlon let his hand drop from his head and wrapped his arm around her. The other hand draped over her leg, making her skin tingle at the warm touch.

"They need talk therapy." He leaned his head against her side. "I can't believe Rochester never allowed me that, I might actually have learned how to deal with loss instead of taking S-V."

Tara's chest panged. She pulled his head closer, suddenly feeling an urgent need to hug him tightly. She hadn't had a talk therapist after the well incident, but when Ma died, Patrice had dragged her to one she had vetted and determined were a good fit. Patrice had, of course, been right.

After the nightmarish trip to Ivory and the murders of Patrice and Adrien, Tara had spent many an afternoon bawling in the therapist office but at least she could now manage the waves of grief when they swept her away. Mostly anyway.

She had set Merlon up with another therapist in the same clinic and while he had been reluctant at first, he had become a firmer advocate for therapy than she was.

Tara straightened again. "Bailey slinked off a while ago. She's still mad about the cat. And she had to report to someone. She mentioned Lennie found you when Fabian and Mira headed to *The Bounty*."

"Yeah, ended up late. He wanted the full story on how mum died and nearly ran straight here to get the sword Mira cut Lady Galantria with." Merlon closed the logbook and stood with a stretch. His joints popped and he grimaced, once more rubbing at the cut on his hairline. His brow had turned dark with a bruise Tara wasn't sure whether it stemmed from Drunk Singer's swinging mug or some other bump.

Tara got up and pulled his hand away from his injury. "That cannae have been an easy conversation." She sought his eyes, but he took two uneven breaths before giving in and meeting her gaze.

His eyes glinted with pain, more brown than golden in the dim cabin light. She realised he hadn't turned the desk lamp on and couldn't possibly have seen well enough to fill out anything in the logbook. He did that when his emotions were too overwhelming, he would sit in his chair and stare at the logbook so he could pretend to have been working if anybody caught him in the stupor.

"I can't wait to be rid of that stupid longsword. If I hadn't promised Lennie to return it, I'd have thrown it overboard." There was almost a tremor to his voice.

Tara brushed a lock of his coal black hair back over his head. "Remember what you told Balfour? It's alright to be sad and cry sometimes."

Lena had died gruesomely. Tara hadn't known her long and she still found herself in tears remembering that day. The day Lady Galantria, a descendant of the horrifying Star-Eaters of old, had driven a dagger into Lena's neck, right in front of Merlon and Tara.

It wasn't often she was thankful her Ma had taken fifteen years losing the fight against a nasty stomach cancer, but whenever she thought of Lena's death, she was. Unlike Merlon, she had had time to prepare herself mentally. Time to say goodbye many times over. Merlon had found his ma after nineteen years apart and then lost her again a month later.

"It's the anniversary in seven weeks. Of her death I mean. It's just…" Merlon's voice grew thick, and he pulled Tara close. Burying his face against her shoulder, he sobbed noiselessly. He held her too tightly and her sore ribs ached, but she didn't squirm or speak.

Instead, she held him fast too, tears of her own escaping her. Would it ever get easier? Some days she missed Ma so much she couldn't breathe. And if it wasn't Ma, it was Patrice or Adrien. Patrice had been gone a year in three days and Adrien four days after that. Sometimes it felt longer, other times like it had happened yesterday.

Merlon had lost as many as she. More even, as both his parents, best friend and his first partner whom he had thought he would spend life with had all passed before their time. How he kept it together more days than not was a miracle.

Much sooner than she had anticipated, Merlon pulled away. Only enough to rub his face although she could see no tears. "Sorry, I didn't mean to wreck your morning." Merlon's smile was wobbly. His rough thumb wiped away a tear from her cheek.

"It's alright." She took a deep breath and when she blew it out again, the tightness in her chest eased. Merlon still looked embarrassed, so she elaborated. "If I didnae cry I'd feel worse. I'll be able to enjoy breakfast with Mira better now I've allowed myself the grief. When I try to hold it back, it's like I try to pretend they didnae mean that much to me."

Merlon watched her face, eyes searching like he thought she was telling fibs. Then he nodded, relief flickering in his gaze. "I understand what you mean." He cleared his throat. "So, breakfast with Mira? I doubt you'll manage that without Fabian on her lap. He couldn't stop crying with joy last night. The rum might've been terrible though, wouldn't be able to tell if *that* was his issue."

"True," Tara snorted, "but it's all of us. If you want of course. Once the kids are awake, I promised they'd get a tour of *The Bounty*. Ola will be there, not sure on Kieran and Hakim, they're even worse than Mira and Fabian. They helped tuck the kids in though. It's too bad they'll never be allowed to adopt so soon after signing up on the list."

The chamber door scraped across the floorboards and Tara turned. Cary stood in the door. "I only wanna be adopted if they promise they dun't hit me all the time and I can read all the books I want."

297

"Nobody's going to beat you." Merlon sounded as disturbed as Tara felt. Of course, it happened sometimes that parents turned out not so well equipped for a child, but with how difficult it was to get permits for having one, it was rare. Most families spoiled their kid.

"And I hate boats." Cary added.

Tara exchanged a glance with Merlon. That ruled out sailing tier families. If Cary got to choose. She wasn't sure how it worked when their tiers were unknown. Cary was dark enough he could be a sailor, but Balfour and Elin would suffer with their fair skin. Even Kieran and Derek were darker and still had to stay covered in hopes they wouldn't die of cancer before forty.

"I have a friend who'll help sort your tiers and papers. For now, you'll have to make do with *Lucia*," Merlon said.

Balfour peeked from behind Cary. "I'm hungry." He was chewing on his fingernail.

"Let's get dressed and get to *The Bounty* then. Mira promised to order a cooked breakfast for us." Tara herded the kids back into the chamber and made a mental note that they still hadn't bought new clothes for them. That would have to happen after breakfast.

"The kids are starving. Can we do the tour after eating?" Tara gave Mira a brief hug after they stepped onto *The Bounty's* main deck.

"Sure," Mira said. She kept hold of Tara's hand for another second before nodding at Merlon. Then she shifted back to

Fabian's side. She intertwined her fingers with Fabian's, smiling briefly at him when he raised her knuckles to his lips.

He looked worse for wear and Tara suspected they hadn't slept much at all, but she didn't blame them. They had barely had a minute alone since Mira's da heard about their relationship.

"Long as I get a nap after, I don't care." Fabian yawned.

"It's hard growing old, eh?" Tara poked his arm and leapt out of reach when he swung a lazy fist.

They settled by the makeshift barrel and planks table that had been set up on the deck. A spread like no other covered every inch of the table. Cary's eyes were about to fall out of his head and Ola, who had settled next to the black-haired boy, had to restrict how much he piled on his plate.

Surprisingly, Ola knew exactly how careful they had to be when getting used to eating again after starvation. He explained in a few words that Lena had been starved when she crashed on his planet, but he had also previously mentioned it was a real fear to run out of food during Outer Universe space travel so *astronauts* – whatever that was – all got trained in how to deal with fasting, famine and the aftermath.

"They only had goose eggs, but I ordered them scrambled with chives." Mira explained each dish, from the turkey rashers to carrot sticks. Tara found herself excited to have soft sheep's cheese and fresh blackberries. It had been months since they had fresh anything.

The kids finished within ten minutes, agonising about how hungry they still were. But when Kieran and Hakim arrived,

Ola stood. "Why dun't we go looking round the ship? Then in an hour or so, you can have seconds."

Elin sprung up, Balfour following suit, but Cary didn't move until Merlon leaned towards him. "If you ask nicely, Ola might have some books you can borrow."

Cary straightened, eyes aglow. "Really?"

"I've half a library's worth. Mira thought I brought so many we'd have to use them as ballast." Ola smiled. The wrinkles by his eyes and mouth grew deeper, for a moment betraying his age. He didn't look a day over fifty and Tara still had to remind herself he was nearly sixty-four. His youthful looks a courtesy of some technology from Outer Universe.

"Where are they?" Cary was on his feet.

Ola chuckled. "Let's finish in my cuddy and you can pick however many you can carry. Mind you," Ola kept speaking while he led the kids towards the forecastle, "I expect you nut to stain or dog-ear any pages…"

Tara turned to Mira. "Alright I still donae know how you gave your da the slip. When did you leave Twin Cities?"

"Oh, it was easy, really." Mira giggled.

Merlon raised a brow. "He's usually star-cursed annoying to get rid of once he's decided to take a dislike to something."

"It was Bailey's idea—"

Tara groaned. "Of course it was. She's the most ridiculous little troublemaker."

"I was already thinking about saying burn it and leave, but Bailey arrived the day after my brother."

"Benrit?" Merlon said.

Mira shook her head. "Kian. Dad had sent him to warn me to keep to the schedule. We'd been one day late on the previous trip between Amule and Trachna and Dad completely lost it over that. And over the fact I'd shaved my hair again. I actually like it short, much easier than to try and tie it up with one hand."

"I'd help ya, but sort of hard when we's never together," Fabian muttered then quickly added. "Not that I don't like it short. Ya's pretty either way."

Tara couldn't help smiling. Even though Fabian still looked like he needed a serious nap, he radiated a quiet joy she hadn't seen in his face for a long time.

Mira patted his hand and continued between bites. "Dad must've thought I'd listen to Kian more than Benrit. I feel bad because Kian will be hearing for it *forever* but at least Dad won't know Kian helped me pick the new crew. Though he'll probably guess when he realises I swapped cargo with Kian."

"Why'd he swap with you? Does he have a Fristate run? Can't say I've ever spoken to Kian." Merlon was pushing his food around on the plate. Tara leaned over and stole one of the rashers he clearly wasn't going to eat anyway. Merlon flicked her hand but smiled when she met his gaze.

"Kian's just registered with his girlfriend and really didn't want a trip to Fristate when she's doing runs to Haven Galaxy. He's been trying to get out of the Fristate runs for a year, but Dad wouldn't let him because it's lucrative and well, prestigious, I guess. But with all the stuff happening in Blacklock's, Kian gets too nervous." Mira finished eating and Fabian took her hand in his, all but sleeping at the table, head on her shoulder.

Tara pilfered Merlon's plate when he pushed it towards her. "That checks. Kian was only a year above me and our years were small, so we often had classes together. Always struck me as a bit of an anxious person. Does he nae see how much calmer you are once breaking free off your da?"

Mira shrugged. "I don't know. He was freaking out about the cargo swap because of what dad would say when he found out. I for one am glad I listened to your advice."

Tara snorted. "Yeah, take it from a nervous wreck, I know what suffocation looks like." *Sadly only in others, or I'd have figured out what's wrong with my navigator's vision months ago.*

The gangway groaned and they all turned to look. A pale-green seven-foot Squamate stepped aboard. Lennie was decked out in jewellery. A necklace dangled around his neck and his belt was studded with so many different gemstones it winked like the rainbows of a sail catching energy.

His tail was longer than his body, tapering to a thin whip at the tip. An uneven skin-flap rose off the back of his head, giving him a plume-like crest that made him look taller yet. Piercings and gemstone rings winked from the crest and his back sail alike. His fingers and toes were exceptionally long with sizable black claws, some of which had been tipped with silver.

Tara pushed her chair out, but Lennie waved at her. 'No need to stand, I join the table.' He took the vacant seat between Merlon and Kieran. He tilted his cone-shaped head at Merlon. 'I have enquired for ways to gain papers for the children. There are options but the price will be high.'

Merlon seized Tara's hand, his eyes holding her hostage. "We'll have to decide what those papers should say."

Tara's mouth went dry. What if she made the wrong choice and the kids ended up miserable?

Chapter 33

Tara looked up from her sketchbook when Merlon's desk chair scuffed on the nailed-down rug. After breakfast, both her and the kids had napped and while Merlon had joined her for a short while, she doubted he had slept at all.

She hadn't yet bothered to scoot out of the bunk, but she leaned forward a little to peer past the solid head-end of it. It was getting towards such a lack of sleep where Merlon got hyper-emotional and she followed his form, stalking back and forth in the cabin.

The kids had tiptoed into the hold not ten minutes ago. Kieran's voice sounded from somewhere in there, probably talking their ears off explaining how the ship stores had been restocked or some other thing they hardly cared about.

Or maybe Gaunty would let them help prepare lunch in the galley. In any case, they were occupied for the time being.

What a sigh, Tara stretched and swung her legs out from the bunk. "What's up?" She tossed her notebook in the scrunched-up sheets.

Merlon paused, frowning at her like he hadn't realised she had been sitting in the dim light for the past half hour, drawing her waking nightmares. She didn't dare carry the notebook around anymore in case one of the kids should see those drawings again, so now it stayed in or near the bunk.

"You act tense." Tara explained when he didn't immediately answer. She sauntered over and put her arms around his neck. "So, what's the deets?"

Merlon reached around her arms to rub his face although he took care to avoid the dark bruise around the cut by his hairline. "I need sleep," he mumbled. He didn't meet her gaze. He smelled more of wood lye than starlight today, but that was down to the misty haze that covered Fristate.

Tara cocked her head. "That's nae surprise but you're nae pacing because you need a nap."

Merlon grimaced and finally met her eyes. This close, she could see the faint black line around the edge of the iris and the golden undertones nearer his pupils.

His arms slipped around her waist, holding her gingerly, like he thought she might try to break free. "We should go to Lennie's contact before heading off. A leather bracelet is barely enough here in the Outposts, but once we reach larger cities…"

Tara's stomach clenched. This time she was the one who avoided his eyes. She clasped her hands behind his head as hard as she could to curb the tremors threatening to course through her body. Her throat seemed to constrict her voice, but she managed to speak in a croak. "What do you want to do?"

"That depends on what you're comfortable with, Tara." He sought her eyes and she relented. "They need foster families at the very least. Fosters get a say in where the kid goes and that way they won't be in an orphanage that'll gladly split them into three homes to maximise profits."

Dizziness overwhelmed Tara. Letting her arms drop, she turned away. Merlon instantly let go of her. She slumped in one of the desk chairs. The armrest creaked characteristically, reminding her of Adrien. It had been his chair once, now she was the only one who used it habitually. "There's at least two non-profit orphanages in Trachna. My bonus aunts adopted from one." Her voice sounded odd to her own ears.

She turned her arm over, running her fingertips over the bumpy scabs. It was tempting to press against the sore spots, let the pain drive away the stutter in her chest. She clenched her hands, refusing to give into the urge. She had never done so, and she wasn't going to start now.

Merlon didn't speak for so long she knew he was carefully bottling up whatever emotions were trying to rule his thoughts.

In the end, she couldn't bear the silence anymore and looked up, finding him leaning on the desk. She couldn't tell what he stared at, but his knuckles were white against the loose papers and notes scattering across the table's surface.

Ignoring the stiffness in her knees, Tara drew her legs to her chest, resting her heels on the edge of the chair.

Merlon looked up. "I think I'd like for us to foster them until…until we reach Trachna." He cleared his throat and straightened. The hurt in his face vanished. His business-as-usual face hid his thoughts. "I still have cargo for Jeweller City, and we will need some sort of fake papers for them to avoid more kidnapping accusations both there and especially when we get back to Twin Cities."

"We could send them back with Mira. She's only going to Intrapolis." Tara kicked herself mentally the moment she had uttered the last word. Merlon's face twitched, but it was the fact he turned his back on her that proved she had pushed him away with that suggestion. "Merlon, I was only adding options." She knew it was a lacking excuse. Her voice had no conviction.

He nodded but didn't turn back to face her. A hollow pit formed in Tara's guts. She made herself get up and walked around the desk. It took several deep breaths, but she had to speak up. Had to try and make him understand. "I'm scared I...I donae know I willnae ruin these kids' lives. I donae doubt you or us, I doubt myself."

Merlon's shoulders dropped. He faced her, searching her face with those warm brown eyes she hated herself for putting hurt into. "You have nothing to doubt about yourself. We can try and sign them for Kieran and Hakim but since they're on separate ships…"

"You put too much trust in me. I cannae even…" Her voice broke. She couldn't do it. Couldn't tell him she would have to quit, that she couldn't see energy properly anymore. That the thing her tier was meant to do was beyond her reach. The one thing she had always been good at. The best at.

Merlon shook his head, folding his arms around her. "I might be *dense*, but I know this. You're stronger than you give yourself credit for."

Despite herself, a chuckle escaped her at the old joke. It seemed like a lot more than a year since Fabian had drunkenly jested that Merlon was too slow to realise if someone had a crush on him.

Fabian had been right of course, it had taken months before Merlon realised, she returned his feelings. His worry of breaking the law since she had technically been in training under his command probably hadn't helped.

"We'll ask Mira if we can do a swap," Merlon said. "I'm not much about giving up Fabian for Hakim until we're home but if that's what you prefer—"

"Nae." Tara shook her head resolution forming in her mind. She wouldn't let him down like this. She couldn't let herself down. Just because she was useless as a navigator didn't mean she shouldn't be able to handle a couple of kids.

"It's what, six or seven months until we're home? We can call it a trial." By the end she would surely know if she was cut out for motherhood or ought to quit sailing and return to tutoring teens.

"Only if you're sure and not saying yes to avoid hurting me," Merlon said. His face was serious without a hint of what was going through his mind.

Tara let out a breath. She already felt better although that nagging anxiety roiling her stomach didn't go away entirely. She couldn't screw this up, the kids had already been through enough. "I'm ridiculously, seriously sure." She dared a small smile.

Merlon's face split in a grin and he tightened his arms around her. He bent his head, kissing her with a desperate passion that caught her unprepared.

Her body responded with longing and intensity. She leapt, wrapping her legs around him, returning the fire his touch sent through her. If his hands hit any bruises, she didn't notice. She folded her fingers behind his head, forcing his face closer still.

The hold hatch burst open with a clatter. "Capten! Oh, burn me, sorry."

Tara held onto Merlon's neck, lowering herself back to the floor carefully. She counted to five, eyes shut and attempted to drive out the longing to launch herself back at Merlon. Between her injuries and having three kids in the – far from soundproof – next door chamber she was getting desperate to have him to herself for a little while. But this sort of interruption was getting a habit it seemed.

Merlon's embrace tensed when she tried to turn to face Kieran. He panted, resting his forehead against her shoulder and muttered curses under his breath.

Tara twisted her neck to look at Kieran. "This better be important." At least they hadn't had time to get undressed. Everyone might hear almost anything aboard this ship, but it was another level of privacy lost when crew walked in on them. Mostly, the crew knew to knock but that wasn't fool-proof and Tara had lost count of who had, in fact, walked into the cabin when they really shouldn't have.

When Kieran still didn't speak, she raised a brow at him. "So, is it important?"

He crumbled his soft hat between his hands, looking at anything but them. "It's, ah, them kids. I left them to play with the big cat. It's down in lower hold, chasing mice and such. But then they must've got tired of that and wandered. And I's busy ye know, still got a few things to load before te'morrow. I figured they's fine, nothing's dangerous down there, all secured and such and—"

"Stars, spit it out, man!" Merlon snapped. He straightened to glower at Kieran, one arm still under Tara's shirt, burning against her waist. His fingertips, tracing unseen patterns over her skin, left her shivering.

"Oh, yes the point." Kieran swallowed. "They's ah...they ate half a crate of apples between them, and Cary's started puking all over. The little ones don't look too good either. They's crying for ye, but I settled them in the sick bay with buckets before running—"

"Thanks, Kieran." Merlon let out a breath. "I guess I asked for this."

Tara snorted. "Campaigned for it, more like."

With a nudge of her side, he extracted his arm and pushed his hair back over his head. "Is Yorik around? The healers in Fristate don't see kids for free and that emergency call last night was plenty expensive so unless we need one..."

"I'll find him." Kieran whirled and vanished through the hold hatch.

Merlon caught Tara's hand when she made to follow. He kissed her neck, sending tendrils of heat through her again. "Thank you," he muttered. Then he crooked a smile. "I guess we'll have to find time later."

"We should find a less ditsy nanny then." Tara snorted.

Merlon nodded with a chuckle and stepped sideways through the narrow hatch. She followed.

When they rushed through the hold to the sickbay, the mirth in Tara's chest left. Instead, a black shadow of panic settled in her mind. How dangerous was it for them to have eaten too much? Had Yorik ever mentioned if they might die? Could kids die from eating too many apples even if they weren't half-starved?

A part of her tried to stop herself from following the line of thought spiralling into more and more dire consequences but she struggled to hear that voice above the screaming fear.

Merlon shoved the sick bay door open, and Tara hurried in after him. The sharp, acrid smell of vomit blew into her face. She gasped, all but gagging herself.

Elin lay curled up in the corner of the cot. She had wrapped her arms around her stomach, hollering in agony. Her freckled face was red, tears pouring from her eyes like a tap had been attached on the inside.

Balfour held a wash basin under her face, patting Elin's shoulders despite the fact he had half-digested apple drooling down his chin and clearly was the one who had almost filled the small vessel he held. Balfour looked up, eyes glassy.

Cary's head was buried in a bucket, the sounds of his barfing echoed up from it. He didn't even seem to notice they had entered but considering how violently he was throwing up, that was no surprise.

"Can you get water? And rags, probably," Merlon said.

Tara nodded and spun out of the tiny cuddy. She heaved down a breath of fresher air and grabbed a jug hanging on one of the supporting pillars. She ladled water into it, trying not to spill any of the precious liquid despite her shaking hands and rush. Seizing an armful of old rags from the cleaning cupboard, she returned to the sick bay.

Balfour hurled into the water basin now. Vomit coming out of his nose as well as his mouth, his breath wheezing in the short intervals between the forceful ejections.

Cary had backed himself up against the wall, bucket still between his legs and hands shaking violently. He glared at Tara when she offered a rag and a mug of water. He clearly wasn't ready for either item, so Tara placed them on the stool beside him and turned to the cot.

Merlon sat on the edge, rubbing Elin's back while holding the tub for Balfour. The boy had a pause in the stream of puke, but judging by how he panted, he might not be done yet and the basin was nearly full.

Tara pulled another tray from under the medicine cabinet. It was dusty from disuse, but she swapped it out and left the stinking, full vessel outside the sick bay hoping it might help the smell marginally. Kieran could take care of that when he was back.

After awkwardly standing in the middle of the floor, she made herself sit on the mattress. She wiped Balfour's mouth with a rag and offered him a mug. He shook his head but keeled sideways and curled himself up against her side. She patted his shoulder, unsure what she could possibly do to help.

"Wha's happened?" Yorik skidded to a halt outside the sick bay. "Kieran's gone all panicky and I's not staying to listen to his babbling."

Tara straightened, spilling half the mug of water on her own lap in the process. But Balfour still rested against her, and she couldn't get up without disturbing him. "They ate maybe half a crate of apples and are puking their guts out." She could hear the tremor in her voice and hated it.

"Ah, I see." Yorik didn't say anything else but checked Cary's pulse, made Balfour meet his hooded gaze and took Elin's temperature with a wrist against her forehead. Finally, he sat back on his haunches. "I think they's fine. If they's over-eaten a week ago, I's much more worried. But apple acid is probably the main issue here. They might also, ah, need a toilet in a little bit."

Tara wrinkled her nose at *that* prospect, but relief flooded her, nonetheless. Realising Balfour had gone quiet she glanced down and found him asleep, head on her lap. Warmth washed through her.

Merlon grabbed her hand, a faint smile on his lips. To her surprise, she easily returned it.

Chapter 34

"Come on," Tara said. "We've got to get you all cleaned up and into your new clothes." She put the large wash basin on one of the chairs in the chamber. Three rag cloths and three, newly bought, towels were already laid out on the tiny fold-out table.

The kids had slept for a dozen hours once their stomach aches began to clear. They had got up bright and early, seemingly unharmed from the previous day's overeating, much to Tara's relief. Balfour – or Cary, Tara wasn't sure who – had already devoured the bowl of salted nuts she had left on the table overnight.

"I'm hungry," Balfour said, eyes growing round and panicky.

Tara pulled a wax wrapping with Manihot crisps from her pocket. "Share." She lifted them out of reach when both Cary and Balfour leapt for the snack. She sent them a sharp glance and their hands dropped to their sides. She emptied the crisps into the metal bowl the nuts had been in. "Share, and we'll see how your stomachs do. I'll just get the kettle so the water's a bit warmer."

She left the chamber but stopped and peeked through the gap between the door's hinges to check they weren't fighting over the food. Cary picked up the bowl, holding it out to Elin before Balfour and then himself grabbed a handful each.

Heart warm and fuzzy, Tara went to the galley and picked up the recently boiled kettle on the stove. She checked the solid iron plate had been shifted over the spiral heat elements so the orange heat powder wouldn't keep burning. On second thoughts, she grabbed a couple of oat cakes from the jar, then returned to the chamber.

She wasn't sure she had made the right choice last night, but she would do her star-cursed best to give the kids some good months until it was finally decided who would adopt them. If the stars were kind, she wouldn't mess it up horribly.

Three pairs of eyes turned to her when she re-entered the chamber. The crisps had vanished, and the oatcakes did likewise while she poured the steaming water into the wash basin.

"No stomach aches?" Tara looked from one to the other. Shakes of the heads met her. "Good. If you can still eat something, I'll go heat the rice pudding Gaunty prepared for you. Get the dirty clothes off, wash up and call if you need help getting the new clothes on. Alright?"

She left both the chamber door and the hatch into the hold open. Luckily, the galley wasn't far from the cabin and chamber. She should be able to hear them without straining. Still, she waited anxiously at the galley door for a minute, ears pricked. When it didn't sound like they were fighting or screaming for her, she turned to the stove.

Tara used a hook to slide off the solid plate that covered the cast iron spiral. The striker rod dangled in a leather cord from the handle of the oven below. A couple of hard raps sent sparks between the spirals, the leftover heat powder catching on and burning with a hot glow. Gaunty had graciously left a tiny pot of rice pudding specifically for the kids. Xe knew how much Tara hated cooking.

"Hullo." Karl's voice made her jump.

Tara looked up from her glare at the sticky pudding and smiled. "How'd you sneak up on me with crutches and all?"

"Hardly snuck anywhere, you's simply not listening." Karl shrugged and leaned a shoulder against the doorframe. "How's you doing? Not seen you much the last few days. Skipped the last night in town even. Gaunty and I missed you."

Tara sighed. Karl had dropped by the cabin to borrow her lipstick, some of which he hadn't quite managed to wipe off this morning from the looks of it, but she had been half-asleep beside the kid's bunk, Elin's hand clutching hers. "Kids take up a lot of time, who knew, huh?"

Karl snorted. "*I* did, which is why I never wanted one, let alone three." He grabbed an oatcake from the jar on the counter and nibbled on it as he continued, "You's looking more relaxed in the role though. It suits you." He smiled.

"I donae feel the least bit relaxed." She shook her head. "I thought we'd killed them last night. Then today they're healthy as anything."

"Nah, kids are like cockroaches." Karl huffed and put the oatcake down, he had barely eaten any of it. He wiped sweat off his forehead, shifting his stance but keeping the weight of his broken leg.

Tara narrowed her eyes. "How hungover are you? Nearly fooled me for a moment."

"Ha! Twas a long night alright. Not sure painkillers and ale is a very good combination." Karl rubbed his temple. "At least the rum was too dear or I've not a doubt I'd been worse off. Gaunty only got up to make that pudding xe had promised you, back to sleep now. Xe and Boomer's having a snoring competition, does my head in that."

Hangovers were the worst and didn't exactly ease with age. Tara was sort of glad she hadn't gone out, however much she had wanted to dance. It wasn't like Karl or Gaunty were very sprightly at the moment anyway with all their ankle sprains and broken shins. "Do like Edur used to, sleep it off down in the hold on the cotton sacks."

Sorrow passed over Karl's features. "Gracious stars, I miss that crazy rat." He shook his head, a sad smile grazing his lips.

Tara nodded, staring at the rice pudding she had been stirring all the while. She pulled the pot off and replaced the solid sheet over the heat element, shutting off the air so the powder stopped burning once more.

"So," Karl cleared his throat and straightened. "We're leaving today? Do you know when? Fabian's not been around and Cap'n left before I was up."

Tara measured out a generous ladle for each of the kids' bowls and scraped the leftovers into her own. She blew on the pudding, replying while she waited for it to cool enough, she could eat it. "It'll be this afternoon if things go to plan. Merlon's gone to meet Lennie to talk about this contact he has. I donae like this fake-papers business, but after the pirate hunter incident where Fabian nearly got his ass whooped…"

"The kids needs identity papers eventually. If you get good fakes it'll help in Amule too and—" Karl turned away, frowning towards the rear of the ship. "I think they's shouting for you."

"Burn me!" Tara dumped her bowl on the table, scrambling to scoop up the other three. "Sorry I better run." She pushed past Karl.

A kid, Balfour she thought, squealed. A slight dizziness threatened to overwhelm her. Had something happened? Were they hurt? Or afraid?

She sped through the hold, nearly dropping one bowl as she stepped over the tall floor panel of the hatch. Balancing the bowl on her fingertips, she somehow managed to get it back against her arm without spilling or flipping it upside down.

"Tara!" Elin shouted.

Tara threw the bowls on the desk. "I'm here, what's wrong?" She burst into the chamber. Chaos met her. There was water everywhere but in the wash basin.

Cary stood with a towel around himself, teeth chattering. Balfour's hair was wet and mussed while Elin hadn't even got out of her hastily made tunic although that too was soaked through and clung to her thin frame.

"What in Tomaline's grace has happened?" Tara blinked. "Have you even washed?"

317

Balfour stared at his feet, shifting a wet sludge of a rag with his toes. Cary turned his head, staring at a wall.

Elin giggled. "Water fight!"

"Water fight? What were you—" Tara stopped herself before she raised her voice further. She realised they couldn't have known. They came from a planet where Tara herself had seen how much water they had everywhere.

She cleared her throat and checked her expression. Hopefully she didn't look too mad, but upset enough they would understand not to do this again. She replied with a level voice, "It's my fault nae explaining sooner, but we have very little water here. You're nae on Quarantine Thirteen anymore and water fights are...nae allowed."

Cary turned his gaze to meet hers. "Where are we?"

"In Fristate Galaxy." Blank stares met her, and she elaborated. "It's one of the main Edge Galaxies in Inner Universe. Quarantine Thirteen is in Outer Universe."

Cary pulled the towel tighter around himself. "I dun't care long as I dun't get to be put in a cell or on an island to die again."

"You willnae, ever," Tara said. Then she picked up the wash basin. "You willnae starve or lack for clothes or a home but you cannae waste expensive water like this again, alright? You'll have to clean yourselves up with what's left."

"*I'm* clean." Cary scrunched up his nose.

Tara picked up a sopping rag and began mopping up the water, wringing it back into the vessel. "You help the little two and get yourself dressed then. There's proper breakfast on the desk in the cabin."

At least the floor's cleaned in the process. There might even be enough water left she could get the cabin floor washed later. It sorely needed it with all the dust from Cave Fourteen stuck everywhere. She hated washing floors but if she did that, she could probably get Merlon to patch up the tears in the clothes she had worn on Quarantine Thirteen. Cleaning was much less tiresome than clothes mending.

By the time she had got most of the water up, the breathing wood greedily drinking the leftover dampness, all three kids had eaten and Cary was fully dressed. He had used his fingers to rake his black hair out of his face and suddenly looked very proper. Like a boy on the first day of school after one of the holiday weeks.

Balfour was fumbling with the narrow belt, the Fristate style darker, tighter clothing making him look very small and sombre. Tara was sure he would look more at home in some loose-cut, earthy coloured Amulean clothes.

She helped him thread the end of his belt through the buckle and tightened it so his trousers wouldn't slip down. The clothes weren't tailor made and didn't fit all that well, but there hadn't been time for that and at least it was better made than what had been created from two of Karl's sarongs.

Elin had managed to pull on her trousers but was stuck inside the shirt. She fought with an increasing level of frantic squeals, arms flailing.

"Easy, Elin. Try standing still and I'll sort the shirt for you." Tara caught her wrist through the fabric and slowed her movements.

Elin kept making frustrated sounds, shifting from foot to foot until Tara succeeded in pulling the shirt around to face

319

the right way. She made a mental note to get one where the buttons went all the way down the front next time. Tara glanced aside, although that had drawbacks too; Balfour still fought to get his last buttons closed.

"Will you put up my hair?" Elin said.

Tara faltered, then resumed tucking Elin's shirt in. "I'm nae sure I can do braids yet." *Or ever.* The cuts on her hands were getting better and she would soon have to either learn to braid hair or admit she had no clue how to do it.

"Uh, okay," Elin muttered and stepped on the toes of her new boots.

"I can put it into a ponytail or bun?"

Elin shook her head. "It's okay, I has it down."

Tara bit back the disappointment swirling in her stomach and stood. "Alright, all ready?"

"What are we ready for?" Balfour frowned.

There was a knock on the chamber door. Merlon stood in it, smiling. "We're going to get your identification papers, so we don't have trouble with pirate hunters again." The hint of a frown built between his brows when he took in the floor that still had a couple of wet spots.

"Donae ask." Tara sighed. "I'll explain later."

Merlon's brows rose but he nodded. "Do you all know your last names?"

Elin blinked, then shook her head. Balfour nudged her arm. "You know our last name." Then he looked at Merlon. "I know our last name."

"Perfect." Merlon held out a hand. "Ready to go then?"

Chapter 35

Something brown scurried towards Tara's leg when she stepped from the gangway onto the jetty. Instinctively, she stomped and leapt sideways. But the rodent shot up her leg undeterred. She all but screamed, strangling the sound in her throat before it made its way out.

Merlon faltered and turned back, Elin's hand still in his. "What's…oh I see."

"Tuh! That's not a very nice way to greet a friend." Bailey crawled onto Tara's shoulder.

A shiver coursed through Tara, and she rolled her eyes. "Rushing out from between crates and barrels like some gross street rat isnae nice either." Tara grabbed Balfour's hand and caught up with Merlon.

"Where're we going? I need to be in Intrapolis in seven days," Bailey said. She began prodding and pulling at Tara's hair, yanking locks from the bun.

Tara bit back a remark. The rat usually made sure she wasn't visible while perched under her hair so while it was annoying, there was a purpose. "We're leaving later. The kids need papers first. Where have you been?"

"I requested more refined portal powder but was declined. Something about me having overspent the extra allowance I already had or something stupid like that." Bailey sighed mournfully.

Tara shook her head. The rat seemed to always think she was owed something, but at least her da, General Rum, had finally put his paw down.

Still, Bailey had grown somewhat more sensible in the past year. She had gone very fast from full-blown irresponsible teenager to a young adult *trying* to follow the Tracker society's rules. At least from what Tara had gathered.

It was a bit difficult to judge since Bailey was the only Tracker they were in regular contact with and sometimes it was easy to forget she wasn't the only talking animal that scuttled around the human cities.

What the Trackers did, skulking around in the shadows secretly, was a mystery to Tara. Bailey would come with unhelpful explanations like "we're ensuring you humans remain in the dark". Tara knew better than to ask General Rum what the purpose of the Trackers was. A rather grumpy rat wielding a tiny sword with terrifying precision when it came to main arteries, she didn't want to anger him.

"So, you're staying aboard *Lucia* for now?" Merlon said.

Bailey shifted under Tara's hair. "No, I'll be on *The Bounty* since she's headed to Intrapolis."

They strolled off the jetty and Merlon led the way past the harbourfront and into the narrow streets of the town proper.

Balfour kept eyeing Tara, or rather the spot where Bailey was hiding. He was clearly still wary of the talking rat. Tara didn't blame him. It had taken her quite a while to get used to Bailey as well.

After a moment, Merlon spoke. "We're travelling towards Intrapolis together. I don't intend to moor though. We'll head to Jeweller City while Mira unloads her cargo. Depending on what she picks up there, she might come to Jeweller City afterwards. Why do you need to go to Intrapolis?"

They passed some early morning vendors and Tara reached up her hand, nudging Bailey's little warm body in warning. The Tracker stayed silent until they turned down a narrow alley, desolate of people and Squamates.

Then she slid down Tara's arm, making Balfour jump when she used him for a springboard to reach Merlon. "They want my witness in the Tracker tribunals of Intrapolis. Boring stuff."

"The Trackers have tribunals there too?" Merlon raised a brow at the rat scrambling up his arm. "What do they need you for, is that part of your education too?"

Bailey tsk'ed and dove into his shirt pocket. She shuffled around, making it bulge and billow until she seemingly felt comfortable. Her voice piped out, slightly muffled by the fabric. "Not my education no. I thought it would be simple enough to report the kids but of course the high up's want a full statement."

Merlon stopped so abruptly his boots scuffed against the partially paved street. "You *what?*" He snarled.

323

Tara's heart froze in her chest as Bailey's statement sunk in.

"I *had* to report them since they have seen me talk." Bailey sounded indifferent.

Tara clenched her free hand so hard the wound on her palm split open. She didn't care, barely noticing the pain. "How could you? You said they'll ki—" She managed to stop herself, suddenly aware Elin's eyes were large, and Balfour stared at her like he contemplated bolting.

Cary had already taken a step back. "What does report us mean? Are you locking us up?" Hurt and distrust contorted his expression.

"Tuh! Not like *that* reported. I said they were slave children you found and rescued from some pirates. I'm not heartless, you know."

It took five seconds before Tara's breath eased from where it had been stuck in her throat. She blew it out, her joints feeling like jelly. "You could've led with that."

"Should've," Merlon said. He rubbed his face. He winced when his fingers ran over the bruise on his brow. "You lead a dangerous life, Bailey. I nearly pulled you out to stomp on you."

The rat huffed and wriggled inside his pocket. A second later her head popped out. "Oh, and there's reports of a huge amount of portal powder disappearing out in Portal Galaxy. I pretended to not know a pair of dragons stealing several warehouses' worth of raw powder to help some humans get back to Inner Universe…so, you owe me there."

"I think that's the dragons owing you. We didnae ask for them to steal portal powder." Tara was getting a headache

324

and judging by the sharp pain of her jaw clenching together, that was where the headache stemmed from.

Merlon nudged Bailey through the pocket. "Will Visca and Vincent get in trouble?"

"Bah, no. We have no power to dispatch a dragon let alone two. They've probably forgotten what they did anyway."

They reached a leaning, crooked doorway. On the nearest street corner, a tall, wiry person with a broad hat loitered. It wasn't till Merlon waved and the person pushed the hat back, Tara realised it was Ola.

She looked at Merlon, but he answered her question before she had uttered it.

"It'll look more official with another high tier signature on the documents. Mira's too busy stocking the ship so he offered to come."

Tara nudged his arm with a smile but didn't comment. She knew Merlon was rather ambivalent about Ola, the man who had replaced his da in his ma's life.

It didn't help Ola was a scholar. Merlon harboured a strong dislike towards that tier. Not that Ola was the least bit up himself compared to the other scholars Tara had encountered. If anything, he was quite the opposite and Tara admired him if for nothing else then his calm resolve to not let anything dampen his enthusiasm for knowledge.

He had bawled like a leaky fountain when he learned of Lena's death by Lady Galantria's hand. Himself having nearly lost his life that day too, he hadn't been able to stand up for her hole-drop and had insisted on being carried down to the funeral grounds to be present for the ceremony.

"I worried I'd gone to the wrong place." Ola nodded at Merlon and drew Tara into a brief hug. "You'll need walking me through what's needed. I dun't know but assume it's different to when I registered meself and got assigned me tier in Amule."

Cary sidled up to Ola. "What is that book?" He pointed at the volume Ola had under one arm.

Smiling wrinkles creased the corners of Ola's pale blue eyes. "I bought it for you, since you liked me library so much. It's supposedly more fun than textbooks."

Cary stared from the book held out towards him, to Ola's face. Then he glanced back at Tara and Merlon. Merlon gave a single nod.

Hands trembling, Cary snatched the book and threw the cover open. "Adventures of the Edge," he muttered. He looked up, tears spilling. "I've never *owned* a book."

Ola squeezed Cary's shoulder. "Let it be the first of many."

Tara noted the kid didn't shirk away from Ola's touch like he did anytime she or Merlon got too close to his personal space but then he was already engrossed in the first page of the book so he might have not noticed Ola.

"Right." Merlon cleared his throat. "Should we go in?" When Tara nodded, he knocked on the crooked door and stepped back to wait.

Tara held her breath. She didn't like they were having fake papers made but it wasn't just pirate hunters that would bring trouble if they tried to return to Amule with three kids that had no identification documents and no tiers.

Ola had been granted his scholar's tier and residency within Gulborg Castle's scholars wing quite fast, but he was old and knowledgeable enough he could present his skills in biological studies to the other scholars.

Elin was so young she would only be about to start school so maybe the Population Chancellor would let her pick a tier – as long as it wasn't one that was already in abundance.

But the boys, with them Tara wasn't so sure. Cary was eleven and should soon be starting his first school year in his tier's specialism. At least he could already read and – hopefully – write and count too or he would have lost the main opportunity for learning those skills.

Balfour was young enough he could possibly be allowed a tier choice. He had four more years of foundation after all.

The door swung open with a shudder, pulling Tara from her thoughts. Merlon stepped through with Elin. Ola and Cary followed, and Tara shut the door again behind herself and Balfour, throwing the hallway beyond it in shadows.

The walls leaned to and fro, the ceiling so low all three adults had to bow their heads to go through the second door at the end of the narrow corridor. It smelled dank and a pressure settled in Tara's chest.

Once they reached the office at the far end, she forced herself to breathe calmly. Despite her attempts to remain serene, Merlon turned to her, worry on his face. "You alright?" He mouthed.

She swallowed hard and nodded. Why did it have to be dark, dank, *and* cramped?

Indifferent to her struggle, the man they had come to see settled in a groaning chair. He rubbed the white powder of a desk lamp between his thumb and forefinger. The powder hissed, drawing up through the narrow glass tube and filling the bulb at the top, casting a painfully bright light around the tiny room.

Tara's ribcage seemed to become more flexible, and she drew in a deep breath to steady herself. She couldn't wait for this to be over and be back out where the walls weren't closing in on her.

"Please, take a seat." The man behind the desk gestured.

There were four chairs, Balfour and Cary shared one while Elin readily settled on Merlon's knee. Tara perched at the edge of her hard, wooden chair, fighting not to fiddle with her hair.

She took in the man opposite. He was short and stout, his face square, with the bridge of his nose seeming pinched and too narrow for his otherwise broad features.

His hair had a mud-brown colour Tara knew to be the more common shade here in Fristate. That had been the exact colour Lanier had, except Lanier had had long curls he brushed forward to tumble down his forehead. *Stop thinking about him, you'll only start thinking about the well too.*

Licking her lips, Tara glanced around the room. There were no identifying features. No paintings on the walls, nothing on the desk beyond the lamp and a couple wads of papers.

"Thes'eh the kids in question then?" The man raised a non-existing eyebrow. Together with the grey tone of his light brown skin and thin lips, he looked exactly as suspect as Tara would have imagined someone who forged identity papers for a handsome sum would. There was something...greasy about him.

Merlon nodded. "I assume Lennie has filled you in?"

The man smiled. A sinister sort of smile that seemed to make Merlon nervous too. He put his arms around Elin and pulled her a little closer to his chest.

This man wouldn't turn around and take the kids to sell them off to the highest bidders, would he? Tara was vaguely aware there sometimes ran trials about that sort of thing. She didn't remember the newspapers ever mentioning trial settlements which probably meant a lot of coin shifted hands under tables.

"And you're sure you prefer to have papers made for them and not'eh…well, sell them?"

Tara's heart froze in her chest. Her ribs shrunk so her lungs once again didn't fit. Had he read her mind? Were her fears so evident in her face? Her fingernails dug into the chair's armrest, so hard pain thudded up through her hand.

"Sell them!" Merlon thundered. He sprung to his feet, clutching Elin in his arms. "Do you think we're crooks? Do we look like pirates to you?"

The man's forehead creased; slight amusement twitching his lips. "They'd fetch a pret' penny, but A guess you are right'eh. You are decidedly *very* Amulean." His tone was accusatory. He probably thought they had bribed someone to give them the kids.

Merlon was trembling with barely hidden anger.

Tara steeled herself and placed a hand on his arm. "Let's nae freak the kids out." She directed her gaze at the Forger, channelling her panic into controlled spite. "We are here to get papers on them so we can bring them to Amule. Their parents have gone beyond the stars, and we would go the legal way if we could without risking them being split up."

The Forger only smiled broader. "Of course. Well then'eh…" He glanced at some papers before him. "In this case, A'll need some details off you all and you can be on your way."

Tara squeezed Merlon's hand and his shoulders eased some of the tension. Elin scooted a little forward although she still clung to Merlon's sleeve when he sat again.

"But before we begin, A must let you know, if A sign over three kids in your names, you will be questioned. These papers won't hold up to scrutiny in Twin Cities Galaxy. We can do two but a third will most definitely result in one or all of them being confiscated from yourselves. A assume Amule has som'eh roomy jail cells for people with fake papers." The Forger smiled sinuously.

Tara thought her heart sunk into her gut. What would they do if they couldn't foster the kids?

Chapter 36

Tara stared at the Forger. There had to be a way. But it made sense, and she couldn't believe they had been this mindless. Nobody was *ever* allowed to adopt three kids.

The fact Mira had two siblings by blood was a huge anomaly and only due to her father being the head of the captain's tier. He had no doubt bribed the Population Chancellor for years, just as he had bribed the former Foreign Affairs Chancellor – and now High Chancellor – Horatio Corncockle.

Ola cleared his throat and ran a hand down his front. He still favoured his Outer Universe blue-chequered shirts although he had taken to the looser Amulean trousers. "At what age does scholar's apprentices begin?"

Tara blinked in confusion.

"If you'd like to become a scholar, that is." Ola looked meaningfully at Cary.

The kid straightened in the chair, his eyes growing. "Can I read books all day? Like you do?"

"You'll have to study hard, but yes there's a lot of reading involved with most subjects. Nut many story books though. Mind you, you'd live with me in the scholar's wing, nut with Elin and Balfour down in the city. You can go visit anytime they're home, but Merlon and Tara travel a lot."

Cary turned his gaze to Tara then Merlon. "Please can I do that? Ola said he lives in the library!"

Ola chuckled. "I dun't live *in* the library, but down the corridor from it yes."

Tara looked at Merlon. She didn't want to admit it, but she would be relieved if Cary went with Ola. Three kids were a lot of work. It did mean Ola would have to give up travelling with Mira. Or at least not do it full-time as Cary was of an age, he would be required for class attendance at least nine months out of the eleven a year.

"It could work," Merlon said. When Tara gave a small nod, he turned to the Forger. "Can it work? Cary's eleven so a couple years short of regular apprenticeship, but scholars are allowed to foster even if they're single, I believe."

The Forger eyed the fairly new partner tattoo on Ola's right hand. "Your partner?" He raised a brow.

Grief slipped over Ola's face, suddenly making him look older. "She's gone to the eternal stars." He had had that partnership tattoo made a month after Lena's death. A single daisy springing out from between a cracked rock. Cobblestones and weeds. Lena had muttered that whenever a panic attack was about to overcome her. In the end, she had bled out amongst those very things on Amule's harbour.

Tara reached out and patted Ola's hand.

332

Merlon made a choked sound. Tara closed her eyes, willing the blurry memories of Lena's murder out of her mind. Merlon had been so close to saving her. But his ma had died in his arms. And poor Ola hadn't even known till he woke up, days later.

Ola looked at Cary, tears glimmering through the small smile he sent the boy. "It'd be nice to have company in the apartment but dun't feel you have to say yes. And if you dun't like scholar's life, we'll find something else out."

"It'll be difficult to change his tier later." The Forger looked indifferent. Like he didn't care in the least Ola had evidently recently lost the love of his life. "The girl's five, yes? She's the only one you might have success changing for another year. The boys' pick will lock them in'eh."

"I wanna live in the library with Ola." Cary shrugged. "I hate boats."

Merlon nodded. "It's a good choice. You'll be as high ranking as you can. They don't let anyone into the chancellor's tier after all. Balfour, what would you like? Since both Tara and I, are in sailor's tiers it would—"

"I want to be like you." Balfour broke in. "You're never scared, and I'm always scared." He began picking at a scab on his wrist where his shirt had crawled up a little.

Cary whacked his hand and hissed something under his breath.

Balfour blinked. "I'm hungry."

Tara whipped a wrapping of cashews from her pocket and handed them to Balfour before he had a panic attack.

"Right." Merlon smiled. "I think that settles it. Captain's for Balfour and Elin since they can't become navigators without being able to see energy."

Tara winced and fought to keep her face straight. The worry she thought she had dismissed successfully, that she might get kicked out of her tier, resurfaced with a roar.

Merlon didn't appear to see her internal battle but continued. "Elin will be able to change when we reach Amule if she wants, right?"

"I mak'eh no promises, your government is…easy to bribe though." The Forger raised both brows with an overbearing smile. "Scholar and two captains. They've done well, ey? All you need is a healer, and you'd have one in each of the highest three tiers."

"They deserve it. With what they've been through…" Merlon trailed off.

The Forger pulled a wad of papers in front of himself. "Let's get started then."

They couldn't have been in the office more than thirty minutes, but the pressure built fast in Tara's chest. The bright light of the powder lamp did little to alleviate the feeling of the walls closing in on her. Maybe it was the dampness. Or the low ceilings and lack of a window. The longer they sat silently while the Forger stamped and scribbled papers, the worse it got.

She tugged at her shirt collar. Next, her bandeau seemed to have been wrapped too tightly. Letting her gaze roam the room, she wondered if she could ask for the toilet and readjust the chest wrap. But she knew that wouldn't help. The feeling of slowly choking would resume the instant she was back in this cramped office.

She didn't hear anything the Forger said when he next spoke up. Nor did she pick up Merlon's calm responses to queries. It all seemed very proper and official considering these were fake id papers to ensure the kids would at least not be removed without their assent to be placed in an orphanage.

At some point, Elin's blue eyes fixed on Tara's face. When Merlon leaned forward to add his signature to the documents, the girl slipped off his lap and toddled over to Tara. "You looks sick," Elin said. Her brow had a tiny crease and she grabbed Tara's hand.

Tara swallowed the lump swelling in her throat and managed a smile. This kid was too perceptive for her age. They all were. She squeezed Elin's hand and took the pen Merlon offered.

Her hand trembled when she dipped the tip in the inkwell, but a deep breath and her signature was there, clear and from a seemingly steady hand. She signed the six or seven documents the Forger slid over to her, shifting the papers to her left where Ola sat. He then put his signature on as the witness on some documents per the Forger's instructions. Tara wasn't sure which document was which, but she had signed the witness box for Cary to become Ola's foster child and apprentice, probably.

She rubbed at the ink spot she had gained on her left thumb from holding the inkwell still. She would read those documents properly later, when her mind wasn't screaming that she was stuck in a well and needed to get out.

Merlon had read through it all, meticulous as he was, and she trusted his judgement in this matter like she did with everything else. He had been fostered by Tara's ma and da and then later Captain Rochester, after all, and knew a fair bit more about the process than she did.

"How much do we owe?" Merlon pulled the coin purse from his belt.

The Forger held up a hand. "Your Squamate friend has covered that. Something about a blood debt owed to you?" He leaned forward, clearly eager for Merlon to explain what that had meant.

Merlon frowned and met Tara's gaze.

She shook her head. "The longsword?"

Lennie had given them an unwieldy longsword he had wanted them to use on Lady Galantria. Apparently, an ancient sword with the blood of an ancestor of the Star-Eaters would go for a decent amount of gold and jewels in the right circles.

While neither Merlon nor Tara had actually tried to use the far too long and heavy sword, Mira had jumped through a portal to help them. She had hacked Lady Galantria with the sword but had then missed the counter defence and lost her left arm from the crazed woman's onslaught.

Surprisingly, the law enforcers hadn't confiscated or cleaned the longsword but had let Merlon retrieve it after being discharged from the hospital.

"Seems her blood's worth more than I thought then," Merlon muttered. He pulled the straps of the leather purse back through the hoop on his belt.

Tara was surprised the Forger didn't charge them twice. But perhaps he worried rumours would spread when they inevitably discovered Lennie had also paid. Surely the clientele he usually dealt with weren't the forgiving sort.

Despite the papers being fake, it felt like they had officially taken on the kids and Tara discovered her breath didn't ease when the Forger got up and handed the documents over in a thick yellowed envelope. "As you saw, A's backdated two by a couple of months to raise less suspicion. The scholar kid's dated last week, we're already pushing it with him only being eleven'eh. A hope for you he's a prodigy, so it'll make sense he's apprenticed three years early."

"He's a bright kid, I'm sure he'll manage," Merlon said.

Tara wondered if he saw any similarities of himself in Cary. He had left school and taken his exams early due to Rochester's harsh learning-by-doing schooling. In any case, his words left Cary two inches taller, eyes glinting with a hint of pride. How different he already looked to the wary kid they had picked up from the island.

Getting up, Tara felt lightheaded. She welcomed Elin's warm little hand clutching hers. They went back out through the narrow, leaning corridor. The Forger didn't say anything before closing the door on them, returning the alley doorway to its former crooked anonymity.

They walked back towards the harbour together. Silence stretched for the first minute of their return to the main thoroughfares of the small outpost town.

Ola was the first to break the quiet. "Do you want to stay on *Lucia* for now with the others or come stay on *The Bounty*?"

"I wanna read all your books." Cary all but rolled his eyes. "They dun't want me there anyway." He shoved Balfour's shoulder, but it wasn't an entirely unkind gesture.

Elin looked at Cary, a whimper escaped her, and Merlon handed Ola the envelope.

He stooped and picked her up, but he spoke to Cary. "We'll be sad to see you go. And you can always change your mind. We're travelling together towards Intrapolis for the next week. If you decide you want to come back to *Lucia* when we go onwards to Jeweller City, you can do that too."

"I dun't change my mind," Cary said.

"Regardless." Merlon smiled. "You just have to let us know and we'll sort it."

They stepped out from the end of the street and were back on the harbourfront. In the time they had been gone it had been filled with market stalls. Carts wheeled this way and that, and newspaper distributors scattered amongst them all. The latter shouted about pirate traps and riots in Blacklock's still ongoing.

They all walked first to *Lucia* where Ola went into the chamber he had once shared briefly with Lena, and helped Cary grab the few things he had. Merlon had ensured the kids didn't just have two sets of shoes and clothes each, but also combs, toothbrushes and other small essentials they had lacked while abandoned.

Tara knew Merlon wasn't exactly rolling in coin these days. He had spent most of Adrien's heritage getting *Lucia* back in space.

The income from selling his house had vanished to bereavements for the crew they had lost on their trip through the galaxy river and past Ivory. Still, he hadn't as much as grimaced or asked Tara to cover anything for the kids. She would make up for that next time either of the kids needed something.

"You have everything?" Tara asked Cary. "If you forgot something you can always get it before we split ways in a week's time."

He had his new book under one arm, Ola carrying the bundle of clothes.

"I didn't smell anything else that was his," Bailey said. She perched on Ola's shoulder, busy grooming herself. She had been remarkably quiet today.

Ola nodded at the cabin desk. "It might be an idea to get Cary's papers. I assume we might need them in Intrapolis."

Merlon had gone to the head, so Tara shook the documents out of the envelope. She shuffled through them, pulling out the three pages for Cary's apprenticeship when they appeared.

She put Elin and Balfour's identity and tier proof documents aside. At a quick glance, it all looked like she would expect. There even was a stamp that looked identical to the Fristate stamps on the mooring documents Fabian had returned with the other day.

Finally there was Cary's tier document but when she picked up the single piece of newly waxed paper, her eyes fell on the title of the last couple of sheets.

She read the title once. Twice. Her gaze strayed to the bottom. There was her signature, next to Merlon's, with Ola's witness below and a name for a registrar which she was quite

339

certain hadn't been the forger's name as it looked suspiciously like that of Lennie's handwriting.

That wasn't what had stopped her breathing. She stared at the title again, skimming down the page. But she had read it right. She picked the sheet up, almost hoping it would prove to be a figment of her imagination.

The door to the head clicked open at the same moment. Tara whirled, fighting not to crumble the paper in her hand. "We signed a fake partnership registration!"

Merlon blinked and took a step back, hitting the closed door of the head. "Ah, yes?" His brows drew together, confusion on his face. "They'd never accept two unregistered people fostering. We're not scholars."

"So we *faked* getting registered?" Somewhere at the back of her mind Tara knew she shouldn't raise her voice that much, but her heart thudded so hard she was sure it would soon leap from her chest.

"We talked about it. You agreed," Merlon said. His voice was level, but his fists were clenched, and his jaw worked.

Tara had no recollection of such a conversation. And she certainly wouldn't have agreed to fake their registration. If they were caught, they would be banned from registering properly with *anyone*. "When? When did I agree?" Her voice was a croak. The cabin air was stale.

"An hour ago, in the office," Bailey said.

Tara shook her head. "I was trying nae panicking. Stars burn me if I heard anything. You *knew* I was panicking."

"You can't hardly blame me if you weren't listening. We agreed to go through with fostering them for now, what else had you expected? It's not like there's time to register.

Outposts like this one have several months' waitlist." There was a hint of anger in Merlon's voice now, but he still kept it low, and it infuriated her.

Ola stepped between them. "Maybe take a breather, Tara? I get it's a lot to process but you're getting quite worked up and—"

"Shut up and keep out of it," Tara growled. But he was right. If she stayed, she would start saying things she didn't mean. She grabbed her night shirt off the back of Merlon's desk chair, her notebook and pencil. "I'm staying on *The Bounty* until Intrapolis."

Her chest hurt as she stalked out of the cabin, painfully aware Balfour and Elin were watching her with betrayal in their faces.

She didn't allow herself to slow down until she was halfway across the harbour but by then it was too late to turn back around and make amends.

Chapter 37

Tara stalked across the gangway to *The Bounty*. "Donae say anything. I donae care if I'm sleeping on the floor, I'm staying aboard for the week."

Mira opened and closed her mouth, a furrow built between her blue eyebrows. Everyone on deck stopped their departure preparations to stare at Tara.

She didn't know where else to hide than Mira's cabin and ducked through the narrow door under the only slightly raised quarterdeck. She stepped inside the cabin that was a third the size of Merlon's and bumped straight into Fabian.

"What're *you* doing here?" Tara grumbled and rubbed her shoulder at the impact site. She had a bruise there that she had forgot about until now. It was but one of a hundred after all.

Fabian raised a brow and crossed his arms. "I swapped with Hakim for the week. Same can't surely be said for ya, but no way ya's sleepin' in here."

Tara dropped her notebook on Mira's desk and slumped in the only chair available. A pile of clothes that looked like it could be Fabian's occupied the seat of the other. "I'll stay in the forecastle, I'm sure." Casting about for something to do, she grabbed her notebook again and leafed through to a blank page.

"What's up?" Fabian said. Instead of leaving her alone, he sat on the edge of the desk, facing her. "Did the fake paper stuff fall through?"

Tara huffed. "Nae, it went splendidly easy."

"What's the storm cloud for then?" Fabian nodded at her notebook, the page quickly filling up with dark pencil marks.

Tara frowned at the page. She had left space for a central object but hadn't quite decided what would go into that meagre spot of light amongst all the darkness. "Listen I donae want—"

The door opened and Tara twisted in the chair. Mira's head popped through. Her short blue fuzz barely covered her round scalp. She was still ridiculously pretty, the black eyeliner against her dark brown skin highlighting the slight tilt of her eyes but it was the only makeup she wore today. "Fabian, I need you on deck. I hate to break it to you, but I can't afford to let you dawdle. Tara, Merlon wanted to know if you're not going back to *Lucia*?"

"In a week. I'm nae talking to him while I'm still mad so he can go back and make his ship ready." Tara knew what she was drawing in the storm cloud now and began pulling dark strokes across the page for the outlining.

"He's not here. Sent a message through Ola."

Tara's hand froze on the page. She had right stepped in it. He was more hurt – or mad – than she had expected. And rightly so if she thought even a little about her actions. Why couldn't she have kept her cool? Did it matter so much they had faked their partnership registration?

But she knew the sick feeling in her gut wasn't because she had stormed out. It was the fear of discovery. Of never being able to sign a real registration. She didn't want a huge ceremony and party – you always had to invite people you didn't really care for to those sorts of things – but she had thought Merlon at least would have asked if she wanted to register for real instead of faking it.

Mira sighed. "Alright, there's a spare hammock in the forecastle. It's not the most comfortable but you didn't warn me I needed space for you." She shrugged. "Fabian, come on."

For once, Fabian didn't sling a joke at Tara. He simply squeezed her shoulder in passing. The door closed behind him, and she was alone in the small room, glowering at the outline of *Lucia* coming out of the grey haze in her notebook.

Mira left Tara alone for a full day before asking her to work. By then, Tara was going insane from lying in the holed hammock, glaring at the overhead or a snoring sailor in turns. If Mira *hadn't* asked her to work, Tara would have made herself busy aboard anyway.

Bailey seemed to live with Ola in the cubby between the forecastle and hold, but she kept a low profile since none of

Mira's crew knew about the Trackers. Ola however had taken Cary's apprenticeship seriously and had already planned out an easy two-hours-a-day learning plan for him.

Tara had thought Cary would protest or dislike suddenly having to read certain chapters and writing summaries of them, but she didn't hear a single grumble although Ola did mention he needed to improve his spelling and could barely calculate simple numbers. "But he's eager to learn and I'm sure we'll make good progress," Ola said during lunch.

His dedication only served to make Tara feel more like she had abandoned the kids – and Merlon – on a whim and it didn't exactly help her mood.

"I better get back up." She shovelled down the last pieces of pear and walnuts and dumped her bowl in the tray. At least she didn't have washing up duty with Ola. He wasn't exactly poking or judging her but his every word about Cary's progress still stung.

She breathed a little freer back on deck. *Lucia* had taken the lead, and they kept close on her rear starboard side. Not so near Tara could see anybody aboard as anything more than little dots moving but it still set a churn to her stomach.

She *ought* to be over there, not here moping about like some moody teenager. But she still didn't know how to explain to Merlon everything that jumbled around in her head. Not without getting over-emotional and shouting. And she didn't want to raise her voice at him. He hadn't done anything purposely malicious after all.

"So, are ya talkin' about it yet?" Fabian said.

She shot him a glare through the corner of her eyes. He had settled to change over a set of lines right beside her, and since they were only tacking slowly to port to turn towards Intrapolis proper, he wasn't likely to sod off anytime soon.

She let out a breath, maybe she would feel better if he could remain serious for long enough. "I didnae realise we signed a fake partner registration."

Fabian's hand stopped moving and he frowned at her. "How'd ya not notice? Can't see Cap'n not talkin' that through first."

"The Forger's office was tiny and damp." She avoided his gaze.

Fabian resumed working. "I see. Seems a bit risky, fakin' the registration, right? Fake id papers for them kids could lead to trouble too addin' to the possible charge…at what point do they give up finin' ya and just throw ya in jail?"

"You're nae helping." Tara gritted her teeth.

Fabian continued, seemingly musing more to himself, but he shot her quick glances between sentences. "So, are ya gonna register proper before gettin' to Amule? That'd help some at least. Maybe even bein' honest and tellin' ya found them kids would be best. Not the Outer Universe part, mind." The last sentence was a whisper and Fabian looked around like he feared someone was eavesdropping.

Tara wasn't entirely sure Mira's crew wouldn't just think he was joking or a bit star-crazed. Nobody but Merlon's crew even believed Outer Universe existed.

"I donae know," Tara said. Then she drew in a deep breath and made herself elaborate. "I donae even know if I should foster any kids at all. Elin and Balfour need the best family possible. But I either get too angry or run away or both when things isnae what I thought. How's that supposed to be good for them?"

Fabian straightened and faced her. "Ya worry too much. No family's perfect. Look at Mira's. Her dad and older brother is terrible people. School thought her lazy and dumb. Then ever'body said she'd never sail with just one arm. But she's managed. In large, thanks to ya supportin' her."

Tara followed Fabian's sweeping gesture. *The Bounty* was calmly alive with crew.

Mira stood to their right, by the bow. She had wrapped a brown scarf around her head today, the light seeming a little brighter than out at Outpost 9. A yellow ribbon was tied around the short sleeve of her arm stump, and she held a silver gilded spyglass in her hand but wasn't using it. She belonged here, on deck of her small schooner, not stuck in Amule living off her parents like her da had tried to convince her to do after she lost the left arm.

"It's easier to see potential in others," Tara muttered.

Fabian nudged her arm. "Exactly, so trust me when I say ya'll do fine. If only ya'd believe that."

She turned her head. Fabian was unusually serious, and she was both thankful and slightly annoyed.

"Although ya might wanna learn countin' to ten before storming out, eh?"

She punched his arm but couldn't help herself grinning. "So, what are you and Mira planning? I've seen you whispering."

Fabian's face split in the goofiest grin. "She'll come to Jeweller City. Just need to change over the cargo in Intrapolis and then she'll try catchin' us up. Lennie knows a nice ceremony hall and union official. Her dad'll lose it but it's not like we can register in Amule without him using bribes to deny us a union."

"That's fantastic!" Tara exclaimed, hearing the too-high pitch in her own voice.

Fabian didn't appear to notice but nodded eagerly. Then his face brightened even more. "Hey!" He bored a knuckle into Tara's arm, right on a cut that was only partially healed.

"Ow!" She whacked him.

He waved her off, hands flapping in her face. "No listen, I've had the *best* idea."

Tara rolled her eyes. "Donae be ridiculous you're too silly to ever have the best ideas." But she raised a brow in expectancy when he jumped from foot to foot.

"How about ya register with Merlon too? If ya want a proper union, I mean. We'd go get tattoos together, have the party afterwards across both ships. But Mira and I goes first because I ain't havin' ya throw a fit and ruin the mood until after we've said our vows."

Tara's brows had drawn closer and closer together while Fabian spoke, to a point she wasn't sure if it was her frown or the annoying light of the space, they flew through that was giving her a mild headache.

She didn't manage anything but a weird, garbled grunt in response. The bell calling the shift change saved her and she turned to walk up to Mira by the bow.

She wasn't sure Merlon would like that. She wasn't sure if she would. Or at least that's what she kept repeating in her mind. If she allowed herself to think it through, she liked the idea a lot. But if she didn't make up with Merlon, she wouldn't get a chance to propose the idea to him. Why had she been so stupid to run off? Couldn't she just have told Merlon to shut up and talk about it later? That's what her therapist had suggested for situations like that, where she lost her temper and knew she was about to say stuff she didn't mean and couldn't take back once spoken.

"Did he annoy you?" Mira had a mild smile on her lips. She glanced at Tara before directing her gaze ahead once more. "I forgot how bothersome he can be, but I missed him far too much to care."

Tara scoffed. "He donae treat you like a verbal punchbag."

Mira shook her head. "You're as bad as each other and don't pretend you don't love that sibling energy. I wish my brothers would be more like you two instead of hating one another."

"Will he join your crew?" Tara said. Mira looked at her quizzically so Tara elaborated, "He told me you'll register in Jewellery City."

"Oh no, not yet anyway. Maybe if Kieran ends up ready to be a first mate but Fabian won't let Merlon down. If Merlon hadn't given him that chance of employment five years ago…" Mira trailed off. Suddenly she lifted her spyglass and peered through. "That's odd."

Tara squinted ahead. "What is it?"

"There's a ship stationary in empty space."

Tara took the offered lens and brought it to her eye. She found *Lucia*, but forced herself to not stare at Merlon. She searched ahead where Mira had pointed.

There, a schooner not much different from *The Bounty* hung. It was plain brown with faded gold lettering across the rear. "What's the ship Fabian's brother sails on again? I swear that ship there's called *Iliana*."

"What?" Mira hiccupped, then she turned and called. "Fabian?"

He legged it up to them. "What's the matter, ya missed me face?" He grinned.

Mira sighed. "Yes, but that's not the matter. Is your brother working a ship called *Iliana*? Because that's the ship that's hovering for no apparent reason."

Fabian snatched the spyglass when Tara offered it to him. His hands trembled when he brought it to his eye. "That's the ship he works on alright." Fabian's voice was but a croak.

Why would a ship lay for anchor a full day from the nearest outpost? Something wasn't right and Tara's stomach clenched when she saw the fear in Fabian's eyes.

Chapter 38

Tara shaded her eyes. She should have brought her hat from *Lucia* but maybe Mira or one of the crew had one she could borrow. There was a shimmer in the air and when she blinked rapidly, it was like there were the hints of energy being pulled at something below *Iliana*. If only she could make her eyes focus.

"What do you see?" Mira glanced at her.

Fabian snorted. "Nothin' you don't. She's been havin' trouble for months but seems to think nobody knows."

The bottom of Tara's stomach fell out. She caught the railing, fingernails boring into the wood. She vaguely heard Mira shout to put the energy diversion anchor out to stop them at a good distance from *Iliana*. *Lucia* was already slowing down too. But Tara stared at Fabian, thinking – hoping – she had heard wrong.

"Don't look at me like that." Fabian rolled his eyes "Ya didn't really think we's all blind, eh? I had me suspicions but once Merlon mentioned it, I wasn't doubtin' no more. He's rather hurt you didn't trust him enough to tell him, ya know."

Tara had yet to find herself capable of breathing. There was no point trying to deny what he already knew was the truth. "How long? How long did you know?" Her voice was but a hoarse squeak.

"I suspected a while back. A few months outta Amule perhaps? I didn't know what was wrong at first, ya's very good at pretend. Merlon mentioned about two weeks ago. Sounded like he'd figured it out almost immediately." Fabian shrugged. "He's dense in some points, but he's pretty quick pickin' up when ya's strugglin'"

"Why didn't you say anything? Either of you?"

Fabian tutted in a perfect imitation of Bailey, but Tara didn't laugh. He let out a breath and shook his head. "What'd ya think would've happened? Ya doesn't exactly take kindly to offers of help if ya hasn't asked for it. I thought some teasin' would eventually make you annoyed enough to say but ya's a stubborn tramp."

Tara opened her mouth to protest but closed it again. Was she that bad? A tiny voice whispered he was right on every count, and she hated that. If she thought rationally, she knew she would likely have reacted no more tactfully than she had yesterday. She let go of the railing and clenched her fists until they shook. The scabs in her palms panged. Would she never bloody learn?

"Now if ya'll let me, *I'm* gonna panic about what in the star-cursed universe me brother's ship's doin' sittin' there." Fabian gesticulated at *Iliana*.

Ola came trotting up to them. His hat hung between his shoulder blades thanks to a string around his neck. From the interior of the hat, a small pointy nose poked out.

"Bailey said something's up." Ola panted. "God, I'm out of shape. Dun't get a morning jog on a ship." He waved a long-fingered hand as if to dismiss any comments despite the fact he undoubtedly was still more fit for running than anyone else aboard *The Bounty*.

"There's a ship hovering. It's an odd place to stop," Mira said.

Ola raised his hand to shade his eyes. "Ah, so that's nut something you normally do?"

Tara shook her head, but Fabian spoke before she could. "Not so close to an outpost. And that's the ship me brother's workin' on. I've had a bad feelin' 'bout him since we entered Fristate. I was mainly worried I'd bump into him and have 'nother argument 'bout Mira but this…" He wasn't chewing his thumb, but it wasn't far off.

"Who has the letter tube?" Bailey whispered.

Mira turned her head and nodded at *Lucia*. "I last sent it to you, when you were on *Lucia*."

Tara cursed under her breath. Would Merlon know where it was? "Maybe we should—" The air shimmered before her. Energy diverted around a small circle, giving her a split second of a warning. The wooden cylinder flew at her face. She ducked.

"Star's burn it!" Fabian yelped when he got smacked in the head by the tube.

Bailey snickered. "I really must instruct you all to not picture your faces but your hands or bodies. Then again, it's so amusing when you do it wrong."

Fabian rubbed his chin and Ola plucked the cylinder from where it had tumbled on the deck. He fiddled with first one end then the other, finally popping the lid off. A crinkled single sheet of paper slid into his hand when he shook it. Ola narrowed his eyes.

Tara sighed. "Let me, he has terrible handwriting." She grabbed the page. Her heart thudded as she skimmed the few lines. Why was she disappointed it wasn't addressed to her? "It says; *Has Fabian seen the name of the schooner? His brother's surely onboard. Something's not right. Stay put while we investigate. I'd advise to get blasts and bows ready.*" Tara looked up.

Now Fabian *did* chew his thumb. When he noticed her watching him, he stuck both hands under his armpits, not exactly looking the least bit more relaxed. "I should be over there, checkin' up on me brother."

"I'm sure nuthing crazy's happened," Ola said.

Tara nudged Fabian, she hated seeing him this anxious. "Maybe they wanted a day off without paying the mooring prices."

"You don't believe that any more than I do." Fabian started pacing by the railing like he thought about leaping the two hundred yards to *Lucia* and then *Iliana*.

Mira scribbled a few words in reply and Tara replaced the letter tube's lid, picturing Merlon when she threw it. It vanished with a soft plop. Not a minute later it reappeared, this time shooting past Tara's head and hitting Ola's chest.

354

Mira read the single sentence and looked around them. "Merlon will check and we're backup if anything's out of the ordinary." She stuffed the paper in a pocket and took Fabian's hand. "I'm sure Tara's right and they wanted to avoid paying in Outpost 9."

Tara licked her lips. Despite the air having a pleasant warmth to it, she had goosebumps on her arms. If *Lucia* struggled it was unlikely Mira's crew, one third the number of people and without the experience and loyalty of Merlon's, would be any help at all. But she kept those thoughts to herself.

"All hands!" Mira left to call orders when *Lucia* moved towards *Iliana*. The large ship turned her bowsprit, heading straight towards the schooner but the anchor stayed out at nearly seventy percent, so she only glided slowly forwards.

Fabian paced back and forth again.

Tara focused on his anxiety instead of the one gnawing at her guts. She ought to have been on *Lucia*. Who was with the kids? Was anyone ensuring they weren't on deck or got scared when Boomer began hanging buckets of blast arrows by the shooting stations? When the archers on board grabbed their gloves, stringed their bows and watched the hoovering ship with mistrust?

Cary came onto the forecastle deck, a frown on his face. "What's happening?"

"We dun't know yet. Best get back below," Ola said.

Bailey transferred herself from Ola's hat to Tara's shoulder when he passed her, leading Cary back towards the main deck hatch.

The rat slipped under the mess of Tara's hair. "You smell nervous."

"Why do you think that is?" Tara spoke through gritted teeth. But she let her hand drop from her hair. Bailey would only yank it down if she tried to push some of the locks back in the bun.

Lucia slowed again, her anchor cranking further out if the flickers of energy Tara caught were anything to go by. The larger ship slid close to *Iliana*.

Mira returned to the bow, looking through her spyglass and making Tara regret having left her own lens on *Lucia*.

Fabian nudged Mira's arm and she handed the scope to him without a word. He finally stood still, staring through it. "There's someone on the deck. I think Cap'n's greetin' them. Don't recognise the person on *Iliana* though."

"Does the ship look like it's taken blasts?" Tara said. Everyone seemed to hold their breath, waiting for Fabian's reply.

"Not that I can see, no." He frowned. "Cap'n's got his hand on his sword."

Tara thought Merlon took a step forward, but without a spyglass she couldn't tell for sure. Why was there only one person on the deck of *Iliana*? Even if most of the crew were off for a spell, it seemed risky to have but one person on watch when they were this close to Blacklock's Galaxy.

From what Tara could see with *The Bounty* closing the distance, Boomer hadn't lit the buckets of blast arrows on fire. That had to be a good sign.

Barely had Tara had that thought when her breath hitched. She blinked. But there really was something moving with a

356

shimmer of the air. Shifting up from below and behind *Iliana*. "There's something—" Her voice died.

A ship appeared as if out of thin air.

A gasp and shout rose across *The Bounty*. Crew hanging in the shrouds were crying out, pointing, half a second before those on deck. "A ship! A pirate ship!"

"Uh-oh," Bailey muttered. "Did you know about the haze illusions?"

Mira whirled. "The *what?*"

Fabian's fist beat the railing with a thud. "Stars burn me! How didn't I see it? How didn't the Cap'n?"

Tara raked her brain. She had heard about this. Pirates hiding in plain sight. That was how they had remained successful in Fristate despite the growing number of hunters.

Due to the mist hanging thick throughout Fristate Galaxy they could manoeuvre ships close to merchants unseen. If anyone should have known or seen the ruse, it was Tara. She had seen the energy the pirate ship commanded if only for a glimmer of a heartbeat.

"Anchor in. Light the blast buckets. Archers ready!" Mira shouted. She ran across the deck.

Fear pulsed through Tara. The energy around her flared up. Or was she only hoping she saw it clearer for a few blinks? *Tomaline help me be right this time.* "Ten degrees starboard! The energy's stronger there. Hurry!"

Fabian gave her a hard glare.

"I see *some* energy still," she hissed, letting the flare of anger seep through her so the fear didn't freeze her to the spot. She spun. "Mira, spare bow and arrows?"

Mira bobbed her head. "Hinna, run to the armoury, bow and gloves."

"Make it two bows!" Fabian called. He rushed to the windlass and helped the sailor already there, winding up the anchor.

Hinna, the young midship sailor dove into the hold through the main deck hatch.

Tara faced front, blinking fast in an attempt at catching more glimpses of energy. Her fury against Fabian was fast fizzling out and with the tremor of her heart, the energy around her waned again.

The pirate ship, flying a black flag with jagged blue triangles edging the top and bottom, pulled up on *Lucia's* port. It was a long, streamlined cutter and it was already shooting volleys of blitz arrows.

Lucia turned her nose downwards.

Meanwhile *The Bounty* had nearly reached shooting distance to the pirate cutter. Grappling hooks were thrown, and the pirates' axes chopped the rigging of *Lucia's* main mast the second they landed on her deck.

Pirates welled out and onto *Lucia* from both the pirate cutter and *Iliana*. They kept pouring over, loosing blitzes left and right, blinding, and incapacitating Merlon's crew. How were they so fast? Tara couldn't breathe. Merlon had drawn his sword, but his chops were wild, uncoordinated. The strong flashes of light from the blitz arrows had to have blinded him.

The Bounty needed to be careful, or they would be overrun too. "Trim the top gallant sails. Mira we should ascend!" Tara yelled. She sprung to the boom of the foremast; the jib sail needed tightening too.

A young sailor popped up beside her. "Bow and gloves. Blast bucket station over there." It took Tara a moment to remember Hinna, whom Mira had shouted to get spare bows.

Tara seized the breathing wood bow. It hummed in her hand. She yanked the gloves on, pressing the leather straps over a rivet to fasten each glove around her wrist. They were too large but better than burning her fingers on every metal arrow she touched.

Fabian joined her. *The Bounty* was drawing close now.

Tara scanned the deck of *Lucia*. How had the crew been overwhelmed that fast? Her heart thumped painfully, there was Merlon, lying still on the deck. Was he bleeding? Dread darkened the edges of her vision. She staggered, Fabian caught and held her elbow until she had managed a gasping breath.

A pirate stumbled over Merlon's boot as xe rushed past. Merlon jolted and shifted but didn't get up. Alive. She could work with that.

The Bounty slowed once more. They had raised to be a dozen yards or so above the decks of the other ships. Giving a perfect view down on the pirates.

There were at least two scores. How they had all fitted on the cutter, unless they had taken *Iliana* a while ago, was a mystery to Tara. But they were splitting up again. Yanking tied up crew from *Lucia* to whichever ship was nearest by the looks of it. Gaunty tumbled into the hold of *Iliana*. The tightness grew in Tara's chest.

She grabbed a flaming blast arrow. Nocked it. A little closer and she could see who she was shooting at. Had to make sure the pirates didn't carry anyone she knew.

She drew the bow. Those pirates would regret whatever they had done to Merlon. Regret kidnapping Gaunty, Kieran and was that Jara being rolled across the deck of the pirate cutter?

They moved with slightly frantic motions, constantly glancing up. They clearly hadn't planned for a second ship to be nearby when one went into the trap they had laid with *Iliana*.

As Tara loosed her arrow, she saw the blonde curls of Elin. Her mouth was open in a scream that didn't reach through space to Tara. A pirate practically lopped her right over the railing of *Lucia* and onto the pirate ship.

Tara twisted her stance, diverting the arrow at the last moment. But had she moved enough? If she blew Elin up, she would never live with herself. Her knees shook as the arrow sped downwards.

The blast exploded. Smoke billowed up. Tara blinked, eyes watering. She swiped the tears away. Where had she hit? *Stars let Elin be safe and not in pieces.* Tara stared below, waiting for the smoke to clear.

Chapter 39

Tara rubbed at her eyes again. But they were already moving past the pirate ship beneath them. *The Bounty* banked to port, going around the cutter's two masts on the outside.

She couldn't breathe. The pressure in her chest made her ribs rigid, refusing to give space to her lungs. She grabbed another arrow. Her hands shook too much. She was too scared of hitting the crew being dragged from *Lucia* to the cutter.

The pirates were shouting. There was one with crimson hair another with sulphur yellow locks. Far Galaxians. At least those two. Everyone else could easily be outcast Edge Galaxians.

Elin came into view again, in one piece. She was dragged below, screaming and thrashing. Alive but kidnapped. Tara gritted her teeth.

The Bounty continued to turn. If they could incapacitate the cutter, cut the pirates off from escape then, maybe, they had a chance. Tara's eyes slipped past Merlon. He lay still on the deck. *If he's dying…*

She shook herself. If she thought like that she would freeze. Inaction would stop her from saving Elin. And Lennie! The Squamate was hauled to the railing. They lobbed him across. His arms and legs twisted and tied behind his back. Tara swallowed hard. She had heard rumours of what pirates sold Squamates for. Not into slavery. Somewhere in the Far Galaxies, they sacrificed Squamates.

Pirates ran from *Iliana*, leaping across *Lucia's* deck and back onto their own ship. Kieran had been dumped beside the hatch on *Iliana*. They began shooting at *The Bounty*. There was near panic to their movements now. Tara saw faces of surprise instead of the smirks and grins before they realised *Lucia* hadn't come alone.

Their blitz arrows were swapped for blasts. *The Bounty* groaned and shivered as they started bombing her. Smoke forced upwards. The heat being drawn up from under the keel to the sails. It rendered the deck smoggy and hotter than an oven. Tara loosened an arrow, knowing it would go wide. She couldn't aim. Couldn't see.

Fabian coughed beside her, clutching the railing. *The Bounty* swung round, lowering herself all the while. Whoever was Mira's helmsperson, xe was highly skilled steering through this.

The pirates shot forward, their anchor wheeling in and sails primed. But Mira couldn't pursue now her ship faced the wrong way. They would need to complete another tight turn around *Lucia* and *Iliana* to get on the pirates' tail.

Tara glanced back. One of *The Bounty's* main sails had taken a hit and smouldered from large holes in the middle. They would be slow. Catching up nearly impossible.

"Fasten to *Iliana*! Quickly!" Mira's shout cut through the moans of the damaged ship.

They weren't pursuing. The realisation hit Tara like a punch in the gut. But there were injured on the Amulean ships. Merlon and Kieran were the two she had seen thus far. But there would be others. Gaunty in the hold on *Iliana* and who knew who else had been thrown in like sacks of produce.

Tara dropped her bow when Hinna shoved a grappling hook in her hands. She gritted her teeth. Her wounds panged but the pain was secondary to her fear. Paled against the rush of dread burning through her body.

She swung the hook. It caught on the railing across the narrow gap. Tara pulled, alongside the other crew. Behind her, the anchor chain clicked.

The rigging and sails flared once, then the colours diminished to a weak, steady glow. *The Bounty* rocked against *Iliana*, both schooners complaining from their breathing wood scuffing against one another.

Mira placed her hand on the rail and vaulted herself over. Her boots had barely thudded on the deck of *Iliana* before her sword whistled out. Tara scrambled across the railings not half as gracefully as Mira.

Fabian followed.

Tara's heart thundered. She ran a hand over her eyes, clearing them of the tears from the smoke. She scanned the deck. Mira ran to Kieran. No pirates.

Mira held up her sword, her thumb jutting upwards. Kieran was alive then. Tara let out a small breath, the pirates had scampered, but they had Elin and Lennie and Jara. She wasn't sure who else they had taken to their ship. It had all gone so fast.

Mira waved and pointed into the hold with her sword. "Quick now." She spoke in a hush. Three of her crew rushed past Tara. Fabian followed them below, cutlass drawn and a hard look on his face Tara had never seen before.

Tara picked up her feet. Mira's crew could deal with any pirates hiding on *Iliana*. She trotted across and found the gap between *Iliana* and *Lucia* was longer. The ropes were stretching at the strain, the three ships not quite catching the same amount of energy. *Lucia's* sails were badly damaged. Halyards whipped in the energy, chopped free from their holds by the pirates. The sails luffed and made *Lucia* bob and list.

Tara sheathed her sword and climbed onto the railing. She sucked in a breath. Merlon's listless body on the other side of the deck gave her the courage. She leapt across. For a brief second, there was nothing but the black emptiness of outer space beneath her. But then she soared past the rail of *Lucia* and landed with a hard roll.

Her knees screamed at the impact, but she fought back up. Stumbling across, she reached Merlon. Her hands shook. His body swam before her and only when her fingers reached his shoulder did the surroundings settle. She shook the dizziness from her head. "Merlon?" She squeezed his shoulder. There was a slight grunt.

364

She hauled at him. He was too heavy and her fingers too shaky. She looked up, Fabian leapt across to *Lucia* in that second. "Fabian! Help me get him on his side."

"He wasn't there. They've took him. Me brother!" Fabian skidded to a halt. He dropped beside Tara. "He's alive?"

Tara looked at Fabian. The tremor in his voice was as bad as that of her hands. She nodded. "They took Lennie and Elin too. We cannae let them escape."

They heaved Merlon onto his side. Tara bent his knee so he wouldn't roll. He murmured but didn't wake. Blood spread on his left side and the cut on his temple had reopened.

She yanked his shirt out of his trousers bracing herself for the worst. But the cut on his side wasn't deep. It was unlikely to have damaged a vital organ. Breathing out slowly, she sat up. "Yorik?"

"Not on *Iliana*." Fabian shook his head. He stood and scanned the deck. Then he shaded his eyes. "We's got to catch them."

"Down 'ere!" Karl's voice carried up from below.

Tara sprinted to the hatch. There was Karl, lying at the bottom of the ladder. He flailed to get up.

"Thank the stars!" She slipped more than climbed down. Then she discovered Bailey on Karl's shoulder. She didn't know when the rat had left her hide under Tara's hair.

"Merlon will live. I already checked," Bailey said. "Deyon and Derek's in the forecastle, drugged by the pirates. Six are below if my ears don't deceive me."

Karl nodded. "We were trying to lock ourselves in the armoury once we saw them arrows."

Tara knelt by Karl, helping him to stand and handed him a crutch. "Let's get you to the sick bay. You might need to be the one tending the others. Bailey, what do you mean by drugged?"

"Coconut water, the Jungle Galaxy variety. It's old and weak but I smell it on the arrows." Bailey scurried up Tara's arm.

Tara settled Karl on the cot. "I'm sorry, I've got to keep going."

Karl squeezed her arm. "Any dead?"

Tara swallowed hard. "I donae think so. But many were taken." A shout on the main deck sent her whirling. She sped back out of the hold. Jumping out, she stopped and let her gaze run across the decks.

Fabian waved at her. "We've gotta pursue before we lose 'em."

"Let's not rush. We need a plan, or we'll all be caught," Mira said. She stood by *Iliana's* railing.

Tara checked Merlon's pulse again, then joined Fabian on the *Lucia* side of the railing. "They took most of *Lucia's* crew. Who's in *Iliana's* hold?"

"Gaunty, Boomer and about a dozen others. Some seem to be *Iliana's* crew," Mira replied.

"They took Hakim. And both kids." Kieran coughed and gagged. He was fighting on all fours, panting, and heaving but not quite throwing up.

Bailey jumped from Tara's shoulder to the rail. "They will have put the most desirable ones on their own ship."

Tara stared at the rat. She didn't want to understand what Bailey meant. That the pirates had taken those they knew would fetch the best prices in the slave markets. And whatever market they planned for Lennie. "We need to follow. We cannae let them get to Blacklock's."

Fabian nodded. "We go on *Iliana*. Any below who can sail?"

"It'll be suicide. Or enslavement." Mira spoke through gritted teeth.

Kieran made it to the rail, pulling himself to standing. "I's going. They's got Hakim!"

Fabian picked up a strangely blunted arrow from beside his feet. The fletching was painted black and blue, the pirates' colours. "We go on *Iliana*, and you follow when you can." He pointed at Mira with the arrow. "*Lucia's* out of commission. Merlon needs tending to." He reached for the tip of the arrow as if to test it.

"Don't touch the end!" Bailey sprung at Fabian's face. He dropped the arrow with a jolt. It hit the railing and bounced, falling between the two ships. Tumbling down it left the atmospheres of the breathing wood and kept falling into the dark mists below. "It's got coconut on it," Bailey explained. "Makes you fall sleep."

"We go back to Outpost 9, find pirate hunters to help us," Mira said.

"There's nae time!" Tara hissed.

Kieran pounded his hand against the rail. "We go now. And you follow as backup." He rarely had such clarity of expression. No babbling today. Not when his partner's freedom was at stake.

"It's me brother," Fabian said, voice suddenly soft.

Mira blew out a breath. She turned and stalked back and forth. Ten seconds later, she stopped. "Alright, but we need a plan. A good one."

"Remember you have me," Bailey said.

Tara looked at the rat, an idea forming. "You still can't pick locks, can you? What about sniffing out more of that coconut drug stuff?"

Bailey sniffed offendedly. "Of course, I can! I took extra classes in lock-picking after I couldn't help you out when Lady Galantria had you imprisoned. Besides, I'm a lieutenant Tracker and a *rat*. I'm the best at sneaking around, that I can promise you."

Tara swallowed hard. She glanced back. Merlon was shifting. "Mira, do you have anybody with healer's skills?"

"Yes," Mira half-turned, "Uthak's already seeing to those...Uthak!" A tall, black man straightened beside *Iliana's* deck hatch. "Please, we have more injured on the Intergalactic Traveller. How are those below?"

Mira had barely finished before Gaunty appeared. Xe looked groggy and nauseous like Kieran. Xe raised a hand when Tara gave a cry of relief.

"Minor cuts. I's cut them free of their bonds," Uthak said. Without a pause, he leapt across the gap and stalked over to Merlon.

Tara turned to follow, but Fabian grabbed her arm. "I'm takin' *Iliana* now. Are you stayin' or comin'?"

"He won't die," Bailey whispered in Tara's ear, once more back on her shoulder and hiding under her hair.

Tara clenched her teeth. Her heart was heavy. But they had to rescue the kids. Elin's little face, mouth open in a soundless scream. The memory overlaid itself with that of Ramson, crying while he roasted alive, hugged tightly by his ma. Tara flexed her shoulders and followed Fabian when he jumped back to the schooner.

Other crew, people Tara didn't know, appeared after Gaunty. They looked about, dazed. A woman spotted Fabian and ran across the deck, seizing his arm. "Fabian! They've taken Pietrek! And our Cap'n."

"We know, Inia. We're goin' after them." Fabian patted her arm. Then he raised his voice. "Remove the grappling hooks! Let *The Bounty* and *Lucia* reattach. We're goin' to hunt us some pirates. Anyone *not* up for that, get off *Iliana*."

Tara fought to focus her gaze. She had to get it right. It was nothing more than a flicker but that would have to do. "Energy's stronger a few degrees up. We need to tack to starboard."

"What is the plan?" Mira spoke through gritted teeth, planting her feet on *Iliana's* deck. "You're not going off without a plan."

Fabian grabbed her and gave her a short and heated kiss. He smiled when they broke apart. "Tara has one."

Mira turned her head, still in Fabian's arms. "You do?"

Tara found herself staring at Merlon, supported by Uthak he held a bandage to his side but was still lying down more than sitting. She pushed away the longing to run and kiss him as passionately as Fabian and Mira had embraced one another.

Tara faced them again with a nod. "We let ourselves get caught."

Chapter 40

After the initial uproar, the remaining people of *Iliana's* crew gritted their teeth and worked fast. Kieran stayed aboard but Tara made Gaunty crawl back to *Lucia*. Xir ankle wasn't quite healed yet and would only hinder xem.

A couple of other people swapped back and forth, but in the end, they were a dozen sailors on *Iliana*. Not at all enough if they were going to attack the pirates with no backup. But that wasn't their plan.

In two minutes, the ships had shifted. *Iliana* bobbed by herself, but still near *The Bounty* who was now lashed to *Lucia*. Bailey had vanished and reappeared, carrying a tiny letter tube in her yellow teeth. Tara stuck it into her bandeau for later. "We're ready."

Fabian nodded and called across to *The Bounty*. "Gem, we're off."

"Be careful, please. We'll follow soon." Mira ran to the bowsprit and held up her arm in goodbye. Behind her, the damaged main sail was being mended hastily.

Fabian blew a kiss and turned. "Let's get movin'. They're fast but a cutter won't hold that speed for long when their cargo is full."

It felt like a lifetime had passed since the pirates took off, but Tara had glimpsed the clock in *Iliana's* captain's cabin a moment ago and barely ten minutes had passed.

She drew in a slow, deliberate breath. She had to get this right, but her navigator's vision was no better than it had been for months. So she had to rely on the faint flickers of colour. "Raise us five degrees." The anchor chain clinked in, and *Iliana* shot forward. *Thank the stars she's a fast ship.*

Tara blinked rapidly, was that a whirl of disturbed energy up ahead? It turned down and hard to starboard. It looked like the sort of slip stream a quick-moving ship left. The emptiness of outer space remained disturbed for a long while. Except these swirling threads of turquoise were still close together, tight, and neat enough it hadn't been many minutes since the ship passed.

She narrowed her eyes, but the energy had vanished from her sight. If they steered after this and she had seen wrong or even imagined that slip stream…

No, she gritted her teeth. She had to trust what she had seen. She clenched her fingers around the handle of the wheel. "I see their path. We'll go hard to starboard in thirty seconds. They're heading down but energy's nae strong there."

Fabian raised a brow at her, but something about her expression made him nod. "Good." He raised his voice. "Sailors! Hard to starboard, we're divin'." Fabian sprung from the helm to help the crew.

Bailey's whiskers tickled against Tara's neck. "Stop panicking. We can do this. It's not that hard to get caught by pirates after all."

Bailey's words did little to still the shudder in her chest.

"The plan better work or we're all going to the slave markets in Blacklock's Galaxy," Tara whispered.

She had already messed up running off *Lucia* like that and she wasn't letting more bad things happen to Elin and Balfour. She didn't know if she would make a good ma, but by the star-cursed universe, she wasn't going to see them sold into slavery.

Adrien had never spoken much of his past, in fact Tara had only known through her da that Adrien had been kidnapped and enslaved for a number of years. Merlon had filled a few gaps although he hadn't known much either. But she knew slaves were branded and beaten and tortured if they didn't do as they were told. The thought alone set her heart in stone.

She flexed her shoulders and wriggled her fingers, one at a time around the wheel's handles to get some blood back into her hands. She would need her full focus and strength.

Iliana turned, groaning, and straining against her rigging. Tara blinked and picked up another glimpse of energy. They were on the right track. She could feel it in her bones.

Then *there*, a flicker of colours. Not energy, but the shine of sails. The pirates had stopped! "Fools," Tara muttered. Then she raised her voice. "They're below us! Prepare for a short fight. Donae get yourselves killed!"

The pirates were clearly overzealous. They probably didn't expect for there to be a navigator who – despite struggling to see energy these days – could follow their secret paths. They thought they had made it away or hoped nobody would look down as they passed on the regular altitude for human space travel. And they didn't know Trackers existed and one was onboard *Iliana* right now.

Tara wanted to let *Iliana* slip overhead, pretending they hadn't seen the pirates and then move at them, but that wasn't for her or *Iliana's* crew to do. They were here to get caught, after all.

"Bailey, note this location and add that Mira should pass overhead like she hasnae seen them. Rapid turn and descend to hit them in a surprise attack. Donae send the letter yet."

"Clever. I like your thinking." Bailey slipped under Tara's shirt and yanked at her breast support. A few tickling seconds later, she yanked once more and reappeared. "You could have made a good Tracker if you weren't so unfortunate to be born a human." Bailey patted Tara's cheek with her tiny paw and vanished under her hair.

Tara snorted. She pressed the altitude pedal, letting *Iliana* dive straight for the pirates. "Anchor at forty percent diversion! Fabian, shoot a blast but donae kill nobody or they'll shoot back to kill too."

"I know." Fabian nodded and aimed.

Tara assumed he too had heard stories from Lennie. Stories of pirates killing a random crew member for every person they had lost during a raid or kidnapping. She was suddenly thankful Merlon had been blinded by the blitz arrows and unable to use his sword skills. If he had been in a fair fight, he would have killed a handful at least.

She wasn't sure if any had perished from the blasts, she and Mira's crew had sent. There had been too many of their own amongst the pirates she didn't think anybody had dared direct shots. She had certainly regretted the first one she had shot where she nearly hit Elin.

Fabian's arrow found the top gallant sail on the main mast. It exploded in an orange flash of heat and destruction. Wood flew to all sides. The canvas caught fire, dripping embers onto the main sail the pirates seemed to only have been about to change from one half-burned sheet to a new one.

The pirates sprung about. Arms pointed and Tara opened her mouth to shout for the anchor to come out more, but Kieran was already on it, Inia helping. The schooner slowed abruptly. She was much quicker to halt and manoeuvre than the larger *Lucia* Tara had become used to.

They slipped past the pirates, turning to get the broadside on them as if they intended a full volley. Blast arrows did fly from *Iliana*, but they went upwards, hitting the top sails of the small cutter when Tara would normally have said burn the law and shoot straight at the pirates, it wasn't like any law enforcers would arrest them for killing pirates who had kidnapped half their crew.

But they couldn't have won a direct fight anyway. There were at least thirty pirates and only a dozen, mostly injured and groggy, sailors on *Iliana*. They would never be able to kill enough pirates before they shot back and boarded.

Tara had barely had that thought before the pirates' cutter was moving forwards. They would ram into *Iliana's* side. Her already damaged hull best hold.

Tara swallowed hard. *Tomaline, watch over my friends. Protect the kids and let me live long enough to apologise to Merlon.*

Then the cutter's bolstered bow hit them, and she was thrown sideways. Tara dangled on the wheel. Pain shot through her ribs. Her breath became a gasping wheeze. Her right knee threatened to buckle under her.

Forcing herself to straighten, she pressed down the rudder lock and grabbed her sword. Pirates swarmed onto the deck. It looked like more than thirty, but that had been Inia's best guess and she had been knocked out along with the others in the original attack on *Iliana*.

Tara didn't get a block in before not one, but two pirates were on her. One kept her cutlass engaged while the other came in with a bludgeon. Tara half-dodged, but mentally stopped herself from fully twisting away. The wooden club clipped her ear. She threw herself on the deck with a cry of pain, dropping her cutlass. *This better work.*

Her wrists were instantly seized. Coarse ropes wound around them. She dangled her head, hoping it seemed like she was out of it. Tara's arms were wrenched back and by the time she dared a peek through her eyelashes, she was being hauled towards the pirate's ship.

"Bloody fools. Yi really thought yi could'a getaway attacking us, huh? Freeing yir stinking friends, huh?" The man's accent was heavy and foreign. He vaguely sounded like the Moonside sailor who had accidentally knocked Merlon out the other day.

"Typical Twin Cities folk. They think'eh they come here and makeh a good deal in Fristate. Flies have more brains."

This voice was sibilant and genderless but had a Fristate accent.

Tara dared let her eyes flutter open for an instant. She jigged at the sight. A man with long black hair, specked with grey, and ochre red skin grinned down at her. His teeth were a crystalline blue and the canines were longer and slightly pointed in both top and bottom jaw. Her throat shut and no air would pass. *A blue fang from the Far Galaxies!*

He had a crazed look in his eyes making the gruff person also lugging Tara look like a friendly parent in comparison. Why did he speak Old Galaxian? She supposed the blue fang might have lived in Moonside for a while.

Then she was swung upwards, and her stomach flipped as she did, mid-air flying over *Iliana's* railing. She landed on the pirate cutter's deck with a thump that forced all air out of her lungs, leaving her gasping and groaning in pain. Those stupid ribs weren't ever going to get better.

Someone kicked and rolled her along. The deck vanished under her suddenly. She tried flailing but landed hard again, this time in the hold. Dizziness overwhelmed her. They had underestimated how efficient these pirates were.

She understood now how entire crews vanished without a trace. The thought almost made her laugh bitterly. She intimately knew two very different reasons ships went missing. Portals storms *and* efficient pirates. *What more will you send our way, Tomaline?*

"Tara!" That voice. So tiny and scared.

Chains rattled. "She dun't care about us," Balfour's whisper wasn't so quiet, and Tara found tears slipping down her cheeks as she was dragged across the floor. His words cut

376

her more than the ropes around her already injured wrists. More than she had thought sincere words by someone she barely knew could.

"Are we keeping that one here? Look's scraggly." Someone grumbled.

Tara caught a glance of her current captor. The pale woman shrugged. She bent and clamped a chain around Tara's wrists, yanking the rope off. "She was steering the ship, must be important. Might get a ransom, you know."

Tara was thrown into a pile of people in the hold. A barred door clicked shut with a grating screech. She took a few deep breaths before sitting up. With a bit of a hassle and panging ribs, she eased her chained hands in front of herself.

Elin and Balfour stared out from behind bars of a tiny cage to her right. They wouldn't be able to stand up inside it, but at least they weren't also chained.

Tara shuffled towards them. "We'll save you. Donae worry, we'll—"

Balfour pulled Elin away. Huddling against the bars on the far side of the cage. "You left us. Like all the other adults," he said. He stared at her, so serious and with only the barest hint of the hurt she had caused him.

Tara's chest tightened. How would she ever regain their trust? How could she make them see she hadn't run from *them* but from her anger at Merlon? Stormed away to escape her own fear. As always.

She let out a breath. Nothing but honesty would help her. "I'm sorry I left like that. It was wrong of me to do. I can understand why it would seem like it was because of you but it wasnae. Sometimes…I get scared. When I'm scared, I say

377

and do things I donae mean. I didnae want to scare you too, so I went to Mira's ship to think but I see now my actions only scared you more."

Balfour's face was closed, but Elin wriggled free off his skinny arms and shuffled over to Tara. She reached through the bars and Tara grabbed her hand gingerly.

"I'm sorry Elin, Balfour." She held Balfour's gaze. But he turned his head away, arms hugging himself like he physically hurt. She knew that feeling.

Tara swallowed hard. "I willnae run away again. Maybe with time, you'll trust that I will stay. Maybe you'll believe it wasnae you I ran from but myself. If you let me, I'll show you by always being there for you."

Holding Elin's trembling hand, she realised she meant those words like she had never meant anything before. The truth hit her chest and stole her breath. She grabbed the bars between her and Elin, leaning her pounding head against the cold metal. She was so terrified about everything else right now, parenting didn't seem all that impossible. She could do it, if she let herself have a chance.

But what did any of that matter if her plan didn't work, and they all got sold into slavery? She heaved an unsteady breath down, but she managed to hold back a sob.

She wished they were back on *Lucia*. Dreamt how she would curl up beside Merlon, soaking in his warmth. That there weren't bars and chains in the way so she could draw Elin into a proper hug. She tried to embrace the child, nonetheless. "We'll get out of here."

Elin peered up at her through the bars, arm wrapping around Tara's. "I miss my mummy. And my Spot."

378

It took Tara a moment to remember the kitten Elin had claimed. She petted Elin's curls, glancing round the hold to get the lay of things. Only then did she realise Fabian had been thrown into the same barred cell, chained hands, and feet.

He sent her a weak smile. "Plan better work, eh?" he pointed at another pen across from theirs.

Tara's heart skipped a beat, and she sat up straight. "Cary! What are you doing here?"

"I wanted to help." He hung his head.

She shook her head. "But where were you? Hiding? How did you even get off *The Bounty* without Ola stopping you?"

Cary picked at a knot in the wood beneath him. "I'm really good at being quiet. Had to, so my stepdad dun't remember to beat me." His voice broke, his shoulders quivered then he sighed. "I wanted to help free them two, so I hid behind some barrels."

Tara could only stare, speechless. It was quite brave of him to want to help rescue Elin and Balfour, but it meant there was a third kid Tara needed to get off this pirate cutter alive and well.

Cary shifted and the shackles around his wrists rattled. Unlike Elin and Balfour, he had been thrown into a cell with four others. One was Hakim, still looking dazed with blood staining the shoulder of his yellow shirt. Another stared at Fabian with eyes about to roll out of his head.

"Good to see you too, brother." Fabian winked.

Pietrek stood, grabbing the bars. "Stars burn me, what are you doin' here?"

"Savin' ya stupid arse. Or well, havin' my love save ya arse so ya can't refuse meetin' her no more." Fabian grinned although he licked his lips, a hint of nerves twitching across his face.

They didn't look the least alike, but then, Pietrek was adopted so it made sense. Where Fabian was tall, long-faced and wiry, Pietrek had broad shoulders and a square jaw. His eyes were deep set and a large partner tattoo snaked up along his right wrist and beefy arm. Pietrek's hair was reddish brown and braided in tight rows across his head.

He wasn't handsome but had a seriousness to his expression that reminded Tara of Merlon. It sent a pang of longing through her. *Hopefully Merlon's back on his feet now.* She tried willing that into being true.

Bailey slipped down from Tara's shoulder. "Was that my cue?" she whispered.

Tara scanned the hold. The pirates were stomping around on the main deck, switching out the burned sails judging by how the last had left with new canvas in their arms.

She caught Fabian's gaze and discreetly indicated Bailey, now hiding in her lap.

Fabian rubbed his hands together. "Let's do this. Have we sent Mira the coordinates?"

Bailey poked her head out, nodding. "We're ready as can be."

"You're a trained rat, remember, no chatting," Tara murmured and prodded the rat in the chest.

That last part would be a challenge for Bailey. The Trackers' true identity being revealed wasn't a major concern for Tara though.

380

She was far more occupied with getting everyone freed before the pirates realised or the plan would backfire badly.

She swallowed hard. "Let's go."

Chapter 41

The chains around Tara's wrists clicked open and fell away. She blinked. *That was fast.* "Hang on a moment," she whispered and picked the rat up. "Pst, Derek, Jara." She waved a hand at the two in the cell opposite.

Derek ran a hand over his face, but then straightened on his knees when he noticed Bailey. "Is that—"

"The *trained rat*," Tara said, willing him to understand. If she could avoid angering the Trackers in this escape, she would. "She…it-it can pick locks, remember."

Jara raised a perfect brow. She had a smear of lipstick and blood across her chin from her split lower lip. "I didn't know it could."

"Oh yes, new trick we taught it." Fabian's chains jingled and he settled beside Tara. He gestured at one of the three strangers in their cell to move closer. "Come, we've a plan."

One of the women got up but a bald, older man with a pot belly, skinny arms, and the spongy nose of someone who drank too much grabbed her arm. "Rashida, it's a filthy rat!" He hissed.

"And that's Pietrek's brother, ye dolt." Rashida, a Haven Galaxian like Kieran judging on her accent, whacked the man's knobbly hand. "Capten's somewhere below so it's up te us te get out. Let's hear what he's got te say." She moved closer, a crease forming between her dark brows. Her long, black hair hung in braids down her back.

Tara sighed, even prettier than Jara. She glanced at the helmswoman in the cage beside Pietrek's. She was watching Rashida with an interest that made Tara decide to introduce them later. If there was a later.

Tara shook herself before her own lack of real interest reminded her of that hard spot in her stomach that had formed the moment, she saw Merlon lying face down on the deck of *Lucia*. *He'll be fine, concentrate.*

Clearing her throat, she held Bailey out, simultaneously showing her freed wrists. "I know it's weird. It's like a pet goose or chicken I guess, but we taught her things." Tara glanced at the hatch, but no pirates were moving down. "She'll pick any lock she sees. We have backup coming."

Rashida's frown didn't let up, but eventually she nodded. "A'right, what's the plan? Bash their heads in when backup arrives?"

"Somethin' like that." Fabian grinned. "We get out and explain to the others. Can't have anybody screamin' cause of the rat. Surprise attack or we'll be dust."

Rashida made a motion as if to brush her hair out of her face despite it being gathered behind her head. She eyed

Bailey, then held her shackled wrists out. Bruises discoloured splotches on her brown skin. "How long till backup's here?"

Bailey turned her nose and stared up at Tara. She clearly knew but Tara didn't know at what point the rat had sent the tiny letter tube with coordinates to Mira. Probably when Fabian had asked. She had to make a guess. "Around half an hour."

A tiny paw patted Tara's finger twice. Did that mean she had messed up or guessed right? Tara had no idea. She wondered if Bailey could speak Squamate but then her fingers were so tiny, and she had no thumbs so it might not help them anyway if she learned.

"Rat better be quick," Rashida said.

Tara held her hand closer, and Bailey leapt at Rashida's wrist. The sailor jolted, but pressed her lips together around a faint yelp, eyes full of distrust. Bailey reached her tiny paws straight into the lock. Half a second later, the first chain fell from Rashida's wrist.

"Tomaline's grace, never thought I'd see *this*." Rashida lifted a hand and gestured a star towards the bulkhead above them. She had a vaguely different accent to Kieran and Tara wondered if she had spent a lot of time around Outpost 5-9-6. It would explain why she invoked Tomaline rather than Haven Galaxy's main star, Amlarin.

Bailey hopped from Rashida's now bare left wrist straight to Fabian. Incredibly, she hadn't begun chatting yet. She would surely talk everyone's ears off when they were back on *Lucia*.

The sceptical drunkard didn't let Bailey near, but the other woman in the cage freely offered her shackles, although her face was twisted in disgust. Then Bailey was scuttling up Tara's shoulder whiskers tickling her ear. "Lift me to the cage door lock. You need to tell the others not to shriek when I free them."

Tara barely stopped herself from responding to the whisper. She held out a hand near the square of the cell's lock. Bailey slipped down her arm and reached into the keyhole.

The hatch ladders groaned. "Someone's comin'!" Fabian hissed under his breath.

Terror twisted Tara's stomach and she threw herself backwards. She stumbled on the chains, sending them rattling across the wooden boards. Snatching for them, she realised Bailey still dangled with her little arm inside the cage door lock. Tara plucked up her chains, clasping one around her wrist and grabbed Bailey. The rat squeaked, legs pedalling. "Sorry!" Tara breathed.

Bailey flew up her arm and under her hair. "I'll be…alright." She sounded like she wasn't, and Tara's chest ached. What if the rat had broken a bone in her tiny little arm?

The unnamed woman and Rashida fumbled to hold the chains around their wrists. Fabian did likewise after holding a finger to his lips at Elin and Balfour. They looked terrified enough Tara doubted they would have dared to speak anyway.

Tara dropped to the floor as the pirate's boots thumped hollow in the hold. She pushed the right-hand shackle around her wrist and gathered her hands in her lap so it hopefully didn't show that the chains weren't quite closed and would fall away if she lifted her arms.

It was one of the pirates Tara had noticed earlier. Sulphur yellow hair, reddish brown skin and tall cheek bones that made xem look entirely foreign. A Far Galaxian, there could be no doubt about that.

There was the occasional immigrant in Amule, but it was rare. Supposedly more lived in Fristate and more yet in Moonside, a few months closer but still years of travel to the nearest Far Galaxies.

Tara doubted this pirate had flown the entire way though. Da had said they used portals. That's how Adrien vanished after being kidnapped and sold into slavery. They had to have mountains of portal powder out in the Far Galaxies to travel so far.

Even before it had been outlawed in Amule, nobody travelled beyond the city limits due to the price of the powder.

Except when the former Foreign Affairs chancellor had sent Tara through to *Lucia* along with Mira and Patrice. Tara had thought it wouldn't work but it seemed she had pictured Adrien well enough as they had arrived in Merlon's cabin a few seconds after stepping through the portal.

The pirate didn't spare them a glance but stalked through the hold and vanished into what Tara assumed was the forecastle. *How many are resting in there?* She turned her head but couldn't see Bailey hiding behind her neck. "We need a count of the pirates," she mumbled.

"I smell at least thirty. Maybe forty." Bailey pipped quietly. "I-I won't be able to run down and find the sedative."

Tara gave half a nod. Bailey was injured, that much was certain. Could she even still pick locks? Gritting her teeth,

Tara turned to Rashida. "Any idea how many pirates are aboard?"

"Dunno." Rashida shrugged. "Two-score mayhaps? They don't travel far or long. They hit a couple of ships and hurry back te their stinking galaxy and the slave markets there."

"Two-score? That's a lot for such a small ship," Fabian said.

Rashida shook off her shackles again. "As I said, catch and run home. Blacklock's only 'bout a week away. No other cargo than us so plenty storage for supplies for themselves. We's been given nothing but a bowl of water te share for nearly a day."

"I'm hungry." Balfour pipped at the same moment.

Tara stuck her hand in her pocket. Empty. She tried the other, relief washing through her, a small parcel of dates was extracted. She opened it. Seven dates would hardly satisfy the kids. She looked up, realising Rashida and the other crew from *Iliana* were staring at the treats in her hand. "I'm sorry, the kids they've already been starved..."

"They's not been stuck for a day!" Drunkard growled.

Rashida whacked his arm again. "They's kids, have some passion."

Tara sent Rashida a thankful smile and reached through the bars to the cage Elin and Balfour were in. "Save two for Cary."

Balfour stared at the dates but didn't move closer to take them despite his hands trembling.

Elin, however, did take them and shuffled over to Balfour. "It are those sweet things."

"It is," Balfour said and rubbed snot off on his sleeve. Then he gingerly took one date. He stuffed the entire thing into his mouth and swallowed barely chewing.

"Donae eat the seed!" But it was too late, Balfour had already scarfed down the second date. Pit and all. Tara hoped it wasn't dangerous to eat it.

A creaking hinge made Tara jump. Fabian stood with Bailey in his hand, peering at the forecastle door. His knuckles were white where he clenched the barred door, he had pushed partially open. But nobody came to investigate.

Tara let out a breath and got up. She took two dates from Elin and went straight to Cary, who, despite her warning words, also ate the dried fruit whole. She sighed. Next time she would have to buy pitted dates, that much was clear.

"We should block the forecastle door," Rashida said. "But dunno how."

Tara regarded the door. It would be little help if they didn't also block the opening that went straight from inside the forecastle onto the main deck. Unless there wasn't one. She tried to bring back the dazed images from her capture. Some small ships only had one entrance to the hold and forecastle both through the middle of the main deck. But she couldn't recall if this cutter was one of those ships.

Fabian put a shoulder against the forecastle door. 'Crates, barrels?' he gestured.

"Willnae hold long." Tara shook her head. She scanned the hold for something better.

Bailey scurried around, letting people free. Tara noted the rat only used her left paw now, and kept the right front leg tucked near her chest while she bounded back and forth. Her fur puffed out in a way that told of pain.

Everyone was being remarkably quiet. But then, it didn't take many seconds to realise they were being freed and that there was a plan in the works. Nobody in their right mind wanted to be sold as a slave to some Far Galaxian maniac.

Yorik had never liked the Tracker much but still lifted Bailey up to unlock the cage door nearest the forecastle. His face was screwed into a grimace. Relief washed over him when the lock on his cage clicked.

The barred door swung open, and Tara smiled. 'I know how,' she signed. "Rashida, find some rope, please," she whispered.

The sailor nodded. "I'll go get Capten, she's not going te be much help though, they broke her arm." Rashida crept away into the darker side of the hold.

Bailey had barely finished freeing the four people in the cage opposite Yorik's before Rashida returned.

Iliana's captain was indeed not looking great. Blood caked down the side of her face. She looked dazed, shuffling dumbfounded after Rashida. Her left arm hung oddly, like the shoulder had been dislocated and the elbow bent the wrong way. It was a wonder she even stood on her feet. She didn't seem to have enough presence of mind to comment on the plans.

Tara waved Fabian away from the forecastle door and pushed first one, then the other cell door completely open. It was a terrible design, but pirates clearly weren't too clever. When both doors were open, the last two bars of each

389

overlapped the other, blocking the forecastle door more or less entirely.

"Was the Squamate with you?" Rashida asked and continued straight away. "Xe's in the lower hold, wanted doing som'thing before coming up here."

"Thank the stars," Tara muttered. She paused tying one of the two ropes around the bottom of the cell doors and turned. "Derek, go check if Lennie needs help."

The young sailor saluted and ran off. Fabian followed with a single gesture. 'Weapons.'

Tara nodded and finished lashing the bottom of the doors as Rashida stepped back from tying the upper part together. Tara took the hand offered and tried to bite back the grimace of her panging knees when she stood with Rashida's help. She hurt everywhere.

"You alright?" Rashida frowned, hand slipping onto Tara's shoulder.

Tara managed a smile. "Who knew being tossed around by pirates makes bruised ribs worse?" Painfully aware Rashida was *still* holding her shoulder, she cleared her throat and gestured at Jara. "Rashida, take Jara and scout the galley. Bring knives, frying pans anything like that. I suspect the armoury will be locked and the rat is hurt."

Rashida let her hand drop from Tara's shoulder, embarrassment in her pretty face. But when she turned and met Jara's gaze, she blinked, then smiled. "I wanna find food too. We're famished and useless for fighting like so."

Rashida led the way and Tara sighed. As cute as Rashida was, her mind kept circling back to Merlon. Would he be on his feet again now? Maybe slowly following Mira for extra backup? She hoped so.

There was a small tug at her trouser leg. Tara stooped to pick Bailey up. She would see Merlon again soon. She had to believe that. "Are you alright?"

"Sleepy," Bailey murmured. She slipped into Tara's shirt pocket, yawning. So, she had been hurt more than she let on. The Tracker always slept for days when she was seriously injured.

Tara pushed the worries about Merlon and Bailey away. She grabbed the door to Elin and Balfour's cage and gestured for them. "Come quickly. You need to hide behind the ladders. Fabian or me or Mira will call when you can run up and get back to Mira's ship."

Elin crept out, but Balfour had wrapped his arms around his legs. He shook his head when Tara waved at him again. "You'll leave again. They always do."

Tara gritted her teeth, biting back any remarks. She deserved that one. "Please, Balfour."

He stared at her hand. She tried to bend her beaten body enough to crawl inside to, gently, pull him out. A shuddering boom echoed through the ship from above.

The forecastle door burst open an inch then smacked into the barred doors. "Get lost! They're 'scaping!" A Moonsider shouted. Time was up.

391

Chapter 42

"**B**alfour come, please!" Tara reached for him, but he jerked further into the cage's corner, terror paling his face. Her heart was trying to escape through her throat. She swallowed hard. "There's nae time."

Balfour shook his head, tears streaming down his freckled cheeks. His entire body shook, and his breath had hitched.

"Tara! Gotta go!" Fabian screamed.

She flicked a little finger at him. A quick glance showed her Rashida and Jara were handing out knives, the still shackled grumpy drunkard climbing out first, the next sailors ready to follow.

Tara shifted to her knees, head bent to fit in the door of the tiny cage. "Yorik, get Elin and Cary out."

With a grunt, he seized Elin's hand, but Cary jumped backwards.

Tara had really messed them up, running away like that. Her gut throbbed in a painful twist. She shuffled back out of the cage and turned to Cary. "Please, you have to come with us. I'm sorry I ran. I'm so, so sorry I…" Her voice broke, she didn't even bother swiping the tears away.

Yorik hauled a shrieking Elin towards the hatch. Someone fell down the ladders and landed in the hold with a hollow thunk. Tara didn't dare look if it was someone she knew, who had been killed.

Derek reappeared from the hold. "Lennie's coming."

Cary stared at Tara for what felt like a lifetime. It was probably less than three seconds before he dived into the cage and grabbed Balfour's elbow. "We've got to leave. The pirates will only send us back to the island. Back to die."

Tara opened her mouth to say the pirates wouldn't know where the island was but only a squeak and sob passed her lips. She held out a hand when Cary dragged the hyperventilating Balfour out of the cage. "I willnae let that happen. Never."

"Maybe," Cary said. He let go of Balfour. "But at least you feed us."

Explosions and the flashes of blitz arrows flickered down into the hold through the hatch. The booms left the breathing wood groaning.

Tara wrapped her arm around Balfour and tried to stand. But he curled up on the floor, eyes blinking without seeing. *Burn us there isn't time for a panic attack.*

The clamour of weapons reached her. She tugged at him. He rocked back and forth, breath shallow. "Balfour you need to be strong. Just this once. Pirates are like ants smelling sugar. If they smell fear, they'll only get more ravenous."

Mira and her crew had to have boarded by now. How many pirates were on deck? Those in the forecastle were bending the hinges of the cell doors, screaming, and throwing themselves at the blocked door. It would be minutes if that much before someone with a knife reached around the door enough to cut the ropes that lashed the cell doors together.

The noise. How would she ever get Balfour to breathe slower while people fought and howled and beat on the door right beside them?

Cary knelt, knuckles white as he held Balfour's shoulder. "Elin's crying for you. We need to go to her. Stop whining and get up."

"Cary!" Tara stared at the boy. But, to her amazement, Balfour gasped in a deeper breath. Once, twice. Then he uncurled slightly. He still looked dazed. His body trembled under her hands.

"Where's Elin?" He asked. Eyes round with terror.

Tara helped him up, keeping hold of his shoulder to steady him. "She's up on deck. Yorik's taking her back to Mira's ship. You'll be safe there. All of you." Her voice was hoarse, full of the terror coursing through her.

She turned Balfour towards the ladders. Cary staggered along, the ship rocking from the blasts Mira's crew were directing at the hull. Were they hoping to blast a hole so the pirates couldn't pursue?

"Donae look at xem." She pushed Balfour's face against her side so he couldn't see the dead pirate by the ladder. At least xe was face down, blood seeping out in a pool around xem. Tara didn't think the pirates would show any mercy now they didn't have the upper hand and stood to lose their living cargo.

Lennie appeared from the lower hold when Cary skirted around the dead person and started up the ladder. The Squamate stopped and tilted his head. His hands fluttered, far too quickly for Tara to understand in her panic.

"Lennie you're speaking too fast, I—"

'Blast, below, soon. We run,' he signed each word carefully and stuck to a simplified version of his language. 'I carry, tell no scream.' He reached up past Cary.

"Cary hold on! Lennie will get you…" The Squamate was already out of the hold, a green lighting darting away with Cary in his arms before she could blink. She gulped down a breath and stopped Balfour from crawling up. "I go first, to check there's no pirates waiting."

She sought the hold. She had nothing akin to a weapon. An old broom stood between two cages. She snatched it, kicking the head off. The wood broke with a crunch and left a sharp point.

"Quickly after me when I shout for you. Wait on the ladder," she said. She nudged the dead pirate aside and pulled an empty sack over them, hoping Balfour hadn't looked.

Climbing ladders with one hand was luckily something she had practice in. She checked once over her shoulder. Balfour was halfway up, hands grasping the third rung from the top. He had tilted his head, large eyes watching her.

She stepped onto the grey light of the main deck. A woman flew at her, cutlass raised. Tara blocked but the broom snapped. She took a step back, and nearly fell into the hold. The blade came towards her head.

She fought to keep her balance and couldn't duck away. So much for a rescue. With a swing of the shortened broomstick, she hit her attacker's knee, slowing the descent of the sword.

Behind the pirate, Tara glimpsed Lennie. He leapt across to *The Bounty*. Elin cried out, already over there. Only Balfour left. Then Tara lost her battle with gravity. As her sore knee buckled, another sword winked in the grey light. And the cutlass coming for her head clanged in a hard block.

The blue fuzz of Mira's head flashed by. She stepped forward, boring a heel into her opponent's foot and disengaging her sword. A flicker of iron and the pirate screeched.

The cut was shallow, but Mira's sword continued across the woman's face, shearing off the nose, digging into her cheek. Mira kicked and the pirate fell, spluttering and howling to the deck.

"Get the sword!" Mira shouted. "Where's Balfour? He's the last one."

Tara scrambled across the deck and snatched the cutlass the nose-less pirate had dropped. Then she rolled and called down the hatch. "Balfour, up now!"

Mira blocked another attacking pirate.

Tara fought to her feet. Her muscles screamed. They burned like she hadn't had a break for a year. "Balfour, where—" A shimmer of energy warned Tara and she spun, meeting a strike a hair width before it cleaved her shoulder.

Mira ruthlessly cut another pirate down. She kicked again, spinning the screaming man, and slashed at the back of his knees. If Tara hadn't *known* Mira only had one arm she wouldn't have realised. If she hadn't seen Mira struggle with basic sword play during sparring but a year ago, she wouldn't have believed Mira had *ever* struggled. She lacked the finesse and technique Merlon had, but with pure strength behind each chop, she saw results.

Tara struggled to keep up. Her injuries were catching up with her. Each second passing, she moved slower, wheezing more for each painful breath after painful breath. She fought off one wiry, almost skeletal guy whose eyes had that slightly vacant look she had seen in the people in the addiction clinic Patrice had once volunteered in.

Fabian stabbed his back, cutting the erratic, unpredictable attacks short. The man had barely buckled before the next pirate came at Tara. There were so many. Far too many.

Tara stumbled over something. She suppressed a gag when she realised it was an arm. Clearly, Mira's crew had shot blasts straight at the pirates while there were no friends on deck. That explained the stench of burned flesh and blackened marks of explosions streaking the boards. The sails were flaming, embers swirled down and left searing trails where they landed on Tara's arms and face.

Mira screamed.

Tara spun to find her friend.

Mira staggered, blood staining the side of her pale-yellow shirt. The dark patch spread fast, faster than Tara could reach her. But Mira fought on, face to face with the black-haired man that had captured Tara. He bared his teeth. Those sharp, blue fangs glinting in the dim light of Fristate Galaxy.

"Tara!" Fabian shouted.

Her head whipped around. He was holding back pirates coming up from below. Her throat tightened. Where was Balfour?

She pirouetted around an already stumbling pirate, jabbing her stolen cutlass at xir ribs as she passed. The sickening sound of metal against flesh and bone. The feeling of the sword pressing into a body. She knew it would haunt her forever.

"Fabian, get to Mira! I'll hold them!" Tara panted. She grabbed the broken shaft of the broom and stabbed at the head of the pirate climbing out from the hatch. The woman screamed and flailed but still pressed up and out. *Where's Balfour!*

Tara couldn't look away. Fabian had run to save Mira from the blue fang and pirates popped out of the hold like ants from a hill.

Sweat stuck her hair to her face. Blood splotched her shirt sleeves but how much of it her own, Tara didn't know. She didn't feel pain. No more than usual for the past week or two. She slammed one pirate with the broken broom and blocked another with her cutlass. She couldn't hold much longer.

Behind her, people were shouting. It sounded like Derek, or Yorik and Jara. Why were they howling so? If the pirates had started swarming back onto *The Bounty*... She didn't dare finish the thought. *Tomaline, protect the kids.*

"Get out of there! Get away!" The words became clearer. "Tara! Fabian!"

"Balfour!" Tara yelled. She had promised not to leave him. Was he already back on *The Bounty*?

A pirate leapt at her. She whirled to meet xem, but there was no sword to block. The pirate was heavier and used xirself as a battering ram. A head and shoulder hit Tara's side. Right where her ribs hurt the most. She twitched in the stab of agony. Her feet lost the solidness of the deck. They tumbled, the pirate on top, driving all breath from her lungs. Her head smacked against the boards.

The world blacked out and came back with a haze. She gasped for breath. Her ribs throbbed. The beefy-armed person was still on top. The pirate drove an elbow into Tara's sternum. Everything dimmed for another five seconds. Tara's fingers groped, but she had lost the grip of the sword and broomstick.

A pale green shape flitted past. So fast Tara thought it was a blur of energy in her daze. The pirate's heavy figure vanished, rolling across the deck with a screech.

Claws scraped on the breathing wood, there was a low hiss and a distinct snap. The person's head dangled as xe dropped to the deck. Xir eyes still quivering but they saw no more.

Tara rolled over and gagged. Long, green fingers wrapped around her arm. Lennie pulled her back up. He was bleeding from a cut on his side, but the scales had somewhat protected him, and the wound was shallow.

'Run now, bomb soon,' Lennie gestured.

Tara still heaved, both struggling to breathe and to not throw up when the neck breaking Lennie had done kept replaying itself in her mind. She staggered and he dragged her across the deck.

His tail whipped at a man rushing them. The cold anger in Lennie's yellow eyes almost had Tara pull away in fear. She had never seen him like this. Never known how dangerous he could be. "Wait! Where's Balfour?"

Rashida and Jara were fighting, side by side, holding pirates off. Fabian was yanked back across to *The Bounty*. He kept throwing insults, but blood poured between his fingers, trying to stem a cut on his right arm.

Mira already stood on her ship. She looked like she could barely hold herself up at the railing. She clenched her cutlass, the blade broken and stained with blood. There was still a fury in Mira's gaze and Tara realised Hakim was holding her *back* more so than holding her upright.

"Ain't we forgetting som'thin'?" A gruff voice cried out.

Tara stopped so abruptly Lennie staggered sideways and lost his grip on her arm. Even as she turned, the deck began to lurch. Her fingers bored into Lennie's scaled arm.

There, held between two pirates, Balfour hung limply. His blond hair had fallen forward, hiding his face. His legs dangled against the deck, head lolling. Blood trailed from his nose. It dripped, slowly, onto the deck.

Chapter 43

I t was the blue-fanged pirate. He leered at Tara, baring his crystal blue teeth in a vicious grimace. There was no kindness. Not a grain of compassion in his face. Long scars drew down his neck, puckering the skin pinkish. They weren't old scars.

Tara sought the faces of the pirates gathering behind him, realising it had to be their captain or leader. One or two were eyeing their dead friends, strewn across the deck of their ship. Several were in…smaller pieces. Mira had been ruthless with the blast arrows during the initial attack, but that might be how they had made it this far.

It didn't matter. The pirates had Balfour. Tara made herself let go of Lennie. She took a step towards Blue Fang. She refused to let the tremors show. Gritting her teeth against the weakness of her voice. "Hand him over and we willnae kill the rest of you."

To her horror, Blue Fang laughed. A high, grinding chortle. Blood seeped down his face from a cut on his forehead. Had Mira hit him with the pommel of her sword? Tara vaguely recalled seeing that action in the fight but whether it had been when Mira faced Blue Fang or someone else, she couldn't remember. Mira was vicious. And she had clearly trained rigorously since she lost her arm.

"Clever ruse, I gave yi that." His accent was foreign, not exactly like that of a Moonsider, and he wasn't quite used to Old Galaxian judging by the grammar. How did he manage to speak while maintaining that terrifying snarl of his teeth anyway? "Yi could be pirates for such clever thinks. Maybe yi are."

Weren't blue fangs cannibals? She was sure she had heard that somewhere. If Far Galaxians sacrificed and ate Squamates, she wouldn't put it past others to eat humans too.

Lennie nudged Tara's elbow. 'No time,' he gestured when she dared a glance at the Squamate.

Her stomach twisted. Time or not, she wasn't leaving Balfour. How would she ever forgive herself if she did? Cary and Elin certainly wouldn't. She steeled herself. "Hand him over and we'll let you go." They all deserved to be burned to dust. But the dagger in Blue Fang's hand pressed against Balfour's neck in threat. He wouldn't truly harm Balfour, would he?

Tara heaved down a breath, somehow filling her lungs and keeping her shoulders squared. These were pirates. They had been willing to capture and sell not just adults, but kids to the slave trade in the Far Galaxies. Of course, he wouldn't hesitate to hurt, maybe even kill, Balfour. That poor kid had seen enough horrors in his short life. Had been ill-treated more than anyone else she had met.

"Yi hand over half of crew." Blue Fang gestured with the dagger. "We chosen who. The kid go free." He tightened his grip on Balfour's arm.

Balfour whimpered. His head shifted and Tara caught his eyes fluttering open. Balfour made a squeak of fear and thrashed when he regained his senses.

Blue Fang whipped the black dagger up. The blade once more against Balfour's neck, and the boy went stiff as a board. His blue eyes met Tara's. Pure terror shone from them.

"I willnae leave you." Her words stuck in her throat, whispered so low he couldn't have heard, but a lone tear slid down his cheek.

"Tara, come back here, we'll think of something," Mira called.

She shook her head before Mira had finished talking. If she stepped off the pirate ship, Balfour would have his throat slit. She knew it like she had known her ma would die from the day the healers told them the cancer had returned a mere two months after Ma's first surgery. And Balfour would never trust her again if she turned her back now.

Tara's skin tingled. Nausea churned in her gut. She kept running her fingertips over the scabbing wounds in her palms. They were healing well now. But would leave scars forever.

That, she knew too. Some scars remained tender. Like the gashes inside her mind every time she lost someone. Some days they would seem hardened and strong, other days as tender as if the wounds had barely healed.

She stared at Balfour. All other adults had forsaken him, and she could already see him closing down. Readying

403

himself for his death. He still didn't believe she wouldn't leave him to die.

A thought whispered from somewhere in the dark cloud over her mind. A memory of something the kids had said. Bailey had proved it untrue, of course, but the pirates didn't know that.

Lennie reached out and grabbed her arm, but Tara twisted free and took another step forward. She held her hands up when all the pirates raised their weapons. "I'm nae dangerous. But he is." She nodded at Balfour.

Balfour's jaw quivered. He thought she was abandoning him. Thought she would treat him like his ma had. He would understand later. Had to. Unless this didn't work. Then he would think himself rejected all over again, whether he lived or died. Tara felt sick to the bone, but she was out of ideas. Had to follow this one through.

Tara lifted her hand and coughed. Suddenly it was good her ribs were bruised. She buckled sideways, wheezing at the pain the pretend cough had brought on. No need to fake *that* agony. "He's sick. It's the lung rot. Do you nae see how skinny the kids are?"

Did people get skinny from lung rot? She thought Merlon had mentioned something about wasting away but she didn't know if he meant literally losing weight.

Blue Fang didn't react, but half the remaining twenty-odd pirates took a step back in unison. Tara noted one who looked like a Moonsider. Skin pale yellow and hair with almost a purple tint. Xe would know better than anyone. Xe looked old enough xe had to have at least heard of the epidemic that killed thousands in Moon City. Moonsider sidled towards Blue Fang. "They're diseased!" xe hissed.

"Bluffs and lies," Blue Fang said. His eyes flashed black and deadly at Moonsider.

Tara shook her head. "We-we're on our way to…" She paused and coughed again. "…to Intrapolis for a specialist healer."

Balfour stared at her. She tried willing him to catch on but the hurt in his eyes betrayed he was only thinking about abandonment. There was a weak cough from behind her.

Tara whirled then thought the better of turning her back on the pirates. She caught a glimpse of Cary, coughing into his hand. He actually sounded phlegmy. A twinge of worry tightened the knot already twisting in her gut. *Tomaline don't take my lie for a challenge.*

Cary's cough sent a shiver through half the pirates. They muttered amongst themselves, several shifting further away from Blue Fang and Balfour.

"It checks out. The Squamate was 'board protecting them kids. Squamates din't get human lung rot," Moonsider said.

Tara's chest fluttered with hope. She had forgotten that. Merlon and his crew had been in Moon City and never got sick themselves because they had all had the Squamate lung rot a year earlier.

Moonsider kept hissing warnings, now indistinct under the chatter of fear from the others. Blue Fang leaned a little forward, glaring down at Balfour in front of him. There was a hint of uncertainty in his eyes.

"I'm a monster." Balfour bawled. "Mummy said so."

Tara's stomach clenched. She held out her arms. "Please, he'll die without the healer. The last one said we're in the most contagious stage. That's why he was attended to by the Squamate." She gambled. She didn't know if Lennie had been the only one near the kids when they were taken.

Blue Fang's grip tightened, and Balfour squeaked, but when Lennie yanked Tara backwards, the squeak turned into a sniffle. The choked sob sounded like a cough in disguise. Had he caught on after all? She hoped he had.

Blue Fang's eyes enlarged in perceived comprehension and fear. He shoved Balfour forwards, away from himself.

Tara twisted free, lunging for Balfour. The boy staggered, losing his feet and arms flailing. The same instant Tara's arms wrapped around his bony shoulders, catching him before he hit the deck, something grumbled. The sound came from deep within the pirate ship. The breathing wood groaned.

Then the deck seemed to rise. It was all so slow. Tara had time to remember what Lennie had signed below. Time to twist around, Balfour still in her arms. She managed five steps back towards *The Bounty*. She made to jump at the railing, but that's when the explosion burst out through the deck.

Lennie's long, green fingers snatched for her. His claws drew burning cuts across her skin. His tail whipped in the air. They were flung through space. Wood splinters and rigging pieces flew past. Tara hugged Balfour closer.

She closed her eyes then. Would they die instantly or starve to death, floating through the cool grey mist of Fristate's space? Suppose Balfour couldn't breathe away from the ship. At least he would go quicker then.

He twitched in her grip. Her eyes snapped open. There was Lennie, whirling and spinning through the air. Pirates, or parts of them, were hurtling all around them. She held Balfour closer, hoping her body and arms hid the sight from him.

The flickering rainbow of a large sail spread out before them. Tara tucked her head down. Like Merlon had taught her when rolling in a Squamate fight. Her shoulders hit the canvas.

She expected a bounce. But the fabric gave and gave. And it seemed to suck them closer. Heat blasted her face. Wood fragments bounced against the canvas. Splinters tore through the sail. A pirate, leg torn sideways in a grotesque mess of bone and tendons and blood, rolled down the canvas.

Balfour clung to her when they began the unendingly sluggish descent. Slowly, as if the sail was sad to let go of them, they rolled down. They gained speed when the heat from the air vanished, flashing through, and absorbed into the energy-catching sails.

She blinked, smoke itched her throat and eyes. The sail spit them out, hanging on for half a second as they reached the bottom, then gave them up. The deck suddenly came fast. Tara landed on her side. Her shoulder smacked against the deck.

A cry of pain escaped her when Balfour's body hit her other side. If she hadn't already had bruised ribs, she did now. She lost her grip on him. His small body writhing away. A small brown critter shuffled away too and was picked up by a hand, passing out of Tara's field of vision.

Her surroundings blurred into darkness. She blinked and struggled onto a knee. Gasping. No breath filled her lungs enough. The searing, burning pain along her side grew in sharp bursts.

Weapons clattered. Voices shrieked. Or maybe it was her ears. There was a high whine, like a whistle of a faraway dock master. Blood dripped onto the planks beneath her. Her hands thrummed but she couldn't fight further up. She remained on her hands and knees, panting and wheezing.

Hands grasped her shoulders, and she cried out. The pain was too much. It flared red hot under her skin and down her arm. Someone caught her elbow, kept her from hitting the deck.

She lost track of time. Someone sat her up. Back against…a crate? Maybe a barrel. Tiny hands grasped hers. Something warm slid down Tara's face, blinding her on one eye. Or was it because her eye had swelled up? The skin thumped painfully above her ear. It was that cut from some days ago. Open again. Probably.

She put a trembling hand over the little dimpled one clutching hers. Blood stained the fair skin. Pressure got applied to the side of her head and Tara winced, but she kept hold of the hand.

She drew the child closer. She couldn't remember any names. Her eyes refused to focus on the face beneath the blonde tangle of hair to her left. "It'll be alright," she whispered when there was a whimper and sniffle.

There was a nudge of her arm but when Tara turned her head, everything swam. She kept her breath shallow.

Avoiding the pain on her right side and hugging the child on her left tightly.

Another body pressed, embracing the child. Another blond head. She felt certain she knew both these kids. Surely they were under her care from the wash of relief swirling in her chest. She wound her arm around the second kid, pulling them both close, despite how much that hurt to do.

She didn't recognise some person talking at her. Not from the hazy image that was all her eyes could manage. But then, she also couldn't quite hear what was being said. It felt like she had been placed inside a silk cocoon and all she knew was the hot wetness of blood slipping down her face and pain tearing through her body in short spasms.

Someone lay on the deck beside her. Another person was tying off bandages, but blood had seeped through the wrappings on the arm already. Even in the fog there was something familiar about the prostate body. But shouldn't there have been a long black ponytail? An annoying, cocky smile? A thousand bad jokes spilling out in even the most absurd situations?

She attempted to speak. Wanted to ask who it was and if the person was alright. The body seemed very still and there was so much blood everywhere.

Then there were shouts again. And movement. She thought she saw a flicker of energy move out past the other side of the ship. Had there not been several ships?

Then her head seemed to tilt sideways, and she gave up holding it upright, leaning it on whatever she sat propped up against.

Her eyes fluttered open an instant when heavy boots thumped towards her. The blurriness gave way to a face. Drawn and furrowed but so familiar she smiled. Or tried to, she felt odd and cold.

"Merlon, I was so worried you...so worried..." Her lips refused to move, and she closed her eyes. Warm, tender arms wrapped around her, and she curled against his body, one hand still clutching both the children's.

Chapter 44

A rank taste lingered on Tara's tongue. Her mouth tingled from some odd herb. Had she been in pain before drinking a tart concoction? Time slipped out of her conscience. She was floating and weighed down at the same time.

Slowly, the faint sighs of a ship's breath enveloped her, like she had long had her ears stuffed and only now began to hear once more. She thought it was dark, but maybe she hadn't opened her eyes. The stillness of the ship sent her heart racing. Or was it because her hearing remained muffled?

It took an unfathomable amount of time before she regained the sense of touch. Sheets felt suddenly scathing against her skin. She gasped for breath, fighting, and realising she had rolled and pulled the pillow over her head.

Sounds grew sharp when she threw it off her. Or they returned harshly to her left ear. The other remained somewhat muted. It took another while before her raw fingers found their way to her head and discovered a bandage

411

wound around her right ear. It constricted. Pressing against the swollen soreness of her temple.

She worked at the bandage. It had to come off. Panic reared when it didn't budge at first. She yanked and scratched. It had to come off. Now!

Then rough, but gentle hands grabbed hers. A voice spoke but the terror coursing through her, the shallowness of her breath, it drowned out the words.

"Get it off! It's too tight!" Her voice cut through her brain. Too loud. She clamped her lips shut again. Her head pounded, starting from the sore spot by her right temple. Or was it from a spot inside her ear?

The pressure eased. Tara swallowed gulps of air. Her heart slowed. She fought to open her eyes but whatever she had been given made it difficult.

She glimpsed someone above her. But her eyelids closed again of their own accord. The person shifted, unwinding the last piece of the bandage, gingerly yanking the cotton wad from her right ear. The movements brought a scent she knew. Starlight and wood lye. *Merlon.*

She forced her eyes to open again. There, she could make out his silhouette against the grey window of a half-drawn curtain. She wasn't in the sick bay but in *Lucia's* cabin, in the bunk they shared. She couldn't focus her eyes enough to see his face.

He turned away as if to leave. Her hands groped, found his and held on. "Please, donae leave."

He turned back. Her eyes cleared a little more, although her eyelids fought to close again. He placed a hand against the side of her face that wasn't throbbing in agony. A faint smile spread on his face, and she let her eyes shut.

"I'm not going anywhere." His voice was a soft whisper. His lips touched her forehead and she let the herbs lull her back into a cocooned sleep.

☼

A weak mewling woke Tara again. The pounding of her head had retreated to a small spot around her ear. Her eyes fluttered open more readily this time. She stared for a long while at the overhead of the bunk. She knew every knot and grain of the wood.

The growling snore of Merlon came from nearby. How she had slept from that, she didn't know. Normally it kept her awake half the night when he actually did sleep at the same time as her. Today, the sound filled her with warmth instead of annoyance.

It took a while for her to determine that the meowing sound, which certainly had nothing to do with Merlon, came from near her feet.

It took even longer before she dared move. Slowly, her ribs protesting and trying to steal her breath away, she propped an elbow under herself. A pile of pillows had been placed beside her. She dragged them behind herself and sat up proper.

Dizziness lasted a few breaths, then her eyes settled on the shifting bunch of blankets at the foot of the bunk. A pair of yellow eyes appeared in the middle. The mother cat's triangular ears pricked towards Tara. *Not sure that's very hygienic.*

413

But she couldn't make herself shoo the animal. The kittens piped and shuffled blindly around against the mother cat's belly.

Merlon had moved his desk chair to beside the bunk. A book was still in his hands although it looked a hair width from falling from his lap to the floor. His head leaned against the stern wall and windowsill, mouth agape in the vicious snore.

Tara found herself smiling. There was space enough he could have crept into the bunk beside her, but he was always so afraid of bumping her accidentally when she had an injury.

Her neck prickled and she turned her head to find Elin standing by her. Blonde curls welled around her head, freckles dark against her pale skin. "You've woked," Elin said. "You dropped this. Your ear bleeds." Elin held out a blood-stained bandage.

It took Tara a moment to remember her earlier panic and that Merlon had removed the bandage. She gingerly touched the side of her head. Yorik or maybe Mira's healer had glued the cut above it together, again. Something had run out of her ear too, but it felt dry. Crusty brown sprinkled her fingertips when she lowered her hand. At least it wasn't currently bleeding. It explained how muffled sounds were to her right.

"Thank you, Elin." Tara took the bandage but placed it at the corner of the bunk. "Is…is Cary and Balfour alright?"

Elin nodded. Her chin began to quiver, and her blue eyes filled with tears.

Tara grabbed her trembling shoulder. "Oh hey, hey. Come now, it's alright. We're alright. You're safe now."

Before she could blink, Elin crawled into the bunk and howled into her nightie.

"You're alright, Elin. You're safe now." Tara's voice grew airy from the pressure against her bruised ribs. But she couldn't make herself hug Elin any less tightly.

"I-I-I..." Elin sobbed, heaved in an unsteady breath, and cried even harder.

Tara petted her curls, rocking despite the pain that motion caused her and found herself humming lightly. The melody was Trachnan. One Ma had hummed every time Tara had a panic attack when she was little. She hadn't thought she remembered that tune, but it came on its own. Slowly, Elin's sobs eased.

"There, feeling better?" Tara smiled when Elin pulled away and rubbed a fist at her eye.

Elin's lower lip trembled but she nodded.

Balfour inched up to the bunk. He looked like he too had cried, but his tears had long since dried. The wariness he regarded Tara with stabbed her guts, but she smiled and held out a hand. After a short pause, he took it, but made no move to crawl into the bunk where Elin still snuggled against Tara's side.

"Reddy is in your bed," Balfour said.

Tara looked at the cat and three kittens and realised Balfour's kitten, the white one with a few orange-red spots, had one eye partially open. The kittens had grown a lot in the mere ten days since birth.

Tara gave his hand a gentle squeeze. "You can crawl up and play with them if the ma will let you."

Elin clambered down to the cat.

Balfour hopped into the bunk with another cautious glance at Tara. She would have to explain everything to him. Let him know she had lied to get the pirate to release him. That she didn't believe for a second, he had any diseases.

Even then, it might be a long while before he trusted her again. She had no one else to blame but herself. But regardless of whether he ever trusted her, she wanted to prove him wrong by never running away again. By always being there for him.

"They named her Miss Hissy," Merlon said. "The mum cat, that is."

Tara's eyes snapped to his face. He was watching her, with the touch of a smile on his lips. His eyes glowed. For a moment she thought his expression was relief or even an "I told you so" but looking closer, she noticed the sweat beading on his forehead despite the coolness of the cabin.

"What's wrong?" She jolted out of bed, biting the pang across her ribs back. She ignored the dizzy spell that came over her.

Merlon's smile turned into a grimace as he tried sitting up straighter in the chair. "I'm sore, that's all." He was pale under his normally dark tawny complexion.

Tara put her palm against his forehead. "You're burning up!"

Tara's teeth started chattering. The cabin floor was cold, and she felt faint from not having eaten anything in too long. But Merlon clearly needed a healer. She remembered he had been cut down by a pirate, blood spreading along his side.

Pulling a sheet around herself to keep warm, she knelt and yanked his shirt from his trousers, ignoring his weak protests.

"Now's nae the time to be self-conscious, let me see." She whacked away his hands and gasped. "Merlon, you fool!"

A bandage had been wrapped around his middle. Soft padding had been added on his left where the wound was. Blood and some yellowish liquid had seeped through even the extra fabric, staining the outside of the bandage with a sickly colour.

Without having seen the wound Tara knew he hadn't had the bandage changed when he should have and was practically cultivating an infection.

"Uthak may have mentioned it needed stitches…" Merlon muttered and winced when Tara prodded the swelling around the bandage. "I might have run off to find you right about then."

For two painful heartbeats Tara could only squeeze his hand until hers shook. There were a million things she wanted to talk to him about. But the timing had never been worse. As if on cue, Merlon keeled sideways. He pressed a fist against his gut and his face twisted in pain.

Tara stood, but she had moved too abruptly, and her knees gave from under her. Merlon shot up from the chair, catching her when her head knocked against the bunk. She blinked, somehow back inside the bunk, or at least partially. Merlon leant against it, panting, and growing so pale as she hadn't thought possible.

"You need a doctor," Elin said. Her little palm rested against Tara's forehead. She had a frown between her fair brows.

Tara forced herself to sit up and smile. The faintness was subsiding, but she didn't dare get back up. *What a pair of star-*

mad fools we are. "Balfour, do you know where Yorik is? Or Uthak, if we're still near Mira's ship."

"Yorik's playing dice with Karl," Balfour said with a nod.

Tara removed Elin's hand from her face and patted it. "Could you run and get him? I was only dizzy, it's Merlon who needs tending to."

Balfour bobbed his head again and gingerly placed Reddy back with Miss Hissy before scooting from the bunk. His bare feet patted out of the cabin with a speed Tara doubted she could match even when she wasn't so beat up. The kid could run.

Tara shifted Elin down to the cats' end of the bunk and got out. "You've got to lie down."

"I don't need no stitches." Merlon grimaced.

Tara rolled her eyes. "You're ridiculous sometimes. Lie down, please." She guided him onto the bunk, making him stay sitting while she began unwinding the bandage.

"Don't say how it looks." Merlon looked about to throw up just at the sight of the blood on the fabric.

Tara turned to Elin, realising she probably shouldn't watch this. "Can you run and get a jug of water for me, please?"

Elin, who had crept up beside Merlon and stared intently at the unwrapping of the bandage, hopped out of the bunk. She picked up a jug from the folding table by the windows and returned instantly.

"It's maybe best you—"

"I wanna see." Elin broke in, standing with the water jug in her arms. "Will you sew him up? My mummy once cut her arm on the fence wire and the doctor sewed her skin back together."

Tara sighed, there wasn't time to argue. "Alright. If you feel sick, look the other way. Merlon, make sure you donae look or you'll certainly spew."

She clenched his hand, then resumed unwrapping the gauze. "You'll be alright." Despite her words, her chest tightened. The cut opened when she removed the last string of soaked-through fabric. What if he wasn't going to be alright?

Chapter 45

A knock on the cabin door jolted Tara. She looked up from her notebook, closing it as she did so nobody saw the severed limbs scattered across the pages.

Merlon slept calmly, only a mild mixture of regular valerian, chamomile and nettle tea had been needed after the exhaustion of getting sixteen stitches it seemed.

Tara kept thinking he had died, especially after he had rolled to his right side and wasn't snoring intermittently anymore. She leaned sideways, making sure she heard his breath over the sighs of *Lucia's* wood and finally got up at a second thump on the door. "Who's knocking?"

A glance at the clock told her it was nearly dinner time. Merlon had slept ten hours which both made her relieved because he had needed it, and worried because it told of how poorly he was. She stepped her boots on, not wanting to bend to tie the laces and tiptoed through the dim cabin.

She opened the door and found Fabian, limping back out the other end. Tara closed the door behind her so Merlon wouldn't wake. "Hey," she called. "You're too slow at knock-a-door games."

Fabian turned, a smile brightening his face. "Thought ya'd fallen asleep too."

"I asked who's knocking." Tara tsk'ed and goaded him out of the narrow passage. "How's your hip?"

Fabian dismissed her with a wave. "That's fine, it's me star-cursed arm. Sword hit a muscle. Uthak and Yorik agrees it'll take months to heal. At this point I should just chop off me right arm at the shoulder, eh?"

Tara smiled. She had thought Fabian was all but dead from the amount of blood, but it turned out he had hit a pirate's neck and most of it hadn't been his own. "Rest it and it'll be fine, I'm sure. Bailey's still sleeping?"

Fabian nodded then replied, "She'll be right. I however asked Cap'n for time off. I've already moved everything I need to *The Bounty*. Gonna miss annoyin' ya, I'll have to admit." Fabian reached out and Tara didn't quite escape his hand stirring up her hair.

She punched his good arm, and they stopped their stroll when they reached the bow of *Lucia*.

The pirate's cutter had gone. The explosion Lennie had rigged using rum and wheat flour had blown such a hole the main mast had broken and apparently the entire ship fell apart. The pieces would drift forever in space, or until some other ship hit them. Sails could tear up badly hitting old pieces of wreckage but at least that was a rare occurrence.

Rumour had it there were debris-eating creatures cruising around the less populated parts of galaxies. She had never seen one but wasn't going to discount it as myth, with dragons existing and Trackers being talking animals, it didn't seem too far-fetched.

Fabian yawned and brought her attention back on him.

"How long are you staying with Mira? Until we're all in Amule again?"

"Nah, Cap'n wouldn't let me squander *that* long. We're meetin' in Jeweller City, remember. Bailey's arranged for a Tracker to change some names and dates around. There'll be a spot for the two of ya at the registration office, if ya want to double up."

Tara picked at the smooth railing. Everything smelled of newly sawed wood and lye. She had missed the main repairs, but it wasn't like she could have helped much with the extent of her injuries. "We've nae spoken yet. He sort of keeled over the minute I woke up."

"Ya's got like a month to speak about it." Fabian shrugged. "No pressure, but ya better still be on good enough terms for us to invite ya both to the party."

The pure thought of falling out with Merlon to a point where they wouldn't be able to be in each other's company twisted her guts. Tara swallowed hard. The last thing she wanted was to break up with him.

She stared across to *The Bounty. Iliana* was at the stern. The three ships were lashed together in a triangle while everyone recuperated. *Iliana* had lost her captain and the man who had tried to escape still wearing shackles. Somehow, those two were the only fatalities aside from pirates. Many had severe injuries, however. "How's Pietrek?"

Fabian sent her a long gaze but replied without commenting on the change of subject. "Back on his feet but

422

neither Uthak nor Yorik's sure his left hand ever gets full function. He's very smitten with Mira, though. I knew he would be." Fabian grinned by the end.

"I'm glad you finally made up with him." Tara bumped her shoulder against Fabian's.

He sighed. "Me too. I know I've had ya support all this time, the entire crew's support, but he's me brother. Always kept his hand over me when I got into trouble. Ya know what big brothers are like. I hated the thought of him not acceptin' her."

Tara nodded, although she didn't quite know as she had never had a sibling. Merlon had lived with them for a year, and Ma had said to treat him like a brother, but he had never been that to her.

She clenched Ma's pendant. Ma had known, somehow. Even though Tara had never told her anything and only kissed Merlon that one time in secret. Kissed him goodbye on the day Captain Rochester took him away and banned Merlon from visiting them. But Ma had known Tara had been in love with him then.

She had fallen out of love with him as the years went by and she met others to fall in love with, yet Merlon was the one person Ma had mentioned Tara should invite for the funeral. That had been a terrible day. When Ma knew she was nearly at her last breath and had made Tara write down all her wishes. But it had helped make the hole-drop smooth. No less painful, but less confused.

Merlon hadn't come of course, and Tara remembered the cold fury of that slight. Adrien had tried to say Merlon had reasons. Only now did Tara understand. Lanier's death had been too hard. Merlon's abuse of S-V too recent.

Adrien too had still been rattled by it. Even months after Merlon nearly died from an overdose, Adrien had struggled with the hole-drop for Ma. *Thank you, Tomaline, for letting Adrien find Merlon in time.*

"Hey, what are you up to?" Mira's shout tore Tara from her thoughts.

She straightened from the rail and discovered where the kids had vanished to earlier. Balfour was sitting on *The Bounty's* deck. Cary was beside him and Ola told them some story or other with an animation Tara hadn't known the scholar to possess. Elin trailed after Mira, reaching up and touching the lace frill of the shortened sleeve at regular intervals.

Fabian swung his legs over *Lucia's* railing and before Tara could tell him to stop being reckless, he leapt across.

Mira caught him, the muscles bulging where her shirt sleeve was pushed up. "You're star-mad." She smiled, pulling him forward and kissed him.

"And ya love it." Fabian grinned and climbed over *The Bounty's* rail.

"Donae ever do anything like that," Tara said, holding Elin's gaze.

Elin shook her head, frowning at Fabian like she too thought he had been reckless. She stalked closer to the balusters and looked through them. "How do I get back?"

"We'll get Boomer to lift you again," Mira said. "Are you done investigating *The Bounty*?"

"I wanna be with Tara." Elin's words solidified something in Tara's chest.

She didn't need to force her smile as she reached over the rail and took Elin's hand stretching through between the balusters. "Maybe if Mira and Fabian helps."

They did, and Elin was hoisted back over the gap and happily sat on the rail while Tara held on to both her legs so she couldn't fall off. "You got through that fight alright?" Tara asked. She hadn't had a chance to speak with Mira yet.

"Yeah. Training two hours a day has paid off."

Fabian slipped an arm around her waist. "Captain Mira Cobalt, pirate hunter." He waggled his eyebrows.

Mira snorted. "Hardly. I just imagined each pirate was my dad all those times he's told me I can't do one thing or another. Turns out, he's wrong."

"I donae want to say I told you so but…" Tara smiled.

Bailey stuck her head out of the brown scarf Mira had around her neck. "You're talking loudly."

Relief washed through Tara. It was a good sign Bailey was somewhat awake and coherent. It meant her injuries were healing. "Still napping then?"

"You broke my arm in two places, yanking me from that lock. Yes, I'm napping." Bailey grimaced and her face vanished again.

Tara felt sick. "I'm sorry."

Bailey's muffled voice came from the scarf. "It's not like it was on purpose. I'll heal *if you'll all shut up*."

Mira smiled apologetically. "I think that's my cue to get back to work. We've got to leave for Intrapolis in twelve hours. Did Merlon say if you're coming along? Would

425

probably be best with extra statements with the whole pirate affair."

"And we know what to do with Cary?" Fabian said.

Tara frowned. "What do you mean? He wants to apprentice under Ola."

Mira glanced over her shoulder before meeting Tara's gaze. "He had the id papers in his pocket when the pirates found him. They tore them up and threw them overboard. He was quite upset but Lennie thinks with the evidence for a pirate attack we should be able to get legal papers for him."

"We have evidence?" Tara looked around. The ships were still getting repaired, but other than witnesses from three ships, two if Merlon decided to avoid the high mooring prices in Intrapolis, she couldn't tell what evidence they might have.

Mira shifted from one foot to the other and Fabian answered. "We uh, kept some bits. Their flag and...parts."

The way he said it, looking meaningfully at Elin, still dangling her feet from the railing with an innocent look on her face, Tara gulped. There had been limbs all over. She supposed some of those might not have been thrown overboard. She hadn't looked closely but several had been tattooed with zigzags and blue triangles, the symbols of Blacklock's Galaxy. Her stomach roiled at the thought of a barrel somewhere in *The Bounty's* hold being stuffed with hands or arms with tattoos on them.

Mira cleared her throat. "Right, we're setting up a big celebration dinner here since Intrapolis will be too expensive. It'll have to be on *Lucia*, she's got the best deck space. You think Merlon will be up in an hour?"

"Possibly but I'd rather he sleeps as long as he can," Tara said, unable to hide the relief at the change of subject. She lifted Elin down and the girl dashed across the deck to where Kieran and Hakim were sitting. "Are we keeping Hakim until Jeweller City? You willnae swap permanently, will you?" She looked at Fabian.

"Nah, Cap'n needs me. We talked 'bout that already, right?"

Mira leaned her head against his with a despondent nod. "It's the best. I can't pay as much as Merlon even if I needed a new first mate, and we want to save up to have a kid one day."

"Once we get to that stage, we'll see about changin' it up." Fabian gave her a squeeze.

Tara shook her head. They were way better organised than her and Merlon and it was mildly embarrassing considering Fabian was five and Mira nine years younger. As if she felt his presence, Tara turned at the same moment Merlon opened the passage door. Even from across the ship, she could tell he should have waited to leave the bunk.

"Remember we want ya both at the party," Fabian called. There was humour in his voice, but Tara held up a little finger, not even glancing back at him. Sometimes he was a jerk.

Tara reached Merlon before he had managed more than the first step up from the passage. She grabbed his arm. "You should be lying down until dinner."

"Dinner?" He blinked at her. "How long did I sleep?"

She steered him back into the cabin and while he wouldn't lie down, she got him to sit in the bunk at least. "Ten, almost eleven, hours. You needed the rest. How's your side feeling?"

He ran a hand over his eyes. "Don't remind me." He reached out and held her shoulder. "How are you? I was so worried…"

Tara kicked her boots off and curled up against his right side, knees drawn up gingerly to avoid hurting her ribs too much in the process. He wrapped an arm around her shoulders and leaned his head against hers.

Slipping her fingers between Merlon's, Tara closed her eyes. "I'm sorry I ran off." Her throat tightened.

"You can just tell me to shut up for a few hours, you know. And I should've clarified with you. I thought you were struggling. It was too small and dark that office, wasn't it?"

She nodded. "I willnae run another time. But I *will* tell you to stop talking so I donae say something I donae mean."

"Fair." Merlon chuckled, relief filling the sound.

"I also…well I should've trusted you more. With the whole nae seeing much energy thing. Fabian told me you guessed it pretty much right away. It's so embarrassing, and if I cannae do my job, what right do I have to stay as your navigator? Maybe they'll even kick me out of the tier."

"I do wish you'd have trusted me with it sooner. I'm glad you are now." His voice sent a pleasant hum through her. "They can't throw you out though. It's pretty normal to have issues after lots of trauma. Lanier couldn't see any energy for half a year after…" Merlon's voice cracked. He cleared his throat and continued, "After we buried Lamia and Epona. The Moonside epidemic was rough."

Tara clenched her fingers around his. "I'm sorry."

Merlon kissed her hairline but didn't reply.

She turned her face to rest against his chest. She breathed in his scent and wished for this moment to never end. But she had to press on before she lost her nerve. Her voice came out a wordless squeak and she forced herself to sit up and meet his gaze.

Those warm brown eyes, searching hers. He almost looked scared. But he didn't need to.

"I love you, Merlon. I donae know if I will make a good ma, but we have two kids who needs a home. Who needs comfort and love and..." Her voice died on her lips.

Merlon squeezed her hand gently. His eyes were blank and this time not from fever. His chest heaved and he nodded, tears spilling when he smiled at her. "I love you too. We can make this work, together."

The teal energy of his thundering heart sent tendrils around her. Stronger than it had looked in a long, long time. Not perfect, but better. She blinked and it had gone.

A sob-laugh escaped Tara and she threw her arms around his shoulders, burying her face against his chest again. "We'll make it work," she whispered.

"Together," Merlon muttered and kissed her right ear gingerly. "Just don't die on me, alright?"

She sat back with a laugh, wiping at her wet face. "You're the one to talk. Running away from getting *sixteen* stitches."

Tara pretended to protest when Merlon caught her face between his hands, but her fingers curled around his neck. She pulled him close for their first kiss in what felt like a lifetime.

Chapter 46

They unlashed the ships twelve hours later and set sail for Intrapolis. Merlon had grumbled about the mooring prices but in the end, everyone agreed it was best they went to the anti-piracy agency together, especially since *Iliana's* captain lay dead in the ship's hold. The more people who could back up Mira's statement, the better.

It took them five days to reach the floating city. Less steeply inclined than Amule or Trachna, it splayed out as a flat dome of grey, white, and brown buildings when they drew close.

The harbour was intensely busy, at least a third of the ships flying a banner Tara had never seen before with a silver explosion and between one and three silver stars above.

"Those are the pirate hunters," Merlon explained when she asked. "The ones with a single star on the flag are the least experienced or only part of the crew have taken the required courses. Three stars are the ones you want to avoid, tough and rich, they're assholes."

And that's how she knew which building was the anti-pirate agency when she later walked up along the harbour with Merlon, Mira, Balfour, and Elin. "That's where we're going." Tara smiled at Elin.

Elin blinked up at her, her fingers sticky from the pitted dates Tara had bought them when passing a stand. Elin had been sucking and holding the last dry fruit for some time but had eventually eaten it all.

Balfour however had swallowed his handful. It made Tara slightly apprehensive she had forked out as much coin as she had for something he wasn't even going to taste, but there was nothing for it. She ought to know by now he would inhale any snack.

He had refused to hold anyone's hand, but Tara knew he would never run away when Elin was here. Cary had stayed on *The Bounty* with Ola until they had scoped out how Balfour and Elin's fake papers were perceived. Everyone else were busy unloading, repairing, or restocking the three ships.

Tara wasn't sure what would happen with *Iliana's* crew, but she had promised to put a word in for Rashida next time Merlon hired. She was pretty sure Jara would do the same.

"Do you think we should have brought the barrel? Or a bag with a couple of the main…parts?" Mira said.

Tara grimaced. She hadn't seen the barrel of pirate body parts and hoped she never would.

Merlon shook his head. "This'll only give us an appointment for a full investigation. They're busier than the goods office in Amule. *Lucia's* not staying past the six-hour mark as I don't have any cargo that justifies the mooring prices so Tara and I will hand over our statements that we

431

wrote on the way. You'll be asked to return with all three first mates and I'd advise to bring Ola for his scholar's leverage."

"Have you had to report an attack before?" Tara asked.

"Many years ago. *Lucia* got away then, thanks to Yuan's steering, but we had some material damages. I've reported twice in Jeweller City as well but at least Squamates only steal goods, not people."

Mira pursed her lips, fiddling with the brown scarf around her neck. "I might reconsider this Intrapolis run. Not sure my dad won't make it fall through anyway just out of spite."

"Maybe you could you take the pirate hunter course?" Tara said.

"Do they offer it here?" Mira looked at Merlon.

His brows furrowed. "It's expensive and takes over a year, full-time last I checked. It's mainly former pirates and rich merchant captains who get the certification although if you have the course, your kid would get a free pass for it. Give it a decade or two and pirate hunter be a new sailing tier."

"I doubt Dad will help pay for it even if I had time." Mira sighed.

"I'm sure Lennie can help sort you a Jeweller City trade deal," Merlon said. "If you're willing to pay him for the connections, that is. It'll be safer and it's lucrative enough to pay off in a year or two."

Mira's face lit up. "Could you put a word in for me? It won't always fit but we might bump into one another every few months if we have the same route."

She was obviously thinking about Fabian and Tara found herself relieved she was working on Merlon's ship. She couldn't imagine not knowing how rarely they would see one another.

As if he heard her thoughts, Merlon glanced at her and grabbed her hand. "Sure, Mira. Lennie was impressed with your fighting, so you already put in a good word in a way."

They paused outside the agency where a queue came out through the open door and took a sharp left turn along the front of the building.

A white powder lamplight shone through the bubbled glass window they stood by, making it impossible for Tara to see anything inside. It was midday in Fristate, but the light remained the same hazy grey no matter the time and most buildings appeared to have lights on.

Not five minutes into their wait, Elin tugged on Tara's hand. "I need to pee."

"Oh." Tara bit her lip and scanned their surroundings. Merlon had made both kids go before they left the ship but that clearly had been a furtive attempt at avoiding this. She met his gaze, forcing down the worry rising in her stomach. She should have paid attention to whether there were public toilets here like in Amule.

Merlon squeezed her hand. He didn't look the least worried although Elin was already beginning to bounce on her feet. He leaned forward and gestured to the Squamate in front of them in the queue. 'Hello, sorry, do you know if there are toilets anywhere? Our little one needs the loo.'

'In the pub maybe. And there is a toilet in the agency,' the short geckoid Squamate replied. Then he twisted his gold earring between two finger pads, tilting his head to look down

433

at Elin and Balfour with one huge, unblinking eye. 'They were kidnapped? You might get ahead in the queue if you ask.'

Merlon smiled. 'Thank you, we will try.' He turned to Tara. "I'll see if they'll let me in." He left her and Mira with the kids, vanishing inside after a couple of muttered excuses at the five people in front.

"I need to pee." Elin was pulling at her trousers now and stepping on her feet.

Tara tried to peer in through the window but could see no more than earlier. "Sorry Mira. Balfour stay in the queue with Mira, please." Tara moved around the Squamate. "Quickly, we'll ask for the loo inside." She pulled Elin along.

"You won't make us go to different houses, will you?" Balfour's small voice sounded frightened.

Tara glanced over her shoulder, Mira had her hand on his shoulder, holding him back when he strained towards Tara and Elin.

Then she walked right into Merlon coming back out of the agency office. "It's not too late? I've found the toilet. Over to the right, in the corner." He gestured and raised his voice. "Mira, Balfour come along. There's another line for people bringing kids, we're up next."

Tara rushed Elin through to the tiny toilet, focusing on the kid to avoid her breath hitching too much. Once back out, without Elin having had an accident, she let out a breath of relief.

While the agency was also cramped, the ceiling was high and the room itself large enough she could manage, at least when Merlon took her hand again.

"You alright?" He watched her with a frown. "If it's too small or anything you just have to say."

Tara swallowed hard. "It's alright, the ceiling's not too low." The light geometric patterns painted on the walls helped too.

"Next." A clerk behind a high desk waved at them. She looked from Merlon to Tara and then Mira over the edge of her half-moon glasses. "Material or person damage'eh?" She had a faint Fristate accent but seemed to take care with her pronunciation.

Mira glanced at Merlon, wiping her hand against her trousers from nerves.

"Both and two casualties." Merlon spoke quietly.

"Sorry about the loss," the clerk said but there was no empathy in her voice.

Merlon cleared his throat and extracted the two envelopes with his and Tara's statements from his satchel. "Three ships were hit, the captain and one midship crew were lost. I have a tight Jeweller City schedule, but Captain Mira Cobalt here will be requiring a full investigation and will lead on the statements for *Iliana* who lost her captain. These are the statements of myself and Navigator Tara Polendi." He indicated Tara as he placed the statements on the tall desk.

The woman nodded along, scribbling in an incredible speed. "We'll need the bodies to be wrapped and brought round the back for examination. You can then decide if they should receive a free hole-drop here or a ship drop a minimum of a day's journey from Intrapolis. Your name and ship?" She shifted the statements down beside her note papers.

"Captain Merlon Ricosta, my ship is *Lucia*, registration IG501 out of Amule."

"And the pirate ship?"

Merlon's jawline tensed, his brows drawing closer to one another. "Blown to pieces."

The clerk's eyebrows rose but she didn't stop writing. Finally, she stretched her neck when she had finished her minutes. "And the children? Kidnapped? We have a surgeon in'eh the back who can look them over shortly. Will you require a referral to trauma therapists? It's free if they suffered trauma for an extended period."

Merlon met Tara's gaze. They *had* suffered for an extended period, but not due to pirates.

Tara cleared her throat. "Does the referral help us in Amule?"

"Probably not without a bribe'eh." The clerk scoffed. "But if you're in a hurry you will need to sign over the investigation responsibility to…" the woman's finger ran down her notes. "Captain Cobalt, then she can accept any Fristate compensation and referrals on your behalf'eh. If you trust her not to keep it."

Tara ground her teeth together. The clerk was clearly strongly biased against Amuleans and the culture of bribery that ruled in Twin Cities. "We trust Mira, if this will allow us to leave later today, we'll happily sign the responsibility over."

"Assuming the kids can still come with us today." Merlon added.

Tara put a hand on Elin's shoulder when she pressed against her leg. Balfour shuffled closer and took Elin's hand.

436

"Very well'eh." The clerk nodded and leafed through a book on her right. "The first appointment for a ship inspection is in five days. Repairs needs to be noted by one of our approved shipwrights." She pulled a page from a wooden rack on the desk and gave it to Mira alongside the appointment slip.

"Anyone who goes to a healer before then will need to ask for a letter confirming *every* injury sustained to receive compensation for the treatments. You accept you won't receive ship damage compensation if you leave with the Intergalactic Traveller right away."

Merlon nodded. "*Lucia* only sustained minor damages."

"Very well'eh. The surgeon can see the kids now." She gestured behind herself. A narrow yellow door opened into what looked to be a light, grey room. A sign on it was too far away for Tara to read but she suspected it was the name of the surgeon who had xir practice as an extension of the agency.

"Um, we have some, well body parts of the pirates," Mira said.

Once more the clerk's eyebrows lifted, her lips almost twitched as if amused. "Put them in a salted water barrel and our investigator can take a look'eh and dispose of them at your appointment. It might help move your case along faster." She added two words at the bottom of her notes page, put it and the enveloped statements to one side.

"Is it really that easy?" Mira whispered when they walked through the narrow yellow door to the surgeon. "Couldn't we have lied about it all and just messed up the ships ourselves?"

Merlon shrugged and steered Balfour towards the surgeon who looked up with a pleasant smile.

"Who've we got here, eh?" The man leaned forward on his knees. His face and eyes crinkled with his smile which didn't falter even though Balfour grabbed Elin and slipped behind Merlon and Tara. "No need to be afraid. I won't take you off your guardians."

"Sorry, they've been through a lot," Merlon muttered.

Tara bit back the pain in her legs and knelt beside them, letting Elin shuffle into her arms. "This nice man is a healer, like Yorik or Uthak. He just needs to take a look at you. Make sure you're eating enough and such."

After the examination, Mira carried Elin back to the ship since neither Tara nor Merlon were fit enough.

Tara stared at Merlon's satchel all the way back to the ships. Not only had the surgeon confirmed the kids were severely malnourished but safely on the road to recovery, he had signed them into Merlon and Tara's foster care without asking for their partner registration papers. That satchel now held an official, non-forged document

If they registered officially before returning to Amule, they should be able to use these new documents to ensure the kids weren't put into an orphanage and split up.

"You'll come to Jeweller City after?" Tara helped Elin off Mira's back when they reached *Lucia*.

Fabian sauntered across the gangway. "I sure hope so or Cap'n be cross with me." He grinned. "It gone alright?"

"An investigator will come check the ships in five days," Mira said. "We'll switch over the cargo, get repairs sorted and head to Jeweller City when we have the compensation."

Fabian took Mira's hand. "Good." He looked at Tara and Merlon. "I hope the two of ya figure out what ya's doin'. Ya's invited to our party no matter."

Tara's heart thudded harder. Then she met Merlon's gaze and his smile warmed her. She took care not to bump his wound when wrapping an arm around him. "We'll be at the party for sure."

Epilogue

Tara half-turned when she left the passage to the cabin. "Balfour, please close the door or the kittens escape."

He picked up the mostly white kitten, now nearly eight weeks old, returned it to the cabin and sped out before Reddy could run after him. Balfour's cheeks had finally begun filling in while Elin looked like she had never been close to starving to death.

"Can we go see the markets again?" Elin's eyes glowed as Tara and Balfour exited onto the main deck. She was twisting her hands in the dress Tara had caved and bought for her last week. It was a blue, lacy thing and even though it was a nightmare to keep the ribbons around the skirt tied into little bows, Elin loved it enough Tara could withstand the hassle.

Tara shook her head, both exasperated and unable to not smile at the kid bouncing on her feet. "It's still only on one day a week. We can go again next week." She reached for Elin's hand, paused to tug the girl's very skewed dress back to front facing and then took the hand waiting for her. "Let's go wait for Merlon at the inn."

Balfour took Elin's other hand, he didn't often accept Tara's, but he let her and Merlon tuck him in alongside Elin or asked them to sit by the bunk if he had a nightmare.

They stepped off the gangway and turned towards the quay.

A lanky kid came running down the jetty. It wasn't till he stopped three steps away, chest heaving, Tara realised it was Cary. He too had put on some weight, but like Balfour, he had retained a certain thinness to him, like the long starvation was desperately trying to keep hold of him.

His black hair had been cropped short in almost the exact same fashion as Ola's. "Hi." He looked at his feet and kicked at the dead wooden planks under them.

"Cary!" Elin twisted free from Tara's grip and threw her arms around the boy.

He took a staggering step back, surprise, then relief on his face. "I thought you'd have forgotten me," he muttered.

Tara gave his shoulder a squeeze. "We never would."

"You're our stepbrother." Elin rolled her eyes and Tara was a little disconcerted with how much Elin had begun copying her. She really had to watch herself to not use too crude words or gestures when Elin was around, or the kid would get in trouble around more polite people than sailors.

Balfour stuck his hands in his pockets. "Hi, Cary." He didn't look as enthused as Elin, but Cary didn't seem to notice.

"Where's Tiki? How big is she? Can I see her now?"

Tara blinked. Cary had never been excited about anything except books. She glanced longingly at the inn they had been on their way too but decided Merlon would come find them on *Lucia* if he got to the table and found them missing. "All the kittens have grown a lot. Tiki is quite scared of everyone."

"She's nut going to be scared of me," Cary said and clearly fought the urge to run ahead when Tara herded them back to the ship.

Tara unlocked the passageway door again. "Where have *The Bounty* moored? Ola or someone didnae accompany you here?"

"Oh, they're just over there." Cary gestured vaguely towards the portside. "Mira saw *Lucia* and Ola said I could go ahead and see Tiki."

Tara stretched her neck while the kids filed into the passage. She thought she glimpsed a blue head, Mira, between the rigging and masts of half a dozen ships.

She wanted to trot over and see how Mira and Fabian were doing, ask Ola how it went with Cary and if Intrapolis had issued Cary proper id papers. With a sigh, she followed the kids. Ola clearly didn't recall that Jeweller City wasn't all too safe for foreigners to run around on their own.

The black kitten, Tiki, allowed Cary to pick it up within five minutes of him lying on his belly and coaxing it out from under Balfour and Elin's bunk. The most surprising part was the kitten neither hissed nor clawed at Cary.

"Ah that's where you are, I was looking—Cary?" Merlon faltered in the chamber door. "Good to see you kid. *The Bounty's* arrived then?"

Cary nodded, not paying much attention to anything but the kitten in his arms.

Tara entwined her fingers in Merlon's when he grabbed her hand. "I've had nae chance to go see them. Cary came running to see the kitten."

"Should I invite them for dinner?" Merlon said.

"Sure." Tara frowned. "Nae paying though? We cannae afford to feed them all. Fabian eats like a horse."

Merlon chuckled. "No, I meant I'll see if they want to come. I guess Ola won't be paying all the time anymore either, I suspect it wasn't cheap if they got new papers for Cary."

Cary looked up, still cradling the purring kitten in his arms. "Oh, Mira got some big reward for killing that nasty pirate with blue teeth. You can ask her to pay. It didn't cost nuthing to get id papers either since the pirates took the other papers."

Tara exchanged a glance with Merlon. Maybe it would have been worth it to stay in Intrapolis a few days. They had paid a handsome sum to turn the surgeon's foster care statement into complete paperwork for Elin and Balfour here in Jeweller City. But she didn't get to comment before Balfour's face drained of colour.

Tara twisted from Merlon's hand and caught Balfour's shoulders. "Balfour, keep breathing. Stay with me. You're safe."

He had the most awful panic attacks almost daily. Anything might set them off. They had sought a therapist in Jeweller City, but the two specialists in human trauma victims had months long waitlists. Once they got to Amule, she

443

would ask her own for a recommendation. In Amule, children had priority in healthcare.

Tara kept talking, calmly but Balfour trembled and curled his arms around his head. His heart thumped so fast the energy emitted created a faint teal haze around him. His panting breath disturbed the swirls with lighter, turquoise threads of energy.

Tara blinked and the energy had gone from her vision. It still wasn't very reliable but for a few seconds every day, she would see it clearly, like she once had been able to all the time, and that was enough for her.

She kept speaking, only looking up when there was a faint knock on the chamber door. Ola stood there, his smile turned into a crease between his orange brows.

"Panic attack. Happens a lot," Merlon explained in a hush.

"Can I do anything?" Ola said.

Tara shook her head. She stayed on her knees, ignoring the growing pain in them, and held Balfour until his breathing slowed and he writhed to get out of her arms. "You're safe, alright? Nae bad people will get you. We'll protect you." Tara put her hand on top of Merlon's, now resting on her shoulder.

Balfour nodded and wiped his nose in his sleeve.

"Hey now, we talked about that. Use your handkerchief." Tara tugged it free from his pocket, sending a handful of raisins and sunflower seeds flying. He had been stashing away again. But that kept some of the panic attacks at bay, so she didn't comment. Rather, she scooped the snacks up and stuffed them back in his pocket while he blew his nose.

Tara realised she also had snot all over her shirt. "I'll just get changed. Merlon, could you run ask the others about dinner? I'm starving."

Merlon hesitated.

Ola smiled and waved Merlon along. "I'll watch the kids." Then, to Balfour he said, "You know, Lena, your step-grandma if you will, she used to get scared too. She was a strong woman, but bad people hurt her, and she fought the memories too. But you can win over them."

"I-I can? How?" Balfour hiccupped.

Thankful for Ola's calmness so easily cutting through to Balfour, Tara pulled the chamber door too and quickly switched out of her shirt to a clean one. She attempted to fix her hair, but it instantly began tumbling out of the bun at the back of her head. With a sigh she turned and nearly toppled Elin. "Sorry, love, you're so quiet."

"I want my hair up."

Tara gestured and Elin turned around. Carefully, and cheating a bit with a broad-toothed comb, Tara untangled the curls into sections. She was still lousy at plaiting hair, but Elin never complained. "Do you want one or two braids?"

Elin jerked around and stared at her like she had suggested some heinous crime. "I dun't want a braid, I wanna have it like you."

Tara stared for so long Elin repeated her request. Then she complied, swallowing emotion in thick lumps in an attempt to avoid crying. When she had tied Elin's hair back in a bun it quite naturally looked messy from the fine curls refusing to do what Tara wanted. But Elin hopped up and down when she saw herself in the mirror.

445

While Tara managed to do nothing but smile and laugh that day, and the next when she sat down with Mira, Fabian, and Merlon to plan their joint partner ceremonies, she sobbed with joy the first time Balfour crept in to snuggle between her and Merlon. And she bawled like a baby when Elin a year later, on the day of their official adoption, asked if that meant she could call them mummy and daddy.

Elin was allowed to join the healer's tier she kept begging for. Meanwhile Balfour got assigned to the sailor's in Amule with the promise he would be uplifted to captain if he managed to sit the full exam after a work placement. A thoughtful, kind kid, Tara had no doubts he too would do them proud.

Acknowledgements

This year has been crazy in so many ways. There are more people to thank than I could possibly hope to remember to list properly so I'll keep it brief.

My family, first and foremost, deserve a big **thank you** for their never-ending support. You all keep shoving my books at everyone who's willing to listen (or are trapped with you such as your hairdressers and co-workers) and your instant acceptance of any of my special interests and minor obsessions keeps me going.

As always, I want to thank my writing friends, both those from Scribophile, twitter and beyond. This year has been incredible, and I wouldn't be here without you all.

Finally, I'd be remiss not to mention Jessica and Sophie, you don't know each other but you both help me get the book to that final stage, ready for publishing and I'm ever grateful for it.

About the Author

Storytelling and inventing new worlds have been a part of Natalie's life since before she could read or write. Nowadays she mostly writes in English, but you'll often discover hints of her native Danish or some of the other languages she has picked up along the way.

Danish by birth, Natalie now lives in the green hills of Yorkshire, UK. She spends her evenings writing, drawing, and creating while only mildly hindered by her adventure cat.

Follow Natalie on Twitter
@NatalieKelda

Get updates, free short stories, and see official Inner Universe artwork on her website
NatalieKelda.co.uk

Printed in Great Britain
by Amazon